[illegible] ...tress and campaigne[illegible] in Sussex. She is the author of three previous novels – *50 Ways to Find a Lover*, *The (Im)perfect Girlfriend* and *Unlike a Virgin* – which have been published in ten countries. Lucy is also the founder of the No More Page 3 campaign. To find out more about Lucy follow her on Twitter (@lucyanneholmes).

Also by Lucy-Anne Holmes

50 Ways to Find a Lover
The (Im)Perfect Girlfriend
Unlike a Virgin

Just a Girl, Standing in Front of a Boy

Lucy-Anne Holmes

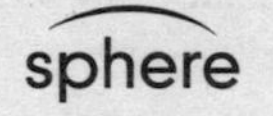

SPHERE

First published as a paperback original in Great Britain in 2013 by Sphere

A CIP catalogue record for this book is available from the British Library.

ISBN 978-0-7515-4765-8

Typeset in Caslon by M Rules
Printed and bound in Great Britain by
Clays Ltd, St Ives plc

Papers used by Sphere are from well-managed forests and other responsible sources.

MIX
Paper from responsible sources
FSC® C104740

Sphere
An imprint of
Little, Brown Book Group
100 Victoria Embankment
London EC4Y 0DY

An Hachette UK Company
www.hachette.co.uk

www.littlebrown.co.uk

For all the amazing women
I've met, and those I haven't,
who battle with the dark days

Chapter 1

My name is Jenny Taylor but everyone calls me Fanny. I admit, it isn't ideal being called Fanny on a day-to-day basis, but it could be worse. 'It could be worse' is my catchphrase. I have need for it a lot. I don't have the best of luck. Take, for example, the reason I am called Fanny. When I was at school my classmates realised that if you said Jenny Taylor again and again very quickly, you got the word genitalia. For years I was called a creative array of private-part slang but it was Fanny that stuck. Thankfully. I wasn't keen on Bald Man in a Boat. See. It could have been worse.

So, my name is Jenny Taylor, or Fanny, and there's not much else to say about me really. I'm quite unremarkable. If I rubbed a lamp and a smiling genie appeared offering me a wish, I wouldn't say fame and fortune, I wouldn't even say world peace. I would say, 'Hello, genie, please could I just be happy for the rest of my days.'

As an answer it hardly dazzles with ambition, does it? But happiness is important to me. It's important to me because there was a time when I wasn't very happy at all.

I've got what is hilariously known as 'a history of depression'. Phew. There, I've said it. I always feel like a bit of a failure when I admit that. I try not to. One in four women is affected by depression, apparently. I wonder whether they all get paranoid that people are thinking, Woah! She's a freak! when they mention their depression too. I hope not. Philippa, my best friend, credits my father as the cause of my depression, because my father HATES me. Seriously, his favourite thing to say to me is, 'Jenny, (tut) you're so useless.' By and large, he's got a point, but it's probably not the most empowering thing you can repeat to your child. So, my early years were a bit testing, and then my first experience of love was pretty grisly. I was wildly in love with this fella and he pooped on me from quite a terrific height. That's when the depression kicked in. But that was years and years and years ago now.

These days, I'm all about happiness. Happiness is so important to me that I have my own happiness manifesto pinned to the back of my bedroom door. It is pithily titled the Smiling Fanny Manifesto and was written by Philippa who had just seen a documentary on telly entitled *Making Slough Happy*. Basically, she pinched the main points that the psychologist people on the programme were making. The Smiling Fanny Manifesto, by Philippa Flemming, reads as follows:

Fanny, you MUST do these tasks every day
or I shall burn all your clothes!
DAILY TASKS FOR FANNY

1) Phone a friend. You can always call me. Just say, 'I am calling you because I have to tick it off my list.'

And then we can chat about the usual: what we shall name our future children, our top five sandwich fillings, what you would say to Robbie Williams if you bumped into him on the street.

2) Grow something – not like something different every day, just always have something growing, like a plant! (Mould on an old cup of tea doesn't count!!!!)
3) Count your blessings – before bed you have to think of things from the day that were good and that you're grateful for. One, very random, off the top of my head example could be 'my best friend, Philippa'!!!
4) Have a face-to-face conversation with somebody. Skype doesn't count, you actually have to leave the house – it could just be, 'Lovely day, today, isn't it? Do you know what the forecast is for tomorrow?' to the man in the corner shop.
5) Give yourself a treat (doesn't have to cost money – a nice bath, a trip to the charity shop to try out new outfits, that sort of thing).
6) Laugh – my favourite – see attached gift!!!
7) Exercise (can just be a ten-minute walk round the block).
8) Smile or say hello to a stranger (has to be a different person to number 4).
9) Do a kind deed – either helping someone or going out of your way to be nice to someone.
10) Watch no more than two hours of telly a day.

There are two things you can tell about Philippa from reading this, one is that she is a slave to the motto 'why use a full stop when you can use 6,000 exclamation marks instead', and two is that she is the best friend a girl could ever, ever, ever (and on ad infinitum) wish for. The gift she mentioned was three DVDs of my favourite stand-up comedians doing live routines.

Now, I love the Smiling Fanny Manifesto. Not only has it kept the dark days at bay but it has also led me to meet some wonderful/terrifying/magical/totally maverick people and on many occasions have wonderful/terrifying/magical/totally maverick adventures. The only slight hiccup about the Smiling Fanny Manifesto is that basically it is ten things that have to be done every day, so it can be rather exhausting. Fairly regularly I can be found at two in the morning (after careful consideration we decided that in the case of the Smiling Fanny Manifesto the day should end when I go to sleep, rather than at midnight) grinning manically at random people, desperately trying to engage them in conversation or shrieking, 'Please, can I help you with something! By that I don't mean sexual favours!'

I met my flatmate, Al, in this way. It was by the chip van, Posh Nosh, which sits outside Tiddlies, Tiddlesbury's one and only nightclub. Arty, the Posh Nosh chef, was making my cheesy chips and beans. I was keeping an eye on him. It's very important the salt and vinegar go on the chips and then the beans go on top of that and then the cheese on top of that. No other variable works. So I was calmly averting cheesy-chip-and-bean catastrophe when I noticed this strange-looking bloke standing next to me. He looked to be about six foot five with long reddish hair that didn't so much hang as float like a cloud about his head. He was reading the menu and rubbing his chin.

'Can I help you make a decision?' I asked him gleefully. I quite often sound gleeful when I'm asking people if they need help, especially in the early hours. It's something I need to work on.

'Ermmmmm,' he mumbled.

'Oooh, no, the beans next, please, Arty,' I hyperventilated.

'Ermmmm,' the strange-looking fellow mumbled again.

'You're going to have a lamb doner.'

'Sorry?'

'Blokes always do this.'

'What?'

'Fanny about for ages looking at the menu and then order a lamb doner with extra garlic sauce.'

Arty, who was now sprinkling cheese on my chips, smiled.

'Am I not right?'

'She's right.'

'Please can I have a small blob of barbeque sauce on the side for dunking?' I asked. It never lets you down.

'I'll have a lamb doner.'

'See?'

'I don't think I was going to, I think you mind-tricked me into it.'

'We do a lot of that in Tiddlesbury.'

'Are you from here?'

'Well, I went to school here. I grew up a few miles away, and then I moved here when I was eighteen. It was London, Edinburgh or Tiddlesbury. What about you?'

'I moved here today.'

'Welcome. Will you be doing the open-top bus tour tomorrow?'

'Is there a . . . ?'

'No, I was joking.'

'Oh.'

'But me and my best friend Philippa can show you round if you like.'

'Oh, er, great, really, wow, thank you.'

That's tomorrow's good deed sorted. Tidy.

'I would introduce you to Philippa now, but . . .' I turned my head to the right, towards the nightclub rubbish bins. Philippa was behind them, snogging the bloke who worked on the cooked meats counter in the supermarket. She likes to end the evening with a little snog. 'Er, she's a bit busy at the moment.'

'Are you sure you don't mind showing me round?'

'No, not at all, meet you here at five. Wear comfortable shoes and bring money for sundry spending. What's your name?'

'Al. You?'

'Jenny. But everyone calls me Fanny. Welcome to Tiddlesbury.'

'Thank you.'

And with that I left him to his lamb doner. Not knowing that five days later I was going to move out of Philippa's dad's house and into the spare room of his flat, which is where I still live, which is where I am at this very moment, lying in bed listening to him clanking and crashing about in the kitchen. He calls it cooking. Quite often he gets up before work to do it. This morning he's baking a cake. I think it's some phenomenal chocolate extravaganza. The aroma reaching me is sweet, it's making my tummy gurgle and my mouth fill up with saliva, something that doesn't happen when he's up early making duck ragout.

So the Smiling Fanny Manifesto has shaped most of my life up to this point. In fact, I dread to think where I'd be without it.

'Fan!' It's Al, tapping on my door.

'Come in,' I call.

'Fanny, Fanny,' Al swings open the door and lunges onto my bed. He's dressed in his acid house smiley face boxers, his towelling dressing gown with the missing belt that barely reaches his knee, and he is covered in a considerable dusting of flour. He's holding a small plate on which sits a massive slab of chocolate cake.

'Fanny, I nailed it.'

'What did you nail?'

'Nigella's chocolate cake,' he informs me proudly.

'Ooh, that could be misconstrued.'

'Eat up your breakfast,' he says placing the plate on my duvet-covered lap. I beam. If there's ever an early indication that the day is going to be a cracker, it's chocolate cake for breakfast. Ooh, I'll say that again. Chocolate. I love the stuff. I tuck in greedily. Al observes me, a contented smile on his face. He really is watching me very closely. I stop chewing and eye him suspiciously.

'Are you looking at my man moustache?' I ask.

'You what?'

'My man-tache,' I say, sadly stroking the downy fur above my top lip. It's all I can see when I look in the mirror at the moment.

'Fan, you haven't got a moustache.'

God, I love Al. He is utterly and completely lovely. Although he is rather huge and scary looking. Seriously, if he followed you home you'd poop a brick, I must have been off my knockers that night to have started talking to him by the chip van. Aside from being the tallest man I've ever met and having hair like flaming candy floss, the only other striking thing about him is a nearly permanent bruise on his forehead from constantly being hit in the head by lampshades. He's kind, thoughtful, loyal as a puppy but he does work for the council so is prone to moan. Oh, and he's also remarkably good in bed for one so clumsy. I have first-hand experience of this because I've slept with him once. All right, eleven times. OK, it might have been nearer fifteen. But it was during that incredibly cold spell the year before last and our heating had broken down and I hadn't had sex for about a billion years, so you can hardly blame me. But please don't think I'm a floozy. I'm depressingly far from it. I've only slept with three people and I'm twenty-seven. It's a source of endless disappointment.

'Uh, oh, my God, this cake is amazing,' I moan.

'I never thought I'd nail Nigella's chocolate cake,' he purrs.

'Please, I'm getting a picture.'

'I wouldn't mind—'

'Change subject now,' I say putting a hand up. 'Right, now, Al, I need your honest opinion. You see, I've dyed it blonde . . . '

Al looks at me blankly.

'My man-tache,' I hiss. 'Don't you think it looks weirder now? Like a golden guinea pig? I can see it out of the corner of my eye.' I squeeze one eye closed, look down with the other and stick my lip out to prove my point. 'I don't know whether to cream it, or wax it or what. It's a—' I'm stopped short in my conjecturing by my mobile ringing on my bedside table. 'Someone's up early,' I say, picking it up. I see my old home number. 'Oh, no, it's my dad,' I whisper, a familiar tight knot forming in my chest.

Wow, that's quickly felled my early morning chocolate high. I haven't spoken to my parents for weeks. It could be well over a month. We don't have the best bond. It's complicated, as they say.

'Hello?'

'Jenny! Oh, oh, dear. Jenny, I've got to go, but I'll see you later!'

The phone goes dead.

It wasn't my father at all. It was my mother. And this is very, very strange.

Chapter 2

'Arrrrggghhhhhhhhhh!' I scream like I'm experiencing some very intimate depilation. 'Arrrrggghhhhh!'

'Fan, should I be concerned?' Al yells, banging on the bathroom door.

'No, I'm all right,' I shout over the shower.

'Sure?'

'Yeah, I've just had a lot of sugar this morning and my mum called and uttered the dreaded words "see you later". Arrrrggghhhhhhhhhh!'

'Fair dos, Fan, fair dos.'

This isn't an unusual reaction to a potential parental visit. I try to see Mum and Dad as little as possible. I realised a long time ago that it's kinder on my mental health not to see them too much. There's only so many times I can hear my father ask, 'Have you achieved anything since we last saw you, Jenny? Have you found anyone to marry you? No? And why doesn't that surprise me?' It's also kinder on my liver, because I normally need an entire bottle of wine and a DVD of something very, very funny to recover from a parental sighting.

'Arrrrggghhhhhhhhh!'

Growls in the shower are very cathartic. Although it's unusual for me to need them on a Friday. I love a Friday, me. People smile on Fridays, something they tend not to do on any other weekday. But the best thing about Friday is something called Fashion Friday, which Philippa invented. Every Friday at 8 a.m. on the dot, Philippa and I take it in turns to text each other with a dress code for the day. At first the texts would say 'floral' or 'gothic' but over the years they've got more and more extreme. Last week was 'Rainy Ladies' Day at Ascot', the week before was 'Yoga Teacher with Penchant for Tantric Sex'. We live in Tiddlesbury, a small town in the middle of England, so we need all the excitement we can get.

'Arrrrggghhhhhhhhh!'

The bathroom clock says 7.57. That will have to be my last growl. I climb out of the shower and into a bathrobe, and then I perform my first daily act of the Smiling Fanny Manifesto. I water Matilda, my plant.

'Morning, beautiful,' I say, because there is a school of thought that believes talking to plants helps them grow and, if you ask me, this school of thought is onto something because Matilda is practically the size of a fully grown cow. She used to live in the lounge but there was nowhere she could be without blocking a doorway or the view of the telly. So now she resides here, in the bathroom. We had to take out the free-standing set of drawers to accommodate her, which was a shame. You don't get much back on the conversation front with old Matilda so I don't go overboard. I just like to leave her with these few uplifting words. If someone was only going to say just two words to me a day, I'd be happy with 'morning, beautiful'.

I wander back into my room. I sit on the bed, place my mobile phone on my lap and await the Fashion Friday instructions. I pick up my book, planning to grab a few minutes reading prior to the arrival of Philippa's orders. The book I am reading at the moment is brilliant. It's about a woman called Rosie who's thirty and has her own drive-time radio show; yes, she's very cool is Rosie, although she does keep accidentally making libellous statements on air, so I'm a bit worried about her job, and her relationship too, actually. She goes out with this lovely bloke who is in a soap opera but she's ballsing it up with him because she's desperate for him to propose. I've barely been able to put the book down, but this morning, before I've even started to absorb the words, I'm looking out of the window and blowing breath through my lips like a horse. Have I forgotten that I was supposed to be meeting my parents later? No. Definitely not. I know this because Matt, my boyfriend, is taking me somewhere special tonight on a date. I definitely wouldn't have double-booked. I breathe out through my lips again. My mother calling is very strange. My mother never even uses the phone. My father has always been funny about her using the phone. He didn't like her answering it, and he used to scrutinise the monthly itemised bills, quizzing her about her calls. As a result she stopped using it. All of which makes my mother calling today so extraordinary. *See you later*, she said. She definitely said it. I wouldn't mind seeing my mum later. My mum is nowhere near as ghastly as my dad. On the whole we got on well together when I lived at home, although we haven't been as close since I left. But I have some nice memories of her from my childhood. She tried as best she could to stand up for me against my dad, she made the best roast chicken and shepherd's pie you'll ever taste and on Thursday nights when Dad played squash and we had the telly to ourselves we'd sit laughing at *Only Fools and Horses* together. But my dad hates her going anywhere without him, so if I'm seeing my mum today it means I'll be seeing him too.

My mobile phone vibrates with a text. I gasp as I always do. It's 8 a.m. It's today's dress code from Philippa.

Friday Fashion this week is . . . Dinner ladies!

It's a wind-up. At least I hope it's a wind-up. Philippa is peeved that I'm going out with Matt tonight. Normally Matt spends Friday night having beers and a curry with his workmates, so Philippa and I go out together. However, much as she'd love me to go out on my hot date this evening dressed as a dinner lady, she will also be going out later too, to our favourite club night, Bomber. Philippa will definitely be intending to pull and even Philippa would find it hard to pull dressed as a dinner lady. She'd get mistaken for a cleaner. She'd get asked to sort out a mess in the toilets. I keep hold of the phone, waiting for the next, more glamorous, option. Ah, here we are.

As if! Fashion Friday this week is . . . The Child of Destiny!! xxx

I text quickly back.

Nice! Xxx

The Child of Destiny is what Philippa and I call the esteemed girl band Destiny's Child. We love Destiny's Child and have since school.

I hop out of bed and scan my room hoping for inspiration. I love my room, but it is crammed to the point of probable pain with clothes; most purchased from charity shops, some donated to me and a few special items bought new from proper shops or websites. Clothes cover the entire room and are colour-coded, creating a pleasant, trippy rainbow effect. Behind the clothes my walls are pale pink woodchip but only I know that. I tidied last night. I always tidy on Thursday because every Friday the room gets massacred when I have to come up with an outfit and be at work by 8.45. As is happening now. I'm already in the silver corner and have thrown some possibilities onto the bed. It may sound extreme that I have so many clothes, and it may well be. But Philippa's the same. So at least I have company in the realms of extremity. This is why we introduced Fashion Friday, so we could get the chance to air some of our more outlandish purchases without having to wait for, say, a special occasion or a fancy dress party.

The third dress I try on is the one. A long-sleeved minidress, in pewter sequins. It's tight on the bottom and baggier on the top, which is ideal because I work in a doctor's surgery and people mainly see the top part of me as I sit behind the front desk. I stand and look at myself in the mirror. And then I sigh. Some days, it's just hard to look in the mirror. Today is evidently one of them. Although that might be because thinking about my father makes my eyes droop and my mouth set to a frown, the combination of which doesn't create the prettiest face.

'Come on, JT, it could be worse,' I say to my reflection, forcing a little smile. 'That's better.'

I don't want to feel glum about how I look. I've got this face and body for my whole life. I may as well make some sort of peace with them. And I definitely look a lot better than I used to. When I was a child people would say that I was funny looking. They weren't wrong. I've got the pictures to prove it. I had big sticking-out ears, with a huge mouth and long limbs, which I couldn't quite control and which meant I was always knocking into people and things, something that infuriated my father. Nowadays, I don't look like the girl I used to. No one's called me funny looking, at least not to my face, for years. Although, once you've been called funny looking you always feel a bit funny looking, to be honest. Maybe that's why I love clothes so much. And dying my hair, I'm a big fan of that too. Maybe it's just to disguise the fact that beneath it all I'm just a funny-looking gangly girl who had her ears pinned back. Who knows? Bit of a morbid thought that.

Moving on. My hair is a mousy brown colour, or it was when I last looked, seven years ago. Right now, it's a raspberry red colour in a fifties-style bob with a little fringe. I have slim legs. Yay. But no waist to speak of. Boo. And one of my small breasts is obviously bigger than the other. Apart from that, I have brown eyes and, although I still have a big mouth, I don't really mind much any more. Sometimes people tell me that they like my lovely big smile, and I love hearing that so much. No, I don't mind my mouth, it's useful for talking and eating too, both of which I do a lot of, and it's useful for other things, if you know what I mean, which I do a fair bit of too, now I have a boyfriend. So I can't be a complete minger because my Matt is buff. Happy days.

Or at least today would feel like a happy day if I didn't have this nagging suspicion that my mother and father are going to make a surprise visit. And if there's one thing I know about my father it's that he won't be impressed by my pewter sequin minidress and will tell me at passionate length why not. Urgh. Stop thinking about your dad, Jenny. Think about your boyfriend. That's much more fun.

Chapter 3

I don't know whether it's me being oversensitive but I think that people often look surprised when they learn that I have a boyfriend. They can't be as surprised as I am. Matthew Parry is his name. Jenny Parry. Jenny Parry. Not that he's proposed. But it's been a year, so you never know. Jenny Parry. No genital connotations at all. A fact that never fails to make me smile. Not only is he six foot two with sandy blond hair, he goes to the gym and hence has arm muscles. But he's also driven. Yep, driven. He works for a big finance company, and is tipped to be a partner. I know! And he's mine. He has just taken up golf though, which proves that you can't have everything.

If it wasn't for the Smiling Fanny Manifesto we would never have met. Although it wasn't what you'd term a romantic first meeting. You'd have been forgiven for not noticing the fervent sexual chemistry, what with him threatening to call the police on me.

I should first explain that although point nine on the Smiling Fanny Manifesto is without a doubt the point that brings the most joy into my life, it is also by far the point on the list that is the biggest pain in the bottom. There are 365 days in a year. I've been following these rules for over six years. I've done over 2,000 good deeds. *Over 2,000 good deeds.* Day in, day out, with no vacations, I have to find a way to help someone. Hence, I always keep a stash of pretty notelets in my handbag so I can write a kind, anonymous note for a stranger should the situation arise. I love note writing. I love the thought of a slightly insecure-looking pretty young girl coming home and finding a card in her bag telling her that she looked beautiful tonight in that pink jumper, and that all the boys were clocking her twice and all the girls wanted to look as good as her. Recently Philippa and I have even tried setting people up with our note giving.

Anyway, back to the first time I met Matt. It was one Friday evening and, contrary to his usual practice, Matt wasn't having beers and a curry with his workmates, he was in a pub in Nunstone. Now, Nunstone is a small town that lies seven miles from, and bears an uncanny similarity to, Tiddlesbury. Like Tiddlesbury it has:

1) a church that no one goes to
2) a doctor's surgery that everyone goes to
3) six estate agents, all next door to each other
4) an underlying drug problem
5) no less than five charity shops
6) seven pubs, three of which serve Thai food
7) a kebab shop which claims it's a Turkish restaurant
8) a nightclub where someone was once stabbed.

Philippa and I go out in Nunstone on the first Friday of every month, as she will be doing tonight, because its nightclub, Original Sin, hosts a night called Bomber where Jägerbombs are half price. Philippa and I love the Jägerbomb. A shot of Jägermeister dropped into a small glass of Red Bull is the perfect nightclub beverage. It's quick to drink, meaning you're hands free on the dance floor, you don't consume too much liquid so reduce the need to visit Original Sin's terrifying toilets and it doesn't make your mouth smell manky like wine, or make you feel as though an HGV has crashed into your head the next day like wine also does. I'm digressing, Jägerbombs make me do that. Back to the story.

Philippa and I were in Nunstone, having a drink in Nunstone's premier (premier because it's the only one) gastropub before we went to Bomber. As it was a Friday we were dressed as 'Air Hostesses Who Work for a Budget Airline'. We were dressed as air hostesses largely because we'd found two matching military-style jackets in a charity shop and thought if we teamed these with miniskirts, high heels and a lot of Jägermeister we might pull.

So there we are in Nunstone's premier gastropub, dressed as air hostesses and scanning the room for a suitable person on whom to bestow a well-meaning note.

'Her!' hissed Philippa, leaning over the table and tapping me on the arm with a pointed finger and then using the same finger to draw my attention to a pretty girl sitting opposite a handsome young sandy-haired man.

'Oh.' I sighed. 'Oh, the poor thing.'

She was probably my age and was wearing a lovely flowered shirt-dress. She was exquisite, her skin was creamy and unblemished and her hair was thick and chestnutty with what looked like a natural wave in it. But I didn't even have natural-wave envy because the poor girl didn't look at all happy. Her eyes were heavy and her mouth turned down. She reminded me of me before the Smiling Fanny Manifesto. I shivered a little, remembering the scared me at eighteen who would cry in Philippa's spare room and didn't like to leave the house.

'Philippa, you do know that every night you're my first blessing, don't you?'

'Yep.'

'Cool.'

'So what we going to write?'

'I might write out the Smiling Fanny Manifesto for her.'

'Nice,' said Philippa with a smile. 'I hereby lend you the copyright.'

'Much obliged.'

So I went into my bag. I call it a bag, because that's what girls do, however, holdall might be more appropriate given the size of it. Another byproduct of point nine on the Smiling Fanny Manifesto is the amount of 'might come in handy for helping people stuff' (some might call it crap) I constantly carry around. I don't leave home without painkillers, plasters, a local map, pens, two macs in sacs, sweets, mints, gum, bottle opener, and, my pièce de résistance, an array of pretty stationery. I pulled out a small postcard I'd been carrying around for months and on it I wrote,

Hello, you don't look very happy and I hope you're not offended but this might help. My best friend wrote this for me when I was down. It's called the Smiling Manifesto, I've been doing all the tasks now, daily, for years, and it really helped me. If you don't want it, you might know someone else who could use it.

I then somehow managed to cram all ten points onto it. Towards the bottom my writing had gone from beyond minuscule to that which might well be deciphered with only a microscope. Anyway, I managed it, whether or not she'd be able to read it or not, I didn't know.

Philippa and I finished our drinks and stood up. We had to hurry because they started charging on the door of the club in a minute. We didn't even need to discuss the next bit, we'd been perfecting it for years. She got up from the table and walked over to where the pretty girl was sitting with her boyfriend on the banquette. I followed. I saw that the girl's bag (also a holdall) was nestled next to her, open and waiting for me to slip the letter in. This would be easy.

'Am I being stupid?' Philippa started while I hovered next to the pretty girl's bag. 'I can't find the loos in here.'

'Oh,' the unhappy girl starts. I lean down to drop the card into her bag. Seamless.

'Oi! Oi!' Sandy-coloured-hair man shouts, getting quickly to his feet. 'What are you doing with her bag?' He challenged us. We stared back, open mouthed, we'd never been caught before. I couldn't help but be impressed and I found myself thinking how nice it would be to have someone watching out for me in that way. A wingman. I had a wingwoman, of course. I had the best wingwoman in the world in Philippa. But as this handsome man leapt to his feet I couldn't help but feel a longing for a man who cared for and wanted to protect me too. I was getting those urges a lot at that time. I suppose I was lonely for love. He's gallant, I thought, and it struck me that gallant wasn't a word that got used much any more. In Nunstone, anyway.

'It's the oldest trick in the book that, "Where's the toilet?" distraction. Thieves! Thieves!' he shouted. 'I'm calling the police!'

Now, I would like to say here, in my defence, that I didn't start the laughing. It was Philippa. She always starts the laughing. She's been like this since school. We'd be hauled into the headmaster's office for causing some sort of uncool ruckus like trying to smoke oregano and setting off the smoke alarm. We'd be sheepishly receiving a bollocking when I'd notice, out of the corner of my eye, that Philippa was silently rocking back and forward. Uncontrollable laughter always starts with silent rocking and once it starts, it generally takes around four and a half seconds for me to be laughing too. I am powerless to keep a straight face once Philippa starts with the silent rocking.

So the sandy-haired gallant bloke mentions the police and Philippa starts doing some really rather dynamic rocking.

'Check your bag! Check your bag!' he's shouting now, and jumping from foot to foot. 'I thought air hostesses were well paid!'

Four and a half seconds are up. Philippa snorts. I have to sit down, the laughs come so hard. A barman comes over. The girl simply sits quietly squinting at the card.

'It's all right, Matt, they didn't take anything. They left me a note. Let's go.'

'Left you a note?'

'Yes.'

'What's it about?'

'Just a girly note. Saying they like my dress.'

Sandy-haired man shakes his head as though he's never heard anything so ridiculous. The pretty girl nearly smiles but not quite. Philippa and I nod to each other and head for the door.

I had absolutely no idea that six months later sandy-haired man would have seen me naked. Mind you, there would be a few more fateful meetings before we got to that point.

Don't whatever you do get Philippa talking about my meeting Matt. She doesn't think Matt's right for me. She thinks that because cherubs didn't appear and fireworks didn't start flying out of my bottom the first time I met him, he's not The One. She says, 'If he doesn't make your bits twitch then you're banging a square peg in a round hole.' She talks about bit-twitching a lot.

It's strange. My best friend Philippa is the wisest person I know. Her father is a doctor in Tiddlesbury and her mum lives in America and is a life coach/sexual therapist (it actually says that on her business cards), and Philippa herself works for the local paper, so she knows practically everything about everything. She delivers top-notch advice on a whole range of subjects, but bless her, she hasn't got a clue about love. She thinks it exists like it does in a romance novel or a film starring Hugh Grant or Sandra Bullock, she believes that it's possible to totally gel with another person and exist in an unpoppable bubble of bliss with them. I know. Ridiculous.

But I love having a boyfriend. I really do. Matt's my first ever boyfriend, which is a bit embarrassing. But it could be worse, I got there in the end. And at least thinking about him stopped me dwelling on my father, as I carried on getting ready for work.

Chapter 4

I work at the doctor's surgery. That's not the sexiest of sentences, is it? I'm head of reception at the local GP. It just isn't saucy. It just isn't true either. I mean basically I *am* head of reception, on account of the fact that the other receptionist is Marge, who dodges anything that can be construed as work. But I'm not head of reception officially. Essentially I'm head of reception in all but title and pay. It's not ideal. But I'm pretty sure it could be worse.

I love my job, a fact that surprises people. *What? You spend your days with grumpy, ill people!* they exclaim. But that's what I like about it. I'm never happier than when the waiting room is full of sick, miserable people. And then guess what I do with them? I make them laugh. It's not generally me that does it, it's more my extensive selection of comedy DVDs and the surgery telly that does the hard work. They come in looking the epitome of doom. That's the thing about illness, it can be pretty miserable. I mean some of them are literally dying. Now, I can't be 100 per cent certain because I've never done a formal study on the subject, but it's my belief that people don't want to spend their last days, or months, or years being miserable, thinking, I'm going to die. I think they'd much rather watch *Miranda* or *Friends* or *Only Fools and Horses*. Actually I should qualify that, I'm sure they'd much rather be driving around California in a convertible or sipping rum punch on a Caribbean island but as circumstances have them stuck in Tiddlesbury at the doctor's surgery, the first series of *Ab Fab* is what they're getting, or at least it's what they're getting today.

I have been at work for over two hours and so far no signs of any surprise visits by my father, the arse. Thank goodness. In fact, all is as it normally is. Which means we have been ferociously busy and I have been sneakily opening my drawer, whenever things calm down, in order to read a page or two of my book. (Rosie's actor boyfriend, Max Read – Rosie Read! I know, I so hope it works out for her – is lush. He could well make my list of favourite fictional boyfriends. Although, Rosie is getting more and more loopy as she tries to wangle a ring out of him, and I'm a bit worried she's going to cop off with her handsome work colleague.) There's also a box of Lindt truffles in my drawer which I purchased on my way to work. It means that my chocolate quotient for the day will be pretty extreme, what with the cake I had for breakfast. But I operate a strict 'I am allowed all the treats I want' policy on days when I might see my dad. I haven't told Marge about the truffles yet. I'll share them with her in a little while, but I'll just sneak a few for myself first. She gets on automatic pilot with sweet treats and before you know it she says, 'Here, Fan, you have the last one.' It can be quite devastating. Oh, and because it's a standard day at the surgery, Marge hasn't offered to make the tea. Marge never makes the tea. Don't get me started about Marge not making the tea.

Marge is quite frankly astonishing. She is thirty-seven and seventeen stone. But she is entirely happy with her shape. In fact she's so happy with her shape that she might be taking part in a BBC documentary about the larger woman. Although when I say BBC I mean BBC Three, and when I say documentary, I mean a programme called *I Like 'Em Big*. We had a film crew here a while back filming Marge for a pilot. Although when I say film crew I mean one disgruntled bloke called Dave with a video camera, on what I now refer to as The Day When Marge Turned Into Liz Taylor. Marge has a pretty face, a jolly demeanour and she always wears very bright colours in patterns that I sometimes worry could harm epileptics. I am very fond of Marge, I just wish she'd make the tea more often and take it a bit easier on my Lindt truffles. Mind you, you have to be fond of Marge really because she belongs to the hardest family of criminals that we have in Tiddlesbury. I think there's a game you can play where you can match any illegal drug found in Nunstone or Tiddlesbury back to a member of Marge's family. She is in bit-twitching love with a fellow called Tim. He's dodgy. He is in house clearance, but not the sort of house clearance that has been authorised, if you know what I mean. He is about my age, I think, and from what Marge says he is the handsomest man that ever sperm created. I have never met Tim, although I know a lot of intimate details about the man that I very much wish I didn't. They have just bought a house together. Something else I know a lot about.

So, basically, I sit next to Marge on the reception of Tiddlesbury surgery trying to marshal the sick whilst she tells me about the tiles in her new bathroom and where Tim puts his finger when she is climaxing. But it's not a bad place to work. I am quite content here. We can't all be superstars, after all, and I really do like a lot of the patients, most of whom are OAPs. I am a bit of a hit amongst the elderly, if I do say so myself. If I ever had need to summon an army, it would consist almost entirely of ailing but wily octogenarians, and would, I predict, be pretty terrifying for the opposition. The army would most probably be led by my favourite patient, Doris, who's just walking in now.

'Ooh, sparkles today, Fanny!' She smiles when she sees me.

'Morning, Doris.' I smile back.

You can't not smile when Doris is about. She's at least eighty, barely five foot, with the biggest knockers you've ever seen in your life, and I've never seen her anything but exquisitely turned out. Face powdered, mouth lipsticked, old-fashioned stockings with a perfectly placed seam down the back, neat suit over a soft-looking jumper (whatever the weather). But despite her immaculate appearance she very often has the mouth of an aggrieved builder and she loves a party. I adore her. Everyone adores Doris. Doris is the grandmother of the man who pooped on me from a great height when I was younger. It's a shame Doris' big heart didn't rub off on him – a great shame, actually. I would love to be Doris' granddaughter-in-law. Doris doesn't know about her grandson's pooping – Doris holds her Little Stevie on a bit of a pedestal and I think she'd be upset if I pushed him off it.

'Have you heard?' she says excitedly, approaching the desk.

'What about?' I grin.

'A man's moving into Rose Cottage. He's a lone writer apparently,' she chatters. 'It sounds like the start of one of those books you read, Fanny, doesn't it?'

'Oh, yes, we did hear that,' I say. That's the other thing about working at the surgery. It's marvellous for gossip and as Rose Cottage is the most beautiful house in Tiddlesbury, there's no way someone could have moved in there without Marge and I being fully and repeatedly informed.

'I'm in to see Dr Flemming,' she says. 'But I thought I'd pop in a bit early to see my favourite girl.'

'So, how have you been, my lovely?' I ask her.

'Well, just the one funeral this week. Bloody dreadful. Don't know what the family were thinking,' Doris says, sitting down and getting comfortable. She's off. Once Doris is off there's no stopping her. Her funeral tirade is passionate and frequent. She's terribly disappointed with the nature of funerals at the moment. She says that once you're in your eighties they're the only parties you get invited to.

'There was no booze! Fanny! Not a sniff of the stuff. Mildred had her first sherry at eleven every morning, and yet her family didn't lay on any booze at her funeral. And they weren't short of a bob or two, Fanny.'

'Oh, no, Doris. What did you do?'

'Well, I had my hip flask with me. It's happened to me before, you see, so I was prepared. But anyway, it got me thinking. When I go, I want a party. A big bash. The bigger the better. I want everyone legless, dancing till dawn to Rod Stewart, oh, that man, Fanny, I could wear him out. I want pork pies, proper ham sandwiches. Cheap fizz and port to drink. No beer, Fanny, I don't care what the men say, it makes them fart. I want a right old knees-up.'

'Will you have a dress code?' I ask. I love a dress code.

'Ohhhh.' Doris nods. 'Oh, yes, let me think . . . ' She purses her lips and furrows her brow. She really is giving the dress code a lot of consideration.

Marge utilises the break in Doris' narrative to sigh loudly. Uh oh. I think I know what's coming.

'Oh, I'd love a cup of tea,' she says, in her wistful 'I've never had a cup of tea in my life' way.

Here we go. The bane of my working life. This is Marge's first Get Jenny To Make the Tea Tactic. It will be followed in a few moments by some excuse as to why she can't get up and put the kettle on.

'My back's twinging again, otherwise I'd get up and make us both a nice cup of tea now. Ooh.' The 'ooh' comes with a pained wince. 'It is sore. Hmmm,' she whimpers as though she's in agony. 'Ow,' she adds for good measure.

And that's as much as I can take. I stand up. I know. I'm weak. I'm a walkover. I always end up making the tea.

'Here, I'll make you a cup of tea,' I say. I get my phone and my book out of my drawer, take her mug and head to the kitchen.

'Oh, Fanny, thank you,' she says, as though I've just saved her from a burning building.

Once in the kitchen I turn the radio and the kettle on and then lean over the counter and try and get a few pages of my book in before the kettle boils. A Rihanna song comes on air. I am just having a little attempt at a Rihanna grind, when Marge pokes her face round the door. I freeze, bottom sticking out, book in hand.

'I love this song,' I say by way of explanation.

'I can see,' she says. 'There's a woman asking for you.'

She disappears. We can't both be away from the front desk. I pop back into the waiting room but I can't see any woman there who might be waiting for me.

'She went outside,' Marge informs me.

I open the surgery doors and peek my head out into the street.

Blimey. A big bundle of blimey, in fact. There standing on the pavement, surrounded by an awful lot of luggage, is my mother. Absolutely no sign of my father at all. Just Mum, a bit thinner than normal, her long, blue, buttoned-at-the-front skirt and pink cardigan look slightly too big for her. Her light brown hair hangs unbrushed to her shoulders and her eyes look both tired and wired.

'Where's Dad?'

'Work, I suppose. Or with his lover, perhaps.'

'Dad's got a lover?' I whisper.

'Yes, and I've come to stay with you, I thought we could have a bit of fun.'

'What?'

'Fun.' She lifts her shoulders towards her ears and smiles. 'And chats. There's so much we need to talk about. Can I stay with you?'

I stand staring at her with my mouth open. Fun and chats? Has she lost the plot?

'But . . . but . . . I live above a shop. In Tiddlesbury.'

'Do you mind if I stay?'

'Well. No, course not. But . . . but . . .'

'What?'

'Well, what about your work?'

My mum works for a charity. She's a tremendous fundraiser for a local hospice.

'I've handed my role to someone else. I need some me time. Now, can I leave these bags with you? I need to get me a haircut.'

The whole notion of reality seems to be spinning on its head.

'OK.'

'Brilliant. I'll do that first. Can't have fun with my hair like this, can I?'

I shake my head. She's got a point.

'See you in a few hours, probably. I need a colour.'

And with that she's off, and I think she might have just skipped a little down the street. It's not even lunchtime and the day has careered into weird. Two suitcases and a rucksack! How long is she intending to stay? My father has a lover and Mum's come to stay with me. My father has a lover and my mum's come to stay with me. Even when I repeat it in my head it still sounds unbelievable. I put the rucksack on my back and haul the suitcases into the surgery. My father has a lover and my mother's come to stay with me. Nope, still weird.

'What on earth?' Marge exclaims as soon as she sees me.

'Don't ask,' I say, humping the bags to the kitchen.

Alone for a moment, I close my eyes. My body shivers

and there's a fluttering behind my eyes that makes me feel like I want cry. I have to help my mother at this time. Obviously I do. However, I wish this wasn't happening. I like my life as it is, as it was, separate from my parents, separate from my past.

Chapter 5

Mum's only had her hair cut like Victoria Beckham. And that's not all. Oh, no. Oh ho, oh no. She's also dyed it blonde. Blonde. She's fifty-four. Which I know isn't ancient but I would say is bit old to opt for a blonde Victoria Beckham bob. It actually doesn't look bad. But she's not my mother. The woman in my flat at this precise moment cannot be my mother. My mother wears practical clothes, more often than not with an apron over the top because she's cooking, and she never does anything with her hair, let alone sexy styling. She's having a midlife. And she's staying with me. Help.

'Um, so, when did you find out?' I ask, sitting myself at the kitchen table. Mum's looking in the fridge.

'You don't have any wine open, do you?'

Definitely a midlife. My mother only drinks with dinner. On Saturdays. It's 4.30 on Friday afternoon. Even I'd wait until 6 p.m. Well, maybe 5.30.

'I think there's a bottle of wine in there you can open.'

She turns around and smiles, holding a bottle of rosé.

'What fun.'

I get up and fetch some glasses and a corkscrew.

'I wonder whether blondes do have more,' she says shaking her head as I sit down and open the wine. I pour two glasses. I can't have her drinking alone and Dr Flemming gave me the afternoon off when he heard my mother had arrived unannounced. 'I've always wanted to be blonde and Jack said no. No, no, no. Jack said that a lot.'

'So, what happened?'

'Sue. It was Sue. My friend Sue!'

'Bloody hell.'

'I'd go as far as fu—'

'Mum.' I gasp. She was going to say the F-word. I've never heard my mum swear in my life. 'Mum, please don't swear. That would be very unsettling.'

'It has been going on for years.'

'When did you find out?'

'A month ago now. '

'A month ago.'

'He said he had a work do in Birmingham. But I knew he hadn't. I knew. I'd known he wasn't always where he said he was. But this time, as I was sat alone watching the telly, I snapped, I'd had some news that day and it made me snap and I thought, I'll just check Sue's house. So, I got a taxi there. Seventeen miles, so it's not round the corner, it wasn't cheap. But I had a feeling. And there was his car, bold as brass, parked in her driveway. So I paid the cab driver and I got in your father's car, I had a key on my set of house keys, you see. I was insured on the car. The family car, that's what he used to call it. So I drove it home and put it in the garage. Jack called the next morning. "The car's been stolen," he told me, he wasn't happy. "From Birmingham?" I said. "Yes," he told me. "Oh dear, you must call the police," I said. "Yes, yes," he said. "Yes, yes." Anyway, he came back that night, I'd made a lasagne, and I said, "Jack, can you pop into the garage and fetch me some garlic bread out of the freezer while you've got your shoes on." And so he did. And when he came back with the garlic bread he looked furious. So I dropped the lasagne on the floor with the oven dish, which was very dramatic for me, I thought, and I took myself off to bed. Your old bed, in fact.'

'But this was a month ago and you've only just left.'

'Well, I didn't get out of bed for a few weeks.'

I nod. I do that. Stay in bed when I can't face things.

'Then I got up and packed my bags and went to Wales.'

'Wales?'

'Yes, I'd always wanted to go to Wales. It always looks so pretty on *Countryfile*. So I did a coach tour of Wales.'

'A coach tour?'

'Yes, because then I didn't have to think about anything. You just get on a coach when they tell you and get off when they tell you and I had a lot of time looking out of the window and thinking. And I decided that I should come and see you, Jenny. And have some fun with my beautiful daughter.'

'I'm so not beautiful.'

'You are, Jenny, you are. You are so beautiful and I wish I'd told you more.'

She's welling up. Oh, blimey. We could be in a midlife-and-menopause scenario.

'So what have you got planned for your Friday night?' she asks. 'And can I come too?' she adds with a giggle.

Woah, now she's really freaking me out.

'Actually, I'm supposed to be seeing Matt.'

'Can I come?' she asks. 'I can't wait to meet him.'

'Um. Um. Um. Let me call him.'

I leave Mum in the kitchen and go to my room to call Matt. I hang up the discarded silver dresses from earlier, which is very unlike me, but I suppose Mum will be sleeping in here now and I'll be on the sofa. My father's been shagging Mum's friend, Sue, and now Mum's come to stay with me. Nope, still weird, actually I think it might be getting weirder. And she's had her hair cut like Victoria Beckham. I need to sit down.

I perch on the end of the bed and call my gorgeous man.

'Hello, darling, lovely weather.'

'F-a-a-n!' He tuts affectionately. 'It's so annoying when you do that.'

My gorgeous man is not one for chit-chat.

'I just can't help it.'

As soon as Matt suggests that something I do is annoying I want to do it all the time. I do try not to but it's a very powerful instinct.

'Fan, please, I'm really busy and I need to leave early because we're going into London tonight.'

'London!'

'Balls, it was supposed to be a surprise.'

'Matt, my mum's arrived.'

'Your mum?'

'Yes.'

'Your actual mum?'

'Yes, my actual mum. Not the genetically cloned one that I ordered off the Internet.'

'Fan, you're talking nonsense.'

'Sorry, my dad's been having an affair and my mum's come to stay. I'm in shock.'

'Fan, you can't cancel on me, you really can't. Trust me.'

'No, course not, so why doesn't she come with us? Then you can meet her.'

'Fan, I've not planned this evening to have your mum with us.'

'OK, OK, chillax.'

'I hate chillax.'

'I know.'

'Look, I've got to go. Meet me at the station at six thirty.'

He hangs up. My shoulders slump forward as I sit. Sometimes I wish Matt was a bit more understanding, a bit less obsessed with his work. Sometimes it all feels like a battle with Matt. A battle I tend to lose. I know, I shouldn't think like that. He's lovely really, he just gets quite stressed when he's at work. No one's perfect. I hoist myself up from the bed and I shuffle back into the kitchen, Mum's already topping up her wine.

'Mum, I'm sorry, Matt's got something planned for just the two of us, I have to go to London with him. Do you mind?'

'Oh, no, love. Don't you worry about me.' Mum smiles. 'I don't want to spoil your plans. I'll just get myself a nice bottle of wine and watch the telly. Unless . . . unless . . . I don't suppose . . . '

'What?'

'No, no. Don't worry.'

'What?'

'You haven't got any marijuana have you?'

'M-u-m! No, I haven't!'

Oh, my God. She's definitely having a midlife.

'It's about time I started to live a little,' she says, in a voice I don't recognise.

I just nod at her and then start to text Philippa about the strange events of the day.

Chapter 6

Matt's only gone and brought me on the London Eye. Now, I know it's a very loving gesture. Many people might call this the perfect romantic Friday night. They may be overjoyed to share such amazing views with their true love. Not me. I don't do heights. At all. I haven't opened my eyes since we started moving. Matt knows I'm afraid of heights. He must have forgotten. I can't begin to explain how ghastly it is. Miles and miles and miles above and beyond ghastly, in fact. My mother's come to stay and I'm on the London Eye. Someone up there is having a laugh.

'Oooh, look, I can see the Houses of Parliament,' people are cooing.

'Ahhh, there's Big Ben.'

Ahh, there's my dinner, more like.

'Oooh, can you see St Paul's?'

'Oooh, Trafalgar Square.' On and on it's been going.

'Oooh, look there's Nelson's Column.' Although that one did make me giggle.

I don't even like London. Everyone seems to think it's the centre of the universe. But if you ask me it's full of strange people and it smells. Property prices went up in Tiddlesbury when they introduced the fast train from Nunstone to King's Cross. London to Nunstone in an hour and twenty minutes. I was quite happy being an hour and forty minutes away, thank you. A while ago I'd thought I wanted to live in London. But then I went. Why would anyone live here? I got off the train and, OK, it was Friday late afternoon, but I thought some terrible disaster had happened, like there was a hungry lion let loose and everyone was fleeing for their lives. But no. Apparently it was just rush hour. And when I asked an old woman if I could help her with her shopping she told me to bugger off. I kid you not. Angry people and heart attacks, that's what it said to me. Why would you do that to yourself?

Two of my worst things, London and heights, rolled maliciously into one. Oh-ho-oh, it keeps wobbling. I should have stayed at home with Mum. What if she's scouring the streets of Tiddlesbury for some dope at this very moment? She might be arrested. Or she could have passed out somewhere. Or what if she's been robbed? Is asking your daughter for drugs a normal response to finding out that your husband of twenty-seven years has been sleeping with your friend, I wonder? Mind you, it's got to be more normal than going on a coach trip to Wales. No wonder she wants drugs. But even I don't do drugs, and I have pink hair. I stick to Jägerbombs. Oh-ho-oh! Philippa's at Bomber tonight, having a laugh. I am hundreds of feet in the air, dangling in a pod.

'Don't you just love it,' Matt says.

'It's great,' I say.

'Fan, you've got your eyes closed.'

'It's better this way.'

'Fan, come on, baby, open your eyes.'

'Matt, babe, I'm really not good with heights.'

'You'll be fine.'

'I'll be sick.'

'Really?'

'No doubt about it.'

'Oh, come on, Fan, it's all in the mind.'

'The mind's a powerful place.'

My eyes are squeezed closed. The wrinkles I'll get from this will be devastating.

'Fan, come on now, open your eyes. There's a beautiful sunset.'

'Take a photo on your phone. I'll look later.'

'Go on, love,' says a female voice. 'Just take one little peek.'

'Hello, nice lady. I'm afraid I can't.'

Ooh, if I keep her talking this is a conversation with a stranger. Point four ticked off.

'Go on, love. Just a quick one.'

'Can you describe it for me?'

'Well, OK, like he said, there's a beautiful sunset and one of the greatest cities in the world is stretched at your feet. Oh, and there's a handsome man before you on his knees and I think he wants to ask you something.'

'Huh?'

I fling my eyes open and there's Matt on one knee in a crowded pod holding out a box in which twinkles a little diamond ring.

'Jenny Taylor,' even when Matt says my full name it sounds like genitalia. 'Will you marry me?'

'Huh. OH, MY GOD!' I whoop. Followed shortly by the word, 'Oops,' because I accidentally looked down. I looked down in the wobbly pod.

'Oh, uh, uh, uh, Matt. I'm going to be . . . ' Sick.

I've just thrown up a little bit in the pod. It's not ideal. But it could be worse.

'But I will marry you,' I tell him. 'Um, I don't suppose anyone has any tissues.'

Chapter 7

Philippa has this saying, 'you write your own love story', actually, Philippa has many sayings but this is one of her favourites.

'You write your own love story, Fan, gotta make sure it's a good one,' she eulogises.

It's one of the only things we disagree on. And maybe I'm unusual, because I don't want a love story in that way. Love stories have glorious highs and ghastly lows. I should know. I read enough of them, and I love reading about them. But, when it comes to my own life, I'd have to say, no, thank you, you can keep your fabulous highs and I'll happily steer clear of the terrible lows. I've experienced one terrible low already and, believe me, that was quite enough. Philippa's welcome to wait for the whole 'I'm just a girl standing in front of a boy' rom com caboodle. (That's a line from *Notting Hill*, a film that Philippa can quote HUGE chunks of, verbatim.) I'll take the sensible love that won't lead me to despair, please, thank you very much.

My love story may not be the sort you read about in books but this is what I want, I think, as I look at Matt. It's not a heady love, it's a sensible love and it feels safe. I smile as I watch him. He's tapping away at his BlackBerry, his nostrils slightly flaring as he raps at the keys. We need to order our food really, but Matt had a message on his phone when we got off the Eye, it was quite important and since then he's been answering an email. Matt is proper high powered. Being honest, I do have a clue what Matt and the company he works for does, but it's not really much more than that. Something to do with finance companies going bust and Matt's company buying them up, quite often they have to move suddenly, like tonight.

'You're my love story,' I whisper, reaching across and tapping him on the wrist as he pauses in his writing.

'Sorry, gorge. With you in a sec,' he says, looking up from his BlackBerry and giving me a quick smile.

I look at my left hand. The ring was too small. I got it on but then couldn't get it off again, which was quite stressful what with having just been sick and being in a small suspended pod. Matt's going to take it back to the jeweller and have it enlarged. I wish I was wearing it now, though, so that everyone would know I was engaged.

'How can anything be happening now, on a Friday night?'

'Huh? Oh, it's end of working day in Chicago,' he says, not looking at me. 'I'll have to fly out there tomorrow, ready to get going on Monday.'

'Oh, how long will you be gone?'

'Can't say, Fan, can't say.'

'Oh, I wanted to get planning the wedding.'

'We'll get cracking when I get back.'

He smiles again, but this time at his BlackBerry. He is very adept at conversing with someone whilst tapping a message into a BlackBerry to someone else. Much better than I'd be. I'd be writing a load of nonsense in the email. *Dear Mr Turner, Further to our wedding on the 14th* I'd be writing to the very important finance person.

'When were you thinking?' I ask him.

'Summer.'

'Which summer?'

'This summer.'

'This summer?'

'Yes, I don't see the point in waiting.'

'People will think I'm up the duff.'

'Balls! Fan. Sorry, gorge. I've got to take this,' he says, springing up and strolling out of the restaurant to take the call. An older lady at the table next to me gives me a sympathetic look.

'Work,' I say, raising my eyes to the ceiling, hoping she'll respond and this can be another conversation with a stranger.

'My first husband was like that. Worst twenty-two years of my life.'

I nod slowly. Whilst point number four on the Smiling Fanny Manifesto generally leads to pleasant exchanges, I can't deny that sometimes talking to strangers can be a downer. I rummage in my bag for my book. Rosie did sleep with her handsome work colleague and now she's very unhappy, things are uncomfortable for her at work and she's been told off for playing maudlin love songs on her upbeat drive-time show. Ooh, my phone, text from Philippa:

> FAN! What's happened to your mum?? I popped round to say hello to her. She wants to go to Bomber!

Oh help.

WTF! Is this normal behaviour??

There is no normal. Dad listened to Wagner REALLY LOUD for months when mum left. Shall I take her??

We're old at Bomber and we're 27!!

Couple of Jägerbombs and she'll be fine!

Oh. Dear. God.

Chapter 8

It's 2.43 a.m. She's not home and she hasn't called. I'm too distracted even to read. At what point do the police take you seriously? Philippa isn't answering her phone, she's bound to be snogging someone and what will my mother be doing? Lying passed out somewhere, while someone steals her bag, most probably. She's not used to alcohol and Jägerbombs can have an alarming effect, even on seasoned drinkers. I'll give it till 3 a.m. before I call the police. How can this be happening? I don't feel prepared for this. My mum once wrote a letter to the BBC saying that *Question Time* was on too late.

I wiggle under the duvet on my temporary settee bed and try to think of my blessings for the day.

1) My best friend Philippa
2) Matt proposing. I can't believe it. Matt wants to spend the rest of his life with me
3) I will soon be known as Jenny Parry – hallelujah
4) Chocolate cake in bed for breakfast

I pause before number five, mainly because I can't decide what it is, a blessing or a freakish nightmare? I decide that I should at least try to look at it as a blessing.

5) Mum leaving Dad and coming to stay with me.

Oh thank goodness, I can hear a ruckus in the hall. I leap off the sofa and open the door to our flat. Philippa stands on the landing swaying before me, she's holding her shoes and grinning drunkenly. I smile to see her, as I always do.

Philippa is gorgeous, even at 3 a.m. after being out for the night. Her hair is so fabulous it makes hairdressers sigh and children ask to touch it. It's so dark that you assume it's black but then you notice that under certain lights there's shades of toasted almonds or roaring fire in there. And it's thick too. It doesn't have to be backcombed to buggery to create body like mine does. And her ponytails have an eye-watering girth whereas mine look like the well-used head of a child's paint-brush. Now you might think that God would have thought, I'll put a ropey old face on that one with the hair, it's only fair, but no, he didn't. He only went and gave her green eyes. Yep, green eyes and raven hair. Not to mention pale skin, with rosy cheeks and a tiny waist and boobs. She looks like the sort of woman that men went to war over in the Scottish Highlands. I could well imagine mud-splattered men in kilts charging about in the rain trying to kill each other over her. She's mystical and ethereal looking. Well, she is normally, right now she's holding her breath to stop her hiccups and repeating the words, 'I wish Al would hurry up with my kebab,' in an impatient manner.

'Where's my mum?'

Philippa hiccups and then leans towards me conspiratorially.

'Your mum's twatted.'

'Where is she?'

Philippa turns to her right and, with an elaborate flourish of the hand, gestures that Mum is at the bottom of the stairs. We both peer down, and silently watch as my mother, who is sitting on the second step, holds one leg in the air, and tries and fails to unzip one of my high-heeled ankle boots.

'What have you done to my mum?' I hiss.

I don't know what is the more disturbing, the fact that my mother is so bertie bollixed that she is seemingly unable to undo a zip or that she's wearing a pair of my wet-look leggings.

'Fan,' Philippa says. 'Ah, thank goodness for that, they've gone.' She smiles. She hiccups. 'Oh, no, they haven't. Fan, I have to tell you, your mum pulled.'

'What?'

'She had a little snog.' She's holding a thumb and forefinger a tiny bit apart to indicate just how little the snog was.

'My mum snogged someone at Bomber,' I pant. I cast my eyes back down the stairs. She still hasn't managed the zip.

'Yes, and he wasn't that bad. Better than most I have snogged at Bomber, not that it's saying much.' She hiccups again.

'Kebab time,' Al calls, bursting through the communal front door.

'Oh, I could marry you,' Philippa sighs, and then hiccups.

Oh! I suddenly remember. 'Matt proposed. He took me out on the London Eye, and he got down on one knee and I threw up and we're going to get married. There is a ring but he took it away with him because it was too small.'

'Wow,' Al says. He's stopped still in his tracks.

'You're going to marry Matt,' Philippa says, scratching her head as though she's confused. Perhaps I should have waited until she was sober before I told her the news.

'Yes.'

'Wow,' Al repeats.

'Matt! Bloody Matt! You're going to marry Matt!'

I nod. She hiccups and then she starts stomping down the stairs.

'Oh, I'm going home,' she humphs. Then she hiccups.

'What about your kebab?' Al holds up the kebab-filled carrier.

'She's put me off my kebab,' Philippa wails, climbing over my mother who's now collapsed against the wall. 'I didn't think anything could ever put me off a kebab!'

I watch in silence as Philippa lurches out of the front door.

'Um, your mum's passed out, Fan-Tastic,' Al informs me.

'Do you think we can carry her up?'

'Here, you take the kebabs, I'll take your mum.'

I walk down the stairs and take the bag of kebabs from him. Al gently lifts my mum up and walks her carefully back into the flat. There's something almost sombre or funereal about it. But that could be because Philippa's just stormed off having heard the news that I'm going to marry Matt.

Al lays her down on my bed. We both lean over her passed-out figure.

'Philippa will come round,' Al whispers.

'Do you think?' I ask keenly. I sound almost desperate.

'Well . . .'

'I hope so.'

Al gives me a peck on the cheek.

'I'm happy if you're happy.'

'Thanks.'

'Kebab?'

'No, you're all right.'

He leaves Mum and me alone. I stare at her. I'm not sure if she's breathing. I watch her chest. It isn't moving, I crouch down and put my ear near her mouth. I can't hear any breath. She coughs. She's alive. Thank goodness. I unzip her boots then I haul the duvet from underneath and lay it on top of her. What if she's sick in the night? She might choke. I think she's stopped breathing again. I hover with my ear near her mouth. She just exhaled. Woah. The booze fumes are mighty. But she could wake up and not know where she is. She might get up and pee in Al's room. When Philippa's dad moved house, Philippa walked into the wrong room, sat on a chair and peed all over it.

I scurry back into the living room, fetch my bedding from the settee and lay it down on the floor next to Mum's bed. I'll worry less if I sleep in the same room as her.

Chapter 9

I have never seen a hangover like it. This is the stuff of legends. I'm almost tempted to borrow Al's new video camera and capture it on film. My mother could be a one-woman government campaign for sensible drinking. This morning, she got up to go to the bathroom. The bathroom that is next door to my room and it took her seven minutes to get there. All in all it was a half hour round trip and she made little whimpering sounds for the duration.

'Mum,' I whispered.

'Er, huh, huh,' she mewled.

'Are you upset?' I asked. I was worried she was crying. She left her husband of twenty-seven years yesterday and I can't imagine snogging someone at Bomber last night made the single life seem hugely attractive.

'Nooooo,' she whispered.

'What's the matter?'

'I'm concentrating.'

I had to strain my ears to hear her. 'On what?'

There was quite a pause. 'On everything,' she croaked.

I ransacked the flat for all the hangover sustenance I could find. I came up with two paracetamol, two ibuprofen, a Lucozade energy drink, a chocolate Mini Roll, a bag of Mini Cheddars and a bell. I left all these by her bed and told her to ring the bell if she wanted Al to make her a cup of tea and a bacon sandwich, Al would hear the bell and make the sandwich, no words needed to be spoken. Ringing the bell will be a traumatic experience for her, but it was the best I could do. She really should think about getting her own mobile for this purpose.

I am on an urgent mission. I'm on my way to see Philippa. I tried to call her this morning but she wasn't picking up. Now she might well be in the same state as Mother or, and this is a horrible thought I can't shake, she doesn't want to talk to me because I am going to marry Matt. We really need to speak about this. I need her to be happy for me. I can't fall out with her. I'd be lost without her. She has to be my bridesmaid and we need to start thinking dresses. I'm going to quickly pop into the chemist and buy us both a lipgloss of appeasement. I'm also going to get some man-tache cream. It's got to go. After the chemist I'm going straight to Philippa's and I'm not going to leave until we two are completely in shiny-lipped harmony.

In Tiddlesbury we have a Boots pharmacy, which everyone goes to, and one independent chemist, which only I ever go to. I go to it mainly because I feel sorry for the Robinsons, who own it, because I predict they will be out of business very soon, but also because a friend of mine, Leah, works on the till at the back, and she always, always has gossip, even if it turns out to be outlandishly false, which it does most of the time.

I stride along Tiddlesbury High Street in my biker boots. I'm wearing my favourite denim miniskirt and my blue Mickey Mouse T-shirt that I cut into a vest one particularly hot day. I walk into the chemist. It's empty as ever. It used to be lovely in here, with a long rickety wooden counter and old-fashioned display cabinets, but they updated it a few years back and now it's glaring lights and plastic like everywhere else. I apply some purple 'disco elf' lipstick, pick out two plumping lipglosses and spend ages deciding on an upper lip hair removal cream. As with all lady products, I don't go for the cheapest, or the most expensive. (How much? For that minuscule tube?) I opt for something in the middle. When I get to Leah's counter at the back, there's no sign of her and the radio out back starts playing Kings of Leon, 'Sex On Fire'.

'Leah, it's only me. Come for the local tales of lust and depravity and something to sort out the guinea pig on my upper lip. Ooh, turn this up, will you, gossip monger, I love this track.'

She does so.

'Thank you,' I shout above the intro.

I raise my hands in the air and start my rock march when the beat comes in. I haven't had a good dance for ages. Philippa and I always go a bit bonkers to this one when they play it at Bomber. We know all the words and do very good pained rock voices. I'll air mime for Leah, now. I'm not a great singer or dancer but what I lack in ability I make up for in volume and comedic overacting. I think she'll enjoy the performance. After all, she works in the chemist in Tiddlesbury so could do with all the fun she can get. By the time it gets to the chorus I'm on my knees, eyes closed, screeching the lyrics.

'I love this track. When they play it at Bomber Philippa and I get very creative, you should come one night,' I pant.

'Maybe I will,' says a voice that's definitely not Leah's. It's a bloke's voice.

'Wha—?'

I look towards the counter and there stands a man. And he is . . . he is . . . wow, he is so amazing I seem to have lost the power of thought. Where do I begin? He looks like a rock star, like, seriously, the bloke standing by the counter in the chemist of Tiddlesbury looks as though he could be *in* Kings of Leon. He's wearing tight jeans, but wearing them well, he's not fallen into that pit of twat that most men tend to when they attempt skinny jeans, biker-type boots and, you will not believe this. You won't. You can't. I must be hallucinating. He's wearing a Mickey Mouse T-shirt and he's cut off the sleeves. His skin is a colour . . . I don't know what colour exactly, but the right colour. Not mottled white, not too tan. It's creamy. Creamy, that's it. He's got creamy skin and it looks smooth to the touch. And he has muscles, but not in a steroidy way. His hair is a mess, as only men can ever pull off. It's brown, mousy brown, I'd say. And his face. His lovely face! His eyes are smiling eyes, and he has full lips, which is worth pointing out because many men don't, and freckles. I love freckles on men. I think I might be blushing.

'Where's Leah?' I croak.

'Her mum's been taken ill in Sh . . . ' he stops. 'Somewhere beginning with Sh.'

'Oh, yeah. Sh-sh . . . ' I start. 'Sh-sh,' I carry on, but then realise that I have no idea what I'm on about and stop.

'She left suddenly last night apparently. And I've just

moved into town and I was stopping by the shops in the High Street to see if there were any vacancies and they hauled me straight in.'

He's very chatty. For a man. It's lovely.

'I'm Joe, by the way. Joe King's the name. School was fun.'

My mouth falls open. I close it quickly.

'I'm Jenny. Jenny Taylor. School was a riot.'

We stare at each other for a moment.

'Everyone calls me Fanny.'

'I used to get called twat a fair bit.'

We stare at each other again. We seem to be doing more than the usual amount of staring at each other.

'Wow,' he says.

That's just what I was thinking.

'Hmm.'

'Traumatised teenage years locked in your bedroom writing maudlin poetry?'

'No, traumatised teenage years locked in my bedroom crying . . . '

'Ah.'

'And watching comedians to cheer me up.'

'Good. I don't like to think of you locked in a room crying, not when you are so clearly a rock legend.'

'Ah, ha. Yes. That has been said before.'

'I'm sure it has. You know the Kings of Leon song I love?'

'"Use Somebody",' I say, without thinking.

'Yeah.'

'I really like that one too.'

'Wow.' He nods. 'Nice T-shirt by the way.'

'Yes, I have very good taste.'

I smile. And then he smiles. And ... his smile is ... what's his smile like? It's like sunshine. It's not toothpaste ad but more the slightly lopsided, unbridled smile of a child. I think it might be the most beautiful smile I've ever seen.

We stare at each other *again*. I'm still kneeling on the floor, which is just as well, because that is a smile to make knees weaken and women collapse. I try to get up without showing him my pants. I manage it. But then once I'm up I remember that I am holding upper lip hair removal cream and have been since we started chatting. I can't lose the cream now, unless I just drop everything and flee. This isn't fair. There should be an EU rule about attractive young men being allowed to work in chemists.

'Um, just these, please,' I say, holding out the cream and lipglosses. He takes them from me. His slightly calloused fingers touch my hand and I feel a churning in my tummy. Actually the sensation isn't just in my tummy, it's in an area lower than my tummy too. Oh. My. God. Joe King is making my bits twitch.

I pay and flee. When I'm halfway down the street I stop and look at my hand. It's trembling. There's only one thing for it. I'll have to start going to the Boots pharmacy.

Chapter 10

I met Philippa at school. Meeting Philippa is probably the best thing that has ever happened in my life. She started there two weeks into the fourth year. She stood next to me in assembly on that first day. I didn't say hello to her. I disliked school and school really disliked me. I particularly disliked assembly because it was when I'd get my nickname for the day. Michelle Cullet (who is now Michelle Wilmot, because she married a bloke called Steve Wilmot, who was also in our year and broke my heart) would be at the other end of the row and would start it off. It would get whispered along the row of students until it reached me.

Philippa turned to me that morning in assembly. Her pretty face was scrunched up and her top lip was raised.

'I think I have to say "minge" to you,' she whispered.

I nodded resignedly and we turned our attention back to the headmaster who was standing on the stage in front of us. Only, after a few moments, she turned back to me again, still wearing a baffled expression.

'Why?'

'It's my nickname for the day.'

Again she nodded and again we turned back to face the headmaster.

'Why?' she asked again.

'My name is Jenny Taylor,' I told her wearily. 'It sounds like genitalia. Every day I get a new nickname.'

We turned back round and I could tell that Philippa was thinking about what I'd said.

'But that's not even funny,' she said.

'It's about as funny as . . . ' and I really wanted to quote something that Blackadder said to Baldrick about something being as funny as being poked in the eye with a pointy thing but I couldn't remember what it was exactly so I just said, 'It's about as funny as walking across hot coals to get to a Robbie Williams concert only to find it's been cancelled.'

And she said, and this is when I fell in love with Philippa, 'Why was it cancelled?'

'Because Robbie had been to a barbecue and eaten a partially cooked chicken drumstick.'

For some reason at that moment we looked straight into each other's eyes and burst out laughing. The headmaster gave us both an after-school detention. But, quite literally, since that exchange we've been inseparable.

Philippa works for the twice-weekly local paper the *Tiddlesbury Times*, writing news stories. She wants to be a writer. Or should I say Philippa will be a writer. She has already written one novel which, and I am not being biased, is brilliant. It's a story for teenagers about a girl who is horribly bullied at school, but she meets this friend, and together, apparently, or so she tells me, they outwit the bullies and become the cool people at their school. It's based entirely on my and Philippa's experiences at school except for the bit where they outwit the bullies and become really cool.

She still lives with her dad. I don't blame her for still living with her dad at twenty-seven. Not only is theirs a beautiful house, tall, Victorian, with fireplaces in each room, but Philippa has the whole top floor to herself. And, best of all, Philippa's dad's house has a garden, which, as soon as there's any sign of sun, Philippa and I lie in, partially clothed, clutching a Pimm's. Philippa's dad is a legend. He's the main GP at my surgery – Dr Flemming. He helped me get my job there years ago. I love him to bits.

He answers the door to me now.

'Jenny! Small cheer and great welcome!' He smiles. He's charmingly eccentric is Dr Flemming. He is very clever, he does cryptic crosswords and reads Shakespeare for fun. I don't know what he's going on about most of the time. He's very jolly in a bobbing way. His smiling face always seems to be bouncing in different directions. He's taller than you'd expect Philippa's dad to be, but he does have lots of raven hair; you can definitely tell they're related.

'Hello!' I give him a hug. I've hugged him for years. Strange, as I can't think when I last hugged my own father.

'Now, then, Jenny, do you think your mother might be able to bear coming to a concert with me?'

'Oh, how nice, I'm sure she would.'

'Well, perhaps you'd ask her for me. Friday night, Mozart by candlelight.'

'How lovely, that sounds right up her street,' I say. He

doesn't need to know that last night she trundled up the snogging and Jägerbomb footpath.

No, Mozart by candlelight with nice Dr Flemming sounds like a much more suitable evening for Mother.

'Philippa's up top,' Dr Flemming says, walking back to his study.

I climb to the top of the house.

'Hey,' I call, knocking on her door. The TV's on, I hear her turn it down. I poke my head in. She's still in her pyjamas. Philippa sees absolutely no point in getting dressed unless she has to leave the house.

'How are you feeling?'

'Fine,' she says flatly. Her arms are crossed tightly against her chest.

'What's up with you?'

'Nothing,' she says with a humph.

'Philippa, why have you got the hump?'

'I can't believe you said yes.'

'You what?'

'I can't believe you said yes!'

Philippa is shouting at me. We never shout at each other.

'Is that congratulations?'

'No, it sodding isn't!'

'Philippa, Jesus, calm down.'

'I can't calm down! My best friend is making the biggest mistake of her life.'

'But I want to get married.'

'Not to Matt! God, not to Matt. I thought you two were going to split up soon. Not marry each other.'

'What's wrong with Matt?'

'Everything!'

'Matt's a good man. He may not be perfect. But I think I've done quite well.'

'Do you love him?'

'Yes.'

'Why? Why do you love him?'

'Well.' I shrug.

'Come on, what do you love about Matt?'

'Well, he's tall.'

'Oh, well then, forgive me. Now it all makes sense. Now that you've explained that life-long commitment is based on height.'

'Wait, you're not letting me think. He's handsome.'

'Well, I'll give you that. I don't agree, but I'll give you that. What else?'

'Look, I love him. Course I love him. I'm going to marry him.'

Woah. Joe King's face suddenly popped into my head.

'Philippa, course I love him.'

She sighs and sits on the bed.

'I just ...' She sighs again. 'Marrying Matt. It never occurred to me.' She shakes her head and sighs yet again.

'Stop sighing.'

She sighs, really dramatically this time.

I make a moaning sound.

'Ah, do I hear the excited squeals of a best friend marrying the man of her dreams?'

'Will you be bridesmaid?'

'I suppose.' She shrugs, but I think I see a flicker of a smile at the corner of her mouth.

'You just smiled.'

'It slipped out. I was thinking about dresses. I don't want to get carried away thinking about dresses. A dress does not a happy marriage make.'

'Oh, please, get carried away thinking about dresses with me. Please.'

'This is really hard for me, Fan.'

'It's harder for me. This is supposed to be a happy time and you're shouting at me.'

'Sorry.'

'We are cool, aren't we?'

'We'll always be cool.'

'Promise?'

'Yes.'

We hug. But it doesn't feel right. It doesn't *feel* cool. It's as though something has shifted between the two of us and the pain of it is making my eyes sting.

'What are you doing tonight?' I muster.

'There's a gig on in Nunstone, if you fancy it.'

'I've got Mum staying, I don't think I can leave her for a second night.'

'Shall we do the Tiddlesbury Tour for her tomorrow?'

'But she knows Tiddlesbury already!'

'She hasn't been here for years, though.'

Mum and Dad moved away from the area about a year after I left school.

'Okay,' I nod, more because I want to spend time with Philippa than show the tour to my mum.

'What's the dress code?'

'I think air hostesses works best.'

'Your mum likes *Countryfile*, she was telling me last night, maybe we could do wellies and wool.'

'Ooh, I like it.'

'Anyway, we'll decide tomorrow.'

'My mum's staying with me. I can't believe it,' I say as I walk to the door.

'I can. Your mum married the wrong man and eventually left him twenty-seven years later.'

'See you tomorrow,' I say quickly. I have to go or she'll make me cry.

Chapter 11

Mum's still in bed. It's 2.15 p.m. If I let her sleep all day, she'll never sleep tonight, and it's horrible lying awake at night, but then it's not nice being woken up in the day. What to do? I creep in the room and hover over her. The Victoria Beckham bob sticks, sweaty and matted, to one cheek along with most of last night's black eye make-up, the rest of it is on my white pillow. The faint aroma of booze hangs over her. But I suddenly feel a surge of warmth towards my mum. She's finally doing her own thing, away from my dad.

The main rule in our family household was that my dad made the rules. Growing up this didn't strike me as odd because it was all I knew. But some of the things I remember from my childhood make me shiver now that I think about them as an adult. One particularly freaky situation can turn itself over and over in my head if I'm not careful. My mum used to have her own car. I remember how thrilled she was to have a car of her own. It was a little second-hand Vauxhall and every night when my father came home from work he would stand next to the Vauxhall and look through the window of the driver's side. Then he would take a small notebook out of his inside jacket pocket and with a tiny pencil that was always sharp, he would note down her mileage. She literally had to justify every mile she travelled in that car. When the little Vauxhall died and went to motoring heaven years later, Mum said she didn't want another car. I'm not surprised. We both lived in fear of my dad. I know that now. But when I was little I used to wish she'd stand up for me against him. God, it used to hurt me that she didn't. For a long time I was angry with her. But I don't have so much anger now, I feel more sad. She was just scared like me. Yet look at her now. Sleeping off a hangover in the afternoon. I almost feel a little proud. As if in response to thoughts of my father, my mum lets out a good, long, loud fart.

'Oh, you dirty dog!' I laugh.

She jolts awake, then slowly clutches her head. She emits a whispered squeak which sounds like, 'H-e-e-e-l-l-p.'

'You need painkillers and fluids.' I pop the painkillers out of their silver wrappers and hand them to her with the Lucozade. 'Come on, get these down you.'

'What are they?'

'Paracetamol or ibuprofen or something, but beggars can't be choosers.'

She picks up the packet that lies on the bed, squints at it and then relents and takes the pills.

'Now, you should brush your teeth, never underestimate the power of brushing your teeth when hungover.'

'You should be a nurse,' she says, shielding her eyes with her hand and wincing at the light my weak little 40-watt bulb is producing. I yank open one of my bedside table drawers and survey my sunglasses. I pick out my Dame Edna shades with the tiny green and purple feathers sticking out at the sides and slide them onto her face.

'That better?'

She nods. Very slowly.

'There we go, now you're hanging in style. You know, I could be a nurse, a hangover nurse. I could hire myself out to hungover people. That's actually not a bad idea. I'd make a fortune on New Year's Day.'

'How are we, ladies?' Al says, leaning on the doorframe and regarding us both. 'Mrs T, you look charming.'

Mum nods slowly once again.

'I made some frittata.'

'Ooh, yes, please.' I smile.

Could there be a better flatmate than Al? There is nothing he cannot do with an egg.

'He made frittata?' Mother seems baffled.

'Yes, he's amazing at cooking.'

'He's a man and he made frittata?'

'Yes.'

'Why does that make me so very happy?'

'And you haven't even tried it yet. Wait until you try it and then see how happy it makes you.'

'I couldn't eat.'

'Mum, you have to eat.'

'I had a Mini Roll,' she says, a little indignantly.

'Well, I'll leave it in the kitchen for you, Fan-Tastic.'

'Thanks, Al.'

I love the way Al calls me Fan-Tastic or Fanny Fan-Tastic, and I have tried to make a superlative out of his name but I've always failed. Al-Azing? Sensation-Al? See. Rubbish.

Mum's leaning back against the pillows with her shades on. It's not so much a Victoria Beckham bob now, more like some bloke called Bob who fared pretty badly in a pub brawl.

'Oh, Mum, you've been asked out,' I say.

Mum's eyebrows rise above her sunglasses.

'Dr Flemming was wondering if you'd go to a Mozart by candlelight concert with him on Friday.'

'Oh.'

It wasn't an excited 'oh'.

'His number's on the fridge, will you call him and say yes or no? When you can speak.'

Another very slow nod.

'Mum, Matt proposed last night.'

She lifts her shades and sees my smile.

'I said yes.'

'You're getting married.'

She sounds a little surprised. I can't blame her. My dad used to say no one would ever marry me.

'Yes. Soon. Matt wants to get on with it quickly.'

A little tear trickles down her smiling face and I feel myself relax for the first time since returning from Philippa's. A tear and a smile. Now this is a much more healthy reaction to my wedding news.

'Oh, you big softie, stop that crying.'

'I'm sorry,' she sniffs. 'I just never thought I'd see you married.'

And on that flattering note I get up and leave the room to acquaint myself with Al's frittata and finish my book.

Chapter 12

'What we drinking?' Philippa says as we walk into the dingy gig venue. 'Sod it, shall we Jägerbomb?'

'Blimey,' I say, because Philippa was on the bomb last night too.

'Yes! See! See, what your impending nuptials are doing to me!'

We're in Nunstone for the gig. Mum did get up, at 5.15 but was back in bed by 6.03. She said she needed to lie in a darkened room, and that I should go out and celebrate my proposal with my best friend. I didn't have the heart to tell her it's not something that Philippa would ever contemplate celebrating. Anyway, I'm glad to be out and I'm glad it's just the two of us.

'My shout,' I tell her and lean forward over the bar.

When Mum was lying in bed whimpering goodbye to me, she held out her arms as though she wanted to hug me. I didn't know what to do. It would have felt very odd if I'd have gone to her. We haven't been tactile as a family for years and years.

I'm touchy-feely with everyone else in my life, except my mum and dad. Anyway, I pretended not to notice Mum's wide arms and just said cheerio.

I lean further forward to try to get the bar girl to notice me. Oh. Oh. Oh. Oh. Buttocks! There's that bloke again. The bloke from the chemist. It's him. Joe King. I don't want to see him again. He is perched on a stool at the end of the bar in a deep discussion with a portly older man. He hasn't spotted me. He looks serious and passionate about whatever he's saying. The older man is nodding intently back. Ooh, now he's made some joke. The older chap is slapping him on the back. They're laughing. Proper laughing. None of the fake stuff. Real throw your head back, don't care how it looks laughter. It makes me smile. He's seen me. Damn. He's caught me grinning like a loon in his direction. He's stopped smiling. Well, you can't blame him, I must look like a stalker. He's still staring at me though. Oh, now, my breathing's gone all funny, shallow and quick. Do I look away? Oh, I hate this, I don't know what to do.

'Fan, what you playing at? You just missed the bar girl, she was right by you,' Philippa says, smacking me on the bottom.

'Oh, bum cheeks, sorry.'

I look back at Joe but his seat is empty now. Thank goodness for that. Back to normality. Now concentrate, Jen. I focus on the bar girl, trailing her with my eyes so she comes to me next time.

'Two Jägerbombs, please.'

'Hi.' It's him. I recognise the voice. It's quite a sensational voice. I feel his breath on my neck. I turn. Woah, our faces are close. Gosh, he's just . . . beautiful. I am so glad I got rid of the golden guinea pig this afternoon.

'Hi.'

'Hello.'

'Ur, huh, humm, humm,' I say. Brilliant. Meet man. Lose power of speech.

He smiles. I smile too. It's not my fault. His was infectious.

'Can I get you a drink?'

Better, Jenny. Better.

'Nah, best leave it till after. I've had a few beers already.'

'Oh, yeah, course.' I don't know why I said course. I don't know what he's on about. But we're looking into each other's eyes. Wow, his are greeny blue with brown flecks in them.

'Sorry, this is Philippa, the bestest friend a girl could wish for,' I say, leaving his gaze and passing her a drink.

'Hi. I'm Joe. Joe King. Brilliant feat of naming by my parents.'

I love how he immediately comments upon his name before others have the chance to. I suppose it's like me calling myself Fanny. I could have insisted that everyone call me Jenny. But actually Jenny Taylor was bullied and she became Fanny. My name is so much a part of my experience that I may as well acknowledge it. Sometimes I feel a little proud that I'm called Fanny. It's like putting a belated middle finger up to the bullies. Perhaps that's why Joe King makes light of his name too.

Philippa holds her drink in front of her open mouth.

'Right, I better get up on stage. Enjoy the show,' Joe says.

Now my mouth is hanging open. He's only in the band.

'Well, shit a brick.' Philippa exclaims after he's gone. 'Did you not feel that sexual chemistry?'

'Oh, wow, yeah, he seems really nice. You should go for it.'

'Not with me!' She throws her head back and shakes it. 'With you! You tool! The bloody sexual chemistry between you two! Even I need a lie down. You must be on fire. Bloody hell, Fan! Oh, my God!' She starts laughing.

'I don't know what you're on about. I met him earlier in the chemist, that's all.'

'Shut up, you. Let's just see what this very interesting night has in store.'

We knock back our drinks and then move into the crowd.

I'd go out to a gig or a club with Philippa every night if I could. I love experiencing the dark hours in rooms with loud music and no windows, my best friend leaping sweatily about at my side. This hasn't always been the case. When we first started to go out to clubs and gigs, Philippa and I would shuffle about on the edges of the dance floor desperately trying to fit in and not make prats of ourselves. But after about six months of regularly doing this we realised that we weren't really having a good time. We loved putting music on at home and going bananas to it, we could do that for hours. So we thought that nightclubs would be fun like that, but with more people and without us having to do the music and pour our own drinks. But when we did eventually get let inside we became too self-conscious to have a good time. Anyway, rather than give up on them altogether we decided to pretend we were in Philippa's bedroom and vowed not to give a stuff what people thought of us. It took us a while, but eventually we mastered it. We found that alcohol helped. Although, the correct dose took us time to establish. The key is to drink enough to feel uninhibited, but not too much so you lurch into people. Lurching into people when wearing high heels isn't a good idea. It causes injuries, as Philippa discovered on her twenty-fourth birthday, when she sprained someone's ankle.

Nowadays, our gig etiquette is nothing short of perfection. We let rip and dance, although when we say dance we don't mean it in the MTV sense of the word. We don't do restrained conventional dance moves. We do throwing our bodies about in whichever way feels good at the time. Our first mission is always to create some space for ourselves on the floor, because when things get going we like room to move. We do this now, both falling into the classic rock march and nod of the head, trying to claim a bit of sacred dance floor space for ourselves. When the track finishes, Philippa leans toward me and whispers in my ear.

'To fervent sexual chemistry and wherever it may lead.'

'Philippa!' I protest, just as the lights black out and a spotlight falls on Joe King's face up on the stage. He's got his eyes closed in a perfect pained rock expression. He starts singing on his own. No music. 'I want you,' he starts. It's an Elvis Costello song. I love this song. Philippa and I do a good version of this too, no tune or rhythm but plenty of passion. Philippa screams when she realises what the song is and puts her arm around me.

Joe King starts playing the guitar which hangs around his neck and the lights go up on the drummer and the bass player as they join him. We separate, Philippa starts playing her air guitar. I do my rock stomp with head bob, arms in the air, mouthing the words.

'Do your whistle! Do your whistle!' Philippa nudges me when everyone's screaming at the end of the song.

'It's a wolf whistle.'

'Just do it.'

I do some wolf whistles as instructed.

'Hello, Tiddlesbury!' Joe roars. Everyone laughs. We're in Nunstone. Bless him. I do another wolf whistle. Joe spots me and puts two fingers in his mouth and whistles back at me. The sound screeches through the speakers and causes the whole audience to groan.

'Sorry, what could I do? She's beautiful.' He shrugs in apology. I worry Philippa might combust with delight.

The band crashes into another song and in seconds we're all jumping around again. At the end of the song Joe waits for the screaming to subside.

'This one's for my new friend,' he says, and then gives me the shyest of smiles.

'It's Kings of Leon. Oh, my God! It's "Use Somebody"!' Philippa, now exploded, screams. 'He could use someone like you. He's wooing you!'

I freeze there on the dance floor. I don't think I should see this man again. Well, truthfully, I'd very much like to see this beautiful man again. But I really don't think it would be a good idea.

'I like this love story,' Philippa whispers and she hugs me. But I shake my head. I'm happy with the love story I'm writing with Matt.

Although the second time I met Matt couldn't have been more different than this. The second time I met Matt was more weirdy weird than the first. Again it probably wouldn't have happened if it hadn't been for the Smiling Fanny Manifesto. Point number seven is 'do ten minutes of exercise every day' and because of this, I now regularly go running. I say running, but slowly shuffling about in trainers might be a better term to describe it. I started just doing ten minutes like Philippa instructed, but somewhere along the line I found myself doing it for longer and longer and really starting to enjoy it. I loved that I could just drift away with my thoughts and suddenly find that I was nearly in Nunstone. I say nearly in Nunstone, what I mean is two miles out on the road to Nunstone. I should make that clear. Nunstone is after all seven miles away and then I'd have to get back again. Anyway, I normally go after work if I'm not doing anything else. It clears away the day and always makes me hungry for dinner, and I feel I've earned a glass of wine. So one evening I was slowly shuffling in my trainers along the Nunstone Road, which gets quite pretty once you've passed Homebase. I had just turned off the main road because I normally cut down a rural track and then do a circuit of a field and come back on myself. A car was parked against the gate to the field and I was quite excited that it might be some people dogging. So I slowed my pace. I'd never come across anybody dogging before and I'd been looking out for them. I'd hoped that might be another one of the endless benefits to taking regular exercise outside. So I slowed down and I realised that no one was dogging, more's the pity, it was just a chap who'd pulled over to have a pee right by the gate that

I needed to get through. Closer inspection told me that the man was on the phone. Not nice is it, to wee while you're on the phone to someone? I don't care how important the call is. Anyway, I had to come close to him to get to the gate so I ducked by him and went through the gate. But as I did so I looked at his willy. Because why not? And then I tutted. But it was very quiet. Tuts in the open air get easily lost, so I tutted louder.

'It's not nice to wee while you're on the phone to someone,' I said, but I didn't look back.

'I was on hold,' he responded, a bit huffily. But then he added, 'Nice legs, by the way.'

I turned around then and looked, because I was single after all.

'Oh, it's you,' I said.

He looked disappointed with me too. But then, presumably because I was on that freaky high you get after exercise, I started chanting 'You like my legs! You like my legs!' in that sing-songy way that children do, and jumping about. And then he said, very seriously and stupendously sexily, 'You have the most incredible legs I've ever seen.' Then I ran off. But I was chuffed, because say what you want to about Matt, you cannot deny that he has leading-man good looks. I was so chuffed I ran much further than I normally do.

But the second time I meet Joe King he calls me beautiful and sings a song to me. I'll never admit it to Philippa but this is the sort of thing that happens at the start of a love story. It would be an easier one to tell your kids than 'daddy was weeing by the gate and I ran past'. Not that I'm comparing Matt with Joe King.

No, course not.

You've met the bloke twice. He sings in a band. He's probably got syphilis. You're getting married. And, anyway, those sort of love stories are always beset by disaster. Pull self together, JT, NOW!

Chapter 13

Whenever Philippa and I come across a new arrival in Tiddlesbury we give them one of our Tiddlesbury Tours. We love doing the Tiddlesbury Tour. Hence we are always on the lookout for people who look a bit lost or like they could be new in town. We started doing them because they count as a good deed, which is always a bonus, but the thing I enjoy most about the Tidds Tour is the banter between Philippa and me. Perhaps I should be more mature but bantering with Philippa is one of my favourite ways to spend time, somehow we fall effortlessly into a patter where we finish each other's sentences, or go off on surreal tangents of conversation. We never really exposed other people to it before the Tiddlesbury Tour, but oddly, really very oddly because we talk complete guff, people seem to quite enjoy it.

We entertained ourselves throughout school like this. We went to Tiddlesbury Comprehensive, or Tiddlesbury Remand Centre as the locals call it. Philippa and I had an ever-expanding Tiddlesbury Remand Tour which we wandered about the school doing, mainly only ever to each other. We would assume lots of different characters but the ones I remember best were Harry and Barry, builders who liked to scratch their balls, and Marion Cleverbottom and Marjorie Knowingknockers, sex-obsessed learned professors who spoke like David Attenborough.

'Ah, ha, Knowingknockers,' I would orate, squinting fascinated at a big gouge that had been chipped out of the corridor wall. 'This indentation here marks a battle, does it not?'

'Ooooh, I think it does, Cleverbottom. It's a mark of war.'

'Ah ha, and someone, some wordsmith, has carved BUM next to it.'

'Oh, yes, yes, some little Shakespeare,' Philippa would agree, crouched beside me. 'It could be from that epoch in 1999, when Michelle Cullet went through a stage of throwing things down this corridor.'

'Yes, once a month, wasn't it? She'd hurl a ruler.'

'Or a pencil case.'

'Or an empty drink can, down this corridor.'

'Generally in the direction of someone's head.'

'More often than not mine. A bloody good shot!' I would laugh.

Laughing at the absurdity of bullying was the only way I ever found of dealing with it. And I could never have done it without Philippa. For years, if I sat in the dining room, someone, Michelle Cullet or one of her followers would spit food at the back of my head. I know, it was charming! Either as they walked past me or from a little distance away. But the first time the spitting happened in front of Philippa, she got her umbrella out of her bag and put it up, there and then in the dining room and carried on chatting away. We huddled under it and ate our food. We got a detention for putting an umbrella up inside but I thought my heart would explode with delight that I had such a friend.

'Bum,' Philippa, as Marjorie Knowingknockers, would sigh, stroking the word, carved into the wall.

'I do like a nice bum,' I would comment.

'I like a willy,' Philippa would say with a sigh, and we'd be in hysterics for hours. We were teenagers, we'd never actually seen one, but just the word willy could keep us giggling for ages.

I suppose it was inevitable that once we left school we'd comment upon Tiddlesbury Town Centre in much the same way.

We only ever do the tour on a Sunday and we always start promptly at 5 p.m. We tend to wear our air hostess costumes, which we opted for today. We team them with a lot of lipstick and we try to smile as much as possible when we speak. Today we are doing the tour for Mum and Al. Al is videoing it. He said it was important to have a copy of it for posterity, although I suspect he just wants to fiddle with his video camera because there's no football on. So, the tour is really mainly for Mum's benefit, not that she's very excited, she was far more taken with the idea of staying in and snoozing on the sofa. I could have done with a winch to get her out of the flat. 'You can't give in to a hangover for a second day, Mum. You need to get out and get some fresh air,' I told her. It was alarming, as though I'd suddenly become sensible. I'm not sure I want to become sensible. Now we're due to promptly start and Mum's in the newsagents. 'I just want to pick up a bar of chocolate before we get going,' she said and off she trotted. My mother eating a chocolate bar. Too weird.

Philippa and I stand side by side, next to the kebab van. Al squints and fiddles with his camera in front of us. Philippa taps her watch. My arms are folded and I hold a whistle between my lips.

Philippa shakes her head. 'I expected more from your mother. Five, four, three, two, one,' Philippa counts down on her watch. I blow my whistle when she's finished.

'We don't allow tardiness on the Tiddlesbury Tour,' I call shrilly as Mum emerges from the corner shop, unwrapping a Biscuit Boost. A very good choice of confectionary, but Philippa and I start tutting and shaking our heads in unison all the same.

'Whoops,' she says, quickening her step to get to us.

Philippa and I look at each other and nod. The show must go on. We turn to our audience and smile. We both proudly hold our arms out towards the chip van, Posh Nosh, as though we are glamorous women on a quiz show demonstrating a prize washer-dryer.

Arty, who's setting up inside the van, stands squinting at us and clutching three bags of burger buns.

'This is Arty,' I say.

'Hello, Arty,' Philippa says.

'Magnificent buns,' I add.

Al mumbles the word arse. I think it's directed towards the video camera.

'Arty fries things at night for the drunk people in the area,' I inform them.

'Tiddlesbury would not be Tiddlesbury without him,' Philippa states.

Philippa and I take a moment to shake our heads, sadly contemplating what Tidds would be like without Arty and Posh Nosh.

'Thank you, Arty,' we both say, at the same time, with a lot of feeling.

'We should tell them about Bean Gate,' I whisper to Philippa.

'We should,' Philippa hisses back.

'Bean Gate was a period in 2007.'

'A semi-hostile period of time, it must be said.'

'It must.'

'Prior to this semi-hostile period of time in 2007, Arty didn't sell baked beans,' Philippa states, like a newsreader.

We shake our heads in disbelief.

'No, but owing to our forceful negotiation tactics,' I continue in the serious newsreader style.

'Arty now serves baked beans.' We both squeal and then clap heartily. We love baked beans.

'But beans aren't printed on his menu,' Philippa says, suddenly seriously.

'So you have to ask for them.'

'Another gem of wisdom from the Tiddlesbury Tour!' we say in a high register together.

'Now let's say goodbye to Arty . . . ' Philippa starts.

'And his buns,' I finish.

'Bubbeye, Arty and his buns,' we both cheerfully say, and wave.

Next, Philippa and I walk Mum and Al around in a big loop.

'This here loop we are doing, is known as the Hole,' I tell them. 'Al, please look at your mobile phone.'

'Er, not too easy with this camera thing, Fan.'

'But Mother doesn't have one.'

'Hang about then,' he pulls it out of the back pocket of his jeans.

'Al, what do you see?' Philippa asks.

'Um, nothing except I haven't got any service.'

'Yes, Al, because you are in the Hole,' Philippa informs him. 'You won't get any service in this whole area.'

'It is what is known as an arse. If, Al, you say to your friend, "Friend, I'm going to Posh Nosh, can I get you anything?"' I say.

'And he says, I'd like a lamb doner,' Philippa continues.

'Which I'd lay money on will, at some point, happen.'

'Something for you to look forward to, Al,' Philippa says, smiling sweetly.

'Ah ha, but Al, you get to Posh Nosh, and Arty will say, do you want salad, onions, chilli, chilli sauce, garlic mayo?'

'He's a very thorough man,' Philippa interjects.

'But you don't know, so you take your phone out of your pocket to call your friend.'

'But terror has struck,' Philippa says dramatically.

'You have no service.'

We both gasp.

'Then, Al, you must walk to the letter box over here,' Philippa states. Mum and Al both follow us to the letter box.

'Now, Al, you should have service. Will you check, please?' Philippa asks.

'I do, yes, Philippa,' Al says.

'And that, ladies and gentleman, perfectly illustrates why we really should be charging upwards of eight pounds for the tour we are taking you on today,' I inform them.

Philippa nods as she murmurs her approval of this statement.

'Now, as we are here,' I continue. 'I would just like to introduce you to the letter box.'

'Useful for posting letters,' Philippa explains.

'And resting your chips on top of should you need to make that telephone call.'

'May we also draw your attention to the error that is printed in black and white before your eyes.'

'The last post is not collected at five thirty,' I whisper conspiratorially.

'No.'

'No, it's not.'

'If you are at home and you look at your watch. It says five twenty-six. You leave home in a hurry, not stopping to even put a coat on to protect you from the autumnal nip in the air . . . '

'Severely disabled Aunt Daphne's birthday card clutched tightly in your paw,' I continue.

Philippa giggles, Aunt Daphne has never been severely disabled before.

'Panting, you reach the postbox by five thirty. You breathe a sigh of relief. Severely disabled Aunt Daphne will know you care tomorrow.'

'Well, no she won't, Al. No, she won't know you care. She'll think you've forgotten,' I say.

'That you're too busy to remember . . . '

'That you hate her. Why? Because Tony, from the Post Office, collects the post at five twenty-three.'

'Five twenty-three, ladies and gentleman,' Philippa echoes.

'At five thirty he is safely in his house up the road, ready for the start of *Come Dine With Me*.'

'I love *Come Dine With Me*,' Philippa says wistfully.

'So the last post is at five twenty-three,' I confirm.

'Poor Aunt Daphne,' we say together.

'If you doubt us, ladies and gentlemen, then ask Tony yourself,' Philippa says.

'He's the man in Tiddlesbury dressed as a postman.'

'Say, "Hello, Tony, did you watch *Come Dine With Me* yesterday, what did you make of that starter?" And he will be off,' Philippa concludes. We move on.

'And here is the one and only dry cleaners in Tiddlesbury,' I announce.

'A word of warning . . . ' Philippa starts.

'Don't give them anything that's silk,' I elaborate.

'Or velvet.'

'Or velour.'

'And write your name inside your shirts as you will quite often take in your white shirt and be handed back someone else's,' Philippa advises.

'It will be very well ironed, though,' I add.

'And they do do repairs.'

'Although bring your own cotton,' I counsel.

'Mona is colour-blind,' Philippa explains.

'Red is green to her. Now, as this tour can be incredibly stimulating, we like to point out that on Sundays this pub, the White Hart, serves a free bowl of roast potatoes when you buy more than four drinks,' I suggest.

'So if you would like to rest your legs and mind for the duration of an alcoholic beverage we can accommodate that.

We might even be able to introduce you to Damien the Dealer. Damien the Dealer kindly risks his liberty to supply the residents of Tiddlesbury with eighths of weed.'

'Damien the Dealer uses the term "eighth" loosely,' I explain.

'He prefers to sell a ninth of an ounce.'

'But for the price of an eighth.'

'It's not ideal.'

'But it could be worse. Mother, you're to keep away from Damien the Dealer. Now, shall we?'

I hold the door open and Philippa and I swap smiles as we walk in. We love doing the Tiddlesbury Tour.

Once we're at the bar I turn towards Mum. Her mouth is open and there's an odd faraway look in her eyes.

'Are you OK?' I ask.

'You girls should be on the telly,' she says as though she's in a trance. I raise my eyebrows at Philippa in a 'my mum's having a midlife – what can you do?' kind of way.

Philippa gives me a sympathetic look.

Chapter 14

I suspect that the majority of newly engaged women, when they return to work on Monday, have conversations with their work colleagues along these sort of lines.

Newly Engaged Woman: OH, MY GOD! I'm getting married!

Work Colleagues: OH, MY GOD! Let's see the ring! OH, MY GOD! It's beautiful! Where did he propose?

Newly Engaged Woman: The London Eye.

Work Colleagues: OH, MY GOD! So romantic.

So far today, my conversations with work colleagues and patients have been thus.

Me: OH, MY GOD! I'm getting married.

Other person: OH, MY GOD! Let's see the ring.

Me: I don't have it. My finger was too fat for it. I did get it on, but then my finger started to go purple. I tried to get it off but couldn't, Matt started to panic but a lady lent us some face cream which I put on my finger and that did the trick.

Other person: Oh. Where did he propose?

Me: The London Eye.

Other person (stunned): Aren't you ... like ... terrified even to be on a third floor?

Me: Yes. I was a little bit sick in the pod.

Some might think these bad omens for a marriage. Seeing a rainbow or saying I love you at exactly the same time during a proposal scene must surely be seen as positive symbols of love and posterity, vomiting and nearly ending up having to have a finger amputated, not so much.

I wish I had a book to read. I always feel a little bereft without a novel on the go. But I like to leave a few days between books, so I can let one world go before I get involved in another. Rosie got back with Max and he proposed, just when she'd decided that she wasn't that bothered about getting married. I cried. Perhaps, next, I should read a book about someone who is about to get married. Although, they're bound to get besieged by obstacles and tragedy, and that could be a worry.

I wish I had my ring. It doesn't feel properly official without the ring. And if I'd been wearing my engagement ring on Saturday then Joe King might have seen it, and if he'd seen it he wouldn't have flirted, with all the smiling and gaze holding and calling me beautiful. And if he had known I was already taken then I would have had two nights of long, contented slumber instead of taking forever to get to sleep because I find my mind being pulled to him, to his name, to how open he was about his childhood when he mentioned that he spent part of his youth locked in his room writing maudlin poetry. And I repeated how he said I was beautiful once or twice too. Jenny Taylor, funny-looking Jenny Taylor, called beautiful by a lead singer in a band. So, yes, it would have been much better if I had been wearing my engagement ring. The girth of my finger has a lot to answer for. A lot.

My mobile phone rings. I usually have it on silent in the surgery. I pull it out of my bag. It's a number I don't recognise.

'Go on, Fanny, take it,' Marge encourages me.

I pause. As unofficial head of reception I shouldn't really. But, and this is really utter and complete madness to have as a thought, because he doesn't have my number and I'm getting married and I don't want to see him again EVER. But the flicker of a notion that it might be Joe King appears in my mind and I press OK. And then once I've pressed OK, I'm committed, so I hold the phone to my ear.

'Hello, sexy,' says a male voice. But it's not Joe King. I already know Joe King's voice.

Joe King's voice is lovely. It was deep and delicious when he stood next to me at the bar on Saturday. His voice travelled down my spine. I like the way he speaks as though he's carefully placing his words. As though he knows that words can hurt and he would hate for his words to do that.

This chap isn't Joe King and he's definitely not my Matt, so whoever it is has certainly got the wrong number. I love it when people call me and it's the wrong number. Once I picked up my phone and this chap on the other end gushed, 'Baby, I'm so sorry, I hope the swelling's gone down. I never knew that would happen. It looked like a bit of fun when I saw it in the shop. Babe, I'm so sorry. Is it still really uncomfortable to sit down?' It was then I said, 'I'm sorry I think you've got the wrong number.' But I was itching to ask what had happened.

'Hello,' I say back to this strange chap.

'What?'

'Well, there's some things I want to say about when you lived at home and, you know, when you left home.'

I jolt back in the chair. That was ten years ago and probably the worst period of my life. I hardly want to go dredging all that up.

'I have to be quick, I'm at work, I just wanted to say please don't give my number out to random blokes you pick up,' I say, a little frostily, and hang up, bringing the conversation to a screeching halt. Thank goodness it's the Nunstone pub quiz tonight and I'll be out of the house.

Oh, dear. Marge's mobile is ringing now and, of course, she's answering it. I should have led by example and not answered mine earlier. All because of an outlandish notion that my call might have been from Joe King, I shirked my unofficial head of reception duties, and now look, Marge thinks we can all be sat behind the desk chatting away on mobiles.

'ARRRRGGHHH!'

Blimey, Marge has done the rarely seen, she's stood up from her chair. Wow, now she's jumping up and down. Serious boobie jiggling. She could have someone's eye out.

'OH MY GOD!'

'Marge, I think you should sit back—'

'We're doing it! The documentary! We're doing it!' She's flushed and panting. 'Me and my Timmy. We're doing the documentary.'

'Oh,' I say. 'Well done.'

I can't imagine why she's so excited. I couldn't think of much worse than being featured in a documentary. People like my father, and Michelle Cullet who bullied me, and Steve

Wilmot who broke my heart when I was seventeen, would see me on the telly and say, 'See, I knew she'd come to nothing.'

'They're going to film here too! And they liked you, Fanny!'

'Me?'

'Yes, the great girl with the pink hair, they said.'

'Raspberry.'

'Oh, I'm so excited. Stardom beckons!' She whoops.

I watch as she dances about in the four square feet we have behind the desk. I wonder whether if I do end up being in the documentary my head could be smudged, like you see on *Crimewatch*, until I'm distracted by something coming through the surgery door.

'Oh, Marge, look. Look what Tim's done,' I gush, as an Interflora man strides into the surgery. 'Oh, Marge!' He's carrying a huge bunch of roses in a vintage pink colour. They are the most stunning flowers I've ever seen. 'Oh, Marge,' I repeat, because these flowers are talk-drivel beautiful. 'Oh, Marge!' The man places them on the counter so wafts of their fragrance reach me. 'Oh, Marge, they're heaven.'

'Fanny Taylor,' the man says.

'What?' Marge and I say at the same time.

'These are for Fanny Taylor. Here's the card.' He holds it out. I take it and as I open the envelope I have a crazy thought. Perhaps they're from that chap, Joe King. A ridiculous thought.

Beautiful bride-to-be, Forgive me rushing off. Missing you. Love you. Thank you for saying yes. I'm a very, very lucky man. Matt. xxx

Chapter 15

Al takes the pub quiz far too seriously. He even has a stack of general knowledge books by his bed. After we had sex, I would pick one of them up and quick fire very difficult questions at him. Yes, that's right, I, Jenny Taylor, know how to please a man.

Philippa and I join him every week at the pub quiz, although we're more fans of the pub than the quiz. We have no general knowledge and are usually out of our minds with boredom by the fourth question. Al's been threatening to get a men-only team together for months now, although he's thrilled tonight to have found a new teammate in Mother. He insisted she came. I tried to dissuade him, on the grounds that she's liable to, either, get drunk and pull, or worse, try to have a little chat to me about the worst period of my life. But like an Olympian, Al wouldn't be put off his goal. 'Think of the quiz! A whole new age bracket, Fanny! This is very, very good news,' he proclaimed, as he swotted up on World Cup finals.

Poor Al, his good feeling was entirely unwarranted because

Philippa, Mum and I have so far spent most of the evening discussing whether Mum should go out with Simon the Plasterer. Actually it's predominantly Philippa and Mum doing the taking and me groaning into my hands. I am trying to be an open-minded, liberal person. But the idea of Mum with a plasterer twenty years younger than her is a bit weird for me.

'He said you were hot,' I tell her a little flatly.

'Hot!' She giggles. 'Well, perhaps I should meet him.'

'But what about Philippa's dad? He's much more suitable. You have to go out with him to the candlelit concert thing.'

Mum scrunches up her face, which doesn't seem a very sensitive thing to do in the presence of his daughter.

'Mrs T. What does Simon the Plasterer have that my father hasn't?'

'Oh, Philippa, love. Your dad's a wonderful man. But I think he might be looking for someone to have a future with and, well, that's not what I'm looking for at the moment. And this Simon, I, well . . .'

'Oh, I get it, Mrs T. You want a nice bit of rebound sex.'

'Philippa,' I splutter.

'Yes, Philippa, that's exactly what I'm looking for.'

Oh, too weird.

'*Girls!*' Al's not happy. '*Ladies*, who is this?'

He pushes a piece of paper towards us, it's full of photocopied bits of famous people's heads. He prods a blurry picture of some dark wavy hair.

'Penelope Cruz,' we all say as though he's stupid.

'*Ladies!* If I could have your attention then we might do quite well.'

Mum and Philippa concur. I lean back in my chair and scan

the room. I'm not looking for Joe King. I've already done that. I've already scoured the room wondering if he might be here. I could see him being a pub quiz man. There's something comforting about a pub quiz man. Not that Matt does pub quizzes, but then he's so busy, he rarely finishes work before 9 p.m. I'm sure if he did do pub quizzes he'd be successful. He does like winning. Anyway, Joe King isn't here. But that's not the only reason that I'm looking around me. I haven't done a good deed today and I'm hoping I might be able to slip someone an anonymous note here tonight. The pub quiz is a good time for anonymous note giving because most people are distracted by the quiz. I think I might well have hit the jackpot tonight. I've just seen a brilliant opportunity to match make.

'Oh, oh, Philippa,' I say, subtly leaning in towards her and whispering in her ear.

'Aye, aye, captain.'

'If you look over your right shoulder, there's a girl in a pale blue jumper – nice jumper, actually. Sitting sharing a bottle of rosé with her mate.'

I wait a few moments until Philippa casually glances over her right shoulder to find out who I'm talking about.

'Yep. Do you know her?'

'No. Never seen her before in my life.'

'Then why are we . . . ?'

'Now look over your left shoulder. There's a table of five lads. One of them is wearing a denim shirt. He's all right, dishy, in a sort of Italian way. Turn now.'

She does so.

'Yeah, got him.'

'He hasn't taken his eyes off the girl in the blue jumper.'

'Interesting.'

'OK. Look at him again. Do we think he looks nice? Shall we slip her an anonymous note?'

Philippa fixes her eyes on him and pretends to be thinking hard about a pub quiz question. It's a stellar piece of acting.

'Yes.'

'Are you sure he looks all right? You don't think he looks like an arse?' I am quizzing her, but I have to, it's important neither of us has even the slightest inkling that he might be a psychopath. There's a lot of responsibility in anonymous note-giving matchmaking.

'I don't think he looks like an arse,' she says seriously.

'Mum?'

Mum turns away from the page of photocopied facial features, not to look at me though, to shut her eyes and clutch her head.

'You all right, Mum.'

She nods. 'It's just very loud in here. I've got a bit of a headache.' Oh dear, Mum doesn't look very perky and she's hardly touched her wine.

'I've got paracetamol in my bag.'

'No, I'll be all right, love. What were you going to ask me?'

'Can I ask your opinion about something?'

She cocks her head as though she's both surprised and pleased I've asked this.

'Yes, what is it?'

'Literally in front of you, can you see a bloke in a denim shirt?'

She cranes her neck and squints at the man in question.

'I can. He could take my mind off your father, Jenny.'

'M-u-u-m!'

She's on heat.

'Sorry, Jenny,' she says, checking herself. 'Why else am I looking at him?'

'In your opinion, does he look like an arse?'

'What does an arse look like?'

'A very good question.' Philippa nods. 'God, if only we knew, Mrs T.'

'Well, would you say he looks like a nice guy?'

'I think so. And his friends look like nice men too.'

'Excellent.'

'Why are you asking me this?'

'We want to set him up with a pretty girl over there,' I explain in a discreet whisper. 'But if there's any suspicion at all that he might be an arse, then we won't. Rules of the Sisterhood.'

'How will you set them up?'

'Watch and learn, Mrs T. Watch and learn.'

'Welcome to our underground dating club, Mum.'

I put my bag on my lap and pull out a notelet and my special anonymous note-writing fountain pen.

I begin to write.

FYI, the bloke in the denim shirt has been eyeing you up since he walked in, we can't be entirely sure, but he doesn't look too odd and he's handsome, so we thought you should know.

I hold it up to show Philippa and Mum. Philippa gives a thumbs up.

Mum claps her hands. 'This is so exciting!' she squeals. She hasn't quite mastered the subtleties of this art yet.

'Shall we do it now?' Philippa says, pushing her chair back.

I nod. We both survey the scene.

'I think it's an earring scenario,' Philippa tells me.

I nod again. We don't always do the 'where's the toilet?' distraction. The 'I've lost an earring somewhere around here, you haven't seen it' is quite a favourite at the moment too.

We share a little smile.

'One good deed coming up!'

Chapter 16

'OK, got the whiteboard, coloured marker pens. Got wine,' I say.

It's wedding planning night. I did start reading a book about a woman who was getting married but she got a wedding planner to help her. Now, my funds don't stretch to a wedding planner because my funds don't actually exist. So a white-board, Philippa, Mum, me and a bit of ingenuity will have to do instead. But I need to be firm and keep the girls focused on the task at hand. I can't let the night descend into drunken-ness and random gossip. I have a wedding to plan. Kate and Wills, who?

'Oh, sod it. Let's open the wine.'

I pour myself one and sit down at the kitchen table. Mum is looking at me quizzically. It's a little unsettling. I have a feel-ing I know what she's about to say. I start to get up to go into the other room. But she starts speaking before I'm even out of my chair.

'We need to talk about the day you left home,' she says seriously. I knew it.

'I really don't want to talk about that day, thank you,' I tell her. I take a bigger than usual gulp of wine. 'Philippa will be here in a minute.'

'It would be good if we could find some time just the two of us to talk about it. I really need to, Jenny.'

'I really couldn't think of anything worse,' I say, unfortunately sounding like a stroppy teenager.

She nods as though she'd like to say more but thinks better of it.

'So, tell me, Jenny. Why do you work at the doctor's surgery?'

'Because I need the money.'

'But why the surgery?'

'I like it.'

She turns her nose up.

'Why did you turn your nose up?'

'I didn't.'

'Mum, you so did, I like it at the surgery, OK? God.' I blow the breath through my lips.

'If you didn't work there where would you like to work?'

'Mum! Where's Philippa? She's never late.'

'Don't change the subject.'

'I'm lucky to be working there. I don't know what else I would do.'

'Jenny, I'm not saying you haven't done well. I'm just wondering what you'd really like to do if you had the chance.'

'Mum! I'm fine where I am.'

'What do you enjoy doing?'

'Mum!'

'Come on, Jenny, you enjoy doing lots of things.'

'What more do you want from me?'

'I think you could be a presenter.'

I bang my head three times on the table.

'Mum!'

'I think you could.'

'That's the most ridiculous thing I've ever heard.'

'No, it isn't. You used to want to be a presenter.'

'Yes, when I was little.'

'You had a place at college to do performing arts.'

'Mum, that was a lifetime ago.'

'I think you'd make a great presenter.'

'Mum, that's stupid.'

'Why?'

'It just is.'

'Why?'

'Well, I'm too old for a start.'

'You're twenty-seven.'

'And I'm too minging.'

'Jenny, you're beautiful.'

'You have to say that as my mother.'

'But you are.'

'Mum, why can't I be happy at the doctor's surgery? We can't all be superstars. If we were all superstars it would be very hard to get an appointment at the doctor's surgery.'

Finally, the sublime sound of the door buzzer.

'Sorry if I'm a disappointment to you,' I say and I get up to let Philippa in.

'What's up with you?' Philippa asks as soon as I open the door.

'Mum's freaking me out,' I whisper.

'Why? Did she get some dope?' Philippa asks. A bit too keenly if you ask me.

'No, worse.'

'Oh, what's she doing, then?'

'She's questioning me about my life.'

Philippa looks appalled.

'I know.'

Philippa nods seriously and we walk into the kitchen.

'Mrs T. How you doing?'

'I'm fine, thank you, Philippa. So tell me . . . '

I freeze. I hope Mum's not going to start asking Philippa about her life. Or my life. Anyone's life. Talking about life is definitely out.

'Tell me, do you think that couple from last night will end up falling in love?' she trills.

'We can but hope, Mrs T. Ooh, wine!' Philippa says, sitting down at the table.

'You girls are shaping people's destinies, giving fate a little helping hand.'

'Blimey, Mrs T, you can do our PR when we set up in our matchmaking business.'

'Is that what you girls intend to do?' Mum asks eagerly.

'No, Mrs T. Couldn't think of anything worse. I have a career. I am a hard-hitting journalist! Well, reporter for the *Tidds Times*. Some novelist has just moved into town.'

'Oh, he's the chap who bought Rose Cottage!' I exclaim.

'Oh, yeah, probably. I'll be interviewing him soon, and there's an ongoing planning problem I'm about to cover too, Mrs T. Now if that doesn't get your pulse racing I don't know what will.'

'I think you girls could be presenters like Ant and Dec,' Mum says.

Philippa turns to look at me. Our eyes meet and before I can stop it we share a smile. I would never ever tell Mum this, but Philippa and I have long held a secret desire to be the female equivalent of Ant and Dec. When we play fantasy other lives, which, sad to admit, we do quite frequently, the female Ant and Dec is our favourite one. I quickly force myself to stop smiling, I don't want to give Mother ammunition. It's not something that could ever actually happen.

'Ladies, if I could just bring your attention to the task in hand,' I instruct them, tapping the whiteboard, on which I've written WEDDING OF THE CENTURY.

'Sorry, sorry, Jenny.'

'OK. Hit us with it,' Philippa says, arms folded, as they quite often are when my wedding is mentioned.

'OK. We'll start with the all-important dress code.'

'Dress code?' Mum blurts.

'Gotta have a dress code, Mrs T.'

'At a wedding?'

'At any gathering, really,' Philippa conjectures.

'So, the dress code is . . . ' I can't suppress a smile. I'm so pleased with this. 'The Beatles and the Stones.'

Philippa jumps out of her seat and starts punching the air with her fists.

'I LOVE IT!' she yells. 'When did you come up with that?'

'Last night, it took me a while to get to sleep.'

'Fan! Genius! Genius!'

'I thank you, I thank you. So, my dress will be short.'

'Short?' Mum sounds surprised.

'Definitely. I love wearing short skirts.'

'She does, Mrs T. She says she feels playful in a short skirt.' Philippa raises her eyebrows at my mother.

'Yes, and I want to feel playful at my wedding, because essentially it's one big monster of a party. So short, cream, lace.'

Philippa nods. She knows the exact dress I am talking about. Two years ago now, we went into the bridal boutique in Nunstone and tried on dresses. I hope all women pretend they're getting married and go into shops to try on dresses. I'd hate us to be the only ones.

'Beatles and Stones is so great for the guys too.' Philippa is nodding her head in admiration.

'Yep, I know.'

Last night I went through all the men I know, imagining them in a sixties- or seventies-style suit and practically everyone looked great. Especially Joe King. I put him in an early Beatles-style single-breasted suit, with a thin tie and the one button on the jacket done up, tight-ish trousers. Not that Joe King would be coming to my wedding. I just happened to imagine him in the get-up, that's all.

'The only thing . . . ' Philippa stops suddenly and frowns.

'What?'

'Matt's not going to go for it, is he? I think he'd want a more conventional wedding.'

'Oh, would he?' Mum looks concerned.

'No. It's hardly that unconventional to have a Beatles and Stones dress code. And people don't have to do it if they don't want, it's just there if people fancy,' I say.

Philippa is still shaking her head. I ignore her, I know Matt a lot better than she does.

‘Anyway, I quite like the idea of the short dress with biker-style black boots, very comfortable for dancing. But I think I might have to opt for ballet-type pumps, at least for the first bit.’

‘What about the venue?’ Mum asks.

‘Well, Marge’s dad has a marquee, which I’d like to put in someone’s garden. There are a couple of old dears at the surgery who have massive ramshackle gardens, one of them might let me use their garden to put the marquee in. I want everyone to feel relaxed and it’ll be in summer, so providing it doesn’t rain I’d like people to stumble out of the marquee and make out under the stars.’

‘I love it,’ Philippa sighs. ‘Bagsy me making out under the stars. Although it’s more likely to be you, Mrs T.’

Moving on!

‘It’ll be a beg, borrow and steal affair. I don’t want to ask Dad for money. So I have a plan. I know. I’m on fire. Basically I have made three lists. Food. Decoration. Entertainment, as you can see.’ I point to my whiteboard. ‘So under food we have coronation chicken, potato salad, trifle, etc. Under decoration there is jam jar of wild flowers, eight times, and twenty blown-up balloons, etc. Then under Entertainment we have sing a song, play crazy disco on your iPod and on and on. The list is based on eighty coming. Basically everyone has to pick something from one of the lists and do it or bring it. Cheap and ever so cheerful. And we could say bring a bottle as well and then we’d just pay for like Jägerbombs and specialty party booze.’

I stand proudly back reading my carefully written lists on the whiteboard.

'Ooh, I love cheesecake,' Philippa mutters as she squints at the list.

'I just think if everyone mucks in a bit, it will be a right laugh. Don't you think?'

'Yeah, I do. I have to say, Fan, I think it looks wicked.' Philippa nods, but she seems troubled. 'I'm just not sure how Matt will feel about this.'

'What's not to like?' I say, surprised. 'It will save him a fortune.'

'Hmmm.'

'Mum? What do you think?'

'Oh.' she smiles. 'I love the Stones. I saw them years ago at Reading Festival, before you were born.'

'Wow, did you, Mrs T?'

'I think this looks great, Jenny, well done. I can't wait.' There's a faraway look in my mother's eye that I can't place. 'Wouldn't you like to be a wedding planner, Jenny?'

I'll ignore that comment.

'So when shall we go dress shopping, ladies?'

'Tomorrow?' Mum suggests.

I chuckle. 'That's serious.'

'No point in waiting,' Mum says. Now, she seems a little emotional.

'Mum, are you OK?' I ask.

'I'm just so proud of you,' she says tearfully.

'We both know that's not true,' I say, quickly, and to be honest I'm shocked by how unkind I sound. But it's such a ridiculous thing to say to me now. I've no idea why she's suddenly started behaving as though she's in an American sitcom. Proud of me? She doesn't know me, so how can she be proud of me? I look back at my wedding list. Mind you, it is a particularly blinding piece of low-budget wedding planning.

'So tomorrow then for dress shopping,' I say, but the lightness has gone from my voice. 'We've got early closing at the surgery. Philippa, can you get out?'

'You know me, I'd get out of anything for dress shopping.'

At least Philippa's on board. Finally. Now, how can I avoid talking to Mum for the remainder of the evening? A bath with a book it will have to be.

Chapter 17

Joe King just popped into my head again! I'm in a wedding boutique in Nunstone and I just looked out of the window onto the street and thought, I hope I don't see him. The ridiculousness of that sentiment works on many levels. For a start, he works in a chemist in Tiddlesbury, why would he be hanging around a wedding dress shop in Nunstone? But also, more importantly, why should I not want him to see me in a wedding shop? Why? It would be good for him to find out that I'm a soon-to-be-married woman. He continues to pop into my head, even though I'm really trying not to think about him. I really am. I really, really am. I bet he hasn't thought about me once. The beautiful comment was probably just a throwaway that he says to a different girl at every gig. I bet he's lying in bed with nineteen-year-old twins at this precise moment. Not that I care. Really.

On a positive note, we've only just arrived at the wedding dress shop and we've already been given champagne.

'Cheers,' I say, clinking glasses with Mum and Philippa. I feel a bit bad about snapping at Mum last night. Although I don't want to apologise, because then I'll be bringing it up again.

'In the eyes,' says Philippa eyeballing both of us. 'Can't risk seven years of bad sex.'

'Oh, God, is that what happens?" Mum says, sounding concerned.

'Yep, seven years bad sex, Mrs T.'

'So that explains it.'

'Did you call that Simon chap?' Philippa asks, because I try to avoid talking about my mother's quest for rebound sex, if at all possible.

'Not yet. But I will.'

'Now, then, Jenny,' the sales assistant joins us.

'Yes!' I squeal. I've already reached quite a high vocal register. It's the excitement.

'Do you have any thoughts about what sort of dress you are looking for?'

'Yes.' Another yelp. They're very hard to control.

'Right.' She laughs.

'So, what I really want is sixties style, short in length, cream lace, long sleeves, high-ish neck, you used to have one just like that . . . ' I hold my breath, willing her to still have this dress.

'Ah, yes. The Twiggy dress, let me fetch that for you.'

'The Twiggy Dress.' I sigh. 'It's called the Twiggy dress.' I suddenly freeze. 'What if it looks terrible on me?'

'I assure you it won't.' The lady is back. She's holding up a dress bag. It's in there. She's holding my dream dress. I gulp some champagne.

'Ta da!' she says unzipping the bag and manoeuvring the dress so we can glimpse its glory.

Oh, I feel like kneeling in its presence. I couldn't imagine a more exquisite wedding dress. I love clothes. I truly do. I have hundreds of items of clothing and if I had to explain why I would probably end up getting a little misty eyed. There's something magical, something amazing about someone, somewhere designing a beautiful dress and choosing a stunning fabric and thinking, I know what I'm going to do, I'm going to create something exquisite that will make someone feel sublime, feel beautiful, feel whole. When I was little and there were a lot of nasty words being said to me both at school and at home, I would lock myself in my room and put on a pretty dress and it would make me feel better. It really would. I think there's a lot wrong with the fashion industry, I hate to think of starving children in far-flung countries working for pennies to make cheap T-shirts, or young girls starving themselves to look like skin-and-bone models. I hate that fashion has became so complicated and dangerous for women. But then I think back to the twelve-year-old me, who'd been banished to my room by my father and didn't have anyone to confide in, and how she would put on a dress and it would feel like a comfort, like a friend. Clothes have always had the power to transport me to somewhere different, somewhere better.

I gulp some more champagne. Why I am scared to try on this dress? Perhaps because I've pictured this day for years and years, ever since I was that twelve-year-old girl in her bedroom. 'You'll find it hard to get a husband with those habits, Jenny,' my father would always say to me, if ever I licked my knife or blew on my food or sneezed without holding my hand over my mouth. But then at some point it became, 'No one will marry you, Jenny.' Perhaps he didn't mean it to be as cruel as it felt. Sometimes I got the impression that he might have thought he was being funny. But there was no playful wink or loving 'I'm only having you on' hug after. Just those words – no one will marry you, Jenny. Even so, I'd daydream. Daydream that, one day, someone would want to marry me. And in those daydreams I'd always be wearing a cream lace sixties minidress. And now, look, it's here, in front of me.

'It is so beautiful,' I whisper as though it's sleeping and I might wake it. 'What do you think?' I ask Mum and Philippa.

'I think ... it's divine,' Mum says, and again her voice sounds choked with emotion. 'I wish I'd had the confidence to get married in something like that.'

'It's never too late, Mrs T. You'll meet a lovely man and you'll marry him in a minidress.'

'I don't think so.'

'Fifty-four is not too old to wear a minidress, no matter what they tell you in the *Daily Mail*, Mrs T.'

'Shall we pop it on you?' the lady asks me.

I nod nervously. I seem to have finished my champagne. I place the empty glass on a low table near me and follow the lady behind a big swooshy satin curtain.

'This will look great with your lovely hair.'

'Oh, thank you,' I say pulling off my skirt and T-shirt.

The lady undoes the buttons down the back of my dress, a tiny heart is carved upon each button. 'Here,' she says, holding it open as I step into it. 'Oh, look, yes,' she coos and begins doing up the buttons now. 'Oh, it could have been made for you.'

When she's finished I turn to face the mirror. I'm still funny-looking Jenny Taylor. My arms are still too long for my body, my mouth is still too big for my face. I'll never be a great beauty, but in this dress, here, now, I don't care, because I feel . . . what do I feel? What do I feel like in this dress? I suppose, I feel like me, but the best of me.

'Let's show the girls.' The lady swishes back the curtains.

'The two of them sit wide-eyed and motionless, looking in my direction. There's utterly no expression on either of their faces at all.

'What? Do you not . . . ?'

'Oh, Fan,' gasps Philippa.

'Are you crying, you tool?'

She nods. 'You look amazing.'

'Oh, Jenny,' Mum says, standing up and stepping towards me. There are tears in her eyes. She's mouthing the word 'beautiful' and she's holding her arms out as though she wants to hug me. I freeze. We haven't done hugging for a long, a very long, time.

'I think I should get you three some tissues,' the lady says delicately to me.

'I don't need any . . . ' I start, but then I feel a big tear, that I hadn't even noticed come into my eye, slide down my cheek.

Chapter 18

Mum bought the dress for me. The nice sales lady said the price and my mum brought out her credit card and got pretty aggressive when I told her not to be silly. There ensued a lengthy verbal tussle. In the end, she said, 'Don't insult me,' as though she was a psychopath, so I slunk back and let her pay for the dress. And it wasn't cheap. It was the same price as most of the long ones, which seems a bit unjust to me. The last time we went shopping together and she bought me something I must have been about fourteen.

So I love my awesome dress but the only downside is that I want to wear it all the time, I keep unzipping the bag and just sitting there watching it. I absolutely cannot wait to wear it. In fact, I could wear it out before the wedding. It doesn't look like a wedding dress. That's the beauty. I'll be able to wear it again and again. Something you couldn't do with a traditional meringue dress, unless it was Halloween and you wore it with one of those plastic axes sticking out of your head.

Whiteboard wedding planning has been cracking on apace and I think we've more or less covered everything. Now, I just need Matt to get back from Chicago, then Mum and I can do a little presentation for him, he can give the nod and we can get 'Operation Kate and Wills Watch Our Wedding And Weep' off the ground.

I've been running every night too, which I'm doing now. Partly because my wedding dress is short but mainly to get me out of the house so my mother can't corner me.

Ooh, aw. Stitch. Ah, ha.

'I'm doing something healthy here. Why give me pain?' I rail.

I have a confession. One I am very not proud of. Since I met Joe King I've started putting a little lipstick on before I go running. There, I said it. And I've been running a little quicker than usual, you know, just in case, on the off chance, if he were to see me, I wouldn't look a total ploddy minger. It's ludicrous. One, he's just some syphilis-ridden rock star who I've met twice, and two, quickening my pace gives me quite a lot of discomfort and causes me to pull a face like a cow in labour.

Ow! OW! OW! I'll have to hobble to Wee Gate and try and stretch it off there. I turn the corner down the narrow lane. There's a car next to Wee Gate. Ooh, could they be doggers? I don't know why I get so excited about the idea of doggers, probably because I live in Tiddlesbury and need all the excitement I can get. I trundle nearer. I see two people sitting in the front seat of the car, a man and a woman, I can tell from the back of their heads. They can't be doggers. If you wanted to fornicate in a Ford Mondeo you'd surely do it in the back. What a shame.

'One day I'll spot some doggers,' I mutter. It pays to be positive.

I stand in front of their car and use the gate to stretch my legs on. The couple now have a cinematic view of my arse. I feel the back bottom view is better than legs akimbo from the front though.

'Ah!' I jump. The fella's just beeped his horn. Very funny. I turn around and give them a nod.

Oh, my god, I know these two. We match-made them with a note! He's the bloke in the denim shirt who was eyeing her up in Nunstone at the pub quiz while she was sharing a bottle of wine with her friend. We slipped her a note. This is unbelievably exciting. I must be grinning quite scarily. The expression on their faces has just changed quickly from one of amusement to alarm. If it wasn't for Philippa and me, Cilla and Cupid, they wouldn't even be sat there all smoochy. I want to tell them. Imagine if I did, we'd probably get invited to their wedding. We could be godparents to their children or they might even name their children after us. I can't tell them though, because the note giving is totally anonymous. Ooh, I really have scared them. He's reversing the car now. I wave. They don't respond.

I wonder whether she told him that she received an anonymous note in the form of a very pretty card. If so, I wonder who they think sent it. I get my sweaty phone out from the pocket in my shorts and call Philippa.

'Today we have reached a big milestone in the Smiling Fanny Manifesto's life,' I inform her.

'Fan, Fan, where are you?'

'Wee Gate. Listen, guess what I just saw.'

'Fan, I'm having a nightmare. Absolute sodding mare. I'm interviewing that writer tonight, the one who moved into Rose

Cottage. Quite a well-established guy, writes sci-fi for young adults. Philip Hall is his name. I was desperate to do the interview because, you know, I might be able to ask him for advice about my book. Anyway, I said I'd do a light-bite tea, so I made a quiche but it ... Oh, Fan, it looks like something unfortunate happened in a shortcrust pastry case.'

'Chuck some rocket on top of it, make it look posh.'

'That's not even the worst of it. He's bringing some kid. And Dad's here in the living room with his Gushing Arterial Blood lot tonight, I hadn't realised!' Philippa's dad meets once a month with a group of doctors, from what Philippa and I can tell they eat cheese and talk about gore. 'I can't even put the kid in front of the telly, and I can't let it near the Gushing Arterial Blood lot or the poor thing will be scarred for life. What do I do with it?'

'How old is it?'

'Dunno. Must be young if he's bringing it with him.'

"Hmm. Does it have a sex?'

'Does it have sex?'

'No, what sex is it?'

'Oh, boy,' she says confidently. 'I think. Or girl. No, I think he said it was his nephew.' There's a pause. 'F-a-a-n,' she sings sweetly. 'F-a-a-n.'

'You want me to look after the child.'

'Well, you're so good with kids.'

'I'm really sweaty.'

'I'll feed you wine and spray you with deodorant.'

'All right. I'm on my way. Got something very exciting to tell you anyway!'

'You couldn't pick up some rocket, could you?'

I jog to Philippa's. It was only going to be another long bath and book night again. And this book is making me feel a little maudlin because the girl getting married has a lovely dad. He's not only paying for everything, champagne, canapés, beef Wellington, love birds being released on the lawn of the stately home, but he's written a poem that he wants to read at the picturesque village church as well. And he's always hugging her. That's the bit that makes me feel most maudlin, the fact that she has a dad who wants to hug her. Still, I think her husband-to-be has been copping off with her bridesmaid, so you clearly can't have it all.

Chapter 19

I don't mind looking after this child. I love playing with children. Come to think about it, it's the playing I like. I'm not so bothered about the child.

'Can I get the paints out?' I call, diving into the cupboard under the stairs as soon as I arrive.

'Oh, yeah, good idea.'

'Cool. Oooh, we can play the monster game.' I'm already armed with paints and paper, stalking through the house to the back garden.

'Now, I'm jealous.'

Philippa and I do painting and play the monster game not to entertain children but to entertain ourselves. It's not something we tend to tell people though. The only difference between ourselves and seven-year-olds is that whenever we paint or play monsters in the garden we are heavily armed with Pimm's and lemonade. Like most of our activities, these were born from a desire to dress in a certain way. We found two Toulouse-Lautrec-style shirts in a charity shop one day, and we've never been able to resist two of anything in a charity shop ever since we saw two identical wetsuits in Oxfam, wore them out on New Year and had one of our best nights ever. Once we'd purchased our painting outfits we bought some cheap paints, a big pad of art paper and we got drunk in the garden while we both tried to paint a tree. Our trees were rubbish, so we turned them into monsters, then we tried to paint the house and those paintings became monsters too. By the time we'd got through the entire bottle of Pimm's we'd hidden our pictures in the garden, made hats out of colanders and were scouring the garden trying to find the monsters.

'Grab the colanders and the string, will you?' I holler as we walk through the kitchen into the garden.

I place the painting gear on the outside table and go straight to the big horse chestnut tree, the one we couldn't paint, and pull some leaves from it. It's very important to camouflage the colander hats, all you do is secure the leaves to the colander with string.

'Here you go,' Philippa says, bringing me the colanders and string. 'I better go in so I can hear the door. I'll bring the little terror out. Thanks for this, Fan.'

'No worries, I'm shamefully excited.'

I set to work. I wish I'd known I'd be doing this, it would have been nice to wear my green army outfit. I put my camouflaged colander helmet on my head and practise my monster-fighting pose, which for some reason is legs quite wide apart, knees bent and bottom sticking out. I am a monster-fighting hobbit.

'Fan! This is . . . '

I hold my arms up to defend myself, when you are fighting monsters you can't trust anyone, and turn round. I'm Mary Poppins. The child will love me.

'Hello, again.'

A little bit of me withers inside, I think it might be my pride. Because this isn't the sweet innocent squeak of a small boy. It's the gravelly, rich beautiful sound of Joe King. He is wearing his skinny jeans, biker boots and a grey hoodie. He's carrying a guitar and he looks perfect. I am in my sweaty running gear with a colander on my head. I look mental.

'This is Philip Hall's nephew,' Philippa tells me, and something in her expression reminds me that I'm still standing like a hobbit.

'Sorry?' I say, standing up and trying to assume a more sophisticated stance.

'Philip's nephew. The writer I'm going to interview, this is his . . .'

'We were expecting you to be, um, under ten.'

He smiles.

'I made you a hat.'

'And I shall wear it with pride.'

'Right, I'll leave you two out here then. Fan will get you anything you want.'

She walks back into the house.

'Can I get you anything?'

He's put on his colander hat.

'What do you reckon?'

'Suits you, sir.'

It does too.

'I'll never take it off.'

'I think it's a look that should be explored in the music industry.'

'Excellent. I've found my niche.'

'Niche. Such a good word.'

'I missed you after the gig on Saturday. I hoped you'd stay.'

'You were amazing.'

You were amazing!

'I've got a confession. Phil said someone called Philippa was interviewing him and I wondered whether it might be your friend. So I thought I could tag along and ask Philippa for your number. I can't believe I told you that, my elaborate plan. And I can't believe it worked out so well. I think I might be a genius.'

I'm very aware that I'm not breathing how I normally breathe. I feel as though I'm shaking inside, as though I could cry but not necessarily in a bad way. As though they'd be tears of joy and they'd be cathartic, wiping everything away to make way for something new. And I'm pretty sure brides-to-be aren't supposed to feel this way about other men.

'What do you want to do? As your babysitter, I need to make sure you're entertained.'

'What do you want to do?'

'No, you choose.'

'I think I'd like to do whatever you want to do.'

'What if I want to play monsters?'

'Then monsters it is.'

'Actually. The thing with the monster game is it really only works if you're completely sozzled.'

'I wish I'd had a babysitter like you when I was a kid.'

'I think what I'd quite like to do is lie on my back on the

grass and drink beer. I had quite a long run before I got here. What do you want to do?'

'Lie on my back on the grass and drink beer. With you.'

I go into the kitchen and pull two beers from Philippa's fridge. It's only the third time Joe King and I have met. Why am I comparing it with the third time I met Matt? Well, Jenny Taylor, you're comparing it because you're feeling so much more now than you did when you met Matt for the third time. Perhaps I'm feeling more for Joe King than I've ever felt for Matt. No. No. I must have felt something. Mustn't I? Well, of course I did, it just wasn't this physical, this magical, or this terrifying. No way near. I keep my face in the fridge for a while, I'm feeling very flushed.

The third time Matt and I met I was in a foul mood and covered in water. It was just after the bad floods in Pakistan a few years back. I wasn't wet from the flooding though. Philippa and I had had a big night at Bomber the night before and were both premenstrual and we saw a news report about it and got through a whole box of tissues because children were dying and people were fleeing their homes – we agreed we needed to do something about it. It was a nice day so we decided to clean cars in our local supermarket car park to raise money for the relief fund. We can get fit, get a tan and do some good. It seemed a no brainer of a good deed. It turned out not to be entirely legal and ended in the police station but, anyway, back to the story. So we set off in our shorts and T-shirts, black, we weren't that silly, with our mops and buckets and we started cleaning people's cars. Oh, it was ghastly. People expected them to be really spotlessly clean.

One woman refused to pay more than £2 as she said it was only a £2 job. It was for charity, the cheek. Besides that, our arms were killing, and we didn't have a hose, so one of us was lugging two buckets of water at a time while the other cleaned. We were very slow and people were returning from their shopping and we hadn't even started on their car. It marginally improved when Philippa ran home and collected her dad's hose, but not much, because we kept accidentally wetting people. Anyway, so grumpy was I that I didn't even recognise the silver Audi, and he'd paid Philippa and not me, and she was so busy muttering that this was the last time she did anything for besieged people that she didn't spot that he was the bloke who threatened to call the police before. So it wasn't until I was sprawled across his windscreen with a sponge and he beeped his horn, which scared me and made me yell 'cocks!' really loudly, that I saw that it was him. He was inside the car tapping away at his laptop.

'Don't scratch my car with your boots!' he yelled, getting out of the car in a hurry.

Well I'd had enough. The abuse we'd had all day and we were just trying to do a good deed. And my boots were soaking. They never recovered. They stank after that.

'It's for charity!' I screamed.

'Oh, it's you!' he said.

'Hello. Did you get out to have a wee?'

'No, I didn't. Hello, Amazing Legs.'

'Hello ...' But I didn't know what to call him. I didn't know what to make of him.

'I have to ask you out now.' He didn't sound too thrilled about the notion.

'Why?'

'Three times.'

'What?'

'The three times rule.'

'What's that?' I hate not knowing things. What was this three times rule?

'If something appears to you or is suggested to you three times, you should act on it in some way.'

'What if something heinous is suggested to you, like eating kidney.'

'Then you should eat kidney. I like eating kidneys.'

'If you are going to ask me out then never in the history of courtship has the line, I like eating kidneys, been used.'

'Until now. Take my card. Let's go for a drink.'

I took the card.

'Hang about, I'm not calling you!'

I leant on his car and pulled a pen out of my back pocket and wrote my number on the card.

'Watch the car!' he gasped.

'Ooops,' I said.

'You didn't scratch it!' he panted.

'Course not.'

'Thank God.'

'Call me,' I said. 'If you want.' I shrugged.

But what with cleaning another fifteen cars and having to go to the police station when we really wanted to go to the pub, I'd forgotten all about him by the end of the day. It wasn't even a blessing when I went to bed that night. Anyway, how long do you think it took him to call me? Two days, you cry. Two days is the uniform time between number exchanging and phone call, is it not? Well, no, in Matt's world two months is how long it takes. Two months. I know! He said he'd been busy at work! I ask you. However, Joe King engineered our third meeting with cunning. Not that I'm comparing him and Matt. No, Jenny, course not.

I close the fridge door and walk back outside. I stand for a moment just looking at him. He must have heard or sensed me there because he looks up and smiles, and I suddenly imagine that this is our garden, and we have our whole lives together. And I don't think I've ever imagined anything like that with Matt and yet Matt and I *are* going to spend our lives together. I can't be wrong about Matt. I can't. Joe King must be a player. He must. He must woo all the girls like this.

'I wrote you a song,' he says, as I hand him a beer.

'Me!' I exclaim, but he just smiles and starts strumming.

'If I play it to you, you will probably think I am a nutter. And you might be correct. Although I have seen you battling a monster with a colander on your head. But it's one thing writing a song about a girl, it's quite another singing it to her. So after I play this to you, don't say anything. I'll be too embarrassed. Let's just lie on the grass and drink our beers. Deal?'

'Deal,' I whisper back.

He starts to strum. He doesn't look at me. He looks at his guitar or at the tree, everywhere but at me.

She walks in
Singing sex on fire
Red hair
Hands in the air

An answered prayer
But where do I go
From here

Mr Man
On her T
A graze
On her knee
She's got me,
She's got me good
Like I'm in a movie,
Like it's meant to be

Don't know where I am going
Don't know what to do
But it has to be . . .
it's gotta be . . .
with you . . .

'Phew,' he says when he's finished. 'Um, phew, so that's your song. And I don't know why I sang it to you except that if we both die tomorrow then at least you know how you've blown me away. And I thought I was un-blow-away-able. I can't stop thinking about you and I've only met you twice. Now let's lie on the grass and drink beer.'

We lie on our backs on the grass. But my breath is all irregular. I feel light in the head. I can hear my own heartbeat. I need to say, 'I'm engaged' but I don't want to.

'Um, I need to shoot off,' I say quickly and I get up and I rush back to the house, leaving him there on the grass.

Chapter 20

I get home and shower. Then I bring my computer into the bathroom and Skype Matt in Chicago.

His face fills the screen. The poor boy looks shattered.

'You look like you should go to bed and get some sleep.'

'I'm so tired,' he says in a childish voice.

'Run a bath, baby. Go on, start it off now.'

He nods obediently. He's very submissive when he's tired, is Matt. I smile affectionately as I watch his slumped muscular frame stumble into a chest of drawers and ricochet into the bathroom. I hear the sound of running water and then he returns.

'Now, what time do you have to be up in the morning?' I ask.

'Five.' He yawns.

'Matt, what time do you *have* to be up. Not what time does your extreme work ethic feel you should get up?'

'I've got a breakfast meeting downstairs at eight,' he says, with another yawn.

'Set your alarm for seven thirty.'

He shakes his head, reaching for the alarm clock on the bedside table. 'Five thirty,' he says, adamantly.

'Matt, you'll be good for nothing tomorrow if you don't get a good sleep. Seven twenty.'

I watch him programme the clock and place it back on the bedside table.

'Nice try,' I say. 'Show me the time you've set the alarm for.'

He fiddles with it again before turning it to show me the alarm time of 7.20.

'What have you eaten today?' I ask.

'Chips, sandwiches.' He shrugs.

'Are you hungry now?'

He shakes his head.

'Right, get up and turn the bath off and then come back with the room service breakfast menu.'

I watch the tired way he completes his tasks.

'Order yourself fresh juice, muesli and fruit, there's bound to be piles of croissants and muffins at the meeting, but try not to eat too many because they'll just make you feel drained.'

'Thank you, baby,' he says, as he scribbles on the room service menu.

'You don't need to thank me. I just wish I was there. I'd give you a massage.'

He smiles sleepily.

'Get in the bath, handsome and then get into bed. Don't forget to leave your breakfast order outside your door.'

He nods. 'Are you OK, by the way?'

'Yeah, fine. Mother being here is a bit freaky,' I whisper.

'I bet,' Matt sighs. Matt isn't at all close to his own mother. I think we've both appreciated the other's lack of close family ties. I've never met his mother, and his father passed away some years ago.

'She's beside herself to meet you.' I tell him tentatively.

'I'll be back soon.' He smiles. 'Love you.'

I blow him a kiss. 'Love you too.'

I lean my head back against the bath. I don't want to leave the bathroom in case Mother jumps upon me with the whole 'talking about things' again. I close my eyes. A picture of Joe King sitting in the sunshine playing his guitar fills my mind. I shake my head to remove it and I think about my Matt instead.

Two months after I bumped into him at the hideous pop-up car wash, Matt called me.

'Fanny?' he said.

'Yes?'

'It's, er, Matt. Matt Parry. You cleaned my car. And, er, you you have tremendous legs.'

He sounded so nervous that I had a vision of him speaking, and in this vision he was blushing. Like a lot of women I love a blushing man.

'Oh, hello, blimey. How are you?' I said.

'Not bad. Could I, er, take you out for dinner?'

'Yes, wow, thank you, wow, lovely,' I said. I was particularly inarticulate because no one had ever invited me out for dinner before. 'Do you fancy meeting up for a drink?' was the usual, and if you were lucky you might get offered chips after. But something in the way Matt Parry mentioned dinner conjured up images of linen napkins, sparkling water glasses and hand cream in the loos.

'Great, I was thinking Saturday. If you're free.'

'Um, wow, thanks.'

He'd given me a Saturday night. Philippa says if a man asks you out on a Saturday then he's very, very keen. A quick drink after work on a Monday, not that bothered. Mid-week cinema, you might be in there. But dinner on Saturday is practically a box from Tiffanys.

'So, if you text me your address, I'll pick you up at seven thirty.'

'Oh, I live above a kebab shop.'

'Well, that must be handy,' he said and chuckled.

I ended the call feeling like Cinderella about to be whisked away by the handsome prince.

So, he arrived promptly at 7.30 in his shiny Audi. Al was crouched down in the flat, peering out of the window and writing down his registration number, 'Just in case I have to call the police, Fan,' he whispered.

Matt was nervous at dinner as well. Weeks later, after we'd started sleeping together I asked him why he seemed so terrified on our first date.

'Ah, was it very obvious?' he said, with the hint of a blush.

'Yep, 'fraid so,' I said, smiling at his reddening cheeks.

'You were this cool, hot girl. I was intimidated. I didn't want to bore you.'

'Cool hot girl!' I exclaimed. 'I work in a doctor's surgery in Tiddlesbury. I live above a kebab shop.'

'Yeah, but you had pink hair and biker boots and great legs. I was never a cool kid at school.'

'Matt, I was definitely not a cool kid at school,' I protested. I didn't want to mention just how traumatic school had been for me at this point though.

Anyway, on our first date he took me to a lovely, posh Italian restaurant, in one of the affluent villages on the other side of Nunstone. He ordered these gigantic gooey balls of mozzarella, and laughed at the way I moaned with pleasure as I ate them. As he laughed, he relaxed, and I liked seeing him relax. I liked helping him to relax. I interrogated him then. Well, he claims I interrogated him. I maintain I was simply trying to get to know him. He said, 'I don't think I've ever spoken about myself so much.' Although that's not what I remember most about our first date. What I remember most is how halfway through his main course he put his knife and fork down suddenly, wiped his mouth quickly with his napkin and looked at me seriously.

'Fanny, I work extremely hard,' he told me urgently. 'People say I'm a workaholic, and when they say that I don't think, Oh, I really need to take it a bit easier. No, I think, Good, I'm glad you think I'm a workaholic. You see, the thing is, Fanny, I'm going to retire from big business at forty-five, which sounds very young. But that's my game plan. My, er, my dad died two days before he was due to retire at sixty-four. And so, well, that's the game plan. That's why I work so hard now.' And he picked up his knife and fork and, without looking at me, said, 'I just wanted to warn you. I'd like to see you again. But, I should say that my work can make me quite stressed, sometimes.'

'Have you thought about yoga?' I asked him.

He looked puzzled for a moment and then he laughed. I

thought, Blimey, Matt Parry is intense, complicated, nothing like me, nothing like anyone I've ever met before. But I remember thinking, I'd be good for you. I, Fanny Taylor, could be good for you, Matt Parry. I'd never thought of myself as being particularly good for anyone before. But best of all, I didn't feel scared, and that in itself felt like a very good thing.

Chapter 21

Mother was up this morning before I left for work. She was sitting at the kitchen table. I thought, Oh, God, she's going to hit me with another 'let's talk about that day'. But no. She wanted to talk about feelings.

'Jenny, tell me how you're feeling about me leaving your dad,' she said. It was ridiculous. I hate talking about my dad. I hate *thinking* about my dad. Blimey, I wish I never thought about him at all, but unfortunately he does pop into my head fairly frequently. I suppose you just can't help the fact that your dad is a seismic presence in your life, even when he is an arse. It's normally when I see other people with their dads that I think of him. Sometimes dads bring their children to the surgery, and I get a little pang of 'my dad would never have done that', or we'll be out in Nunstone and I'll see a dad doing the pub quiz with his daughter and buying her drinks and meeting her boyfriend. You can see the respect in her eyes and the tenderness in his. That's when I start to think, I wish my dad wasn't so cold, or just, I wish my dad liked me. I have to force myself to think of his positives then, otherwise I'll be stuck in the 'my dad's an arse' headspace for ages. So I'll consider how he's not afraid to wear pink, he speaks very good conversational French, he was visibly upset when our dog died, he plays a phenomenal game of Scrabble, his name, Jack Taylor, could almost be a whisky, until other non-dad thoughts plant themselves in my mind.

I do have one nice memory of my dad though. At least I think it's a memory. It could just be a daydream that I've had so often, I've mistakenly started to believe it was real. It isn't a particularly dramatic reminiscence. I am about three or four years old and we're in the garden, he throws me up in the air and he catches me and swings me round. Afterwards we go inside, I'm tired and I fall asleep on his lap. He cradles me and strokes my hair. But it could well have been a dream, because I can't think of another time when he voluntarily touched me. Nope. Not ever. No pecks on the cheek goodnight, no pats on the back to say 'well done' or 'good luck'. Not one hug. Didn't he ever read any books on parenting?

So if I was about to start discussing my relationship with my father it wouldn't be with my mother at 7.30 in the morning after having spent a large portion of the night thinking about a man who wasn't my husband-to-be. One Mr Joe King. So, I backed straight out of the kitchen. It wasn't safe to breakfast in there. All in all, an unfortunate start to the day.

The cameraman, Disgruntled Dave, is back at the surgery to film Marge. He's more fed up than ever. If he carries on like this I'm going to slip him the Smiling Fanny Manifesto. I actually think he could be quite handsome if he didn't have the unattractive aura of a man who desperately didn't want to be where he is. He's in his early to mid thirties, swarthy, he wears his combats well, but he's just not happy. Mind you, he has been filming Marge all day, in her head-to-toe leopardskin ensemble, so perhaps it's unfair of me to expect him to be perky.

'I met my Timmy on match.com. He'd just moved to the area. He winked at me. Well, at my profile. Then he sent me a message saying, "Hey, good looking, I like what you got cooking." Well, if I'm honest, I wasn't blown away.'

Marge said 'blown away'. Joe King said he was blown away by me. He hadn't been able to stop thinking about me either. Perhaps he wasn't with those nineteen-year-old twins after all. I keep drifting back to last night, in the garden, lying next to each other on the grass, listening to his breathing. The bit before I ran away.

'No, I wasn't blown away by my Timmy's message. But, I was blown away by his picture. *And* he was twenty-seven. I was thirty-six. I wrote back, "It's a sweet chilli chicken stir-fry, thank you very much, and if you play your cards right you can sample it one day." And he said, "I would like to play my cards right very much." And I replied, "Well, then I accept your kind offer of dinner," and he came back with a restaurant and a date. I liked the fact that he'd taken the initiative then. So, we had a great first date and about three months later I made him my sweet chilli chicken stir-fry.'

'Doris!' I throw my arms open to greet my favourite patient as she walks into the surgery. 'How are you, lovely?'

'Oh, mustn't grumble, Fanny, love, must not grumble. And I have been giving my Big Send Off a fair bit of thought. I'll just sit myself here and discuss it with my best girl.'

I wink at her and mouth the words, 'You're my favourite patient,' before saying, at full volume, 'Right, so did you decide on a dress code?'

'Yes, I'm very pleased with it. The film *Grease*.'

'Oh, Doris, I love it.'

'Do you really, love?'

'Absolutely, it's a great one. You can do the sexy Sandy or the sweet Sandy or go for the classic pink lady. It's great for the guys too. All ages know the film.'

'That's what I thought! I hope you'll be there as a sexy Sandy with that man of yours.'

'Oh, Doris, I don't like to think of you not being there.'

'Oh, I'll be there, don't you worry.'

'Just you make sure you are.'

'And it has to be at the community centre. We had a lovely do there for my Little Stevie's christening.' She smiles, the dreamy smile that is always in attendance when she mentions her grandson.

'Doris.' Dr Flemming pokes his head out of his office.

'Oh, I hate it when you're efficient. I was enjoying my chinwag with Fanny here.'

She gets up and tootles into his office.

'We certainly do have an energetic sex life,' Marge continues, wide-eyed and animated, confiding to the camera. Then, she leans forward so that her fully grown hounds escape the confines of her leopard-print top, produces a little breathy giggle and follows it up with a wink.

Next to her, I place my blurry head in my hands and slowly and gutturally utter the words, 'Oh, holy mother.'

'My Tim knows how to pleasure a woman.'

Surely, there's only so much we, or the BBC Three viewers, need to know.

'He's very adventurous.'

'That's enough now, Marge,' I say in my best head of reception voice.

'And he's very well endowed.'

'Now, stop it, now. We are working, Marge. In a doctor's surgery.'

'Oh, Fanny, stop being a prude!'

'Prude, I'll have you know I'm a sex goddess.'

'He likes a little spanking.'

'Marge!' That was my firm puppy trainer voice.

'I know how to keep my man happy,' she says smugly. As though I don't!

'So do I.'

'He likes it outside.'

'Outside?'

Oh, Disgruntled Dave, why are you encouraging her?

'Yes, in the open air. I think it's the risk of being caught he enjoys.'

'Anywhere in particular?'

'Dave,' I sigh, wearily.

'There's a nice field out past B & Q.'

'Marge, I run there. Now I'll have images.'

Luckily, I've never met Tim so the image is somewhat blurrier than it could be. Not that I need to meet Tim. I know all there is to know already.

'There's a little lay-by, with a gate.'

I wait until she's doing her titillating lean forward into the camera before I break the news.

'My boyfriend stops to wee there sometimes.'

I have finally silenced the Marge. I tap away at my computer triumphantly.

'I think I'll stop now for some lunch.' Disgruntled Dave sounds tired. He puts his camera in its bag. 'Will it be all right to leave this under here?' he asks, indicating his bag under the desk.

'I might sell it on eBay. Or shoot myself a little pop video.' I smile.

'Should I move it?'

'No, no, it's fine.' I'm grinning away at Disgruntled Dave, but he's too disgruntled to smile back. 'Leave the bag here, honestly. It'll be fine.'

'Thanks,' he says, with absolutely no hint of a grin, before walking slouchily off to lunch.

That's it. I lift my holdall onto my lap and pick out a neutral bloke-type card and then in capitals, not in my scrawly writing, I copy out the Smiling Manifesto for him. See what I did there? I left out the Fanny. It would be very obvious where it came from if I gave him the Smiling Fanny Manifesto, what with me being called Fanny. I wait until Marge has to go and see the nurse about a prescription and then I slide the card into the side pocket of Disgruntled Dave's camera bag. I don't know what he'll make of it, or even if he uses this side pocket at all. It might lie untouched there for years and years. Disgruntled Dave might buy a better bag and take this one to the charity shop. But then someone could purchase the bag, discover the note and they may just think, Perhaps I should have a go at this.

I have never mentioned my anonymous note giving to

Matt. He knows we gave Trudi, his ex-girlfriend, a note in Nunstone, on that first night. But he's under the impression that it was an isolated occurrence because Philippa and I were moved by her pretty dress and a fair bit of wine. He doesn't know about the Smiling Manifesto at all. He's noticed that I often strike up conversations with random people when we're out together though. He says it makes him feel like a carer for the mentally ill. There's a lot that Matt doesn't know about me. I suppose I didn't want to put him off me by telling him all my stuff. But, somehow, I could imagine myself telling Joe King everything. *Like it's meant to be.* That was a line in his song, I'm sure it was. He thinks that we are meant to be. And what if we are? What if Jenny Taylor and Joe King are absolutely 100 per cent meant to be together? How can you know? You can't. The only way you can know is by taking the dangerous risk of finding out. Oh, why am I even having these thoughts? Why do I feel as though nothing will ever be the same again?

Chapter 22

I had a drink after work with Marge and Disgruntled Dave. It was an avoidance tactic. I didn't want to go home and defend myself against Mother's new-found delusion that she's Oprah and that feelings have to be talked about and trauma revisited. Going for a drink was a win–win. Not only has it delayed any potential discussion of feelings but it's also provided me with a tingle of tiddliness, which could come in handy should the situation arise.

Neither Dave nor I really got a word in, but when Marge went to the loo I found out that he's single and a bit out of sorts at the moment because he's been working abroad, he says it feels strange to be back. He was very direct, articulate and honest when he answered my rapid-fire interview questions. And there's definitely a bit of a young Robert Redford about him. So who can I set him up with? Philippa? Hmmm. Now Philippa is very discerning, but the pro is that he has a creative job. Admittedly I'm using the term rather loosely in the case of *I Like 'Em Big* – and, I think, there might lie the cause of at least part of his disgruntlement. The con with Philippa is that he could well fall in love with her and she will probably snog him and leave him, and then he could feel even worse. Although perhaps a little snog as a pick-me-up is all he needs. And talking about pick-me-up snoggers, what about Mother? Hmmmm. On the whole I am really working on the liberal thing, but the thought of my mother with someone twenty years younger is still really icky for me. And, yes, I know Demi Moore did it. But that was Hollywood, where they have plastic surgery and Botox, and this is Tiddlesbury, where we have a doctor's surgery and Posh Nosh. And even if he is into older women, he would probably prefer a stable one. Still, I'll force Mum and Philippa to come to Marge's house-warming next week and he can choose for himself. I'd call that a good deed.

Later, as I stand wrestling with the lock to get me into the flat, I have a vision of me as a bridesmaid at Mum and Disgruntled Dave's wedding. But it's not Matt who's at the wedding with me. It's Joe King. He looks beautiful in a suit. I press my hands to my face to dissolve his image from my mind. I don't care that I'm smudging my make-up. I so need this to stop. I want him exorcised from my brain.

I enter the flat and walk into the living room. The curtains are pulled shut even though there's a bright blue sky outside. Mum and Al are sitting next to each other on the sofa huddled around my laptop. Fleetwood Mac is playing on the stereo. Fleetwood Mac is always playing on the stereo at the moment.

'Is someone ill?' I ask, flopping in an armchair.

Neither of them look at me but they both shake their heads.

'What you watching?'

'I love him,' Mum says without taking her eyes off the screen.

'You what?'

'Mick Jagger,' Al says to the computer.

'You what?'

'Your mum loves Mick Jagger,' Al repeats. 'We're watching the Rolling Stones on YouTube.'

'But you've got Fleetwood Mac on the stereo.'

'Yeah,' Al agrees.

The video obviously finishes because Al leans back and starts smiling and moving his head along to Fleetwood Mac. While Mum, on the other hand, sits up a touch and begins to open and close her mouth like a child who wants a bottle.

'Mum, are you all right?'

She nods. She's still suckling.

'Mum?'

Mum ignores me and instead turns to Al. The strange thing she's doing with her mouth continues only now there's a slight look of alarm in her eyes.

'Have you got any saliva?' she asks, leaning very close to him.

Al looks at her seriously and then joins her with the baby mouth. Finally, he shakes his head.

'None at all.'

'It's very strange.'

'Hmmm.'

I stare at the pair of them. They're still at it. Together they look like fish.

'Perhaps we should have a cup of tea,' Mum whispers.

'I would love a cup of tea,' Al says earnestly.

'I can't move though,' Mum confides.

'Hmmmmphf,' Al agrees.

They both turn to me. I cross my arms and pretend to be Supernanny.

'What's been going on here?'

Neither of them responds.

'Tell me. Mum? Al?'

Mother's started to giggle. Al's just joined her.

'Mum? Al?'

Mum's rotating her torso as she giggles and giggles. Al's head is bouncing up and down. I spring up from my seat.

'You're stoned, aren't you?'

They think that's hysterical.

'Al, I can't believe you got my mother stoned.'

'She had the stuff.'

'Mum!'

'Damien the Dealer was very kind.'

'*Mum!*'

I flop back into the chair, shaking my head.

'Please make the tea, Fan,' Al pleads.

'Is cocaine like this?' my mother squawks.

Chapter 23

'I can't believe you brought me here,' Philippa humphs.

'It's my good deed.'

'Since when does a good deed involve pimping your best friend?'

'Times are tough.'

Mum wasn't feeling well this evening so decided not to come to Marge's house-warming party. I suggested a little detox might be in order but she just turned her nose up. Al's not at all happy because it's pub quiz night and he's down three men. Well, women. I couldn't interest him in coming here either, which I can well understand, because it's basically lots of people who don't know each other, and are far too sober to chat to each other, standing in a new-smelling home trying not to get marks on anything. Still, at least I've got Philippa, hopefully she'll cheer Disgruntled Dave up. She has been known to cheer many a man up in the past.

'So what do we think of this Dave bloke anyway,' she says, absent-mindedly punching one of Marge's new sofa cushions, a bored expression on her face.

'He's disgruntled,' I say, removing the cushion from her clutches.

'Sounds perfect,' she says, sarcastically.

'But I like him. I think he's a nice bloke.'

'Lovely, Fan.'

'There he is.'

I point to Disgruntled Dave, who's hovering to the side of Marge, filming her, Marge is resplendent in a green trouser suit, holding court and a plate of chicken satay.

'He looks miserable,' Philippa comments.

'How can you tell? His face is obliterated by a video camera.'

'I can just tell. Nice body though.'

'There you go.'

'FANNY!' Marge bellows from across the room. 'Presents in the bedroom.'

'Right you are,' I holler back.

'Did you get her a present?' Philippa whispers.

'No,' I whisper. Then I start shouting back to Marge. 'Where is Tim? Do I get to meet him? This man I've heard so much about.' I fail to add the words 'day in day out for six months' whilst banging my head repeatedly against her brand new door arch, which must mean I have excellent self-control.

'Oh, you haven't met my Timmy.'

'No, although I feel I know him.'

'Well, let me go and find him. Dave, you can turn that off for the moment.'

'Right.'

Marge bustles off.

'She didn't offer us a drink!' Philippa squawks. 'Where's that bottle we bought?'

I fish it out of my bag and hand it to her.

'Screw top. Lovely.' She sighs, gratefully. 'What did we do before screw tops?' She opens it aggressively, swigs from it and passes it to me.

I beckon Disgruntled Dave over to us.

'Hello, Dave. Meet my friend Philippa.'

'Hello, Philippa,' he says, taking the hand she's offering and, ooh, we have a slight turn up of one corner of his mouth.

'Are you having a good night?' Philippa asks, very seriously, her head cocked to one side.

'It's quite . . . astonishing,' he says, completely deadpan.

Philippa grins. 'Would you like to swig some of our warm wine out of the bottle?'

'I couldn't think of anything nicer.'

Ooh, both corners of his mouth are up a little bit. Philippa is very, very good.

'Do you think they'd mind if we turned on the telly? There's a good *Panorama* on,' Philippa says.

'I love *Panorama*,' Dave says seriously.

They're holding each other's gaze. I am a matchmaking genius.

'Fanny,' Marge chimes from across the room. I take the wine from Dave, have another quick swig from the bottle lest it's all gone before I return, hand it back and then leave the others to join Marge.

'Tim, this is Fanny from the surgery.'

The dark-haired man next to her obediently turns round.

'Oh, I have met you,' I say immediately.

He looks blank. But I've definitely seen this fella before. He's a handsome Mediterranean-looking chap. I can see why Marge overlooked the diabolical chat-up line.

'I'm sure I know you. I can't think from where though. It'll come to me, I'm sure. Anyway, Tim, it's nice to meet you properly at last.'

'I don't think I remember meeting you, but pleased to meet you too.'

'Congratulations on your move. Great place.'

'Thanks.'

I gasp. 'I've got it,' I say, but then I stop myself. I know where I know Tim from. Philippa and I match-made him with the girl in Nunstone. The pub quiz girl. He was heavy petting her in his Ford Mondeo last week. I can feel my smile dropping from my face. Poor Marge.

'What?' he says, carefully. I can't work out if he's recognised me. But he must have done. Everyone recognises me. I've got raspberry-red hair.

'Nothing,' I backtrack, trying to force myself to look a bit more cheerful. 'Nothing. I've worked it out. You, I ... er ... you just look the image of someone I haven't seen for ages.'

'I've got one of those faces.'

'Oh, well, they say that imitation is the highest form of flattery ... or something.' Oh, dear, I've got a forced smile and for some reason have now started doing a fake laugh. 'Anyway, great to meet you. I should go and rejoin my best friend. Make sure she's not pocketing your cutlery.' Oh, God, I'm doing the fake laugh again.

Cock and balls, Cilla and Cupid massively messed up. We match-made Marge's man to another girl. I shake my head. I look at Marge still clutching the chicken satay, beaming at her Timmy, This is awful.

'Crisis,' I whisper in Philippa's ear, pulling her away from Disgruntled Dave. 'We need to go. I'm calling a Musketeer Mission.'

'Why?'

'We accidentally match-made Marge's live-in boyfriend to another girl, he's the one I saw smooching in the Mondeo. We need to find her and tell her, so she leaves Tim alone.'

'But I quite like old Disgruntled here.'

'Well, you can stay.'

'Not if it's a Musketeer Mission. I'm a musketeer,' she says indignantly.

'Well, come on then.'

'Where are we going?'

'First stop will have to be the pub quiz in Nunstone, that's where we found her, there's a good chance she'll be there.'

'Are you calling Al or shall I?'

'You do it. I'll make some excuse to Marge.'

'Al will be so excited. He bloody loves a Musketeer Mission.'

Have I mentioned that Philippa, Al and I live in Tiddlesbury, a small town in the middle of England and need all the excitement we can get? So occasionally we go on what we call Musketeer Missions. Basically, if ever I, or Philippa or Funny Al, have a problem that we can't solve alone we summon a Musketeer Meeting, where we three musketeers develop a plan of problem-solving action. I'm not entirely sure how the Musketeer Missions started but I'm fairly certain there was wine involved.

Chapter 24

'Ladies, I've got the headwear,' Al says as soon as we are seated in his Fiat Punto. I know, if I were six foot five I don't think I'd drive a Fiat Punto either. He tosses us both balaclavas.

'Oh no, oh no, oh no,' I mutter.

'Just put them on to discuss the plan,' Al says keenly.

'Al, the balaclavas were a joke. That's all. A joke. Not to be worn and definitely not to be worn when driving around in a car.'

It's all my fault. I bought us all balaclavas for a bit of a lark. I love mine – it's a hand knitted one with Spiderman's face on the front. A brilliant piece of craft. I couldn't believe someone had given it to the charity shop. I wanted to buy it, but I needed a reason. You can't really buy yourself a balaclava without a reason, can you? So I thought, I know, I'll buy one for Al and Philippa as well, and say they're for our Musketeer Missions. But I was joking. Of course I was joking, we can't go around Tiddlesbury and Nunstone wearing balaclavas because we will scare people and get arrested. Al, however, must have missed that key day at school because he's always trying to put his on.

'Put them back in the glove compartment, please, Philippa,' I say firmly.

'Where's your sense of adventure, Fan?' Al humphs, but he concurs and hands his balaclava to Philippa.

'Right, Al, you'll be pleased to know that we need to head for the Nunstone pub quiz.'

As Al starts the car and heads off, I fill him in on the Cupid and Cilla cock-up.

'Musketeer, ready for action,' Al says, when he's got the gist.

'Stop the car!' Philippa screams suddenly.

Al checks his rear-view mirror and starts to brake. Philippa winds her window down and sticks her head out of the car.

'Oi,' Philippa calls. 'Oi! Oi!'

I look out and oh, my goodness. It's him. It's Joe King walking along eating a packet of Frazzles. He hurries away from the car.

'Al, catch that bloke up,' Philippa barks.

Al rolls the car along. Joe breaks into a run. Really rather a good run. We could run together, I think, before I can stop myself.

'Joe, it's us,' she hollers. 'It's Philippa and Jenny!'

He stops suddenly and turns around, then takes a few tentative steps towards the car.

'Get in,' Philippa orders. 'We're on a mission.'

'Oh, hello, there.' He chuckles. 'What sort of mission?'

I'm smiling. I'm smiling just to hear him speak.

'A mission of good, we're like the relief effort. Get in!'

He pauses, then shrugs and opens the back door and climbs in next to me.

'Evening.' He nods, as he gets in next to me. Then he leads forwards so he's close to my face and says, 'Very nice to see you.'

'Joe, this is Al,' I say, because I don't know what else to say. 'Al is a top man, flatmate, raconteur, bon viveur, but he does work for the council so, I have to warn you, he is prone to moan.'

'Bloody place. Pleased to meet you, mate.'

'Al, Joe is new to Tidds, works in the chemist and writes beautiful songs.'

I wish I'd said yes to the balaclava, my cheeks are starting to feel hot from just sitting next to him.

'Good to meet you too.'

'Now, Joe, if you perform well on this mission, we might make you a part-time musketeer.' Philippa tells him. 'What's the probationary period for that, Fan?'

'Six years,' I inform him.

'Well, something to aspire to,' Philippa interjects.

'So dare I ask what the mission is?'

'Philippa and I accidentally match-made a couple,' I tell him.

'How do you accidentally match-make a couple?'

'We were in a bar and we left an anonymous note with a girl saying that a guy had been eyeing her up and that he looked handsome and not too mental.'

'Or so we thought,' Philippa adds.

'But you just never can tell,' I explain.

'And that's not all,' Philippa says.

'They've been hooking up in his Ford Mondeo. I saw them on my run.'

'Good work.' Joe looks impressed.

'Ah.' Philippa raises her hand to ward off his praise. 'We thought it was good work. But then tonight we met Mr Mondeo and discovered he has a long-term girlfriend. We realised this at the party they were having to celebrate buying a house together.'

'I work with the long-term girlfriend. Marge is her name.'

'So what do we do now?' Joe King asks, managing to squeeze a word in between Philippa and me.

'Another anonymous note,' I tell him.

'Shouldn't we leave them well alone?' Joe asks.

'We have discussed this,' Philippa sighs.

'They have, mate, at length.'

'Ultimately, if we left everything alone the world would be ... what would the world be?' Philippa conjectures.

'Balls,' I offer. I do love the word balls.

'Balls, well said. When we reach out to make people's life better, when we take those steps, those risks ... ' Philippa must have had more wine than I thought at Marge's.

'Like matchmaking a girl to a two-timing bastard?' Joe is starting to look confused.

'We're the first to say that this world view is fraught with problems,' Philippa reasons.

'However, we have to tell her. It's one of the Rules of the Sisterhood,' I explain.

'What's the sis ... ?' Joe starts.

'Word of advice, mate. Never get them started on the Rules of the Sisterhood.'

'Thanks for that, mate.'

'So we're going to Nunstone to find the girl,' Philippa continues.

'And you'll tell her?'

'No, an anonymous note.' He's quite slow getting it, is our Joe. 'Stop here!' I screech. 'Here we are.'

I get a card from my holdall. I zone out the others' chatter and think about what to say. The best way is to remain impartial and place the information in her hands.

> Hello. This might be a horrible note to read. Or you may already know this. But the man you meet in the Mondeo. He's in a relationship. Thought you should know.

'Right, you guys stay here. I'll check inside and see if she's there. If I can't drop the note straight off, then I'll return for back up.'

I stride into the pub. I spot her instantly. She's sitting at the same table with the same friend and they are sharing a bottle of wine just as she was when we gave her the note. I had a feeling she would be. She has the rosy glow of someone who's getting a lot of sex after a drought. There's no way I can go over and drop the note without being totally conspicuous. I return to the car. When I sit back down, Joe King is wearing a balaclava. He still looks fit. Colander hats, balaclavas. His is a fitness that keeps on giving.

'Please take that off,' I whisper. 'Or we will get arrested.'

'They said you'd say that,' he whispers back, and starts to take it off.

Al and Philippa laugh. I just watch Joe King's smiling face re-emerge. He catches my eye, and I look away and swallow.

'We have lift off,' I say.

'Right. What's the plan?' Philippa asks.

'I think Al should distract them. They might twig it was you last time,' I tell her. 'Al, so you'll approach them and try to chat them up,' I command.

'Why do you use the word try?'

'The boys should both go and chat them up,' Philippa suggests.

'It's not some jolly,' I say firmly, not much liking the thought of Joe King off chatting girls up.

'No,' agrees Philippa. 'So just very mild flirting.'

'What exactly is mild flirting?' Joe asks.

'Bloody good question, mate,' says Al.

'Have we got time for this?' Philippa asks keenly.

'Briefly,' I concur.

'OK,' Philippa starts.

'Mild flirting . . . ' I announce.

'As opposed to, "What's a beautiful girl like you doing in a shithole like this" heavy flirting,' Philippa continues.

'To which the answer is . . . ' I add.

'Always is . . . ' she stresses.

'Considering becoming a lezzer,' we say in unison.

'These girls are hard,' Joe laughs.

'Tell me about it, mate.'

'Mild flirting is . . . ' I continue.

'Lovely.' Philippa smiles.

'It's just a little smile, and a nod, and a, "How are you doing?" No need to make some lewd sexual overture, no need to drink ten pints and a sambuca beforehand to work up the courage,' I state.

'Wow.' Joe is rightly impressed.

'They make it sound so easy,' Al says mournfully.

'You girls should write a book,' Joe suggests.

'On what?' I ask.

'Everything,' he says, huskily.

We hold each other's gaze for a second before I tear myself away.

'Jump to it. Right, Philippa and I will lead. You boys bring up the rear. But don't take your eyes off me because I will be pointing out the women you need to do light flirting with. So stay alert. I will subtly show you where they are. Philippa will head to the bar and purchase the Jägerbombs. The bomb without the Jäger for the driver though. We gather at the bar. Neck the drinks. The boys go and engage in mild flirting, I will slip in and deposit the note and head back to the car with Philippa. As soon as you boys see me go, you can leave too. Got it?'

'Got it,' says Joe, seriously.

'Welcome, part-time musketeer,' I smile.

'Positions please,' Philippa sings.

We exit the car. We nod to each other. We're off. Philippa and I do our musketeer strut into the pub. She hums the theme tune from *Cagney and Lacey*.

'The pent-up sexual chemistry between you guys is s, s, s, s, s, s, sizzling,' she hisses.

'Hang about, don't distract me,' I say, to direct her attention from the big grin that just spread over my face.

We pass the girls. I do a genius little dance move to signal them out for the boys.

'I'm on fire,' I whisper to Philippa.

'You're on something,' she snorts.

The boys join us at the bar. We raise our glasses and drink a quiet toast to the musketeers.

'I'm feeling a lot of adrenalin,' Joe remarks.

'Oh, mate, the Musketeer Missions make you feel alive.'

'Ready for your mild flirting?' Philippa questions.

'As ready as I'll ever be,' Al says, belching Red Bull.

Philippa and I shake our heads.

'Those lucky ladies.'

'You ready, Fan?'

'Yep. Got the note. I'll drop it down on the slide past. See you back in the car in a few minutes, boys.'

Chapter 25

'It's taking the biscuit now,' Philippa groans.

'It took the biscuit twenty minutes ago,' I humph.

'How long have they been in there?'

'Must be forty minutes now.'

'It can no longer be termed as mild flirting.'

'See, the more I think about it the more I think we messed up tonight.'

'Why?'

'We send a six foot five bloke with aspirations to be a comedian and the most attractive man in the universe—'

'Ahhhh, you love him.'

'Course I don't, I'm engaged. I'm just saying that those two were perhaps not the subtlest of distractions.'

'I didn't think of that.'

'Oh, well.'

'Were they pretty? The girls? I didn't get a look.'

'Yes,' I reply sadly. 'Pretty and nice looking. One had big boobs. That's the wine finished,' I say, shaking the empty wine bottle sadly.

'I think you should kiss him.'

'Who?'

'Who?' She smirks.

'I'm getting married.'

'Yeah, that's inconvenient. Go and see what's happened to them, Fan.'

'You go.'

'All right.' She flings open the car door and stalks into the bar with her hands on her hips. She returns after a minute in exactly the same manner.

'They've sat down with them and everything.'

'No!'

'Yep, chatting and laughing away, didn't even see me, and I was quite conspicuous standing there with my hands on my hips, huffing.'

'Oh, well, at least it softens the blow when she gets the note.'

'Good point. I'm bored though, I don't want to sit in a car all night.'

I'm not bored but I am feeling a little miserable at the thought that Joe King might be falling for the girl with big boobs and that it was I who inadvertently match-made them.

'Why are you looking so sulky?'

'I'm not.'

'Where's your mum tonight?'

'She said she wasn't feeling that great.'

'What's wrong with her?'

'She's fine. She's just toxic. She got some weed from Damien the Dealer. She says it makes her feel better but she doesn't want to do anything except stay at home and talk about feelings.'

‘That is so weird.’

‘Tell me about it.’

‘And how is the talking about feelings going?’

‘It’s not. I run away.’

‘Oh, dear.’

‘I know. I’m finding it all a bit late. It might have been nice if she’d asked me how I was feeling all those years ago when Dad was being foul to me.’

I can’t help but feel that I’m not dealing with Mum being here very well. If truth be told I’m not dealing with it at all. I’m trying to pretend it’s not happening. You see, Philippa’s right. It is weird. She’s my mum, she’s family, and she made me. And you’re supposed to know your family, aren’t you? I’m sure most people do. But Mum and I don’t really have a clue who the other is. We haven’t spent any proper length of time together for nearly ten years and I certainly don’t recognise the lady who’s been getting stoned in my lounge. She’s nothing like the woman I grew up with. And I don’t mind her staying and sorting herself out after the whole Dad debacle, but this wanting to hang out with me and telling me she’s proud of me, and asking me how I’m feeling, is freaking me out. Well, not that I’m freaking out as such. I’m not that dramatic, I’m just trying to avoid her, which is much more civilised.

‘Oh, about frigging time.’ Philippa sighs as Al jostles into the driver seat. I don’t say anything to Joe as he climbs into the back seat next to me. I pretend to gaze out the window. It’s good that he’s found someone else. I’m not going to look at him. I’m not going to look at those freckly eyes and that peskily beautiful smile ever again.

‘Oh, sorry!’ exclaims Al. ‘Were we a long time?’

'What do you think?' Philippa says belting him in the tummy.

'Nice girls. Thanks for that. One gave me her number. I haven't had luck like that for ages. The other one said she'd just started seeing someone, so that must be matey in the Mondeo. We're a good team, mate.'

'We are, yeah,' Joe agrees.

I can't be sure because I'm staring intently out of the window but I think that Joe King is trying to catch my eye. I'm not going to bite. He can't chat up girls for half an hour and expect me to turn and smile, can he? Not that I care.

Chapter 26

'What's that smell?' Mum asks, standing in the centre of the living room and sniffing.

'Urgh, dunno. Have you dropped some perfume?' I ask, my eyes watering slightly.

'No, it's not me, love, I thought it might have been you.'

'God, it's so bad, I'm considering opening the window.'

'Yes, I think that might be wise. It's quite addling on the brain, this strong perfume.'

'Yeah, but the smell of kebab meat is quite addling on the stomach so we tend not to open the windows. Still, needs must. Here goes . . . ' I open one of the windows and lean my head out.

'Oh, good idea,' Mum says, opening the other window and leaning out of it. 'Oooh,' she turns her nose up. 'I see what you mean.'

'Ladies, how do I look?' It's Al, he's doing a pirouette to show off his outfit while trying to avoid the lampshade. Black jeans, shirt, and waistcoat.

'Dapper,' I say approvingly. 'Is there a lady involved?'

'Oh, Al, you haven't dropped your aftershave, have you?' Mum asks.

'What? Have I got quite a lot on?'

'What, you haven't dropped any?' I ask, stunned.

'You just put some on?' Mum's eyes are very wide and slightly watery.

'Yes. Don't you like it?'

'It's not a case of liking it, Al, it's a case of diving for air to get away from it,' I say, gesturing to Mum and me who are leaning out of windows inhaling a kebab shop.

'Really?'

I jump up, leaving my perch to go and sniff him.

'Al, Al. She'll pass out. You need to shower it off.'

'I can't. I've got to leave. I'm late already to meet them.'

'Them? How many are you planning to asphyxiate?'

'Oh, the two girls from the other night and Joe.'

'Joe?' I ask, casually, or at least *aim* to ask casually.

'Yeah. I really like him. Nice guy.'

'Like a little cosy foursome?'

'Yeah, well, you see, the other one, she's splitting up with the guy she's been seeing tonight. Turns out he had a lady. Can't imagine how she found out about it.' Al winks at me. 'So Gemma felt that she'd be out with me and she'd feel bad that Felicity would be on her own and might be upset. So she said why didn't I invite Joe and then she could invite Felicity to come after she's done the break up.'

'Felicity.'

So he's fallen for Felicity. Felicity King. Joe and Felicity.

'What's up with you? I thought you'd be pleased the mission was accomplished.'

'Oh, I am. I'm thrilled. Over the moon. Beside myself. Al, I really can't breathe when you stand close to me.'

'Sorry, Fan.'

'Wow. She's dumping him now.'

'Yes. Good work.'

'And you, musketeer.'

Al nods bashfully. 'Wish me luck,' he says.

I stand on tiptoes and pucker my lips, indicating I want to give him a kiss on the cheek. He bends down for me, so I can.

'You don't need luck, she'd be a fool not to snap you up,' I whisper in his ear.

'Aha, but she might be a fool.'

'You like her, don't you?'

'I do, yeah.'

'So go get her.'

Mum and I stand and see Al off on his hot date. Mum tries to link her arm through mine, but I step away and pretend to check that Al closed the door behind him. I suddenly have a horrible thought, well it shouldn't be horrible, but it is. What if Al tells Joe King that I'm engaged. I stand with my back to my mother and I ask her a question. It comes out of my mouth before I can stop it.

'Do you believe in love at first sight?'

Love at first sight? What am I saying? Of course she doesn't. No one does. It only happens in books.

'Yes,' she answers.

I spin round.

'Did you know as soon as you met Dad?'

'Oh, God, no,' she chokes. 'Not Jack. Someone else. Someone before Jack.'

'Oh, what happened?'

'I lost him.'

'Oh, no. Did he die?' I ask carefully.

'No,' she laughs sadly. 'I literally lost him. I had one weekend at the Reading Festival with him and I lost him on the last afternoon. I'd gone to meet my friend to see this folk band. But it poured with rain, stormy it was, and I lost my bearings and couldn't find where we'd arranged to meet until it was too late.'

Woah. I don't know what is odder, the fact Mum went to the Reading Festival and pulled some bloke or the fact that we are talking intimately and I'm not running away. I want to ask her more about it. But something stops me. As if reading my thoughts she carries on.

'He was lovely. Lawrence was his name. That's all I knew about him. Oh and that he was from London. Big place London to search for someone called Lawrence. I didn't even know what he did. That seems ridiculous, doesn't it? Nowadays we always say, "What do you do?" But then, that weekend, he told me about his dreams. And he made me laugh. Oh, God, he made me laugh. He talked gibberish for hours, like you on that Tiddlesbury Tour you and Philippa do. Seems funny really, you'd never lose someone now. Not with mobiles and Facebook and the Internet. Anyway I think . . . I think it took me about a minute to fall in love with him.'

She's started to cry. She's still looking at me, but there are tears falling down her cheeks. All I can do is watch her. Perhaps I should go and hug her, but that would be such a strange thing to do now so I don't, but I do contemplate it and somehow that feels like something. Although what exactly, I'm not sure.

'Maybe it wasn't meant to be,' I say gently instead.

She shrugs and half smiles. It's one of the most intimate moments we've shared for years.

'Jenny, please let me say a few words about you leaving home . . . '

And now she's just gone and ruined it. I sigh and stomp off. But Mum's taken over my room so I can't flee there. I'll have to stomp into the toilet. Urgh, it reeks of aftershave! I slam the door. Damn, I left my book out there. There's no way I'm going back out there with my mother. It's not safe.

Chapter 27

'Al?' I peek my head round his door.

'Urgh,' he groans into his pillow.

It was evidently a good night, he's opted to vegetate in bed rather than stand in our cluttered kitchen concocting treats.

I look at him sleeping like a baby and I feel a little leap inside of love for him. Al is the kindest man. The times he's hugged me while I cried. And when I pass out on the sofa after a big night, he'll remove the plate of toast that's under my head, take off my shoes, wrap me in a duvet, leave a pint of water nearby and put my phone on charge. And he was oh so lovely in bed. It was well over a year ago, now, that I was slipping into his bed. But really it was all I could do not to stay in it all the time. But it was just a casual thing, caused because our heating broke down during that unbelievably freezing period last February. On the Saturday morning we were both in our separate beds and I texted him.

Too cold to move. Staying in bed all day. If you're making tea???

And he texted back

Me too. Will be watching films if you want to join me. Bring duvets and tea. I'll do next tea round.

So I pegged it into his bed. We watched a movie. *The Lost Boys*. Afterwards we lay snuggled together, deciding what to watch next. That's when I felt it. I thought it might be the remote control at first, but when I saw the remote control lying on his bedside chest of drawers I knew it was his, you know, big erect doo dah.

'Is that . . . ?' I whispered.

'Yes,' he whispered back. 'Sorry.'

I wondered whether something in the film had got him going, but ruled it out. Al is eccentric but I doubted even he'd get a stiffy from *The Lost Boys*. As we lay there, I found that I liked the thought that he had an erection. I was flattered and excited and I loved Al, I trusted him with my life, in addition to all this I hadn't had sex for fifteen billion years. And as I lay there pondering all this I noticed that I could hear our two hearts beating.

'Al,' I whispered. 'Do you think if we . . . ?'

'Um . . . '

'Would it be . . . ?'

'Hmm. Um.'

So once that was sorted, we turned to each other and began kissing. And that's how it happened.

'Al,' I call again.

'Urgh,' comes the same reply.

'That's no way to talk to your favourite lady friend and flatmate,' I say, climbing into his bed with him.

'Urgh,' he turns over, pulling the duvet over his head.

'Al?' I pull the duvet away from his head.

'What?'

Excellent. A whole word. He's finally waking up.

'Morning,' I sing.

'What is this?'

Three words! Although his eyes are still closed.

'It's me having some quality time with my flatmate. Al, man, you still reek.'

'Fan.' He swallows. He raises his eyebrows and slowly opens one eye.

I place my smiling face in its line of vision. 'So how did it go?' I say.

'What?'

'The frigging date,' I exclaim. 'Men,' I mutter. 'So different. A different species.'

'Oh, it was good,' he says, closing the one eye.

'Good?'

'Hmmm.'

'You give me one word, and that one word is good.'

'Hmm. It was good.'

'Al, have you got an erection?'

'No.'

'What's that hard thing?'

'The remote control probably.'

'Oh, so it is. So tell me. Are you in love with Gemma? Is Joe King smitten with Felicity?'

'Oh, yeah, they got on well. She's quite funny.'

'Funny?'

'Yeah, nice boobs.'

'Funny with nice boobs,' I say sadly.

'Yeah, and she'd just dumped that bloke and she still had a sense of humour, so we thought that was a good sign.'

'You thought it was a good sign. So you had a little blokes' chat with Joe after?'

'Yeah, I called him after to discuss how we'd play it next time.'

'Next time?'

'Yeah, you know, whether we should do something the four of us or, you know, go out as couples. See, I'm getting on well with Gemma. But I am a bit of a twat when I'm nervous.'

'No you're not. You're lovely.'

He opens his eyes.

'A bit of a twat,' I concur. 'But a lovely twat.'

'Thanks, Fan.'

'Soooo.'

'So what?'

'Oh, Jesus. What did Joe King say about future dating with frigging Felicity.'

'She's really nice, no need to say it like that. You'd get on with her.'

'I'm sure we'll be great friends. So what did he say about her?'

'Oh, you know, just that she's a nice girl, attractive.'

'Did he say attractive?'

'I can't remember. Fit. Maybe.'

'Fit.'

'Or gorgeous, or something.'

'Gorgeous!'

'Fan?'

'What?'

'Do you fancy Joe?'

'No. Hardly. As if.'

'Oh, because I got the impression he liked you. He was asking all sorts of questions about you.'

'Was he? Like what?'

'Just, you know, how I met you, how long we'd lived together, what you did and liked and stuff. He was definitely interested in you, Fan, a man can tell. When I told him about you and Matt getting married he went really quiet. Anyway, good we split Felicity and that letch up, eh.'

'Yeah, brilliant.'

I don't know why I feel like crying when I know it's for the best. What is wrong with me? Matt's back tonight and I feel as though the bottom of my world has collapsed now that Joe King has found out I'm engaged.

Chapter 28

You know that feeling you get when you suspect that you've really cocked up and things are liable to explode? Well, I've got it. Strongly. Matt's been away for ten days. He got back late last night and was in work first thing this morning as usual. Normally, I'd suggest me popping round to his, ordering us a takeaway, then running him a bath and giving him a massage in bed. That's what I should have done. That's Wife-To-Be-of-the-Year-Award stuff, that. What I've done instead is the stuff of How to Totally Pee Your Husband-To-Be Off In One Easy Step. But Mum has been so excited to meet Matt, and her excitement wore off on me. So I suggested we all have dinner out somewhere together tonight. Matt was humpy about it on the phone when I first mentioned it this morning but then Mum said, 'Let me talk to my soon-to-be son-in-law,' and snatched the phone off me. She seized it in her excitement but Matt's not one for surprises. He tried to excuse himself by saying he wouldn't be finishing work until late. But Mum said that didn't matter, we could do a late dinner at the curry house. So Matt acquiesced. However, if there's one thing that makes Matt cranky it's being placed in a position where he can't say no. It's not boding well.

'I think I want the prawn special, that sounds delicious,' I say, looking at the menu.

'That poor boy does work late,' my mum says, checking her watch, and scooping mango chutney on to her poppadom. 'It's five past nine.'

'I wouldn't poor boy him, he likes it.'

'Jack was like that.'

'Hmmm.'

'It's a good trait in a man, being diligent about his job.'

'Hmmm. Oh, here he is.' I jump up. Matt stands in the doorway, wearing his navy suit trousers and a creased white shirt. He looks tired and unpredictable and wildly sexy, if I'm being honest. He's my man, but somehow when I look at him I'm always surprised that he's my man. I walk slowly towards him.

'Hello, handsome, I missed you,' I say.

He sighs, gives me a peck on the cheek and says, 'This is the last thing I feel like doing tonight, Fan.'

Bugger. Bugger. Bugger.

'Matt, this is my mum,' I say, trying to keep my tone upbeat.

'Hello, Matt! Aren't you handsome!' Mum stands up and holds out her hand. He shakes it. I wish he'd given her a kiss. 'Now sit down, favourite son-in-law-to-be and let's pour you a glass of wine.'

He flops into the seat next to me. I lean over for a peck on the cheek, but he swats me away like a fly and hangs his suit jacket behind his chair instead. Now, I'm used to the after-work Matt swat. But Mum isn't. And I feel embarrassed to be swatted away like a pest in front of her.

'How was the trip?' I ask.

'Tiring,' he says without looking at me.

He's blaming me because he's here. Marvellous. Mum's giving him a look I can't read.

'Poppadom,' she offers. He takes one without thanking her. 'So what do you recommend to eat here?'

'We always have the same. One chicken korma, one lamb passanda to share,' he says, closing the menu, placing it on the table and signalling for the waiter.

'But, Jenny, you were going to have that king prawn special.'

'Yeah, but, I think I'll stick to our usual.'

'Yep, stick with what you know,' Matt says, emphatically.

'Stick with what you know,' Mum echoes. She's looking at Matt in that strange way again. 'Tell me about your work, Matt, what exactly do you do?'

'I work for Sorton Ltd, which basically buys and sells either entire companies—'

'Like Richard Gere in *Pretty Woman*,' I explain.

'Oh, he's devastating in that film,' Mum sighs.

'Or parts of companies,' he carries on. 'I specialise in the finance arena as opposed to say manufacturing or marketing. So it keeps me largely in the UK although I go to Germany and the US a fair bit. The company, and in particular the finance team, which I lead, has shown tremendous growth in the past four years. So much so I'm expecting to be made a partner at the end of the year.' He turns to me and smiles. Finally. And he takes my hand.

A waiter arriving to take our order brings some light relief to the conversation. When he's gone I open my mouth to try to make the conversation a bit more user friendly but Mum has beaten me to it.

'Jenny's dad worked for IJD, well, still does we assume,' Mum tells Matt.

'IJD. You never said,' Matt says to me.

'Why would I say?'

'Because IJD are huge. I modelled my finance team on IJD's when I started.'

'I said he was a finance something or other.'

'What does he do there?'

'Bank-to-bank finance.'

'Interesting.'

'So, is yours a sociable company? Do the wives mix?'

'I think some of them play golf.'

I start strangling myself with my napkin.

'You're not funny,' Matt tells me, but the corners of his mouth do turn up a fraction.

'I am. I'm hilarious,' I say, cheekily.

'We've been having a lot of fun discussing ideas for the wedding,' Mum gushes.

'Yes. Let's tell him about the amazing cheap wedding we've planned. It's practically free, Matt, you'll be very impressed.' Right, now I've got the conversation tiller I'm not letting anyone get hold of it. 'So, we have this big list at home, which we drew up, it's all on a whiteboard to show you. It's in categories like, Food, Entertainment and Decoration. And under each category there are lots of things, so under Food is coronation chicken, potato salad, cheesecake, etc. And under Entertainment is sing a song, read a poem, play crazy disco for an hour on your iPod speakers, bits and bobs like that. Under Decorations are pick eight small bunches of wild flowers and put them in jam jars for each table, buy and blow up balloons, etc. And basically my list is based on inviting eighty guests and everybody says they'll do or bring at least one thing. Two ladies at the surgery have both offered their gardens for free and we can use Marge's dad's marquee that he bought for her brother's wedding and intended to hire out but never got round to it and pitch it in someone's garden. We borrow the chairs and tables from the Rotary Club, a chap at the surgery will sort that out for us.' I pause. This is quite a vigorous presentation, I need to breathe. Still I think I'm nailing it. 'And then we have a wedding, cheap but ever so cheerful, I would say. And we can either do the booze, or ask everyone to bring a bottle and then we just have to pay for the Jägerbombs.' I smile. Phew.

Matt doesn't look well.

'Jägerbombs, jam jars and coronation chicken,' he says quietly. Then he says, 'Jägerbombs, jam jars and coronation chicken,' a bit louder. 'I can't invite my bosses to a wedding where there's Jägerbombs, jam jars and coronation chicken, that they'll have to make themselves!' Ooh, he's getting quite impassioned now. 'And someone doing shuffle on their iPod, Fan. I'd already decided to use my bonus and have it at the golf club. I called them today and booked the eighteenth of August.'

'The golf club!'

'Yes. The golf club that I've just joined, that all the partners play at. That has a function room overlooking the first hole.'

'The golf club. The male-dominated least sexy place in the universe where we'll pay a fortune for horrible food and uptight people serving it!' I'm raising my voice. It's very unlike me. The golf club!

Matt looks shocked, then annoyed.

'We're having it at the golf club, Jenny,' he says, firmly.

'But . . . but . . . I . . . '

I swallow. Tears prick the corners of my eyes. I feel like a child who's been told off.

'But I . . . '

He sighs. 'It's booked. I've paid the non-refundable deposit. Come on, baby, cheer up.'

I think about telling him where to shove his cheer up. I really do give it a lot of consideration. But I don't.

'Can we maybe do a theme?'

'A theme?'

'Yeah, pimps and hookers.' I couldn't resist.

'Fan!'

'I'm joking. No, like a time period. I'd like to go for sixties or seventies. Then I'd have the option of wearing a short dress.'

'Fan, I'm hardly going to invite my bosses to a wedding and tell them to dress up in clothes from the sixties, and you can't get married in a minidress.'

'But you like my legs.'

'I've got the rest of my life to look at them, I don't want to on my wedding day. On my wedding night perhaps, but that's a different story.'

I'm about to make a futile protestation when the food arrives. Mum's looking at me strangely. Matt's fishing his BlackBerry out of his jacket. I spoon the chicken korma onto my plate. I wish I'd ordered the prawn.

Chapter 29

If forced to come up with some adjectives to describe the evening I'd worry that hideous, atrocious, abysmal were falling short and have to insist that they were preceded with adverbs such as unimaginably, eye-wateringly and pant-poopingly. However, even this wouldn't adequately convey quite how uncomfortable the nice Indian for my mum to get to know my future husband felt. I'd probably have to resort to mime and cover myself in chicken korma and then invite rabid dogs to eat it off me. Although thinking about it, even that might not get the point across.

The three of us will have to do something at the weekend together, so Mum can see that he's not all bad. Because he's not, far from it. Well, having seen him tonight, not that far from it, next door to it possibly or a flat above it in the same building. But Matt is capable of being the sweetest, funniest, sexiest man alive.

'Jenny,' my mum whispers. She's crept into the lounge in her nightie.

'Hey.'

'Are you asleep?'

'Yep.'

'Can I come in?'

'Um, yeah. I'll curl up. Sit on the end there.'

She sits down on the sofa that has become my bed.

'Oh, love,' she says, sadly.

I tense. It's going to be another feelings chat.

'What?' I say. It comes out a little testily.

'I don't know how to say this.'

Never a great thing to hear.

'What?'

'I think you might be making a big mistake.'

'How do you mean?'

'Oh, I can't believe I'm going to say this . . . I think you're making a mistake marrying Matt.'

I don't reply.

'Oh, God, Jenny. I'm so sorry. Matt's just like your dad.'

I glare at her through the gloom. That was unforgivable. And untrue. Mum's frozen, staring at me.

'He's nothing like Dad,' I explain. 'He was just stressed tonight.'

'Oh, Jenny.'

'Mum, stop it.'

'Oh, love.'

'Mum, please stop the pitying ohs.'

'Philippa doesn't think you should marry him either, does she?'

'That's different. She's jealous.'

'And Al.'

'What's Al got to do with it?'

'He calls him Twat not Matt.'

I didn't even know that.

'He just does that because he thinks he's funny. I don't want to talk now, Mum. Can I go to sleep?'

'Course, night, love.'

She gets up and goes back into her/my room. I lie still, listening to my breathing getting quicker and quicker. I'm cross. How much longer will Mum stay?

'It's me again,' she whispers.

I pretend to be sleeping.

'I know you're not asleep. I can tell by your breathing that you're awake. But I'll just speak anyway.'

She doesn't sit down this time. She stands above me. I don't move.

'Now, I've helped you plan this wedding, I've bought the dress. But I don't think you should go ahead with it. I think, years from now, you won't be happy if you marry Matt. I think you'll be like me.'

My breathing is getting deeper. I don't want to hear any of this.

'I made the best of it, because that's what you do, you get on with it, you celebrate the strawberries you've got growing in the garden – you celebrate the little things so that the big gloomy fact that you married the wrong man doesn't weigh you down to your toes. And he adored me for that, Jack did, but not enough to allow me any freedom and not enough to keep himself faithful. And it was like looking in a mirror tonight, Jenny, seeing the two of you together. Seeing you succumb to Matt the same way I did to Jack.'

She pauses and sighs.

'Jenny, I want you to be with a man whose face lights up when he sees you, who asks you what you want to do and doesn't assume you'll have what he's having. You're so full of this extraordinary energy and joy and I don't want to see a man douse it, like Matt did tonight. I'm worried that you think you deserve to be treated the way Matt treated you tonight. Because you don't.'

She sighs again.

'Oh, well, I've said my piece.' She tiptoes back to her room.

No, actually, it's *my* room. It's *my* flat. It's *my* life. I am so angry I want to roar and scream and smash these windows. How dare she stand in my home and criticise my life.

I throw the covers off. Within seconds I'm standing over her, as she lies in bed.

'Since when did you become Frigging Oprah?' I'm shouting. I don't know whether I've ever shouted at anyone before. It feels strange and hard to curb. There were so many times I wanted to shout at her when I was growing up. 'Why don't you stand up for me?' I wanted to scream. 'Why don't you stand up for me against Dad?' I never did then. Now I can't stop myself. 'I don't remember you ever giving me advice when I've needed it. And it might have been nice then. When you were the person I looked up to. Or when you were the person who would just stand by as Dad was destroying me. But you can't swan in now and tell me what to do. Because I don't need you now! I'm fine with you being here and having hangovers and trying to forget about Dad. But please don't start criticising my life. You don't understand. *You* may not think I'm doing well, but I do.'

I stomp back into the lounge.

Of course I'm going to marry Matt. You don't give up on the man you're going to marry just because your mum cocked up her choice of life partner or because you meet a rock star who writes you a song. No one would do that. Would they? No.

Chapter 30

'I'm going to kill him.'

Marge has found out about Tim. She went into his phone. She wanted to change the ringtone that came on when she called him to that song that goes 'I'm horny, horny, horny, horny'. But as she was doing it a text came through from another woman. I don't know if it was pub quiz girl or someone else, what I do know is that Marge is terrifying today. She's not shouting. There's no rage. Just cold, calculating fantasies about how she can make Tim feel pain.

'I will make him suffer as he made me suffer,' she says calmly, taking another date slice from the box she brought in from the bakery this morning.

'Do you want a cuppa?' I offer.

She nods. She doesn't even look at me, just chews the date slice with a vengeful look in her eyes.

I wait for the kettle to boil. This is terrible. She's broken. What if she really does kill him? She'll get sent to prison. Two lives ruined. Two careers scuppered, one in illegal house clearance, the other in health negotiations. Oh, and what about

Disgruntled Dave? He filmed last night's confrontation apparently, but he's not here today. He can't film Tim and Marge any more because there *is* no Tim and Marge. I'll have to keep an eye on her. Crimes of passion are more likely to happen in the two weeks immediately after a major disturbance like this. But she could start calmly planning to do away with him. That could take years. Oh, God.

'Jenny?'

'Dr Flemming.' I smile. 'Cuppa?'

'Lovely.' He nods. 'Decaf. Can't take the excitement of the other.'

'Coming up.'

'Am I detecting some turbulence on the desk?'

'You are. Marge caught Tim cheating last night.'

'Oh, dear. What's her mental state?'

'Planning murder.'

'Naturally.'

I don't respond. Dr Flemming's wife left him and Philippa for another man. Philippa was fourteen. Mrs Flemming had been back to the States to visit family when she fell head over heels with another man; her tantric sex instructor. They're still together now.

'Although we should watch Marge, I think someone in her family went to prison for murder.'

'Yeah, I was thinking that. One decaf,' I say, handing him the cup.

'Jenny, did you, er, did you happen to mention that Mozart concert to your mother?'

'Yes. Yes, did she not call you?'

'No, not to worry, perhaps it slipped her mind.'

'Oh, I'm so sorry, she's not been feeling herself.'

'Well, of course. Well, if at anytime she feels like the cinema perhaps.'

'Dr Flemming, I don't think she's ready to date yet after my dad.'

'Oh, Jenny, I didn't mean that. I thought she might like some company that's all. She . . . ' He stops himself.

'She what?'

'Well. I thought she might be low and need cheering up. Do you know in all the times I met her when you girls were at school and I would pick Philippa up from your house or she'd come to fetch you from ours . . . '

'Hmm.'

'I don't remember seeing her smile. She never seemed happy.'

I think about that for a few moments. But I'm still so angry with her I can't muster much sympathy and I can't reply because I fear it'll turn into a rant against my mother. I'm sick of her being here, I really am. I wouldn't turn up at someone's place and loll around the place with a hangover on a daily basis and comment upon their lives. I wouldn't do it.

I take a deep breath and return to Heartbreak Headquarters. I place Marge's tea in front of her. She doesn't acknowledge me, just picks up another date slice.

'You know what we need?'

'I couldn't say,' Marge says.

'Destiny's Child. There's nothing else for it. The Rules of the Sisterhood state that in times of heartbreak we must worship at the alter of the Child of Destiny, the *Survivor* album. You're a survivor, Marge. Listen to the girls.'

I play it on YouTube. Bashing my fist against my chest as I feel the power. I listened to nothing but this track when I was brutally dumped at the age of seventeen.

'Great track,' I say and I give Marge a squeeze when it's finished. 'What I suggest we do this evening is go on a girls' night.'

'Oh, I don't think so.'

'What will you do instead?'

'I don't know.'

'Stay at home and mooch?'

'Hmmmm.'

'Come out. Booze and man moaning is what you need. Come on. Philippa will be up for it. We'll all glam up and then we'll talk about all the awful things that have happened to us and that we've survived and we'll laugh and we'll cry and you'll wake up so hungover tomorrow that you won't even remember who Tim is.'

'Can your mum come? She's been through this too. Will she come?' Marge asks.

'Um, I'm not sure, I'll ask her,' I say, unenthusiastically. 'Now the question is, where?'

'Somewhere Tim won't be.'

I think. But I can only come up with one place that Tim definitely won't be.

'My flat,' I venture. 'It's central, close to buses and, more vitally, booze shops. That is a cordial invite. No, order.'

Chapter 31

'This is a great party!' Philippa shrieks when everyone is in tears. She means it. 'So cathartic. Right, now it's your turn, Fan. Tell us your saddest love story.'

I glance quickly at Mum and then back at Philippa.

'I don't think I can,' I say.

'Yes, you can, Fan,' Philippa replies, and then giggles. It must be the rhyme. Or the wine.

'But . . .'

'If you don't tell your sad love story, I will,' she counters.

'But . . .' My eyes flick to Mum again and I shake my head.

'Fan, it was years ago. Your mum can hear.'

I was adamant that I wouldn't tell this story tonight, but for some reason I nod. Then I take a deep breath. Here we go.

'OK, well,' I look down at the table as I speak. 'This one happened almost exactly ten years ago. There was this boy in my class called Steve Wilmot.'

'Oh, I remember that name,' Mum says.

I nod but keep looking down.

'I like, oh, God, it sounds really stupid but I really loved this bloke, Steve Wilmot. I loved him all through school.'

'She totally did,' Philippa chips in.

'From literally the first minute he came into class on the first day of secondary school. I know it sounds ridiculous, but he burst into the classroom, with his cheeky little face, he was fifteen minutes late, out of breath, with this massive grin. Biggest grin I'd ever seen in my life. And I know I was young, but it was like boom. You know sometimes a tune comes on the radio that makes you smile and tap your feet, that changes your day and your mood? Well, Steve Wilmot was that tune. He was the most exciting person I had ever seen. I was only eleven then, but he remained the most exciting person I ever saw right up until I was seventeen. It was like this powerful never-ending extreme crush.'

'Yep, it was definitely extreme,' Philippa adds.

'I kept his picture under my bed. All my hormonal day-dreams featured Steve Wilmot. I hated maths, but they were my favourite lessons because during maths Steve Wilmot and I sat in the same room.'

I look up at them. I'm going on, they must be bored. But everyone is statue still and focused on me, I put my head back down and carry on.

'He was the most popular boy in our year and I was the least popular girl in the year, so really this was never destined to have a happy ending. But he was kind to everyone, even me, and I had a lot of trouble at school. With, er, er . . . '

Oh, my goodness, I've never told my mum this. I kept it all bottled up.

I swallow. 'I was bullied a lot at school.'

There. I've said it.

'But if Steve Wilmot saw other kids teasing me, or hurting me, he'd say, "Leave her be, she's all right." Leave her be, she's all right, you've no idea how hearing him say that made me feel. He was the only person who stuck up for me until Philippa started at that school.'

I smile at Philippa, we lock eyes for a moment.

'I dread to think how many of my teenage hours were spent daydreaming about Steve Wilmot.'

'And talking about him. She went on and on and sodding on!'

'When we got into sixth form he started going out with this girl called Michelle Cullet, who was the most popular girl in the year.'

'That was a bad day when we found out they were together,' Philippa says, almost to herself.

'But shortly before we were about to leave school they split up. And everyone was talking about it. Then the weirdest thing happened. Steve Wilmot started hanging out with Philippa and me. He just casually started waiting for us after classes or finding us in break and spending time with us. And we had a really good laugh, didn't we?'

'Yeah, Fan made him laugh with her Blackadder impressions and we'd do our itchy balls builders act for him. It was jokes.'

I nod and smile to remember. Making Steve Wilmot laugh was to this day one of the most exciting things that ever happened to me. He wouldn't just laugh, he'd roll off chairs and clutch his tummy. It was exciting for both Philippa and me, because it was the first time we'd had an audience. We bounced off each other, finished each other's sentences, never competed for attention. It was as though suddenly we were the cool ones and everyone else had been wrong all along. They were the best two weeks of my school days. Everything had changed. The bullying was over, I was about to leave school and go to performing arts college, the coolest boy in school hung out with me. Life was just beginning.

'So,' I say, getting back to the story. 'Then one night, Philippa had to go and have dinner with her dad, and Steve asked me if I wanted to meet up and watch this film that we were supposed to watch for Business Studies and so I said yes. Of course. Funnily enough when I told Philippa about it, she said she had a really bad feeling about it but Philippa's psychic feelings were pretty useless, so I thought it was probably rather positive that she had a bad feeling about Steve Wilmot and me.'

'That's true,' Philippa says, with a little nod.

'So I arrived at his house. I was wearing a denim skirt and a flowery shirt.' It's funny how I remember that exactly. But I can clearly visualise looking down and seeing his hand shake as he undid the buttons on that shirt.

'And we went into his room to watch the film. And we sat on his bed because there were no other seats and we didn't even get through the credits before we were kissing. My first kiss.'

I don't go into details for the others. I don't mention how tender he was. How when he held me it was as though I was precious. He cradled my head, he kissed my neck and it felt like butterflies. That's what I remember thinking, which is strange really because you don't get many butterflies in Tiddlesbury. I never felt violated. I felt safe. I felt loved. And I didn't know when to stop or if I had to. So when he whispered, 'I have a condom ...' I nodded. 'Are you sure?' he asked. I nodded again. And when it was over. I cuddled against his chest and that's the moment I remember the best. He kissed the top of my head, on my mousy hair and I moved my hand gently over his nipple and I'd never felt so completely close to someone. And I felt warm. I felt a warmth inside me that I don't think I've ever recaptured with anyone else. Mind you, I've only slept with Steve Wilmot, Al and Matt. But I don't think I've ever felt that since, that magic.

'Well, I'll leave out the ins and outs, if you'll pardon the expression. But it was really beautiful. It was my first time. Afterwards, I didn't want to go home. He kissed me on the front step.

'"See you tomorrow," he whispered.

'"Bye," I said.

'I went home and I couldn't have stopped smiling if I'd been ordered to.'

'I think I remember you coming home that night,' Mum murmurs. 'You glowed.'

I don't look at Mum, I just carry on. 'The next day, I didn't see him in the morning and I couldn't find him at lunch. Then by the end of break there was a rumour that he was going out again with Michelle Cullet. But I still didn't see him. It was the day after that. I walked through the gate and they were there together, sitting on a bench in the quad, she had her legs over his lap. It was as though they were waiting to show me. I stopped walking and Michelle Cullet smiled smugly at me. He looked away. Then at 11 o'clock, Michelle grabbed me and pushed me into the loo.

'"Did you think that was real?" she demanded.

'I looked blank.

'"It was a bet. For money. Did you think he'd do it otherwise? Most of the blokes chipped in a fiver and the winner took all."'

I remember it as though it was yesterday. The feeling of my eyes filling with tears, the sense that my head was swimming and I'd never again know what was real or who to trust, and I really wanted Philippa.

Michelle looked at me for a few seconds and then left me. And I stayed where I was, I locked the door, and I missed the next lesson. I stayed in there and I cried, but I didn't make a noise. I kept my mouth shut and I remained silent as I cried and cried.

'So that's my worst man story. How the bloke I was totally in love with took my virginity for a fifty-five quid bet. Bless him!'

I look up and smile. 'But you know, it made me stronger and all that,' I say with a shrug and glug of wine. But I suddenly wonder whether it has made me stronger. It actually made me pretty scared of the magic that can happen between a man and a woman. I think it's stopped me believing in happy endings.

Oh, God, everyone's staring at me. Mum looks pale.

'How could anyone be so cruel?' she whispers.

'That which doesn't kill us makes us stronger,' Philippa says, trying to perk us up. 'Roar after three. One, two three.'

No one makes a sound.

'Roar. Arrggghhh. After three, ladies. One, two, three.'

'Argggghhhh,' we relent.

'I think that deserves a Jägerbomb,' she slumps across the table to gather everyone's glasses.

'Who's next?' I ask. It's important to keep them coming. 'Marge, do you need another rant?'

'I'll have a quick one. But, Fanny, love, sorry you had such a hard time at school. Kids can be so cruel.'

'It was years ago.' I shrug and smile. 'What's your mini rant?'

'Well, just some advice I need, really. I was thinking that my Timmy didn't operate on the right side of the law. And I could always fix things so he has a little holiday care of Her Majesty.'

'Oooh,' Mum looks shocked.

'Ah, but then, Marge, that's out-and-out war and he could shop—' I stop. What do I say? I can't say your dad and brothers. I'm not used to talking to criminal types. I need more practice.

'Oh, I see your point, Fanny, he could shop my dad to the police.'

'Exactly.'

'No, I don't want that.'

'Mum, do you need a rant?' I say without looking at her.

'No.'

'Sure? Dad wasn't the easiest.'

'He certainly wasn't.' Philippa chokes.

'Oh, dear,' says Marge. 'Because you left him quite recently, didn't you?'

'Yes, a few weeks now.'

'How are you finding it?' Marge asks.

Mum thinks for a few moments, looks at me and then back at Marge.

'Well, I feel as though I'm where I'm supposed to be.'

My eyes widen as I regard her. She's living with me above a kebab shop in Tiddlesbury because her husband's been having an affair. Her daughter was foul to her last night. How can that be where she's supposed to be?

'Well, you can't ask for more than that.' Marge nods wisely.

'Go on, have a little rant,' Philippa encourages. 'The floor is open.'

'I feel . . .' my mum starts and then trails off. 'I feel as though I should rant against myself.'

'Bloody hell, Mrs T, I wouldn't if I'd been married to Mr Taylor.'

Mum smiles. 'No, I should because, well, I can't blame Jack, I can only blame myself. It was all my own doing. I allowed myself to be walked over. I lost a lot of things when I was in the relationship: friends, hobbies, my freedom. But it was my fault because I didn't defend them. I used to have this one friend, Debbie Diamond . . .'

'Debbie Diamond. Great name.' I sigh.

'Hmmm, we were a bit like you and Philippa, we did everything together, had so much fun, we'd go to festivals.'

'Festivals, Mrs T!'

'Yes. In the early eighties. Then I got married and I let that friendship slide. I let a lot of friendships slide. Worst of all by far, I let my relationship with my daughter slide. I lost myself in the marriage. And now I've left him, I realise how much I lost and how sad it was and it makes me cross.'

I'm not going to respond. Mum's obviously saying all this to warn me against Matt. It won't work.

'Oh, don't you get cross, my love,' says Marge.

'Look at you, you're only fifty,' Philippa gushes.

'Fifty-four.'

'We'll call it fifty for a good while yet,' Philippa counsels.

'Mrs T. You can still wear short skirts. We could all go to a festival!' Philippa's up on her chair now. 'Let's book for Glastonbury.'

'I read it's already sold out,' Marge says.

'Reading then. There's bound to be tickets for Reading. It's in Reading after all,' Philippa calls as she runs to my room.

'Oh, I don't know . . . '

Philippa's emerged from my room holding my notebook computer.

'Right, who's up for the Reading Festival? Ooh! Mrs T!' Philippa gasps. 'Your friend you lost touch with. What's her name again?'

'Oh, Debbie. Debbie Diamond she was, but that was years ago, she probably got married.'

'Let's search for Debbie Diamond, see if she wants to come to Reading with us!' Philippa rubs her hands together.

'Oh, I, er . . . what?' Mum asks.

'Debbie Diamond, there's bloody loads of them. Here, Mrs T, have a rifle through these and see if you can spot her, while I do us another Jägerbomb. Did I do the last one or just talk about it?'

'Who's next to . . . ' I was going to say, 'regale us with woeful tales', but the front door's just opened. Al's back.

''Ello 'ello, what's going on here?' he says.

'It's a Rage Against Men Party!' Philippa informs him. 'Jägerbomb?'

'Oh, go on then. Hello all,' he says, sitting down.

'I have to warn you that if you sit in this circle you will have to divulge the worst thing that ever happened to you in the name of love.' I find it best to lay down the rules first.

'This isn't really fair. Have I missed all yours?'

'Yep.'

'Did you tell your virginity one?'

'Yep.'

'Glad I missed that one. It always makes me cry.'

'You're a nice boy, who are you?' Marge asks, squinting across the table.

'This is Al, my flatmate. AL, THIS IS MARGE,' I say very loudly whilst eyeballing him. It's important he doesn't let on about his involvement with her break up.

'OH, RIGHT, THANKS,' he shouts back.

'Come on, Al, just because you're a man doesn't mean you get away without having to divulge your sad love tales. We've all done it.' I fold my arms waiting for him to start.

'OK,' He exhales. 'Well, it was a while back now. And I was going out with this girl and she, oh, how do I put it?'

'Slept with your friend!' Marge volunteers enthusiastically.

'No, no, he wasn't my friend. He wasn't my friend at all but she evidently preferred him to me and that was that. But, yeah, it hurt, that. Yeah, that one hurt a lot. When someone doesn't choose you. And you really like them. You know, it hurts. It has to really.'

'What did you do?' I ask. I haven't heard this story before.

'How do you mean?'

'Well, did you fight for her?' I ask.

'Um. I didn't. No.'

'Not at all?' I exclaim.

'Well, no, she made her choice and it wasn't me. I had to respect that.'

I look about at the scrunched up, disbelieving faces of the ladies.

'You should have fought for her, Al,' I tell him.

'But, but ... how do you fight for someone?'

'Oh, well, what do we think, ladies?' I ask. 'If you love someone how should you fight for them?'

'Dramatically,' Philippa volunteers.

'Yes!' Marge agrees. 'You write her a beautiful letter. You get a plane to fly in the sky with a banner. You surprise her with a song.'

'Hang about, I've heard Al sing,' I counter.

Al looks baffled.

'You should have fought for her, Al. You might have won her back,' I say, gesturing to my lady back-up team.

'Would you have wanted me to fight for you?' he asks.

'What?'

'Damn. Did I just totally ruin talking about our relationship in an ambiguous way?'

'Me?'

'Yeah.'

'But we weren't going out.'

'Well, what would you call it?'

'Sleeping together because it was cold,' I whisper, and then remember Mum is in the room.

'Is that all you thought it was?'

'I didn't . . . you didn't . . . hang about.'

'Is that what you thought it was?'

'Al, I don't know. We never discussed it.'

'I know, and then you came in one day, going on and on about this posh meal that Matt had taken you on and it was all over.'

'Why didn't you say anything?'

'You're my friend, Fan.'

'Damn, this is so riveting but I don't think we should really be here. Right, come on, troops, let's go to the White Hart for last orders,' Philippa says, quickly ushering the others out of their seats and towards the door. 'Now, you two,' she points to Al and me. 'I love you both. Do you want me to stay and umpire?'

'No,' we both say quietly, not taking our eyes away from each other.

'I just can't believe you didn't say anything,' I whisper.

'I just can't believe you didn't think it was anything.'

'Bye!' Marge calls.

'Bye,' my mother echoes.

'What a night,' Philippa shouts.

We're left alone.

'Al, I'm really, really sorry,' I say stepping closer to him.

'Don't be sorry. You couldn't help it. You chose him over me.'

'I didn't think you were an option.'

'It was pretty incredible, Fan, the sex we had because it was cold.'

'I know.'

'And we had it a bit when the heating was fixed as well. So it couldn't have just been because it was cold.'

'No, no it wasn't. I just assumed you didn't want any more than that.'

'Why would you do that? You're beautiful, and funny and the most incredible woman I've ever met or am likely to meet. From the second you mind-tricked me into having a lamb doner, I've loved you, Jenny.'

'I need to sit down.' I sink my weight down onto the sofa.

'Sorry, I shouldn't have said all that.'

'No, but . . . but . . . why say it now?'

'It just came out.'

'No, why not say something when I was crawling into your bed and taking my clothes off. Don't you think the fact that you never offered to take me on a date made me think that it was just sex to you? So, yes, I was excited when Matt took me on a date, because I'd waited and waited for you to ask me out. But you never did.'

'Oh, Jen, you're beautiful. I thought you could do so much better than me. I was waiting for you to say something to me.'

'You were only the second person I slept with.'

'We completely buggered it up, didn't we?'

I nod sadly and look up at him. He kneels down and wraps his arms around me in a big glorious hug. No one doles out hugs of the calibre that Al does. I sink into the hug.

'Totally screwed it all up,' I say, pulling back a bit so I can see him.

'Hmmm,' he agrees.

'Hmmm,' I say.

And I don't quite know how it happened but we seem to be kissing.

Chapter 32

We didn't just stop at kissing. Nope. We had full on … you know … yes … that. I would very much like to stay in bed for the entire day. I open my eyes, Al is facing me on the pillow.

'Was it a full moon last night?' I ask.

'It was from where I was standing.'

'Hilarious.'

'How are you feeling?'

'Like I will probably cry in the shower.'

'Oh, really?'

'It'll be the wedding we've both been invited to on the eighteenth August.'

'Will it? Whose?'

'Mine, you plonker.'

'Oh, yeah.'

'And what about Gemma?'

'Oh, yeah. I quite liked her. Supposed to be seeing her tonight actually. Do you want me not to?'

'No, go and see her.'

'Are you sure?'

'Yeah.'

'Really?'

'Really. It's cool.'

'Yeah, but is that girl cool, which in my experience is anything but cool.'

'No, it's please go out with Gemma. I did a bad thing for the sisterhood by sleeping with you. But as you're only in the early stages of courtship and we had had a sexual relationship misunderstanding in the past I may be forgiven. I'll check with Philippa. I may need to atone.'

'I hear the sisterhood word and it's like everything just becomes white noise. But you don't mind if I go out with Gemma tonight?'

'No.'

'OK, but if you change your mind on that, call me or text me and let me know.'

I smile.

'What?'

'Nothing.'

This is why Al and I could never work together, because neither of us will ever take the lead. Al won't say, 'I'm going to tell Gemma to back off, and see where this goes with us,' and I'd never suggest it either. I reckon a relationship needs at least one person in it who is capable of taking a risk, of being rejected, in order to get things off the ground.

I'll have to tell Matt that I've been unfaithful. It's the right thing to do and I hate secrets and lies. It would be completely impossible for me not to tell Matt. I couldn't imagine sitting there at dinner with him, knowing that I'd slept with someone else and hadn't told him. I shiver at the thought. But if I tell

Matt that I slept with someone else, then I guess, well, I guess, that will be us over. That thought fills me with panic, but then so does the thought of staying with him, for some reason.

'Are you all right?' Al asks.

'Yeah, I better get up and go and cry in the shower.'

'Do you want me to come with you?'

I smile. 'I think Mum would have a heart attack.'

'Oh, yeah.'

I sit up on the side of the bed and start putting my clothes on.

'So, Al. Thank you very much for a very enjoyable evening,' I say when I'm dressed and standing up.

'It's my pleasure.'

I get to the door.

'Fan?'

'Hmmm.'

'A couple of things, I'm just reminding you of a couple of things, that I sort of assumed you knew but I don't think you do. One, you're beautiful.'

'Hardly.'

'I don't know what you see when you look in the mirror but it's not what the rest of us see, I know that. You're hot, Fanny Fan-Tastic. There's not a man who wouldn't.'

'Al!'

He holds up his hand to stop me interrupting. 'Let me continue. I want to say some stuff because, well, I know that you and I won't end up together, I think we had our moment, but what I do know is that we'll always be mates. I'd take a bullet for you, Fanny Fan-Tastic,' he says seriously, nodding.

I smile.

'So, as your mate I can say that you are beautiful. You have this big smile that lights up the coldest of cold hearts, eyes that dance, yes. I know I sound like a wanker, but I mean this, eyes that make you feel like you're the only person in the world. Your legs, your body, I could go on. You are as mad as a warehouse of the craziest frogs, I admit. But in the most brilliant way. I just want to say this because it's like you don't realise how special you are. I could kill that Steve Wilmot fella, if what he did made you so insecure.'

I stare at him. 'That was such a lovely speech.'

'I meant every word.'

'Thank you.'

'Although, thinking about it, you know that bullet I said I'd I take for you?'

'Yeah.' I nod.

'If at all possible could it be in the leg?'

'I'll see what I can arrange.' I smile.

'You're one in a million, Fanny Fan-Tastic.'

'So are you, Al,' I say and mean it. 'What made you so insecure?'

'Just being a funny-looking bugger.' He laughs, and hurls a cushion at me. 'Now sod off and cry in the shower.'

Chapter 33

I am having the strangest day. I was in the shower for a long time this morning, crying. I was happy with Matt. I know he wasn't particularly nice the other evening but he was tired and jet-lagged; normally he's very personable. He definitely didn't deserve to have me sleep with someone else. And it was Al. How did that happen? Stupidly, the thing that was, and is, confusing me most is Joe King. It feels as though Joe King is rattling the cage of my life. If I'm being honest, then I've worried more what Joe King will think of me having slept with Al, than I have about what Matt will think about me sleeping with Al. And yet Matt is the man I'm supposed to be marrying. It doesn't make sense. I don't make sense. I'm sure I used to. I'm sure pre-Joe King I used to make perfect sense. But now I'm all higgledy-piggledy.

Anyway, when I eventually got out of the shower, Mum was standing in the corridor waiting for me. I wasn't overjoyed to see her. Oh, God, I thought, I poured out a lot of stuff last night, I can't do feelings this morning. I wondered how I could escape her.

'I've called in sick for you, Jenny,' she said.

'What? How? Who did you speak to?'

'I called Marge and told her that I thought you needed to get out of Tiddlesbury for the day. I thought you might be confused and want to clear your head.'

'And what did she say?' I enquired.

'She said she totally understood,' Mum says, her eyes wide and innocent.

'What did she say really?'

'She said you owed her two days. She's quite a negotiator.'

I didn't answer.

'Was that wrong of me?'

I shook my head. She smiled.

'Get dressed. I thought we'd get the train to Skegness.'

So I nodded and got dressed and now we're in Skegness. And I slept with Al last night. It doesn't get more random.

I've never done a sicky in my life and I dread to think what's going on at the surgery. But I have had a surprisingly lovely day. We didn't speak much on the train, which was a relief. We both stared out of the window at the land racing past us. When we arrived we headed straight for the beach and kicked our shoes off.

'Ah! The feel of sand beneath your feet!' Mum said, and she smiled as though she was really content. 'You know sometimes I think that this is what it's all about.' She sighed. 'Feeling the ground under your toes and the wind on your cheeks. We over-complicate things, don't we? When really there's nothing like the simple pleasures.'

I didn't answer. But I liked what she said. We walked towards the sea, carrying our shoes, and paddled for ages. The water was freezing, but we waded out as far as we could. The sky above us was blue and cloudless. Mum threw her hands in the air.

'I used to come here as a child,' she said, and again I was reminded of Mum pre-Dad. Mum pre-me.

Then we walked along the beach for a long time, again not speaking. It was such a relief not to have to speak. We were starving when we got back to the main drag so we got fish and chips. The most we've said to each other today has been a debate about whether you are still allowed to eat cod, and if so whether we should get the large one (we did, of course).

We sat on the sand and ate our warm chips in the cool breeze and to be honest, it was the best fish supper I've ever had. I'm stuffed now, although that's hardly surprising – Mum didn't have much appetite so I ate a fair bit of hers, too. Emotional trauma, it seems, doesn't stop me eating. We'll probably have to head back to the station in a little while. I don't want to leave. I like gazing at the ocean.

'Sometimes you need to see the sea to get a perspective,' Mum says. She reaches across and squeezes my hand, and for the first time since she came to stay I don't flinch or try to fidget myself away from her touch. I just glance at her briefly and smile and then get back to staring at the sea.

'I haven't seen the sea for years,' I say.

'I know, I thought that when I went to Wales. I thought, How have I forgotten you? The sea's always been one of my favourite things. Oh, I love the sea, I would tell people. Yet I hadn't seen it for years.'

'Hmmm.'

'Well, for what it's worth. I think Al's a very nice chap.'

'Yeah, he is,' I say and my voice goes up and my eyes fill with tears. 'Sorry, I'm not very good at men.'

'Don't be sorry. Get it all out,' she says calmly. 'No point in leaving it in there,' she coaxes. And something about the way she says it makes me feel as though we have all the time in the world. It's a pleasant sensation. And I snivel for what must be a few minutes, grateful that we don't have to be anywhere or do anything.

'You know, Jenny, I'm so terribly sorry,' she says. Then she leaves quite a pause and makes a groaning sound. 'Oh, I'm so sorry.'

I pull my eyes from the heaving waves to look at her face. Her plaintive eyes are fixed on me.

'I didn't know you were bullied and I didn't know that boy had done that to you.'

I shake my head.

'I just thought . . . oh, Jenny, I don't know what I thought. That you were being a teenager, I suppose, that you'd pushed me away. But' – she squeezes her eyes closed and then opens them again – 'I should have asked, I should have made you tell me what was wrong. I should have been better.'

Now, I close my eyes because I know what she's going to talk about. I can sense it. And perhaps we do need to discuss it. No perhaps. We do. She's going to talk about the day I left home when I was seventeen. Nearly eighteen. Crikey, the world should have been at my feet at eighteen, but all I could do was lie in bed. I spent weeks and weeks in bed in my childhood home. There's a saying about a piece of straw breaking a camel's back. Well, Steve Wilmot might just as well have broken my back because after that happened I literally couldn't move. Just couldn't move. You take for granted that you'll be able to get up every morning and keep going. But I couldn't. I wouldn't. I didn't. I'd left school. My life was ahead of me. Supposedly. But actually my life had collapsed. Other kids were probably out enjoying their freedom, the hot summer, being able to legally buy booze, while I felt exhausted right down to my soul. I would sleep and sleep and still I'd feel sleepy. I would hear Mum and Dad downstairs. They were always shouting at each other. They rowed a lot that summer. About me.

'Do something with her, for God's sake,' my dad would bellow. 'I'm going out.' Sometimes I would hear my mother weeping.

'She's useless,' he would spit, and a door would slam. I would lie upstairs and agree with him. I was useless. Apart from a rather brilliant Rowan Atkinson impression, I was incapable of anything.

Then one day, they came into my room. My dad first, he hauled me out of bed.

'*Pull yourself together*,' he bellowed. '*We've had enough. For God's sake! What's the matter*?'

There was hatred in his voice, and I deserved that too.

'Jenny, we've had enough, you're an embarrassment,' he said. My mum was there too, there in the doorway, she stood with her arms folded. She didn't say anything and I don't think I've ever really forgiven her for that.

After they left my room, I didn't get back into bed, I called Philippa and asked if I could stay with her for a while. I never again spent a night in my childhood home. Luckily, Philippa's dad was a GP, he understood I was depressed, and took me to see someone. A breakdown, that's what people say I had. It took a long time to get over. I never went to college. Instead, I spent months trying to find the right antidepressants and the right dosage. I had a bit of counselling, and a lot of Philippa. And eventually, by the time I was twenty-one, I was much, much, better, I'd come off the drugs and I was working at the surgery. I was still worried about sinking back to that place though, so that's why Philippa gave me the Smiling Manifesto. To keep the dark days at bay. Shortly after that I met Al and moved in with him. The Smiling Manifesto seemed to do the trick. But to be on the safe side, I avoided my father as well, and steered clear of any man who made my bits twitch. I've always tried to keep away from anything that could break me again and take me back to that horrible place. It's why Joe King terrifies the life out of me and why I really didn't want to talk about all this with Mum.

'I wished I'd asked you what was wrong.' She closes her eyes and laughs a very sad laugh. 'I never asked you what was wrong. What sort of a mother does that? And then once you'd gone it was too late. I thought Jack was having an affair, you see, at the time, and I didn't think I could cope with him or with you. You know, you always imagine that at some point, when you become middle-aged, you'll become wise. But it doesn't happen like that. And do you know, there's no point in having regrets. But I do regret that time. I wish I'd held you, and made you tell me why you were so unhappy.'

'I wouldn't have let you,' I say.

I look at her and I realise that for years I've resented my mum for not sticking up for me on that day and all the other days. I've repeatedly had the thought, What sort of mother doesn't help their child when they are so desperately unhappy? But I know that even if Mum had done what she now says she wishes she'd done, it wouldn't have changed anything.

'I wouldn't have let you,' I repeat.

'Oh, love, well, then I should have taken you to get help.'

'It was probably best I went to Philippa's. Dr Flemming diagnosed pretty quickly that I was having a breakdown.'

'Oh, God, Jenny, I'm so, so sorry.'

'Don't be, don't be, but, well, the only thing I want to know is why—' I stop myself. Perhaps there's no point in asking.

'What?' she asks.

'Why didn't you come and get me? Come and try to get me back from Philippa's?'

She sighs.

'Oh, love, Jack put you down so much when you were at home. He was a tough-love dad. He said he'd had a tough-love dad himself, he thought it had made him strive for success. I realised that was damaging for you. But don't forget, you pushed me away. You wouldn't let me in. I didn't know what to do. That's why I didn't stop you leaving home or come and get you. I wanted you to stay, Jenny, but I also wanted you to fly free, to find out who you were. I know that sounds terrible but you did that, Jenny. I thought it was better that I didn't see so much of you because I knew you were finding your happiness. But it wasn't easy, I missed you terribly and I am so, so sorry.'

'Don't be,' I say, and I mean it. I'm looking at her and I don't feel like crying at all. I feel weirdly unburdened. Except . . . 'I should have asked you how you were feeling. I could hear you arguing.'

'But I was your mother.'

'I was your daughter. I should have been your friend. So promise me, please don't have any regrets about it. No regrets, Mum, honestly.'

'No,' she smiles. 'No regrets. There's no point.'

We both look back at the sea.

'Wow,' I say.

'What?'

'I really didn't want to talk about that time. But . . . well . . . it was all right.'

'Hmmm.'

'Let's make it different between us from now on,' I say, looking at her.

'Friends?'

She holds her hand out for me to take.

'Friends,' I say, taking it. 'Good friends.'

Chapter 34

Matt lives in Nunstone Square, a development of new apartments on the outskirts of Nunstone. They are sandy-coloured flats built around a gravel square with potted trees in the middle. The more expensive flats have tiny navy blue balconies and you have to go though security gates, which are also navy blue and need an entry code. It was built shortly after they introduced the 'high speed' rail line from Nunstone to King's Cross. If you mention Nunstone Square I lay down money someone will go 'ooooooooh' in quite a high register. I don't go 'ooooooooh', I'd never say this to Matt but I think Nunstone Square looks like an asylum for posh people.

I know the code to get in the gates, but I need to be buzzed into the main building. It's Friday night, and there's only a small window when Matt will be here before he goes out. He brings his car home after work every Friday, has a shower and then he goes out again and meets some workmates for beers and an Indian. This has been the routine throughout the whole year we've been together. I think the only Friday we've spent together was when we went on the London Eye.

I press the buzzer.

'Who is it?' Matt sounds wary of whoever it might be.

'It's me.'

'Fan?'

Matt is a creature of habit. He won't appreciate me turning up unannounced. I can't blame him. When I'm on my own I am generally wearing odd socks, a dressing gown, hair removal cream on my upper lip and blubbing at a chicklit novel. I'm not at all chuffed when someone pops by. Unless it's Philippa, obviously.

'Yeah, sorry, can I come up?'

'Fan, what are you doing here?' He sounds annoyed.

'Matt, sorry, but I really need to talk to you.'

'Fan, listen, gorge, I'm just out the shower and I'm late to meet the boys.'

'Matt, I'm sorry, but it's really important. Can you let me in?'

'Hang on!'

I wait with my hand on the door, ready for him to buzz me in. But he doesn't. I call again on the intercom, just as I see him walking across the hallway in his towelling robe and bare feet. I look at his calves. I always liked his calves. Perhaps I shouldn't tell him that right now.

'Is your buzzer not working?' I ask when he's opened the door.

'No, I thought I'd come down.'

He's got a girl up there, is my first thought. That's rich, you slept with Al, is my second.

'Matt, you might prefer to do this upstairs,' I say quietly.

'What?'

'I've got to tell you something.'

'So you said. Come on, out with it,' he says, he's sounding more cheerful now and smiling at me affectionately. 'You'd be disastrous in business where time is money.'

'I'm disastrous in most areas.'

'So what is it?'

I can't say it. Maybe I should just go.

'I . . . I . . . I . . . '

'Fan?'

'I slept with someone else last night.'

Matt steps back. 'Say that again,' he whispers.

'I'm so sorry.'

He shakes his head and steps further away from me. He looks as though I've winded him. He takes another step back and then starts moving his neck as though he's going to say something but doesn't. He's starting to look a little Jurassic.

'What? Fan? What do we do now?' he asks. 'Do I cancel the golf club? What do we do, Fan? Fan?' He looks lost.

This is the first time Matt has ever asked me what to do.

'I don't know, Matt, I don't know.'

'I can't look at you!' He sounds so shocked.

'I'm so sorry.'

He shakes his head and turns away.

'Fan,' he says, with his back still to me.

'Yes.'

'This has broken me.'

'I'm so sorry.'

'Why did you tell me?'

His question takes me aback.

'I had to tell you.'

'I've never felt like this.'

'Matt, I'm so sorry.'

'Sorry!'

'Matt, do you want me to come up?'

'No, I don't want you to come up and tell me how you screwed some guy. I feel sick. You know, one thing I thought I knew about you was that you were loyal. I didn't realise you were a slut!' He's still got his back to me.

'Go on,' I say.

In one of the many books Philippa and I read about bullying, one of them said that if someone's abusing you, you should encourage them to elaborate. So if they say 'I hate you,' the perfect answer is not, 'I hate you too,' but is actually 'Tell me more.'

'No, I don't want to go on.'

It really does work. Philippa will be pleased.

'Why are you so calm?' he asks.

'I think I'm a bit in shock myself.'

'You definitely weren't drugged?' He turns his head and looks at me.

I smile sadly and shake my head.

'Oh God, I can't even look at you,' he hisses and walks back to his flat.

I watch him go. His hair doesn't look at all wet for someone who's just had a shower. Once he's out of sight, my shoulders slump forward and my eyes fill with tears. This is such a mess. What have I done?

Chapter 35

On the whole, I think it would be fair to say that my life has imploded in a spectacular fashion and I am entirely to blame. Nice work, Jenny Taylor. Pat on the back. I had a man, not just any man, but one with arm muscles who was driven and who wanted to marry me. Things were good, very good, bloody marvellous, in fact, but no, because I am Jenny Taylor and a total idiot when it comes to men, I ballsed it all up by sleeping with my flatmate. And it's not like men are growing on trees for me. It took me twenty-seven years to come up with Matt. And Joe King is probably writing songs for Felicity now. *Oh, Felicity your boobs are so nice and you make me laugh. It's like I'm in a movie. Like it's meant to be.* But still, still I think of him.

And Mother was behaving very oddly this morning. The buzzer went at 7.20, obviously I heard it because I sleep in the lounge. It was a man delivering a big box for Mum. I signed for it. I took it in to Mum. 'What is it?' I asked. 'It's nothing,' she said. 'Oh, I love it when I get sent big heavy boxes of nothing,'

I said. 'Hmm, hmmm,' she said, all mysteriously. 'Seriously, Mum. What is it?' I asked. And she said, 'I'm not telling you!' I dread to think what's in that box.

Marge and I, the love blunders, sit with downturned mouths drumming away at our keyboards. Marge is so fed up she can't even muster enough energy to try to get me to make the tea, it is unimaginably sad.

'Here, let me make you a cup of tea,' I say, getting up.

She shakes her head. 'No, let me do it.' She pushes her chair back and heaves her weight to standing.

I don't even feel like reading. We are all doomed. There's only one person who can save us. Miranda Hart. I open my desk drawer and pull out *Miranda*. Series 1. I slide her smiling face into the surgery DVD player. I've done this since I was a girl. Ever since I first laughed until I choked at an *Only Fools And Horses* Christmas Special I've sought solace in laughter. I've always craved the comfort of comedy. A tiny smile almost flickers at the corner of my mouth to think of it.

'Do you take sugar?' Marge asks, poking her head out of the kitchen, even though we've worked together for four and a half years.

'One, please. Thank you.'

We reseat back behind the desk at the same time. We pick up our cups of tea. We clasp our hands around them, like you see ladies in cat food adverts do. We blow.

'Oh, good grief, what on earth's happened to you two?' It's Doris.

'Doris!'

'Ladies! Ladies! What is the cause of your pain and can I kill him?'

'Yes, Doris, you certainly can,' Marge says, with quite a lot too much venom.

'And Fanny, where's that lovely smile gone? Your smile makes my day, love, it's worth being in my eighties and falling to pieces to come in here and see that smile. Yours is a mouth for smiling, Fanny.'

My mouth starts to obey Doris, but only because I completely adore her.

'Well, I've had more thoughts about my Big Send Off. After I worked out the dress code . . . '

Oh, uh oh. My bottom lips starts wobbling at the mention of a dress code.

'Fanny, love, what's happened?'

'We were going to have a sixties-themed wedding and I've got the dress but now the wedding's off.'

I do a bit of antenatal breathing to stop myself from crying. Not that we were ever actually going to have a sixties-themed wedding, because he'd booked the golf club.

'What a bastard,' Doris cusses.

'Well, it was her fault, really, she slept with her flatmate,' Marge fills in helpfully.

'Oh, I hate it when that happens!' Doris claps her hands together. 'Now do you like the flatmate or the other one?'

'Oh, Doris, I don't know.'

'Well, if you don't know, then you don't want either of them. You'll know when you want someone, believe me. It will box you between the ears. And then some. Now, I'll just sit myself here,' she says, taking the prime spot for telly watching. 'Oooh, you've got *Miranda* on, I'll have a little watch of Miranda. She does make me laugh. I hope

Dr Flemming's not running to time. I don't think I've seen this one.'

'Have you not, it's classic! Wait till you get to the bit where . . . '

Oops I nearly gave it away there. But there's a scene in this episode where Miranda is dancing in a nightclub and her trousers fall down and she doesn't notice. If I know Doris, and I think I do, she'll find it hysterical. Actually I should take it home and show Mum. Wow. My mum. When I think about Skegness I feel warm and calm and, funnily enough, excited about spending more time with her. What a difference a day makes.

I watch Doris and the other patients enjoying the telly. And then let my mind wander to Joe King. But he's there in my mind with pretty Felicity and her humungous breasts. They get bigger and bigger with every daydream. I shake my head clear of them. Ooh, it's the trousers round the ankles scene already. I glance at Doris, she's rocking with laughter.

'I thought you'd like that bit,' I call to her.

She's still rocking with laughter but she's not making a sound. This is unlike Doris, she normally howls. She hasn't acknowledged me either. And she's still rocking. She looks a bit odd.

'Doris?'

She flaps an arm in my direction. She's still rocking. She doesn't look right to me.

'Doris?' I say, getting up.

She's still rocking but now she's going red. This isn't good. I walk towards her. She makes a choking sound.

'I'll just get Dr Flemming for you, Doris,' I say, calmly. It's very important to stay calm in the surgery. We once had a man slip away quietly whilst he was waiting for an appointment and we all had to be very calm as we carried him into a side room so as not to disturb the other patients.

'Dr Flemming,' I say, knocking on his door. 'We need you for a second in the waiting room.'

Dr Flemming moves very quickly, which I think is what keeps him wiry. He pokes his head out. He knows I wouldn't interrupt a session with a patient unless it was important.

'It's Doris,' I whisper. 'In the waiting room, looks like some sort of seizure. She was laughing.'

He takes one look at her. She's still rocking. She's almost purple in the face now.

'Call an ambulance,' he tells me quietly as he strides quickly towards her.

Chapter 36

They took her away in the ambulance. I'm watching the back of it get smaller and smaller as it drives down the street. She'd stopped breathing and gone purple. I've never seen a face go purple before. It's horrible. I've always loved the colour purple too. It doesn't hold the same allure now I've seen one of my favourite faces sport it. Lovely Doris, nearly done in, by me and Miranda Hart. It's awful.

I sit on the pavement and put my head in my hands. What have I done? I'll have to call her next of kin. A tear springs into my eye. More tears. I let them fall even though, as ever, I have rather a lot of mascara on. Oh, please be all right, Doris, please. They've taken her to Nunstone Hospital. Sometimes these elderly patients go into hospital and they never come out. Another tear slides. We spoke about her Big Send Off but it was just banter. Not something that had a chance of happening at any time soon. I put my head back in my hands. Another tear. I know you shouldn't love patients. But I love Doris. I've known her for years through the surgery. We buy each other Christmas gifts and everything. Last year she gave me a vintage handbag of hers that I'd coveted once. It looks like something that Jackie O would have used. I gave her *The Vicar of Dibley* box set. Oh me oh my, I hate to think of her in hospital, in pain. I really must stop crying.

I've been crying almost solidly for two days. I generally try to avoid crying. It started with crying last time, then before I knew it, I couldn't get out of my bed. But I'm not going back there. Nope, I'm not. I sniff. I hear footsteps along the pavement next to me. I keep my head down, hoping they'll pass. They don't. Whoever it is has stopped right by me. I don't look. They're sitting down next to me. Oh, please leave me alone. With my head still in my hands, I open my eyes and turn my head slightly to see who it could be. All I see is a leg of grey tight-ishly fitted jean with a black biker-type boot on the end. My breathing deepens instantly.

It's Joe King. Although he doesn't speak for quite some time and when he does first open his mouth, it's not a word that escapes, more a groan of frustration.

'I thought when I saw you I'd be really manly and I'd ignore you, because I made a right plonker out of myself that afternoon by singing you a song, and all the while you were about to marry some bloke . . . ' He stops and sighs. 'But now, look, here you are . . . and all I want to do is to put my arm around you and say, "What's the most beautiful girl in the world doing sitting on the side of the street crying?"'

I twist my head a fraction more so I can see his face. But I try to hide my own.

'Hey,' he says softly, and he bumps his bottom a fraction towards me, then he leans forward too and puts an arm around my shoulder. He presses himself against me, laying his head on top of mine. 'Don't cry, beautiful,' he whispers. 'Can I help? Can I do anything to help?'

I shake my head. He lifts his head from mine then and turns it round, crouching down a bit further so he can see into my eyes.

'Is there anything I can do?' he asks again, seriously, kindly.

'I think I just accidentally nearly killed my favourite old lady,' I whisper.

For a moment, Joe King looks like he might laugh. Then he looks frightened.

'It wasn't just me. It was mainly Miranda Hart.'

He's looking baffled now.

'The comedian.'

'You know, Jenny Taylor. When I'm with you I feel as though reality ups it, and leaves the building.'

'Hmmm,' I agree, looking into Joe's eyes again. 'I tried reality and it wasn't much cop.'

'I'm really pleased to have met you, Jenny Taylor.'

I'm blushing. I like his arm around me. It feels like the most natural thing in the world for his arm to be across my back, for his hand to be clasping my upper arm. I could tilt my head and kiss that hand, press my nose to his skin and breathe him in to me. Or I could kiss his mouth. Our faces are so close, I'd barely need to move. Oh, why do I feel as though kissing this man might be the end of one life and the beginning of another?

'So,' he says, squeezing my arm a touch as he does. 'Do you realise that this is actually the fifth time I've met you. I've seen you on your knees singing in a chemist, dancing to my music at a gig, fighting monsters in a colander, musketeering with a balaclava. And now on the street crying. I hate seeing you cry.'

'Sorry,' I say, and I straighten myself up. 'I should head back to work.'

'Where do you work?'

'In the doctor's surgery.'

'Yeah. I knew that. I was just trying to be cool. I'd already asked Al.'

I smile. He doesn't join me.

'Why don't you wear an engagement ring?'

'Oh, well, at first it was too small and now because well, it's all off. The, er, engagement is off . . . '

'Is it?'

'Hmmmm.'

'Like off off?'

'Off off, yeah.'

'Oh. I don't know what to do.' He sighs, more to himself than to me.

'I should go in.'

'My uncle and I are having a party,' he suddenly blurts. 'Will you come?'

'Course.'

'And Philippa and Al?'

I nod and smile. 'When?'

'Um. Um. Saturday.'

'Where?'

'Oh, it's called Rose Cottage, on the main road once it gets a bit quieter on the way out of town.'

'I know the one.'

'Come. Anytime you like.'

'OK.'

I stand up. He remains on the curb. I turn away. My heart pounds.

I push open the heavy surgery doors. Back to business.

'Doctor Flemming thinks you should go up to the hospital and see Doris,' Marge informs me.

'Oh, oh, OK. But I should try to get hold of Doris' family before I go up there.'

I sit in front of the computer and bring up the details of Doris' next of kin. The information flickers onto the screen. I read the words, then I stare at them and then I blink and blink again.

Stephen Wilmot.

I close my eyes tightly for quite some time. I reopen them. The same name swims into focus.

Stephen Wilmot.

I imagine calling this landline number, either Michelle or Stephen picking up the phone, me having to introduce myself. My heart beats like a bass drum. I shake my head.

'I can't make this call,' I announce to Marge. 'I'm sorry, could you telephone him and explain about Doris. And I'm going to take my lunch now and get some air and then I'll take some flowers up to the hospital if you don't mind.'

I don't wait to ascertain if she minds or not. Sorry, Marge. I push my chair back and I bolt for the door. Stephen and Michelle Wilmot. Now, there's an icy cold blast from the past.

Chapter 37

They've only put her on a ward on the fifth floor, and there are windows everywhere in this hospital. It's very difficult to look out of a window and not look down, and if I look down I feel as though the contents of my tummy might emerge through my mouth.

Lily, another patient I know from the surgery, sits up in her hospital bed and smiles warmly at me.

'Lily!' I exclaim.

'Fanny!' shouts another lady from another bed on the other side.

'Oh, blimey, hello, Glad.'

I scan the beds looking for Doris and spot her at the far end of the ward, slumped slightly to one side against her pillows, her eyes closed but fluttering.

'Hello, you,' I say softly.

She opens just the one eye, fixes it on me and smiles.

'The funniest thing I ever saw in my life.'

'I know! It's the way she carries on and tries to make the

fact that her trousers are round her ankles part of the dance!' I exclaim, doing a quick impression.

Doris laughs. I panic. It was the laughing that did it earlier.

'Doris, lovely, I don't think you should be laughing,' I say, leaning over her.

'Oh, Fanny, if you can't laugh, you're buggered.'

'I agree,' I say.

'Sit down, Fanny, I want to talk to you.'

I pull the visitor's chair around so I can sit away from the window and face Doris instead.

'So, have they told you what the matter is?'

'Oh, I don't want to talk about my health. I tell you, Fanny, you get past eighty and that's all anyone wants to talk to you about. It used to be sex, it used to be politics, then all of a sudden it's blood pressure and feet.'

'Shall we talk about sex then?'

'Oh ho, you! Now, Fanny, love, fetch me my bag out of the cupboard there. Fanny, I want to give you something.'

I do as I'm told and pass her her red leather handbag. She puts on her glasses and appears very industrious all of a sudden. She locates a pen and then her cheque book.

'Doris, what are you doing?'

'Wheel that little table up here for me to lean on, will you?'

I hop up from my chair and do so.

'Doris, what are you doing?'

'I'm writing you a cheque.'

'Doris, I don't need money.'

'You will though, love,' she says, looking at me over the top of her glasses. 'One day, when I've popped me clogs. I want you to organise my funeral.'

'Oh, Doris! Don't talk like this!'

'Take it,' she says, ripping the cheque out along its serrated edge and holding it towards me.

'Five grand!' I exclaim. 'Doris!'

'Port's not cheap,' she says. 'Sadly. And even cheap fizz isn't cheap. And I want everyone to get legless.'

'Doris, what about your family?'

'Fanny, you know how to party, and you know what I want. And I don't trust them not to give me some ghastly afternoon tea affair at the golf club.'

I shiver at the mention of the golf club. Doris is pointing at me now. 'If there's money left over perhaps get some of those drinks you like, landmines or whatever they're called.'

'Jägerbombs,' I correct her.

'That's the one. I like the sound of them. I want a party, Fanny. For all of us what come in the surgery. Everyone. Shame I won't be there.'

'Why don't we just have a party, Doris? And not wait for you to pop your clogs.'

'Nah! It's my Big Send Off. And I know I can trust you, Fanny.'

Suddenly Al slides along the central aisle of the ward, doing that slash neck gesture that is supposed to signal cut, but instead looks like a six foot five man skidding along a ladies' OAP ward having a psychiatric episode. Philippa and Al have been on Steve and Michelle Wilmot lookout. I had to enlist the mustekeers on this one. There was no way I wanted to bump into Steve and Michelle. They must have just arrived. This is my cue to leave smartish.

'Doris, I need to shoot. That's my lift,' I say, springing up and giving her a quick peck on the cheek.

'And don't forget, Fanny, that mouth of yours is for smiling, OK?' I catch her saying as Al literally pulls me away by my arm. We race down the corridor.

'Al, you legend,' I call to his back. He doesn't answer but he does stop abruptly, causing me to bump into his back. Then he pulls me through some double doors and gestures for me to stand back against the wall for a moment. I do so, but not before I've spotted two people walking along the corridor we've just left.

How clever are eyes? My eyes only fell upon Mr and Mrs Wilmot for a second at the max and yet I saw so much. I saw Steve Wilmot, ten years on. He's bigger than he was. He's filled out, the ladies in the surgery would say. There's a cuddliness to him that was never there before. The cheeky twinkle he used to have in his eye isn't there either, but then he has come to the hospital to see his nan, so he's hardly going to be scooting about in search of mischief. He would be twenty-seven, like me, but I'd say he looks older. There are lines on his forehead and around his mouth. He looks a little world weary, a touch beaten. But he's not unattractive, far from it. God, I used to adore him. There were a few feet between him and Michelle. She has hardly changed at all. She's a tad fatter, but then she has had two kids. Two girls. A nine-year-old, Stacey, and a three-year-old, Georgie. Doris kept me fully informed about 'her gorgeous girls'. Michelle's still attractive. She's a yummy mummy, not in the plummy, posh sense, more of an Essex yummy mummy who'd try to borrow her daughter's jeans. She's wearing jeggings and Ugg boots and a tight T-shirt that shows off her big boobs. She has that tarty plumpness to her, the type that boys like. Although she's dressed down she's made-up. Dark eyes and red lips set in a pout. She still looks hard. I don't know why that surprises me. I'd always wondered whether she was just a cow at school because of teenage hormones, and once they'd settled down she might have become softer, less bulldog, more King Charles spaniel. But no, she's still very much bulldog, perhaps even more so. I wonder what sort of mother she is, what sort of friend she is, what sort of lover she is. Steve was a lovely lover.

'Bastard,' I mutter as Al and I stand flat against a wall waiting until they've definitely passed down the corridor.

'I could go and hit him for you, Fanny,' Al offers.

'Nah, best not, his nan's ill.'

'Well, I'll keep the offer open for you, Fan. Day or night, if you change your mind, I'm your man.'

'Thanking you kindly.'

'I think the coast is clear,' he says, holding the door open for me.

We walk to the lift. Me trying not to look out of the windows, Al chattering away.

'I think we should find a proper musketeer theme tune, that we can all hum, or have quietly playing on our phones when we're out on a mission,' Al conjectures.

I smile. We stand waiting for the lift and I take my phone from my bag to check it for messages.

Just the one. It's from Matt.

I haven't cancelled anything to do with the wedding. I can't bring myself to. Can we talk? Xx

He couldn't look at me when I saw him before. I stare at the text not knowing how to respond until the lift door opens and Al says, 'Come on, Fan-Tastic. Philippa's got my car round the front for a quick getaway.' Then I put the phone and the unanswered text back in my bag.

Chapter 38

'Ladies! Ladies, ladies,' Al looks at Philippa, Mum and me in turn. 'Help me out here,' he implores. 'Undivided attention tonight! I beg you. At least for the general knowledge round.'

'You're quite sexy when you're firm, Al,' Philippa says, leaning forward across the table towards him and pouting.

'Philippa, Gemma's coming along later, you're not to flirt with me,' he wags his finger at her.

'Oh! Now I really want to flirt with you!' she sulks.

'I've been available for flirting for years, Philippa,' he says smugly.

'But having a lady makes you so phenomenally attractive.'

'Well, I know and I'm sorry. But I'm taken,' he sings.

'Will, um, Joe and Felicity be coming as well?' I ask, *extremely* casually.

'So subtle, Fan. Super subtle,' Philippa splutters.

I cough the word 'cow' back.

'Not that I know of, sorry, Fan,' Al says, rather apologetically.

'Why are you sorry?'

'Oh, just because, you know, you fancy the pants off the man.' Al winks at me affectionately.

Al and Philippa haven't been able to hide their glee at the fact I'm no longer going to marry Matt. When I think of Matt I feel this knot in my tummy. I don't want to go back to him, but his texts make me feel guilty. I'm ignoring them, which I know isn't the best way. Oh dear, Al's right – I do fancy the pants off Joe King but I won't let him know that. I scrunch my face up as though he's talking nonsense and try not to dwell on the picture of Joe King in his pants that's forming in my mind.

'Don't be ridiculous.'

They both start laughing.

'Why are Philippa and Al laughing, darling?' Mum asks.

'Loonies the pair of them.' I shrug.

'Do you fancy the pants off this chap?'

'YES!' shrieks Philippa.

'He's seeing someone,' I protest.

'We don't know that for a fact,' Al reasons. 'Anyway, Gemma will have the lowdown, if there is any.'

'He's with Felicity,' I try to say the name of Joe's big-breasted friend kindly. I try but I'm not entirely successful. 'I'm not getting involved. I can't. Rules of the Sisterhood.'

Al pretends to fall off his chair at the mention of the sisterhood word.

'This young man you're talking about . . . Is this the love-at-first-sight man?'

I open my eyes wide. 'M-u-u-u-m!'

'Did you tell your mum you fell in love at first sight w—?' Philippa pants.

'Well, er, no, she just asked me if I believed in love at first sight, and I felt that was a very telling question,' my mum blusters.

'Thanks, Mum,' I attempt to sound peeved but really I'm trying to suppress a small smile. I love the closeness that's developed between Mum and me.

'Love at first sight! My friend, Fanny Fan-Tastic! Miss I Want A Nice Sensible Love! This requires a toast. Stand up you lot.' Philippa picks up her glass and springs to her feet. Then she looks down at the rest of us who have remained seated. 'Like now, actually get up. Come on!' She hauls Al by up the shirt.

Eventually we all stand huddled round our small table.

'To Fanny Fan-Tastic and her bits finally twitching!' she shouts.

Everyone raises their glasses.

'I will totally twat you all.'

'Hello, hello, what's going on here?' A familiar voice shouts over our noise. I smile. Philippa is instantly in her bag taking out her lipgloss.

It's Disgruntled Dave and he's only grinning!

'Hello, how are you? I didn't know you were still in these parts,' I say, pulling a stool from the table behind us so Disgruntled Dave can join us. 'Sorry, Dave, this is my mum, Pam, my flatmate, Al, and you know Philippa.'

Oh, go, Philippa. Beautiful eye-to-eye contact with a smile. If I had a hat I would doff it to her genius.

'And Al takes the pub quiz very seriously, so when it gets going please help him 'cos us three will just want to talk about boys.'

'Nice to meet you, Al. I love a pub quiz. Do you mind me joining your team.'

'Please do,' I say. 'I thought you'd left the bright lights of Nunstone when you finished filming with Marge.'

'Yeah, I did, I went back to London, but there are still a few shots I need to get of outside locations and whatnot, so I might be toing and froing back here a little.' His eyes dart to Philippa. Oh, bless him. 'Which actually suits me, because there's a little project of my own I'd like to get cracking on.'

'Oh, what's that?' Philippa says, circling the rim of her wine glass with her finger.

'Well, it might come to nothing, but, a strange thing happened to me when I was working here. I was given a note.'

'Oh, right,' I say, my voice a little higher than normal. I keep my eyes fixed on Dave.

'What sort of note?' It's Philippa speaking, well, squeaking. I can't risk a look in her direction. She might start on the silent rocking.

'Well, I was a bit of moody bugger, when I was here before, I'd been out in Guatemala filming with indigenous communities for nearly eighteen months, came back and did this BBC Three thing to help out a friend. But I wished I hadn't said I'd do the job. So I was a bit of a stroppy sod. Anyway, the note was really quite sweet. It said *I notice you don't look too happy. I was down for a while. It may sound weird but now I do these things on this list. Here you are, it may help you too.*

'Oh, that's nice.' Mum smiles.

'Yeah,' I agree.

'Sweet,' chimes Philippa.

'But it was anonymous. A mystery if you like. And I love a mystery.'

'So are you going to discover who sent it?' Mum's getting excited.

'Yes, I hope to. I thought there might be a nice little story there. If there are other notes it could be a little human-interest piece I could film one day. I was going to track you down, actually, Philippa. I remembered you saying you wrote for the local paper and I wondered whether we could put something in the paper to see if anyone else has received a note.'

Philippa hurriedly takes a pen out of her bag and starts scribbling her number on a beer mat. I just sit blinking as I wonder how many notes we've written over the years. It has to be hundreds.

'Oh, oh! Dave!' Mum is literally jumping out of her seat.

'Yes, Pam.'

'If you ever did make a film these girls could present it for you!'

'Oh, why, do you two . . . ?' Dave turns to us.

'They are *terrific*! I've got a showreel tape I can give you to watch of the two of them.'

'M-u-u-m. A showreel. You've got a showreel.'

'Yes, I got some copies made of the video that Al made of you girls doing the Tiddlesbury Tour. I thought it might be nice to give to people.'

'Not that big box?'

'Yes.'

'That couldn't have been just a few DVDs.'

How long does it take for women to go through the crazy marriage break-up stage? Or how long does a midlife last?

Should I be talking to someone about Mum's behaviour? I don't like to talk to Dr Flemming because Mum blew him out. But she's not right. If she bought an entire box full of DVDs of Philippa and me doing the Tiddlesbury Tour then she's definitely not right. I mean, that's bonkers. If she had meant to order just the one and accidentally ordered a hundred then fair enough. But I think she really meant to order them all. What's she going to do with them? I've got this dreadful feeling she's sending them to distant relatives. What if one is a policeman? I mention Damien the Dealer. He might get arrested. If the Tiddlesbury dope smokers found out I was responsible I'd be hounded out of town.

'Anyway, Dave, write your address down for me and I'll send you one,' Mum says, completely ignoring me, the daughter she's brazenly pimping. 'You'll see they're very talented and funny and beautiful.'

"Well, I can see that,' Disgruntled Dave says, looking at Philippa.

'Honestly, Dave.' Mum is nodding intently.

'They are, mate. They're hilarious together. It's something to behold,' Al says.

'Well, I'll take a look at your showreel, by all means. Although, I'm not sure whether this idea will ever get off the ground. There might not be any other notes. It's just a hunch. But I'm sure you two could be fantastic. And the producers at BBC Three loved Fanny when they saw her on the pilot.'

'Did they?' Mum nearly falls off her chair.

'Yeah, she's great on camera.'

Mum's expired. I finally look at Philippa, she's begun to silently rock.

Chapter 39

It's Wednesday. Joe King's party isn't until Saturday. How am I supposed to get through the days? Every time I've met Joe King in the past it's been in a random, bumping-into-each-other way. But now I know, I actually *know*, I'll be seeing him on Saturday. It's very hard to think of anything else.

From what Al gleaned from Gemma, it seems that Joe King and Felicity have seen each other a few times, but so far no kissing. So Rules of the Sisterhood say I should stay away. But even if this wasn't a sisterhood situation I should still steer clear. Joe King terrifies me. Imagine loving and losing Joe King. It doesn't bear thinking about. Although, I still can't wait to see his gorgeous smiling face. It's all I can think about. I haven't even been reading, just daydreaming.

It's Wednesday afternoon so I'm home early. Home alone, in fact. Mum's nowhere to be found, which can only be a worry.

I'm tiptoeing into my room. No idea why. There's no one else is in the flat and it's my room. I turn on the light and stand properly on my feet.

'Hello, lovely clothes,' I say as though they're chubby gurgling babies.

I sit on the bed for a moment to ponder. I'm not going to dress up on Saturday. The rules state that I shouldn't tart up, because Joe and I have flirted in the past, but now he's with Felicity, so I must step aside. Technically though I am single and it is a party, so I could tart up in the hope of meeting someone else. But I have no interest in meeting anyone else. How could I flirt with someone else with Joe King in the room? I couldn't. I flop forward and sigh. Having a monumental crush on Joe King is exhausting, there's just so much to think about. I hardly ever think about Matt, except when he texts, and then I just feel guilty and don't answer. I'm all in a whirl for Joe King. It can't be normal.

'What shall I wear?' I whisper. I can't believe I'm doing this on a Wednesday.

I stand up and walk to the black corner. I spot a dress I'd forgotten I had. It's a faded black T-shirt dress that falls off one shoulder. It's fits well, although it's not too clingy and it's not at all glam. But it has a big heart that looks like it's been drawn in chalk across the chest. That's the one. I pull it off the hanger and throw it on the bed, smiling. Philippa will no doubt have much to say about the fact I'm turning up to Joe King's house with a bloody great heart emblazoned across my chest.

Then I turn, and I find myself looking at Mum's belongings. I was only able to give her a drawer, everything else she's kept in her cases. They lie one on top of the other at the end of the bed. The massive box that must contain DVDs of me stands next to them, it's open, its cardboard wings stand upward. I push them apart and peer in the box. A pile of small jiffy bags and a piece of paper slide slowly out and onto the floor. I knew it. She's jiffy bagging them up and sending them to people. I put the jiffys back in the box and pick up the piece of paper. It's full of names and addresses. I was so right. Mum's writing is quite a scribble. I don't recognise any of the names though, and most of the addresses are in London. She can't do this to me or Damien the Dealer. I leave the box as I found it. And then I turn my attention to her case. I start to pull back one of the zips. The case is tightly filled and it's quite tricky to undo but I manage to pull it back a few inches. All I see is a white paper bag like you get from the chemist, but then I quickly re-zip the bag closed. I shouldn't be snooping on my mother. I turn the light off and hurry out of the room.

I think I'll buy a small cake and take it up to Doris. That could be my good deed for today. I fish my mobile out of my bag and dial the number for Nunstone General.

'Ward E4,' I tell the operator when they ask.

I always feel bad calling wards at the hospital. I always imagine the poor nurse, seeing to a patient, and then having to leave him or her, possibly in a state of undress, to go and wash her hands, in order to answer the phone. Perhaps I shouldn't have called. But then what if I go up there only to discover I'm outside visiting hours.

'Hello. E4.'

'Oh, hi there, so sorry to bother you. Is it all right for me to come and visit Doris Framer in half an hour?'

'Mrs Framer?'

'Yes, she was admitted on Friday.'

'Oh, oh, I'm so sorry. Doris passed away this morning. I'm terribly sorry.'

'Oh. Oh.'

'I'm so sorry.'

'Thank you.'

I hang up. I walk to the window and look out over Tiddlesbury High Street, at all the people coming and going, shopping and smoking and driving and loitering. Mum used to work for a hospice and now I work at the surgery, I've almost got used to death, and the inevitable fact that we're all going to go at some point. But the thing I've always found so odd, is that you can see someone and joke with them one day, and although they might be ill, they're still full of life. Yet, a few days later, that's it. They've gone. I'm not really religious, but that life, that spirit, it's got to go somewhere, hasn't it? I hope it goes somewhere pleasant. I hope there's a big old party for all souls that goes on for eternity. Perhaps they're dancing around me now. I'd rather think of that than nothingness. I just hope, for Doris' sake, there's some booze.

My phone rings. It's Philippa's landline number.

'Hey.'

'Jenny. Hello.'

'Oh, Dr Flemming, hello, have you heard about Doris?'

'Well, yes, I have, that's why I'm phoning actually. I just had quite a ferocious call from her daughter-in-law. The family, it appears, are blaming the surgery for over-exciting Doris and are planning to launch some sort of enquiry. I feel I should warn you, Jenny. Doris made it clear that there was a young lady at the surgery who liked to show her comedy, and obviously they want to blame someone. So I would just keep a low profile. I'm sure you weren't going to, but don't make any contact with the family. If there's a case against us it might affect it.'

'Oh.'

'Yes, terrible state of affairs all round. I'm sure it'll all blow over and it's just a response to their grief. So just keep out of their way, while they calm down.'

And now … the question is … what am I supposed to do about her Big Send Off?

Chapter 40

'Sorry to call you, guys. I didn't know what to do.'

'Fan-Tastic, never apologise for calling a Musketeer Mission,' Al says, he's trying to spoon cold dauphinois potato into his mouth without getting it on his balaclava. I watch him, thinking about telling him to take the clava off. But the sight of him sat there like a giant tadpole is oddly comforting and he is at home after all, there's scant chance he'll get arrested. I leave him be.

Mum strides into the kitchen but stops abruptly when she sees Al.

'What the . . . ?' she says.

'It's only Al,' I inform her.

'I realise that, Jenny, but he's wearing a balaclava.'

'I'm a musketeer, Pam,' he says proudly and winks.

I raise my eyes to the ceiling and shake my head.

'Mrs T, there's not much to do in these parts,' Philippa says by way of explanation. 'Every so often, if we have a task or a mission to complete we don balaclavas and call ourselves musketeers. We're not proud.'

The corners of Mum's mouth turn upward.

'Can I join you?' she asks.

'You certainly can, Pam, there's even a clava for you here in the tea towel drawer,' Al says, putting his dish on his lap and twisting in his seat to open the drawer and rummage for our spare balaclava. 'Here we are, the burgundy for you,' he says, handing it to her.

She puts it on eagerly and sits down at the table between Al and me.

'So, Fan-Tastic, musketeers at the ready,' Al says, digging back into the dauphinois.

'Um. Doris died today,' I say, quietly.

'Oh, Fan, I'm sorry,' he says, looking up from the oven dish. 'And I thought she looked fine when we saw her that day at the hospital as well.'

'Yeah, yeah, I did too.'

'Oh, I'm sorry, love,' Mum says. She takes my hand. She's always holding my hand at the minute.

'It's all right,' I say, squeezing her hand. 'We're all going to go at some point.'

'Hmmm.' Mum squeezes my hand back. 'And at least she got old. It's good to get old.'

'Yeah, but there's more.'

'Tell all, musketeer,' Philippa says, leaning forward, ready for action.

'Well.' I sit back and look at them all before I begin my tale. 'Doris was desperately disappointed with the standard of the funerals that she went to. She would come in moaning, saying that they were the only parties she ever got invited to at her age, and they were rubbish. "I'll come straight out with it, Fanny," she would say. "It was shite." She had quite a mouth on her. So she took to planning her own funeral, her Big Send Off she called it. Anyway, I know all about it. And then when I went to visit her she asked me to organise it for her when she passed away, and she gave me a cheque.'

I slide it out of my diary and push it onto the kitchen table. Philippa pulls it towards her.

'Five grand!' she cries.

'Yep, Doris is serious about this being a major bash. She wants Jägerbombs and everything.'

'I so want to go to this funeral,' Philippa whispers.

'But the problem is, Doris asked me to organise her funeral, but I've been told not to go near the family because they're launching an enquiry into her death and blaming me and the surgery. What do I do? I've somehow got to tell Steve Wilmot and Michelle Cullet how they should organise this funeral without going near them.'

'Ouch.' Philippa winces.

'Have you got this in writing at all, Fan?' Al asks.

I shake my head.

'Was anyone there while you had the conversation?' he tries.

'Not the one in hospital. But lots of people in the surgery heard the jokey way we were planning it and Disgruntled Dave, the cameraman, will have some stuff on video too, I think.'

'You need a lawyer,' Mum states.

'You do, Fan-Tastic, you do,' Al agrees.

'Do I?' I say surprised. 'How can I afford a lawyer?'

'Does anyone know a lawyer?' Philippa asks.

'No.'

'No.'

'No.'

'Can anyone pretend to be a lawyer?' Mum asks excitedly.

I'm torn between feeling quite impressed and terrified that she suggested that.

'I think that might be a little extreme,' I tell her.

'Sorry, it's this balaclava. I'm getting carried away,' she pants.

'Someone must know a lawyer,' Philippa says, bashing her fist to her head.

'I don't know about getting a lawyer,' I say. 'But we do need to do something quickly, she died today. The funeral needs to be soon.'

'So. Why don't you send Steve a letter?' Philippa suggests. 'Explaining what Doris said about her funeral.'

'I thought that,' I agree. 'The only thing that worries me is, what if, for some reason, he doesn't read it. Or doesn't read it until it's too late. He needs all this information, like now, so he can get cracking with the organising.'

'We could talk to him on your behalf,' Al suggests. 'We don't have to steer clear of him.'

'But what if he doesn't want to talk to us?' Philippa counters.

'He'll have to,' Al says thoughtfully.

'We'll have to kidnap him,' Mum says with a gasp.

We all stare at her.

'Mum!'

'I like it.' Al nods.

'You can't kidnap him!' I splutter.

'Why not? We're not going to hurt him,' explains Al. 'We'll just lure him into my car and drive him about for a bit and talk to him about the funeral.'

'You can't kidnap someone in a Fiat Punto!'

'No,' Philippa agrees. 'Al, do you know anyone who's got a van?'

'Joe's got a van.'

'Awesome on every level!' Philippa says.

'Nah, Joe's at band practice, I called him earlier to see if he was musketeering tonight,' Al says.

'Did you?' I ask Al, suddenly very sidetracked from Doris' funeral.

'Yeah, anything to help my favourite flatmate who fancies the skinny jeans off him.' He winks at me.

'I don't. Anyway, he's with Felicity.'

'Jenny lurves—'

'Philippa! Stop it now, back to the mission. There's absolutely no need for kidnap, or anything that hints of a Bruce Willis film, thank you. But I think I've cracked it. You lot just have to go and see Steve Wilmot and tell him what Doris wants for her Big Send Off.'

'Oh yeah, so what was it she wanted again?' Philippa asks.

'Tell you what, I'll write out a letter. All you have to do is make sure he gets it and reads it. Is that OK?'

'Yes.'

'Yes.'

'Yes.'

'Excellent because we have to do it tonight.'

'Tonight!' Three sets of wide eyes goggle at me. They weren't expecting that.

'Yes, people act quickly on funerals. I'll go and write the letter in the lounge. You stay here. I won't be a second.'

An hour and seven minutes later.

'How's it going, Fan?' Philippa says, walking towards where I am kneeling on the floor, bent over the low-slung coffee table writing, surrounded by at least twenty scrunched-up discarded efforts.

'Bloody awful. I keep missing words out, I've spelt funeral wrong and cheque wrong and I can't seem to write in a straight line, my lines look like planes taking off. Oh!' I scribble through the latest draft. 'It's not easy. What am I supposed to say? Hello, you might remember me, you slept with me for a bet years ago, your gran wants me to organise her funeral.'

Philippa looks at me and then looks at her watch. 'Have you still got that Dictaphone?'

I nod.

'Record yourself saying it on there. We'll play it to him. We'll be here all night if we wait for you to write a letter.'

I think my best friend might be a genius.

Chapter 41

'Matilda, help me out here,' I instruct my automobile-sized plant, as I enter the bathroom, Dictaphone in hand. I close the door, put the toilet lid down and settle myself upon it.

I press record on the Dictaphone. I wait until the tape starts to turn. I take a deep breath.

'Hello, Steve,' I say. 'Long time no see ... not since you broke my heart and completely ruined any hope of me ever being able to trust a man again, you complete turd ...'

I press stop and rewind.

'Matilda!' I hiss at my plant. 'You're supposed to be helping me out.'

Another deep breath.

'Do it properly. You haven't got much time,' I whisper to myself. I press record again.

'Steve, hello, it's Fanny, er, Jenny Taylor, here, from school, sorry about the, er, the um, unconventional way you've come to hear this. There are some things I need to say to you, and they're very important, but I've been told not to come near you, and all that. So ...

'Well, before I get to the nitty-gritty, I just want to say, Steve, I'm so sorry about your gran. About Doris. God, you had the coolest nan. So funny, and kind, and full of love. She was full of all the good things. It made my day when she came into the surgery.'

I pause, my voice is getting shaky. I swallow.

'I'll really miss her, so I can't imagine how you're feeling. I know you're hurting at the moment. But I hope you're happy, I mean, I hope that things turned out well for you, in life, since I saw you last. If that makes sense. I wish you well, I just wanted to say that. Despite what, you know, what happened, between us. Anyway.

'You probably want to know why you are now being played this message. Well, it's this. Your nan, Doris, has asked me to organise her funeral. I know that sounds ridiculous and I don't know whether she's told you this, or just assumed I'd be able to contact you in the normal way and explain it to you when she passed away.

'You see, your nan would come into the surgery and we'd joke and she would plan her funeral. I know that sounds odd, but she would. So I think the best thing is for me to tell you what she wants on this tape. And then you can do it all. She gave me a cheque as well, which I can give back to you. The main thing, though, is that she gets the Big Send Off that she wanted.

'So, she wants it in the community centre, she's very serious about this, apparently you were christened there. It was a right knees-up, she said. She'd like some of her old photos on the wall, she said. Ones where she looked nice, not frumpy or double-chinned and none where she doesn't have any lipstick on. That's really important, the lipstick bit. And drawings that your kids have done for her, she'd like them on the walls too. She loved them, she'd bring them in to the surgery and show everyone.

'Food, she wants all her favourite things, proper ham sandwiches, she stressed the proper, if you get that cheapy thin stuff from the supermarket she will haunt you forever. And she wants pork pies, cold sausages, egg mayonnaise, but no fish, especially smoked salmon, she didn't trust that, and absolutely no cucumbers, slimy green bastards she called them. Lots of bread and butter. Proper butter, not marge, but I think you know that.

'Drink. She wants people to get legless. Cheap fizz and port, and Coca Cola out of the little bottles for kids. No beer, she said. She doesn't care if men moan. She said it made them fart.' I laugh. 'Oh, and Jägerbombs if the budget allows. Do you Jägerbomb? It's a shot of Jägermeister dropped into a small glass of Red Bull, if you haven't come across them.

'She wants dancing, she really wants dancing. Till dawn she said, or as close as you can get to dawn in a community centre full of pensioners. It has to be Rod Stewart and Tom Jones, that sort of thing . . . ' I swallow again.

'So, I guess I'll leave this with you. Take the tape and this machine and then you can play it back to remind yourself. Oh! Wow, can't believe I forgot, there's a dress code. She wants a dress code. It's *Grease*. The film, *Grease*.

'Anyway, so, I'm happy to organise all this for you, if you want, or help, but I've been told to steer clear of you. So, well, I don't know what you want to do. But she really wants a shindig, Steve, she said "I had two registry office weddings, this is my big do." It's just a shame she won't be there.' I pause, and swallow again. 'Although, I think she'll be there, knocking back the port and making sure there's not a slimy green bastard in sight.

'So, goodbye, Steve. Oh and if you need me, I live above the kebab shop in Tiddlesbury. You can find me there.'

I press stop and exhale.

Oh, and Steve. I'm not saying that what you did messed me up, but it did take me eight years to sleep with another man. Oh, and when you kissed me that night, I thought I'd never kiss anyone else, I thought I'd found my happy ending. I still think about that . . .

Chapter 42

'I think we need to be playing calming classical music when we capture him, so he doesn't get aggressive,' Mum gabbles as she ransacks her way through our CDs.

I stand gaping at her.

'Mum! I think if we stop referring to it as a capture or a kidnap, it would probably be a good thing.'

'Oh, right, sorry, love. We're just going to seize him temporarily.'

I open my mouth but then close it quickly. I feel this is a battle I am losing.

'Are you all sorted?' I ask, turning to Al.

He nods.

'I feel so alive,' Mum gushes, which seems a little insensitive seeing as Doris isn't, but I don't mention it because there's a knock on our door. It causes us all to freeze.

'Someone must have left the downstairs door open,' Al whispers. 'Are you expecting anyone?'

'Not me,' I tell him. 'I'll go,' I say, as I walk to open it. It could be Steve Wilmot, I think, but then I remember he doesn't know where I live yet. I open the door a tiny fraction. It's Matt. He's wearing his grey work suit with a purple tie. He looks incongruously smart against our tatty landing.

'I hope I'm not disturbing you, you're not shagging anyone are you?'

'That's not funny.'

'I thought it was.'

'Maybe it was a little bit.'

We share a smile, which seems bizarre under the circumstances.

'Why don't you answer my texts?'

'Because I don't know what to say,' I reply sadly.

'Can we have a chat?'

'Matt, I'm so sorry, but it's, um ... yes, I want to chat but ... it's just not a good time.'

'I won't be long. Two minutes is all I need to say what I need to say.'

'OK, but you'll have to say it here.'

Matt's body suddenly jolts, he steps toward me and tries to see round the door.

'You've got him in there, haven't you?'

'No, no, God, it's not like that!'

'Then why can't I come in?'

'Matt, it's just that ... '

'Fan, are you all right?' It's Al, looking over my shoulder. I hope he's taken his clava off. I tip my head to look. No, course he hasn't.

'Jenny, there's a man in a balaclava in your flat!' shouts Matt in alarm.

'No, no, no! It's not like that! It's Al!'

'What the hell's going on?'

'We're just messing around.' I sigh. We'll be here all night. 'Come in.'

I drag him swiftly past the musketeers while he splutters a variety of expletives. For some reason I lead him into the bathroom.

'Jeez, this bloody plant,' he says, swiping at the leaves around him. He is practically in Matilda. Two people and Matilda is quite a squeeze in our bathroom.

'I'm so sorry. It's not the best time,' I explain.

'So who was it?'

'Who?'

'The bloke you slept with.'

Lie, Fan, this is one occasion when it is perfectly acceptable to lie.

'I don't know.'

I really need to work on my perjury.

'You shagged some bloke you don't even know?'

'Y-e-e-s.'

Matt laughs. 'Fan, I've never seen you lie. You're appalling at it. You'd never make it in business.'

I sigh. 'It was Al.'

'Al?'

'Yes.'

'The big bloody ginger?'

'Yes.'

'Your flatmate?'

'Yes.'

'Right, bloody hell. Look, Fan,' he puts his head in his hands. 'I've thought about this, and we're about to make a big commitment and sometimes that makes people do things that are out of character . . . ' He tails off suddenly. 'Bloody massive Al with the weird hair?'

'Yes.'

'Do you want to sleep with him again?'

I shrug.

'That's really encouraging, Fan.'

'I don't know what I'm thinking, Matt. I slept with him, I've been fancying someone else. I really don't want to get married at the golf club. Everyone keeps saying we're not well suited.'

'Who?'

'Just. People.'

'But, but, we're going to get married and have a life together, and I'll take care of you and you'll take care of me.'

'I know all that, Matt, but you do boss me around.'

'Don't be ridiculous.'

'You do.'

'Fan, you're making this up.'

'Why would I make it up? See, I'm not even allowed an opinion.'

'Hang on! You slept with someone else.'

'Yes, because I'm confused.'

'Confused.'

'Yes.'

'Well, I'll still take you.'

'But, Matt, I don't know whether I want to be taken.'

'What?'

'I don't think you really want me, either. The real me. I don't think you even know the real me and that's my fault not yours.'

'I don't even understand that.'

'If I told you that I tried reality and it wasn't much cop, what would you say?'

'What?'

'If I said that I'd tried reality and it wasn't much cop what would you say?'

'I'd say you were talking nonsense, Fan, because you are. But I still want to marry you.'

'I'm sorry, Matt. I really am.'

'But I booked the golf club. I told my bosses.'

'I'm sorry.'

'Fan, please don't do this.'

'I have to, Matt. I'm sorry,' I say, and I close my eyes because I really mean it. I am sorry. But I do have to do this.

But Matt's out of Matilda, out of the bathroom. I've never seen anyone move so fast. I leg it after him, just in time to see him swipe his fist at Al, who ends up on the sofa. Al groans. Mum screams and Matt bolts out through the door.

It seems the wedding is definitely off now.

Chapter 43

It's all done. Steve Wilmot has heard the Dictaphone message. Apparently he cried. Hearing Philippa say that made me a feel a bit strange. Then when she said, 'I'd forgotten how much we used to like Steve, Fan,' I felt even stranger. I don't want to think of him having a heart, it's easier for me to pretend he doesn't have one. Still, at least it's done. Apparently, my mother told him he should be ashamed of himself for how he treated me. She shouldn't have done that, he had just lost his nan and, really, there's no point in bringing up an incident that happened so long ago and making him feel bad for it. I certainly wouldn't do it myself, but I do quite love that Mum did. My mum fought my corner for me; that feels very special. They had already booked the golf club, so it was very lucky that the musketeers intervened when they did. Funny old world.

Actually what is funny, well, not funny ha ha but funny wow, is the extent of my crush on Joe King. I have got more going on in my life now than I've ever had before: Mum having a midlife in my flat, breaking off an engagement, people getting punched in my living room, my favourite patient dying and me being appointed chief funeral organiser. So, you know, I should have stuff on my mind, shouldn't I? Yes, Fanny, you should. But I don't really. It's *all* Joe King. Other thoughts do make an appearance, but they all end up at the same place, with me in the arms of Joe King. I think back to how it felt on the curb when his arm was around me, and my stomach does a little Joe King flip.

Oh no, someone's trying to hand me a sample pot. By far the worst part of my job. I shake my head and point at the letterbox with the big sign saying SAMPLES HERE.

Wow, someone's just pushed the heavy surgery doors open with some serious welly. Marge and I share our 'can't be that ill if they can do that' raised eyebrow look, and then turn our attention back to the door to see who it is.

My tummy tightens in a knot. No, it can't be her, I think. She strides to the counter. It is. She leans forward so that I can see her closely, the way she hasn't blended her foundation on her lower cheek, how she's tried to cover up a spot on her chin, the small shadows under her eyes. She looks as though she's trying to place me. I know I've changed since school. People rarely recognise me. But I recognise her. It's Michelle Cullet.

'I'm looking for Jenny Taylor?' she barks. No pleasantry. She was never one for a pleasantry. And I so love a pleasantry. A 'hello', an 'excuse me', a 'how are you?', a 'gosh, how's Monday treating you?', a 'it's turning into a lovely day'. A pleasantry costs nothing. Little free nuggets of niceness that make such a difference to a day.

I don't answer. She stares at me. Then she furrows her brow. 'It is you,' she says.

She takes a step back and looks around the surgery. Her

expression of disgust increases in intensity by the moment. Suddenly I see the place with her eyes; it's not aided by one of the elderly male patients standing beside her, scratching an egg stain off his lap.

She looks back at me. 'I thought you'd come to nothing. I didn't think it would be quite this bad.' She snorts a laugh. 'I'm just dropping by to tell you that we're having her wake at the golf club. We had to pay a big deposit up front. It's non-refundable. She may have wanted some party of the frigging century but we can't lose that money. And you can stay out of my family's affairs.'

Marge is standing next to me now. I didn't notice her get up. But I am aware that she's tensing an arm and clenching a fist. Blimey. I think Marge the Heavy is going to thump Michelle Cullet! We can't go walloping people. We're a doctor's surgery. Peace and Love, man. I turn to stop her. But I don't think it's my brightest move to put myself in the way of a moving fist with seventeen stone behind it.

'Arrrghhhh!' I cry, as her fist catches the side of my face and knocks me to the floor.

'Fanny!' Marge cries.

'You lot are mental,' Michelle exclaims and walks out.

'Well that got rid of her,' I remark when she's gone.

Chapter 44

'It looks like she's got a good thump on her.' Mum winces as she delicately places a bag of frozen peas onto the side of my face.

'I can't believe she hit me,' I squeak. 'She was like an animal.'

'Shhh,' Mum soothes.

'Twatted in a doctor's surgery. I could probably sue.'

'Shhh.'

'Does it look angry, Mum? Does my face look red and angry?'

'Oh, well, um, perhaps a little cross, yes.'

Brilliant, now I know what I'll be wearing to Joe King's party. A bloody great bruise. That's not even the worst of it. Dr Flemming came out of his examination room when he heard the kerfuffle and suggested that I stay away from the surgery for the time being.

'Two thirds of the inhabitants of this flat have been thumped in the last twenty-four hours. It's practically a war zone.'

'I'll have to watch my back,' Mum says.

'What am I supposed to do now though?' I wail.

'How do you mean?'

'Michelle said that Doris can lump it with a do at the golf club and Doris loathed the golf club. If she knew they were doing this it would break her heart.'

'Well, the truth is, Jenny,' my mum says, stroking my hair with her peas-free hand. 'Doris will never know where she has her funeral.'

'But how do you know that?'

'Darling, she's dead.'

'Yeah, I get that bit. But she might still know. Her spirit might still be around.'

'I didn't know you believed in all that.'

'Well, I don't really know what I believe in. But I like to think there's something else, don't you?'

She nods and then suddenly I see tears welling up in her eyes. Oh dear, I've upset the emotional, menopausal woman.

'Come here, softie,' I say, reaching over to give her a hug. I love hugging my mum now. 'Ooh, watch my face. I love you, Mum.'

'Oh, Jenny, I love you too, so much.'

'Tissue?'

'I'm all right, but I think you should get the whiteboard, the balaclavas and the musketeers and we should hatch a plan.'

'You're worse than Al with the balaclavas.' I laugh.

'Jenny, it's the most fun I've had in a long, long time.'

'I'll get the whiteboard. But it's just the two of us, Al's out with Gemma and Philippa's working late. I could . . . '

I could call Joe King. But I won't. That would a bad idea. Wouldn't it?

'Could what, love?'

'Nothing, let me grab that whiteboard.'

I skip through to the lounge, heave the whiteboard out from behind the shelves and then I stomp back to the kitchen and erect it. I swiftly pull the top eight pages off and stuff them in our kitchen bin. There goes my dream wedding. Mum has already sourced her clava and is sporting it. I quickly fetch mine from my bag and put it on.

'We're going to ambush Doris' funeral,' Mum says with relish.

'Mum, I think it's important to keep the vocab under control when we're discussing these missions.'

'We're going to organise the funeral she wanted.'

'But what about the golf club do?'

'The guests start off by going to the golf club do and then afterwards they go to the big bash that she wanted.'

'Oh, I see. Oh, I see. Oh, I like it. But how?'

'We have to hijack the golf club do.'

'Mum, vocab,' I sing.

'Someone needs to get all the people who are at the golf club to go to the community centre.'

'Yes. Who though? I can't tell them. They don't want me there. Oh. Oh. I know. Doris could tell them.'

Mother wasn't expecting that.

'Dave's got Doris on film talking about her Big Send Off. We play that on a screen at the golf club and then tell everyone that after they've finished their cups of tea there's going to be a knees-up in the community centre. Actually, we get

Philippa to sort that bit out. If anyone can chat somebody up at the golf club to make all this work, it's Philippa.'

'Excellent,' Mum says, as though we've just sorted out the tiny issue of who's going to go and buy loo paper. 'Right, so now we need to get on and organise her big bash.'

'Mum, do you really think we can do this?'

'Jenny Taylor, if anyone can, you can.'

And for some reason that comment makes me feel so happy I give her a kiss on the cheek.

'Right, let's make some lists,' I say, taking off the lid of my marker pen. I'm instantly interrupted by my mobile phone ringing. 'I should turn this off, we have work to be doing,' I say as I fetch it from the kitchen surface. 'Oh, it's for you.'

I hand my mother my mobile phone, which is flashing the words SIMON THE PLASTERER CALLING.

Chapter 45

'Hang about,' I say as soon as Mum walks out of the bedroom. 'That's not a dress.'

'Well, what is it?' Mum asks innocently.

'It's a top, Mum. A top.'

'She looks lovely!' Philippa protests.

'She's going out in a top!'

'My dress is longer than yours,' my mum says, smiling.

I stand next to her. We compare dress lengths. Hers is definitely shorter.

'I just don't want him to get the wrong idea, that's all.'

'I think she might want to give him the wrong idea.'

'Philippa!'

'Come on, Fan, your mother has needs.'

'Enough.'

Mum's off on her date with Simon the Plasterer. I can't work out whether I'm sorry that she won't be able to come to Joe's party this evening and finally meet Mr Love At First Sight, as she calls him, or relieved because she could well hand him a copy of the Tiddlesbury Tour DVD. Perhaps it's for the best she's off with Simon the Plasterer. Although I don't feel that comfortable about it, what if he takes advantage of her? I leave Philippa applying bronzer on Mother and sneak into the bathroom with my mobile phone.

'Matilda, this is between you and me, do you hear?' I say sternly to the plant.

I'll send just the one little text to Simon the Plasterer.

Simon, it's Jenny Taylor again. I just wanted to say, please look after my mum tonight and treat her like a lady. I do have some friends who aren't very nice. So if you cross me you cross them too. That's all. Have a lovely evening.

I read it back. A kiss would be inappropriate, I feel. I press my finger firmly on the send button. I walk back into the bedroom just as the flat's buzzer goes.

'That will be lover boy.' Philippa smiles.

'Woah, nervous tummy,' Mum says, getting up.

'Have you got money?' I ask.

'Yes.' She laughs. 'Have you?'

'Yes.' I smile. 'Have fun.'

'And you.'

Philippa and I give her little air pecks on the cheek, lest we smudge her make-up. When she leaves, we skip to the window to watch her. The mum from my childhood has been replaced by this lady on the pavement beneath my window, with the big smile and the keen laugh, getting into a transit van with a plasterer called Simon who's nearly twenty years younger than her. Simon the Plasterer has clearly shaved and ironed his shirt specially for their date.

'Look at her go,' Philippa says, putting her arm round me and leaning her head against my shoulder. 'She looks gorgeous.'

'Hmmm. She's got so thin, though. But she does look happy tonight.'

'I love how she likes a bit of rough. Now, shall we get ready for the Bit Twitcher?'

'I will twat you.'

'Do you know what you're wearing?'

'Worked out my outfit on Wednesday.'

Philippa laughs. 'I probably shouldn't say this, but I am really bloody thrilled you're not going to marry Matt.'

'I thought you would be.'

'Promise me something, Fandango.'

'What?'

'That you won't run away from Joe King because you're scared.'

'How do you mean?'

'Fan. You're terrified of loving someone. You have been ever since Steve Wilmot. That's all in the past, yet you still equate love with pain. But it doesn't have to be like that. You can have the love story. You can have a happy ending. And I think Joe King is it. Promise me you'll give it a go.'

'He's with Felicity.'

'We don't know that.'

'But . . . '

'Just promise me, your best friend, that if he's not with Felicity, you'll give it a go with him. You won't run away. Please.'

'Philippa!'

'Promise me.'

'He's with Felicity.'

'Promise me.'

I look her straight in the eye, I swallow and then with a timid little voice, I relent and say, 'I promise.'

Afterwards, as I put on a dress with a big heart on the front, I hear my mobile vibrate. I pick it up thinking it will be Simon the Plasterer but it isn't, it's from Matt.

I still haven't cancelled the wedding. Miss you. xx

Chapter 46

Rose Cottage is the most charming house in Tiddlesbury. Although, as it's away from the main drag of shops and modern housing, it doesn't actually feel as though it's in Tiddlesbury at all. If you saw a photo of Rose Cottage you'd think, Wow, where's that? It must be some quintessentially English picture-postcard village, and then you'd arrive in Tiddlesbury and be very disappointed. Rose Cottage is the only pretty dwelling in the area. It's a white stone cottage with thick walls and small windows, partly covered with wisteria, and surrounded by an old stone wall over which jasmine drapes. I used to do a run that took me past Rose Cottage and I would always groan and dance with pleasure as I passed the thick jasmine bushes. The rest of the garden is gloriously topsy-turvey, nothing is too coiffed or austere and, best of all, the air smells like fabric softener.

Philippa and I stand on the doorstep breathing in the scented air while applying lipgloss, she's clutching the Jägermeister, I'm holding the Red Bull. I'm just rubbing my lips together when Joe answers the door.

'Ladies! Welcome! Thank you for coming tonight.'

Oh me oh my. He's been gorgeous in my mind all week. But he's even more so in the flesh. His freckly eyes are sparkling and he's smiling as he steps back to let us walk in.

'Thank you for inviting us,' Philippa says. 'We're very flattered.'

'Ah, well, yes, the thing is, we called it a party, but we don't really know anyone in Tidds, so, well, we think we've just about managed to rustle up nine people. Does that qualify as a party?'

'Absolutely,' I say, finally finding my voice. 'Some of the best parties I've been to only had two guests, me and Philippa.'

'Why do I believe that?' Joe chuckles. As I pass him, he leans towards me. 'How's your favourite old lady?' he says, in a softer voice.

'Oh, oh, she died.'

'Oh, Fanny, I'm sorry,' he says. 'Are you OK?'

'Yeah, I'm all right. Thank you.'

He looks at me closely. 'Oh, angel, what happened to your face?'

'My workmate clobbered me.'

'At the doctor's surgery?'

'Yep.'

'Blimey, it all happens in Tiddlesbury. Right, in we go. Can anyone make a fire? We haven't sorted the heating yet and it's colder in here than it is out there, for some reason. Especially at night. So we thought we'd get a fire going.'

'I'll do it,' I volunteer.

'Great,' he says and he holds my gaze for a second before disappearing.

'Go, pyro.' Philippa snorts. 'Although, I think there's quite a lot of fire already in this room. In both your pants,' she hisses in my ear.

'So juvenile.' I tut.

I love fires. I'd love to live in a house with an open fire. Although the danger would be I'd spend all my time gazing at the flames. I can do that for hours. I'm not sure why. I kneel in front of the fireplace. Joe was right, it's freezing in here. I shiver.

'Do you need a jumper till you get the fire going?' It's Joe again, walking past me.

'Um. I wouldn't mind.'

'Come up.' He nods towards the stairs.

I don't know whether I should go up the stairs with him. What about Felicity? Would she think that wrong? Am I being entirely over-paranoid because I absolutely adore him?

'OK.' I follow him up the narrow stairs to a tiny landing where he opens a door and walks through darkness to turn on a bedside lamp.

'It's a bit of a tip. I haven't really unpacked yet.'

It doesn't look like a tip to me. A double bed rests against the wall, bestrewn with a mountain of duvets and blankets. A guitar lies on the floor, surrounded by sheets of scribbled-on paper. Scribbled-on paper is a prominent feature here. It's in his bed too. He scoops some up and stows them in a drawer.

'Song lyrics, that's what the maudlin poetry turned into. What about you? Did the comedy-watching lead to anything?'

'No.' I laugh. 'Just an expensive DVD habit.'

He holds one arm up and takes a little sniff of his armpit. Oh crikey, I even think he's beautiful when he does that. Oh frig, now he's taking off his T-shirt. I watch. I can't not. He throws the T-shirt on the ground and I so could pick it up and sniff it. What is wrong with me? His nipples are very erect but then it is about minus seventy in here. He clocks me staring. And he just stares back. Then he sighs and sits on the bed and shivers. Then he pulls a blanket from it and puts it round his shoulders.

'Bloody cold, isn't it?'

I nod.

'How can it be warmer outside?'

He lifts one arm, indicating that I should get in the blanket with him. 'For warmth,' he explains.

I hesitate, then leap across and sit on the bed next to him. His arm reaches around me and I nestle into the blanket. My flimsy T-shirt dress is the only thing separating our chests. We sit like this for a moment. I can hear our breathing. And see it in small plumes of smoke escaping our mouths.

'Can you feel it?' he whispers.

If he means this amazing chemistry, then, yes, I can feel it in every nerve in my body.

'I'm not sure what you mean.'

'This thing.'

'Oh, yes, that's narrowed it down,' I say nervously.

'This thing between us.'

What should I do? Get up and leave the room, that's what I should do.

'Yes,' I whisper, barely audible.

'Crikey.'

'Absolutely crikey.'

'It's the weirdest thing. Our names, our clothes. I feel as if I've known you for a billion years. That's mad, isn't it?'

'Yes,' I say meekly.

Oh, strange breathing. I'm breathing from my throat. It sounds shaky.

'Right, I need to stop this,' he says, jumping up. 'One jumper, my favourite.' I take it. It's a soft, black round-neck. 'Hoodie for me, we should get back down.'

I stand and nod. I can't speak. I look at him, my breathing all irregular and I take a step towards him. I look up into his face. He's looking down at me. I take another step. I could kiss his lips. They would be warm and, I know, wonderful. But I don't, I stand only inches from his face, feeling all these crazy surges through my body, just looking into his eyes, and then abruptly I pull myself away from him.

'Thank you for the jumper,' I mumble and race back downstairs.

Oh, Fan, why are you racing down the stairs? I'm racing down the stairs because I know, I just know, that Joe King could smash my heart into a million pieces and all the king's horses and all the king's men and all the superglue in all the world wouldn't be able to fix it. That's why. Philippa administers a Jägerbomb and I get back on my knees and start making a fire. But even making a fire doesn't hold its regular allure because Joe's not next to me.

'How goes it?' Philippa says.

'Confusing.'

'Well, you made a promise to me, Fandango. So just snog him tonight. It might be dreadful. Sometimes you get all the chemistry but then you kiss and it's gone. Cher was right, you know. It's in his kiss.'

'What about Felicity?'

'Yeah, what about her? She's not here.'

'Urghhhhh.' I groan.

'If anyone deserves the fairy tale it's you. Kiss him. He's been put in your path for a reason. May as well find out what the reason is. Get it while you can.'

'It could end in tears.'

'It could, yes,' Philippa agrees.

'But, you know what I was like after Steve Wilmot. I didn't get over that for years,' I hiss, lest anyone hear.

'Well, that was then. That was a seventeen-year-old girl who'd had to put up with a lot of crap from school kids and her dad. But this is Fanny Fan-Tastic, ten years later, the same lovely, funny, caring person she's always been but now, much, much, *much* stronger.'

I nod. 'Thank you.'

She smiles. 'Oh, and, Fan?'

'Yeah?'

'It might not end in tears.'

Oh, thank God, someone's put a CD on. If in doubt, dance. I jump up, my knees cracking, that's from the running, my knees have been very vocal since I took up running.

'Shall we show them how it's done in Tiddlesbury?' Philippa says, as we clink glasses. I nod, we drain our drinks and Philippa pulls me into the floor space. We push the settee backwards slightly to create our own dance floor.

'No worrying about what these cool rock boys think, now!' she says.

'As if!'

I love dancing. I love standing still at first and letting the music fill me up. It tingles in my head until my head starts to nod, then the beat travels all the way down my spine. It reaches my belly and goes all the way down to my toes. I love that moment of surrender. Like diving off a board into water. Like the music is in the air around you. When I dance I feel like I'm inside the song. Sometimes, all right, often, when Al's out I just put music on and dance around the house. I can do it for hours. Whole albums I'll get through. I do get a bit sweaty though. I pull Joe's jumper off and fold it and leave it on the settee. I don't want it to be stinky when I give it back. Ooh we've got some of the others up on their feet too. Blimey, everyone's dancing. The sofa's being moved right to the edge of the room. And now, Joe's uncle, Phil, is standing triumphantly upon it, his hands in the air.

'HELLO, TIDDLESBURY!' he shouts. He doesn't look uncle old, maybe just ten years older than Joe. He wears dark-framed spectacles that make him look geeky chic. His hair is cropped and he's shorter and a bit stockier than Joe. He sounds like a kind man from what Philippa has said, he even said he'd read her book for her. Philippa dances over to the settee and raises her hands towards him as she dances. I close my eyes and start beating my body around to the drums in the song. I can see Joe, he's dancing to the side of the room, talking to the older man he was talking to before the gig the other night. He bounces his head to the music. I start to feel the booze and the beat. I love this feeling. I want to bottle it and revisit it when I'm old. Joe starts dancing towards me. He's been put in your path for a reason, that's what Philippa said. Maybe for this one moment. To feel young and alive. Maybe when I'm old I'll remember this, dancing freely with a cool guy from a band. Maybe that's all it is, one for the treasure chest of memories, nothing more. He's not self-conscious when he dances like most men are. Matt hates dancing. But I don't want to think of

Matt. Joe is closer to me now. We share a smile as our heads nod and our bodies lurch. There's a break in the song, and suddenly we're jumping and laughing. Then as it slows at the end and we're out of breath, we stop, waiting for the next tune, the next surprise, the next surrender. It's got a dirtier, sexier bass line. Joe's uncle yells, 'Turn it up.' Philippa pulls Joe and me to the side of the dance floor and over to the stereo where she's got Jägerbombs waiting for us.

'Welcome to Tiddlesbury,' she toasts. Joe hugs her and I love that he does that. She dances away to offer the other Jägerbomb to Joe's uncle. We carry on dancing but we're closer than before, still in our own worlds, but those worlds are slightly nearer now. Joe dances forward until our hips are almost touching and then backs away slightly, I move my arms so they nearly touch him. We're sharing the song with each other. I can feel I'm sweating already. I wipe my chest with my hand. It's wet. I attempt to dry it on my dress. Delightful. Joe hides his hand in his hoodie sleeve and gently wipes it across my chest. Then using the same hand he wipes the sweat off my neck. But he keeps his arm resting against my neck when he's finished. We dance. We're close enough for my breathing to practically sound orgasmic. I wish I could control it. I can't look at him, not while I'm panting. I'm looking down at the carpet. The song ends, his arm is still around me. He's leading me off the dance floor. I look at him now. I smile, just because I can't not.

'I'm going to do something ridiculous now and you will think I'm a twat,' he says. He's heading for the stairs. I pause at the bottom of the stairs he's already started to climb. But then I follow him. I stand outside his room for a minute. He walks in and turns a light on. He looks back at me.

'Are you OK?'

Should I step into his room again? I think of Matt's text that I haven't responded to. But I don't want to be with Matt. I want to be here with Joe King. 'What about Felicity?'

He looks suddenly pained. 'Ah, yeah. I've ballsed up a bit, haven't I?'

I must look devastated because he springs forward.

'It's not that bad. I should have organised the party for last night really. Tonight Felicity's got some big family bash so she couldn't come, she really wanted to meet you and Philippa. She's heard loads about you. She said you sound like the coolest person she's ever heard of.'

'Your girlfriend sounds like a freak,' I say trying to sound carefree.

'Felicity isn't my girlfriend. Why do you say that?' he says quickly. 'I like her, as friends, she's fun, but she's not . . . We're not—' He stops, and chuckles to himself. 'You know, I only organised this party to see you! It was all I could think of when we were sat on the pavement. I wanted an excuse to see you soon, so I made up a party for Saturday. But then I realised that I barely knew anyone in town. Except Felicity. And she couldn't even come.'

I'm smiling. I step into his room. I can't stop smiling and it would be really useful if I could.

'OK, I don't know why I'm doing this, really, it's so not cool. It really wasn't cool when I did this before. So the very fact that I'm doing it again lifts me into the premier league of twat. Not that I worry about cool. But, God, anyway . . . what am I saying?!'

I laugh. He watches me.

'Your smile is ... Sorry, I'm all over the place with you. Anyway,' he says, 'have a seat, get into bed, if you fancy. I will be down here.' He sits crossed-legged on the floor and picks up his guitar. 'I wrote you another song. That afternoon after we bumped into each other.'

Now I've stopped dancing I feel cold. I climb into his bed. I'm still smiling.

'Oh, God, I'm not sure why I'm playing it to you ... I love your smile,' he murmurs.

'I love yours too,' I whisper.

He starts to play.

I was out for lunch
Meal deal
Credit crunch

You're there on the floor
And again
I want more
But you look at me
And I freeze
And I stall
Is it only me who sees
What he's looking for?
Then I see your tears
I wanna take them away
I wanna hold you today
Reality's
No cop
I just can't stop

'Bit of a work in progress that. But it's your song,' he says, when he's finished. 'Your other song.'

I climb out of bed and I get down on the floor. I can't do crossed-legged because my skirt is too short, so I kneel. I look into his eyes, his green eyes that are flecked with brown, and I feel my heart beating. I'm experiencing such a longing for him I must look as though I'm in pain. I'm just a girl standing, well, kneeling, in front of a boy asking him to love her. Oddly enough, it feels like the most natural thing in the world. I cup my hand to the side of his face and I lean in. Sod it, let's see if Cher is right. We could all be dead tomorrow and then I'd at least have this moment. This kiss.

'Jenny Taylor,' he says softly pushing me away from him. My breath catches and already I can tell there are tears in my eyes. He doesn't want to kiss me. How have I got this wrong? Even *I* couldn't have got this wrong!

'Jenny Taylor, I could kiss you all night. I would love to kiss you all night, but what I'd really like to do now is ask you out on a date tomorrow.'

'A date!' I gasp.

'Yes, would you come on a date with me tomorrow?'

'I'd love to.'

'Do you have a preference for what we do or shall I surprise you with the itinerary.'

'The itinerary!' I nearly have a kitten.

'Yes, the sequence of the day.'

'Oh, surprise me! If you'd like to.'

'I'd love to . . . I shall pick you up at midday.'

I am only capable of smiling sappily at him.

Chapter 47

It's really, really hot. It's that one randomly baking day in mid June that will end up being summer. And I'm going on a date. I'm wearing a white dress, opportunity for disaster high, but at least I'll be cool. It's a gypsy dress, off the shoulder and above the knee and I'm wearing a battered cowboy hat and sandals. I hope I look all right. Oh, God, there he is. I race down the stairs and meet him on the street. He's wearing a cowboy hat too. And a short-sleeved blue shirt and shorts. I want to kiss him right now, sod the date. I want to haul him back upstairs to bed. The bed that my mother didn't sleep in last night. I know!

'I think we must have the same stylist,' I say, but I'm feeling shy.

'Sack her. She's got this one look that she gives all her clients.'

'Does she give you the Mickey Mouse T-shirt too?' I ask.

'Yeah, and the grey hoodie with everything.'

'And the lacy hot pants.'

'Always the lacy hot pants!' He shakes his head and laughs. 'These are for you.'

He hands me flowers. A tumble of lilacs, pinks and greens.

'I picked them. I wasn't being a tight git. But I thought they'd be nice.'

'They're beautiful. Thank you.'

'I would very much like to see you in those lacy hot pants. Sorry. Pervert. So,' he runs to open the passenger door of the van for me. 'Your carriage awaits. You look beautiful by the way.'

'So do you,' I whisper.

'I organised the weather,' he says once we're both seated in the van. 'Blue sky and sun, now belt up and enjoy the ride. How are you feeling musically? Sunday morning chilled? A little of bit reggae as the sun's out? Or maybe some rock?'

'Um.' I think for a moment. 'A little bit of reggae as the sun's out.'

He flicks his eyes to me.

'Of course, because that's what's in there, that's what I had playing on the way over here. Crazy this, our similarities, don't you think?' Joe smiles.

'Yeah.'

'Good crazy or just crazy crazy?' he asks.

'Definitely good crazy.' I nod. 'I've just never had it before.'

'Me neither.'

'So why do you think we're so alike?'

'Well, I have a theory,' he says.

'I love a theory.'

'Of course you do, because I do too.'

'Tell me this theory,' I say, turning in my seat slightly so I can look at him.

'Well, I think we're made for each other. I think the universe, God, the powers of fate or whatever is at work, made us for each other, and we had to go on our own paths and then, when we least expected it, we had to meet. Even though you were engaged to someone else, and I was working in a chemist in a small town in Tiddlesbury because I'd come to avoid distractions and stay with my uncle in the ramshackle cottage that he'd just bought and write an album. So, we had to meet. And the universe, fate, blah blah whatever didn't want us to miss each other, so they had us wearing the same clothes, you know, so we'd pay attention, and they had you on your knees singing a rock classic. We were made the same right down to the silly names so that there'd be no doubt that we were meant to be together when we met.'

He stops speaking and I can tell he's pleased with his theory.

'What?' he asks.

'I didn't say anything,' I whisper. 'I'm too busy smiling.'

'Tell me everything about yourself.'

'There's nothing to tell.'

'Ah, well, there's no rush. You've got the rest of your life to tell me.'

I look at him and he winks. I laugh, but then I stop laughing.

'There is one thing I have to tell you.'

'What?'

'I slept with Al, the other night. I don't know why I'm telling you except I suppose I don't really like secrets.'

'I know about you and Al.'

'How?'

'He told me.'

'Oh.'

'He felt bad because he thought we liked each other.'

'Ah.'

'Yeah, I like Al, brilliant bloke.'

'Hmm. We had a thing before Matt, and I think we were just putting it to bed.'

'Literally.'

'Yeah. But I just don't want you to think I'm a slut. I'm not a slut. Well, Matt thinks I am. But can you be a slut if you've only slept with three people and one of them did it for a dare? Do you think less of me?'

'Nooo, Fanny. Even if you'd slept with a hundred people I'd still think you were the most awesome woman on the planet. We've both got stories and histories, that's life.'

'I think you're letting me off quite lightly. I mean I slept with my flatmate when I was engaged to someone else and daydreaming about you.'

'Well.' He laughs. 'I was a bit surprised when Al called me and told me. I don't know what I thought he was going to say but I definitely wasn't expecting that. But do you know what, Fan, I tell you honestly. I got off the phone and laughed. One thing you're not is dull. I admit, part of my male pride wished you'd been confused and jumped into bed with me. But I sort of just loved the impetuousness of it and I love your honesty now. Jenny Taylor, I'm not playing very hard to get. I need to work on that. I need to be a bit harder to read.'

I smile.

'What?'

'I didn't say anything. I'm too busy smiling. Where are we?'

'Ah, do you not know my secret spot?'

‘That could be misconstrued.’

‘Cheeky.’

‘How can you have a secret spot when you’ve only just moved here?’

‘Have van will find secret spot so can sit underneath tree and write songs about girl with pink hair. What colour is your hair naturally?’

‘Same as yours.’

‘Of course.’ He parks. I go to open my door.

‘Wait! Wait! I do that.’ And he hops out of the car and races round to my side to open the door. ‘Madam,’ he says, giving me his arm to help me get up. ‘I just need to get some bits from the boot.’

He trots away and reappears with a guitar strapped to his back and holding a cool box.

‘Can I take something?’

‘Nope, the lady goes hands free,’ he says as though he’s knackered and it’s heavy. ‘I can manage.’

We walk along a tiny path, squeeze through a gap between two hedges and then make our way past some trees and suddenly we’re in front of a lake. It’s not a huge lake and it’s overgrown on all sides, but there’s not a soul around and it’s so peaceful. There is no sign of man or anything man-made. It feels as though we’ve stepped back in time.

‘How did you find it?’ I ask.

‘I saw it on a map of the area. I miss the sea. I normally live by the sea. And I like a bit of water. It’s calming.’

‘My mum likes being by the sea.’

‘Yeah, there’s something powerful about standing on the edge of the land.’

'*On the Edge of the Land*. You could call your album that.'

'Bloody hell, I may just do that. It sort of perfectly sums up how I'm feeling at the moment.'

I was thinking the same thing.

'Although the working title I'm using at the moment is . . . '

'What?'

'No, can't tell you, need to play it cooler. So, anyway, I saw on the map that there was a lake here, I thought it would probably be used for fishing. It took me a few trips to find. But I persevered and one day here she was. And I've never seen anyone else here, which strikes me as a bit odd, so we might be attacked by dogs or shot at by snipers. For which I apologise profusely.'

'How can you tell if it's safe to swim in a lake?'

'I think you have to swim in it and see if you die.'

I turn my head to look at him.

'Shall we?' he says as if reading my mind.

I nod.

He unbuttons his shirt. I can't take my eyes off him. I kick my sandals off. He takes his shorts off. He's just down to his black pants. I toss my hat off and pull my dress over my head. I stand in front of him in just my white pants and strapless bra.

'Jenny Taylor, you're the most beautiful girl I've ever met.'

'Joe King, I think I've . . . ' Been in love with you since I first set eyes on you. But I don't say it. I run and I make a bomb into the water instead. When I come up, he's still on the land.

'What's it like?' he asks stepping nearer.

'Ah, ah! Eels,' I shriek, flinging my arms about.

'Oh, my God, are you all right?' he pants, hopping toward me through the reeds.

'Yeah, I'm fine, I was just doing some incredibly good acting,' I say, standing up, so just the tops of my shoulders are out of the water.

Joe wades out to where I am. He stops and stands gazing at me.

'I would just like to say,' he says, stopping and looking up at the blue sky for a moment. 'God, universe, whatever is at work here, I would just like to say, thank you.'

I smile at him.

'Do we wait to kiss or do we kiss now?' he whispers.

'Let's wait,' I whisper back.

He nods.

'For five minutes,' I instruct.

'I don't know whether I can.' He makes an 'eek' face.

'Me neither,' I whisper.

'Shall I time it on my waterproof watch?'

I nod.

And we look at each other for five minutes. We just look into each other's eyes and listen to each other breathing, and you'd think it would be rubbish, but it's glorious and sexy and as though we're merging into one, somehow.

'That's actually five minutes and thirteen seconds,' he says eventually. And he steps forward and cups my face in his hands. At first he kisses my forehead, so softly, then my cheeks, then he tilts my face ever so slightly, so his mouth is near mine. And I can't tell which is his heart or mine or whose breath is whose, and then his lips touch mine and I feel like I'm spinning. I cling onto his back, his shoulders, his hair.

We stand and kiss, until our skin starts to feel like dried fruit and we begin to shiver. He takes my hand and leads me out of the water.

We stop for a moment, there, on the edge of the land, with the sun warming our skin. Joe starts to fidget, he moves some of my sodden hair away from my eyes, he's murmuring words, but he's not looking at me. I can't catch what it is he's saying.

'What was that?' I whisper.

'I was just telling you the working title of my album, it's . . . ' He stops, looks straight into my eyes. 'It's *Love at First Sight*.'

Chapter 48

Mother's still not home! I've been trying to be cool, I really have. I know she needs her independence. I know I can't keep her close to me all the time. And, yes, I know, as Philippa says, that she has needs. I texted Simon the Plasterer three times, he told me she was safe. But then I thought, Of course, he's going to tell you she's safe, Fanny, you tool, while he's ripping up his kitchen floor and burying your mother there. So then I called and asked, well, he said demanded, but I think I was polite but firm, that he put Mum on the phone. And Mum did sound fine, a little sleepy, because it was 8 a.m., but I'm not going to feel bad, it was the second night she'd stayed out. So I spoke to her to arrange the plan for the funeral ambush (her words), but she said she didn't want to help with the funeral today.

'I just don't think I can handle a whole day to do with death, Jenny,' she said. And I sort of get her point. She's menopausal and emotional so she'd probably be a blubbing mess, and she's done so much work already, organising today, that I couldn't bring myself to persuade her. Still it feels like quite a lot of pressure on me now. Al can't take today as a holiday from work. Philippa only has a few hours off to sort out the golf club presentation. So I'll be setting up the entire community centre on my own. It is doable. I hope. I'll just miss Mum, that's all. I've been really enjoying hanging out with my mum recently. I feel as though we've become a little army of two. I never imagined we'd have this friendship. It's like receiving the best present and it's not even my birthday or Christmas. And obviously I want her to be here right now so I can tell her all about the most wonderful man in the universe. Mr Love At First Sight. Ooh, talk of the handsome devil. A text!

I think you said you had some time off work. Would you like to practise kissing today? Xx

I'm ambushing a funeral. Would you like to come? Xx

Did I just read what I thought I read?

We can practise kissing there.

I love kissing at funerals. When do I pick you up?

Half ten.

That's in 20 mins!

And can you dress as though
you're someone from the movie
Grease.

You what?

Very important. A dying
woman's wishes. Think tight
black T-shirt and trousers like
Danny wears at the end.
Sexy . . . Xx

Will you be in the black catsuit?
xx

Might be.

Is it right to be this excited
about a funeral?

Chapter 49

'You're the one that I want,' Joe sings, as he Blu-Tacks a Doris picture to the wall.

I had to ring round all the patients I knew who had been friends with Doris to find the pictures, then Mum took them to Snappy Snaps in Nunstone and had them blown up. I think we did well. One lady knew Doris from the sixties and gave us a lovely photo of her in a minidress eating an ice cream in Brighton. Mum got some extras of that one. She said, 'I made the executive decision that she'd want to be remembered like this, young and smiling, so had a few more done and then I saw the offer they were doing on the personalised badges!' Mum couldn't believe the offer on the badges so now we've two hundred Doris badges with this picture on as well.

'You better shape up!' I sing, well, sing-ish. I walk around the food table, checking we've got everything. 'Right, what's the time? Could you look at your waterproof watch?'

'Shall I just kiss you first? It's the blonde wig. It's getting me going.'

Well, it's impossible to do Sandy with raspberry hair, you

can only do Frenchie, and no one chooses to go to a *Grease* party as Frenchie, so I'm wearing my blonde wig. I love a wig and I'm very excited that Joe King does too.

'Yes, I thought you'd never ask, it's been about four minutes since you last kissed me.'

'It's quite hard to control myself for four minutes with you in that catsuit.'

He walks across the empty community centre dance floor, kicking some balloons out of the way as he goes. He reaches me and we stand smiling at each other.

'I think I've spent my whole life waiting for your smile,' he whispers and then he puts his lips on mine. 'Hmmm,' he says. 'Was that a bit cheesy? You're making me very cheesy, Jenny Taylor.'

We kiss some more.

'I think you're a little bit more handsome than you were four minutes ago,' I whisper, because I have completely turned into a tool. I speak a load of tosh and most of the time I speak it as though I am five. 'Ooh, what time did you say it was?'

'Um, um, half past one.'

'I think we've done everything we can for now. The Rod Stewart impersonator should be here at two.'

'You've got a Rod Stewart impersonator coming?'

'Yep, every good funeral should have one. And Doris loved him. Well, she loved the real thing but we couldn't get him. We did try.'

'That I am looking forward to seeing.'

'Ah, well, we won't see him. We have to go now.'

'Where are we going?'

'Dunno. Wherever you want?'

'But you've organised this, aren't you going to stay?'

I shake my head. 'I can't.'

'Why? I think Doris would want you to be here.'

'Ah well, yes, she would. But . . . Hmm . . . It's complicated.'

'Try me.'

'I've been asked to steer clear of the family. They're hoping to sue the surgery.'

'But you were so close to her . . .'

'Wait, it gets even more complicated. Doris' grandson broke my heart when I was seventeen and as if that wasn't enough, he married the girl in my year who used to bully me.'

'Oh, baby, come here.'

He holds me.

'If you want to face them, I'd hold your hand.'

I love that he said that. But . . .

'Ah, well, it's not so much a question of me getting the courage to face them now, as me not wanting to get thumped. You see, the thing is, they've booked a tea at the golf club. They think the reception is going to be at the golf club. But Doris couldn't stand the golf club and she wanted a full-on boozy bash, and I did tell them but there was a non-refundable deposit on the sodding golf club and they wouldn't change it. So Philippa had to chat up a guy who works on the bar there and pretend she was a relative, and, anyway, when everyone gets there they're going to play a video of Doris talking about the big bash she planned. Then Philippa will tell them all to come here. Hence the ambush.'

'Wow. Yeah, that was complicated.'

'Yeah.'

'Wow,' he says again, I can tell he's trying to get it all straight in his head.

'Hmmmm.'

'It's pretty massive what you're doing,' Joe whispers.

'I know. Let's just think positive.'

'It'll be fine,' he says stroking my back. 'It'll be fine.'

'Yeah, hopefully.'

'Wow.'

'Yeah.'

'No, I was wowing you that time.'

'How do you mean?"

'I didn't think anyone as awesome as you existed, Jenny Taylor.'

He kisses my nose. I can't speak because I'm smiling.

Chapter 50

I've had only two texts from Philippa today. The first one said:

Screen's up. Video's ready. Bar guy who's 17 just asked if he could touch my boob!!!

The second one said:

Played video. Michelle KICKED OFF . . . got to get back to work . . . they're driving a RAGE Rover . . . watch out! Gd luck! xxx

I got that fouteen minutes ago, and the first few cars are pulling up now. Joe's inside, the Rod Stewart impersonator is late so he's putting on a Rod Stewart CD to tide us over. I'm standing by Joe's van in the far corner of the car park, watching in the wings. I lean my head against the cool bodywork and close my eyes for a moment.

'Hey, Doris,' I whisper. 'I hope I did the right thing. I hope you enjoy your party.'

When I open my eyes again Joe's standing in the doorway of the community centre doing a drinking sign. I put my thumb up in response and shout the word champagne. He darts back inside. A man with long blonde hair, a lot of fake tan and a white suit gets out of an old Escort. Here's Rod! He walks to his car boot and takes out some black equipment boxes. I look down the road and I can't see a Range Rover so I dash quickly across the car park to help Rod with his equipment. Oo-er.

'Hello, I think you spoke to my mum on the phone. I'm Fanny.'

'Mick, pleased to meet you.'

I try to take one of his bags.

'No, you're all right, love. Just lead the way.'

He stands waiting for me to show him where to go. But I freeze. I've just spied a Range Rover driving too fast in this direction.

'Oh, just go through those doors and you'll see the stage. People should start arriving in a minute,' I say, already jogging away from him.

'Ah, hello there, mate,' I hear Joe call out. 'Come in here. Let's take a bag off you.'

I stand back against the van, catching my breath. I don't know what to do. If I get in the van I might draw attention to myself. But then again if they look over here, I've nowhere to hide.

The Range Rover parks very near the hall. Michelle Cullet flies out of the driver's seat, slamming the door. She's inside in seconds. Steve walks slowly round the back of the car and stops. He's looking in this direction. I'm wearing a blonde wig and I'm dressed as Sandy from *Grease*, he might not know it's me. God, he looks sad. He looks as though he can barely lift his limbs. I know that feeling. I could almost sympathise. He takes a step towards me, and then another. I used to love his face. During the entire time I was at secondary school, Steve Wilmot had his picture in the school magazine twice, once when he was fourteen and once when he was sixteen. I cut out both pictures and kept them under my bed. I knew his face so well. I wonder whether Michelle loves him as I would have loved him.

He quickens his step towards me. Quite a lot of cars are arriving now.

'Is it you?' he says. He's only a few feet away.

I don't answer.

'Jenny?'

I used to love the way he said my name. I used to think that he said my name as though he liked me.

'Jenny.'

I close my eyes.

'Jenny.'

He's really close now.

'Wow,' he whispers. 'You look like a model.'

I don't respond but a part of me knows I'll revisit that comment at a later date and it will have me dancing around the flat.

'You really do, Jenny.'

'Steve!' It's Michelle calling from the entrance. 'There's a bloody Rod Stewart lookalike in here! Steve!' She's walking quickly towards us when suddenly she stops.

'Oh, it's you,' she shouts. 'Blonde now, are you?'

I don't reply.

'So was this all you?'

I don't feel like a scared girl any more. I feel like Jenny Taylor being shouted at by a bully. But this time she can't hurt me.

'Do you know how stupid we looked in there?'

Oh no, a tiny smile escaped my lips.

'Go on,' I say.

'What?'

'Say whatever you want to say, Michelle.'

It seems to throw her for a moment.

'You've got a bloody cheek.'

Funny, I spent my time at school not being able to say boo to a fish. Hearing that I've got a 'bloody cheek' is rather flattering.

'Thank you. And you should probably thank me for organising the funeral Steve's gran wanted.'

'Thank you?'

'Yes.' I turn to Steve now. 'What were you thinking trying to do it at the golf club after we told you what she wanted?' I ask the question gently.

'We'd booked the golf club. It's a non-refundable deposit,' Michelle blusters.

'I'm not having a go. But I'm not going to apologise for what I did.'

I start to smile because Joe is jogging towards me.

'Hello, hello.' He nods to both Steve and Michelle. 'I'm Joe.' He slides his arm around my waist.

'Are you all right,' he whispers to me, obviously feeling the tension.

'Yeah, I'm good, thank you. This is Steve and Michelle.'

'I'm really sorry to hear about your gran, mate,' Joe says.

Steve nods.

'I hear she was quite a girl.'

Steve smiles and nods again.

'I mentioned to Rod Stewart that I played guitar, he was wanting me to play a few numbers with him. But I told him we had to make a move,' Joe tells me. I nod in reply.

'You should go in and thank people for coming,' I say to Steve.

'Don't tell him what to do!' screeches Michelle.

'Come in with us,' Steve says to me.

'I don't want her coming in!'

'Shhhh. Come in,' Steve repeats, and then he looks at Joe. 'And you, you have to play with old Rod in there.'

Joe looks at me. I look at Steve.

'Thank you,' I tell him. 'I'd really love that.'

The four of us stand rooted to the spot for a few moments. Joe breaks the silence.

'Shall I lead you in, gorgeous?' he says, cocking an arm for me.

'You certainly can, handsome.'

We walk towards the entrance of the hall.

'You're the one that I want,' Joe sings in my ear.

'Ooo, ooo, ooo.'

Chapter 51

'That Steve bloke can't take his eyes off you.'

We're smoochy dancing to 'We Are Sailing' along with most of the town. I only booked Rod until 6 p.m. He did stop at 6 p.m. and I paid him, but then he said he'd carry on for free as we were such an appreciative audience. It's 7.30 now and he's still going. Although he's assured us that this is definitely his last number. Doris would have been so proud. It's the sort of night where children are made.

'That Steve bloke's missus, the bulldog, is going to give him a right rollicking unless he stops looking at your bottom,' Joe whispers in my ear.

'Is he looking at my arse?'

'Yeah, but he's not the only one. Your bottom in that catsuit is the stuff of schoolboy fantasies. I have been trying very hard all day not to grab it.'

'You can have a little grab.'

'No, I'm a gentleman. Besides I'd want to unwrap the bottom. Best leave it till later.'

'I can't wait until we . . . you know . . . '

'Until we have our first row in a DIY home store?'

'Yes, how did you guess?'

We stop and applaud the Rod Stewart impersonator. I do my wolf whistle. The ovation goes on for quite some time. Steve Wilmot, of all people, has made his way to the sound system, presumably to put a CD on. A few people drift off to the toilets or the bar but most of the crowd on the dance floor stay where they are, waiting for more music.

'Well, let me tell you what I can't wait for,' Joe says huskily in my ear. 'I can't wait until we have a whole night together. I want to explore every bit of you until you squeak that you can't take it any more.'

'I'm not really a squeaker. I'd probably scream.'

'When you've screamed "I can't take it any more!"'

'Why have I got an American accent?'

'I'm such a good lover it happens. Anyway, once you're screaming I want to slide my massive and humungous penis gently inside you and hold you close so I can hear your uneven breath and then I'm going to tell you that you're the most beautiful woman in the world and then I'm going to give you fifteen orgasms.'

'That's quite a lot to live up to.'

'I know. You might have to bear with me. It could be over in the first twenty seconds.'

'We'd just have to do it again.'

'Oh yes, I think I'd make the forty-five-second mark the next time.'

'Well, then we'd just have to do it again.'

I kiss him on the mouth.

'And again,' he says.

'Oooh, how appropriate, someone's put on Tom Jones, "Sex Bomb",' I snigger.

'Fanny, he's back staring at your arse. At what point should I tell him to stop staring at your bottom?'

'Oh, that I don't know. I don't think The Child Of Destiny mention it in any of their work.'

'The Child of Destiny?'

'Destiny's Child.'

'Oh.'

'The *Survivor* album in particular is practically a bible for the modern woman.'

'But they don't mention how long a fella's allowed to stare at a girl's bottom before he gets a talking to?'

'Not unless it's very subtly put and I missed it.'

'I have to go and say something. I mean how would he feel if I stared at bulldog's arse for half the night?'

Joe releases me.

'I'll be friendly,' he says in my ear. 'Just a little . . . Oh, will you look at that. Bulldog must have read my mind. Ouch.'

I turn around in time to see Steve clutching the side of his face and Michelle storming out of the community centre.

'Ah, that's harsh, hitting a man at his gran's funeral,' Joe says. 'She could have just had a gentle word.'

'Michelle Cullet,' I tell Joe wisely, 'wouldn't know a gentle word if it shoved itself up her—'

Joe kisses me on the lips, cutting me off.

'Such a pretty girl,' he says. 'Such a filthy mouth.'

'I have to tell you, this is one of the best nights I've ever done,' the Rod Stewart impersonator says, striding towards us. 'Argggggghhhhhh.'

Woah. He's just been whisked away and spun around by one of Doris' friends from bridge club, a well-built pensioner in a cheerleader's outfit. Our Rod Stewart impersonator looks very concerned as to whether he'll get out alive. I can't blame him. There are over fifty women on the dance floor, the majority being over seventy and all of them full of cheap, fizzy wine; any man who steps on the dance floor is devoured by bingo wings, handbags and sod-the-hip-replacement dance moves. Most men are choosing to congregate around the bar, cheerfully moaning about the lack of beer.

'He won't be getting out of here in a hurry,' Joe King muses, surveying the scene, and Joe should know. He spent the best part of the last hour being passed around the bowling ladies. Dr Flemming has been dancing since he arrived after the surgery closed. Marge is line dancing with some of the old girls from the surgery. She's gone for the sexy Sandy catsuit as well. Her massive bazooms and rolls of Lycra-ed flesh have been flying about the dance floor for hours.

Now that Michelle has left, Steve Wilmot has started working his way around the sides of the room, shaking guests' hands and thanking them for coming. I watch him, Joe King next to me squeezing my hand. It's ten years ago this summer since he broke my heart. For years afterwards I'd lie in bed at night and close my eyes and revisit the pain and humiliation. But now there are ten whole years between me and that event; days upon days and days. What was once a raw, red wound has now healed to just a thin little white scar that you can barely notice. I look at Steve tonight and all is see is an overweight, tired, sad-looking man.

'Poor bugger,' Joe says.

'Indeed.'

'What's going on in the corner there?' Joe asks, pointing at a huddle of elderly pink ladies busying themselves around a table.

'Jägerbombs in plastic cups for all.'

'Well, of course.' He chuckles. 'Er, Fan . . . '

'What? Why are you looking all guilty?'

'I'm not. I just need to establish whether or not you'll still want to go out with me if I go up on the stage and take the mike for a minute. I don't want to embarrass you.'

'You couldn't embarrass me, Handsome Pants.'

'I love a challenge, Sweet Cheeks.'

'What are you going to do?'

'Surprise!' he calls. He's already jogging towards the stage.

He mounts the stairs two at time, lunges at the amp, fiddles with some knobs so that Tom Jones stops sex bombing and then picks up the microphone and spins round to face us. He smiles cheekily at the crowd beneath him on the dance floor. There are a fair few female murmurs of approval. I do one of my wolf whistles. He winks. One of the ladies on the floor shouts, 'Hello, sailor.' People laugh. Joe holds the mike to his mouth for a few moments while everyone settles. Then he starts singing.

'Summer loving, had me a blast . . . '

Everyone, it really does sound like everyone, cheers. Even Dr Flemming and he's normally such a quiet man. But it's Marge's screams that can be heard above them all. She's quickly waddling up the stairs to the stage. Joe stands open-mouthed as Marge, flushed and a little sweaty, snatches the microphone out of his hand and delivers the next line of the song into it herself. The over-seventies are screaming in delight. The pair go on to perform the whole song, the rest of us joining in for the 'awella wella ahs!' Marge wraps one of her legs around both of Joe's at the end and plonks a huge kiss on his cheek.

One of the pink ladies, who was busy pouring the drinks in the corner, taps me on the arm. 'They're ready, over there, they are, we thought you might like to propose a toast, since you did all this work,' she tells me.

'Oh, I don't know whether it should be me . . . ' I say, but she pats me on the elbow towards the stage. I walk up to Joe on the stage and take the microphone out of his hand.

'Um, hello, hello, could everyone just go and pick up a plastic cup from that table. We're going to have a toast,' I say quickly into the microphone, and then I run back down onto the dance floor, careful to dodge the stumbling exodus of people moving from the dance floor to the drinks table and back again.

I spot Steve. He was already looking at me. I walk towards him. I hold the microphone out. Surely he should be doing this toast.

'Will you do the toast?' I say.

But he shakes his head and nods towards me as if to say go ahead. I stay where I am.

'She'd like you to do it,' I whisper.

I see the muscles in his neck tighten briefly and then after a few moments he nods.

'Will you come up there with me?' he asks.

'Yeah, if you want.'

We take two full cups from the drinks table and climb up

the stairs to the stage. I hand the microphone to Steve and step back. I look at all the flushed, excited faces and a little smile escapes my lips.

'To Doris,' Steve says raising his glass. A hundred voices echo his words.

'I hope you're enjoying this, Doris,' I whisper, so that no one can hear me. 'The only thing that's missing is you.'

Chapter 52

You know that thing I can't wait
to do to you??

Have a stinking great row in B & Q
or give me 6 million orgasms?

I think I said 15 . . .

Yes?

May I take you away at some
point and ravish you?

This is the photo of the smile
that text just gave me.

Beautiful.

Do you want to pick me up now?

I was thinking tomorrow. I'll pick you up at 4 p.m.

How can I cope till then???

Xxxxxxxxxxxxxxxxxxxxxxxxxx
all of these to be applied to your body tomorrow.

Chapter 53

'Did you think this was cheesy?'

'What? Bringing me to a hotel with a four-poster bed?'

'Yeah?'

'And log fires, and champagne and big fluffy bathrobes and a free-standing bath.'

'Yeah?'

'Yes. Very cheesy.'

'Really?'

'But I bloody love your cheese.'

'You bloody love my cheese? That is a remark that could be misconstrued.'

'Most of my remarks could be misconstrued.'

'What does your mother think of your dirty mind?'

'It's my mother's mind that needs the good clean.'

'She sounds like my sort of girl. When am I going to meet her?'

'Um, I don't know. Whenever you want. I haven't seen her properly for days myself, not since I went on a date with this bloke, Joe King's his name. Since then my mother's been eclipsed.'

'Do apologise from me.'

'I shall.'

'We could take her out.'

'Say that again.'

'We could take your mum out, somewhere nice.'

'Are you just the most perfect man in the universe?'

'I hate to tell you this.'

'What?'

'Yes, I am.'

'And I hate to tell you this.'

'What?'

'You owe me thirteen more orgasms.'

'Coming up,' he says, rolling on top of me. He pulls his torso away from me suddenly and regards me with a quizzical expression.

'Fanny,' he asks. 'What are you doing?'

'I'm pinching myself,' I say, as I squeeze a good inch of the soft skin on my upper arm.

'Why?'

'I just can't believe this is real, you and me.'

'Don't pinch yourself. Don't hurt my girlfriend. It is all real, baby.'

'I'm a bit scared, Joe King.'

'Why are you scared, Jenny Taylor?'

'I'm so high, so happy. I'm dizzy up here with you. I'm worried how far there is to fall.'

'I'll catch you,' he says and then he tenderly kisses my lips. 'You know, I think if we're always honest with each other, with how we're feeling, then there's nothing to be scared of. Nothing at all.'

'I like the sound of that.'

'Me too.'

'I hate secrets and lies more than anything.'

'Hmmm. Me too.'

'I should tell you something,' I say, all of a sudden very serious.

'What?'

'It's quite embarrassing. And you'll probably think less of me. But I'd like you to know, for some reason.'

He nods and leans on his elbow by my side, giving me his undivided attention. Then I take a deep breath and I tell him my story.

How I had a breakdown just before my eighteenth birthday, followed by a spell when I was very depressed. I tell him how ashamed I felt during that time, ashamed that I couldn't pick myself up, dust myself off, cheer up, pull myself together. How shame was the overriding thing I remember about that time, that and the feeling that everybody would be better off without me. And it's funny because as I'm telling him, I don't feel ashamed. It's as though depression has become part of my story, part of who I am, just another fact about me. I tell him how I got better. How Dr Flemming helped. And I tell him how grateful I am to Philippa. Grateful isn't even the word. Words always fall short when it comes to describing what Philippa means to me. And then I tell him how, since that time, I'd always avoided falling in love. Until now.

And when I finish my lengthy dialogue, I look at him and

he's still there. He hasn't got dressed and run outside to hail a cab to take him far from me. He's there by my side.

'Thank you,' he says. 'For telling me that.'

'Not many gags in that story. Need to put a few knob gags in it to liven it up really.'

'I really do think you're amazing, Jenny Taylor.'

'Excellent! Now, I'd like thirteen orgasms, please!' I say arching my back like a cat.

Chapter 54

'I can't believe you made scones!'

'Sc-ohns,' he mimics. 'They're sconns, love.'

'Can't believe you made sconns, love!'

We've invited Mum to cream tea at Rose Cottage. She seemed really excited.

'Do you think she'd like it in the garden?'

'Yes, let's put a blanket down and have it on the grass. Ooh, she'll love it. Will you play guitar for her?'

'Do you think she could bear it?'

'Shut up,' I say, moving towards him and putting my arms around his waist. I kiss him gently on the lips. 'She'd love it.'

We kiss again and within seconds it's a full-on snogging-in-the-kitchen situation. The last few days have been like this. Four minutes of activity, and by activity I mean putting the kettle on or running a bath or going to the shop, followed by twenty minutes of kissing and flattery. It's very hard to get anything done, but blimey, it's ... I can't think of a word ... heavenly, blissful, magnificent, glorious? They all fall short.

'We should get the cream and jam set up.'

'Hmmm.'

More kissing.

'We'll just kiss for one more minute,' Joe whispers. 'And then we'll have to give me time for . . . '

'For your erection to disappear,' I answer. 'Seems such a waste. Especially when I'm owed two more orgasms.'

'No,' he says, pushing me away from him and turning towards the scones on the work surface. 'I can't have talk of you orgasming or your mother will feel quite uncomfortable when she meets me.'

'Oh, I want to do more kissing,' I say like a sulky child.

'Beautiful girl,' he says, leaving the scones, and sliding his arms around me this time. 'Beautiful, beautiful girl, when your mother goes, we shall move the blanket to the end of the garden under the apple trees where no one in the world can see us and then there will be plenty more kissing . . . in all sorts of places.'

We're kissing again. The doorbell rings.

'I'll get it.' I giggle.

'OK,' he says stepping back to the food. 'I'm on scones and serious erection deflating duties.'

'I'll keep her in the front garden. We'll sniff jasmine, come out when you're ready,' I say, moving towards him for a final little kiss before I see him again in two minutes.

'Back! Keep back, seductress! Away!'

'Oh, no kisses for Jenny!' I whimper as I go to answer the door. Mum looks lovely. She's wearing the floral dress I haven't been able to wear since I dyed my hair raspberry. I tried it on but the oranges and reds near my hair looked a bit extreme.

'Wow, that dress is gorgeous on you. Have it.'

'No, you don't want to give it to me.'

'You have to have it. It looks so good on you. It's clearly decided it's yours.'

She's wearing my cowboy hat, too, and my sandals.

'Do you mind I borrowed the hat?'

'No, I'm glad, but you can't have that, because I love it.'

I give her a kiss on the cheek and as I do I whisper, 'I can't wait for you to meet Joe, Mum.'

'I can't wait either.' She giggles.

'He'll be out in a sec. He's just waiting for his erection to go down.'

'Oh, Jenny!'

'Sorry, too much information?'

'Perhaps a touch.'

'But I'm glad things are . . .'

'Working,' I suggest.

We both giggle like teenagers.

Suddenly a shadow falls over Mum's face.

'Well, hello, there,' Joe says, striding out of the house.

'Joe, this is my mum.'

Mum takes her hat off and they look at each other properly for the first time. There's a bit of an awkward pause. I regard them both. I wonder what's going through their heads. They both look quite serious. I reckon Joe is regarding my mother physically, because they say that women turn into their mothers. I feel quite proud though, if I end up looking like my Mum does today, I'll be doing quite all right, thank you. And I suppose Mum is wondering if Joe is really one of the good ones, because that's what we women wonder about men. But she doesn't need to worry. Joe is one of the best ones. The best one, in fact.

'Shall we get the blanket out?' I say, eventually.

'Yes, I'll go and get the stuff,' Joe offers. He turns back into the house.

I spin round to Mum.

'Isn't he gorgeous!' I exclaim.

But Mum has a faraway look in her eye.

'What's up?'

She shakes herself slightly. 'Nothing, I, er, he, er, he reminds me of someone, that's all. Couldn't think who . . . '

'Hmmm, I think you'll find he's totally unique,' I say proudly. 'Although he's been working a bit in the chemist on the High Street so you could have seen him around. Smell that jasmine, there, it's heady. I'll go and give him a hand with the stuff.'

I skip back into the house, Joe is concentrating on squeezing everything onto a tray.

'Hey,' I say, sidling up behind him and placing a palm on each of his bottom cheeks.

'Huh?' he says, turning.

'What's up with you? Are you being shy?' I ask.

'What? No. I just thought I recognised your mum then.'

'Oh, she said that too. You must have seen each other around Tidds.'

'Yeah,' he says, turning to me. But he's not looking at me, he's looking through me.

'Earth to Joe King,' I say, waving my hand over his face.

'Sorry,' he says and then he shakes himself just like my mum did.

'Let's take the stuff out,' I suggest.

'Yeah, oh, your phone's been beeping,' he tells me as he picks up the tray.

I walk to my bag, which is hanging on the back of a chair. I take my phone out. Joe walks back out into the garden. I'll leave them for a bit. He and Mum can work out where they know each other from. I glance at the screen on my phone. Two texts. From Matt.

Jenny. I miss you.

It knocks the smile from my face. I feel so sublime and there he is hurting. Is it right to feel this much pleasure at the expense of someone else's pain?

I can't bring myself to cancel the wedding. Can we talk?

I plonk myself into the chair. Do I want to talk to Matt? I can't tell him what he wants to hear. I rub my forehead with my fingers. I've never been in this situation before. I don't know the best course to follow. I'll talk to Philippa before I respond, I decide, and I place my phone back in my bag. Then I skip back out to see my lovely mum and ridiculously gorgeous boyfriend.

Chapter 55

In all honesty, Joe and Mum meeting wasn't the love-in I had anticipated. That's the problem, isn't it, when you visualise something as being sensational it invariably falls short? I mean, it was fine. It was quite nice. However, I was hoping for more than 'fine' and 'nice'. If truth be told, conversation was a little bit stilted although we did all agree that the scones were amazing, so that was something. And today is the first day that Joe and I haven't spent together. We decided that he needed to write some music and I should spend some quality time with Mum. Obviously he's been there, topless and smiling, in my head for the entire day. Now, Mum and I are at the Nunstone pub quiz with Al and Philippa. Al is convinced that tonight's the night to snatch the cash prize, but that's looking very unlikely as we've barely been able to answer a question. Although that could well be my fault, because I'm too busy enjoying this truly lovely fantasy where Joe and I have rented a cottage somewhere by the sea, we sit on the beach in the evenings and light a bonfire, which I doubt is legal, but we snuggle up in blankets by it anyway, toasting marshmallows while Joe plays his guitar. And Philippa's been all jittery because Disgruntled Dave called her and said he was coming here tonight.

'Any idea, Fan?' Al asks.

'Sorry, what?' I say.

'She's lost in Joe King land.' Philippa moans.

'What's the question?'

'Who's that?' Al pushes the piece of paper covered with photocopied faces towards me.

'He looks so familiar to me,' Mum says, shaking her head with a pained expression. 'But it could just be someone I met a lifetime ago.'

Should I be worried about Mother's memory, I wonder.

'Oh, Larry Lemon, he's a comedian,' I say, as soon as I look at it. 'I think. Looks like it anyway. That's a hard one though, it's such a blurry photo. But I think it's Larry Lemon. He's not really a household name.'

'It's definitely Larry Lemon,' Philippa confirms. 'The comedian's comedian.'

'A bit like me,' Al says, writing the name down next to the face.

'Um, no, not really.' Philippa laughs.

'Now, if I could draw your attention to this face here.'

'H from Steps,' I say.

'Thank you!' Al sings shrilly, writing down the answer.

'Should I go to the bar? It looks quiet,' I suggest.

Al places his head in his hands. 'I need to do the quiz with blokes.' He weeps.

'Here, take my purse,' offers my mum.

'You sure?' I check.

'Please. I haven't bought a drink yet.'

'Marvel-arse.'

I walk to the bar. I have to climb over three people sitting on the floor. This pub gets packed when the quiz is on. One girl looks up at me as I'm trying to avoid her legs. We lock eyes. Oh, my goodness, it's Trudi, the girl I gave the Smiling Fanny Manifesto to when she was having a drink with Matt before we got together. She's so pretty. It's her skin. Some women have all the luck. It's like someone's poured caramel into cream. So unfair. If she did skincare adverts everyone would buy the products. I give a tight smile and rush away to the bar. The problem with the creamy-skinned goddess is that she is the only person, aside from Philippa and me, who knows that we give out anonymous notes. She may have told people. Not that it really matters, I suppose. Once I'm at the bar, I discreetly turn back and look at her. She's huddled over the quiz paper laughing with two chaps. It makes me smile. She looks so much happier now than she did the day I gave her the Smiling Fanny Manifesto.

I order a bottle of wine and a pint for Al and am just trying to find a safe way to carry them when a voice says, 'Fanny, let me give you a hand.' It's Dave.

'Hi! How are you?' I smile. 'How's it going?'

'It does not go too badly, here, let me take this, you can't manage all that.' He takes the wine bottle from me. And he smiles.

'Blimey, you look well.'

'Yes, I'm OK.'

'Oh, are you still doing that list thing?'

'I am, I am.' He nods, then chuckles. 'Who'd have thought?'

We're at the table now. Philippa licks her lips and Mum smiles warmly at him. Al's engrossed in the quiz.

'Right, well, I've got some good news, ladies. The Tiddlesbury Tour tape that you sent me, Pam. You were right, it's fantastic. I showed it to my boss and he loved it.'

'You didn't . . . ?' I say.

'Oh, my goodness,' Philippa whispers.

'You two have really got something on screen. A priceless chemistry, is actually what he said.'

'A priceless chemistry,' I echo. Obviously the chemistry between Philippa and me is priceless to me, but for someone else to say it. Someone who works in television. Wow.

'So what should they do now?' Mum asks.

'He said the pair of you should think about getting an agent,' Dave tells us.

'Yes, I thought that.' Mum nods her head.

'Oh, my goodness,' Philippa says again.

'I don't believe it,' I whisper.

And then, at exactly the same time, we both whisper the words, 'Fantasy alternative life number one'.

'That's what he said was great, that thing they do when they both speak together,' Dave tells Mum.

I sit blinking. Dave's not joking. Philippa and I might be able to get an agent and possibly, maybe, you never know, might be able to do some television presenting. It's a dream I haven't even allowed myself to have for ten years. Philippa catches my eye and winks.

'Blimey,' I whisper back.

Chapter 56

'Oh, Al! Stop the car!' I scream. We're outside Rose Cottage. Philippa groans.

'We've had a whole day apart. That's quite enough,' I say, starting to open the car door.

'Oh, no, love, come back with us. We'll have a cup of tea,' Mum suggests.

I look at my mum. I do want to have a cup of tea with her. But I also want to feel Joe King's lips on mine. And kissing beats tea every time, I'm afraid.

'Sorry,' I say with an apologetic wince.

'Let her go to Lover Boy.' Philippa giggles. 'See you, Fan.'

Philippa is in a great mood. Dave suggested they go for lunch to talk about the article they'll be putting in the *Tiddlesbury Times* and she said that if we become presenters, not only will it be jokes, but she'll definitely get a book deal. She says celebrities always get book deals. God, this jasmine is divine. I stand and wrestle with it until I've pulled a good-sized bunch off. We can have it in a vase by the bed tonight. Ooh, bed tonight, goody!

'*Fan!*' It's Philippa running down the path.

'What you doing here?'

'You have to come back.'

'Why?'

'Bit of an altercation.'

'Ooh, an altercation! What sort of altercation?'

'Steve Wilmot is crying outside your flat.'

'You what?'

'Drunk and disorderly and calling your name.'

'Fanny or Jenny?'

'Jenny.'

'Oh, would have been quite funny if it had been Fanny. Do I have to come back?'

'I think you might be the only one who can shut him up.'

'Oh, but I want to see Joe, do you think Al will bring me back after?'

'I'm sure he will.'

I follow her unwillingly to the car where Al and Mum are waiting.

It's true. Steve Wilmot is stood outside the kebab shop staring up at my flat, he's clutching a polystyrene kebab box and sobbing to the point of hiccups, while a chap who's waiting for his kebab shouts. 'She's not worth it, mate.'

'Oooooh,' I mewl as I observe the scene from the car.

'We'll wait in the car, Fan-Tastic, we're back-up if you need it.'

'I love you, Al, thank you.'

I get out of the car slowly.

'Steve,' I call as I cross the road towards him.

'Jenny!' He lollops into the road to greet me.

'Let's try to stay on the pavement,' I say as I engineer him back to the curb. 'Steve, what are you doing here?'

'Jenny.' He belches. 'You're beautiful.'

For years I entertained this fantasy that Steve Wilmot was going to realise that we were destined to be together and woo me with words such as these. Never in this fantasy was he reeking of booze and holding a lamb shish. As if reading my mind he offers me a bit of the lamb shish. I shake my head.

'Will you hold it for me?'

'Oh,' I say, taking his food parcel.

He reaches into his back pocket and produces his wallet.

'I didn't want the money, Jenny! I never wanted that money!'

He's holding a handful of notes out to me.

'Take it. Take this money. I wish I'd given it to you years ago. I didn't do it for the money. I really liked you. But then Michelle told me she was pregnant and I was only seventeen and I didn't know what to do. Oh, Jenny! I cocked it all up.'

Tears are rolling down his cheeks. He drops his body slowly down until he is sitting on the curb.

'I'm so sorry,' he repeats.

I look about me, not knowing what to do, and then I sit down beside him. I pat him once on the back.

'It's OK, Steve, it's OK.'

'It's not, Jenny. I heard you were really bad after. Had a nervous breakdown or something. Jenny, I felt so bad.'

I watch him for a few moments and then I sigh. And then I try to explain something I've been thinking more and more recently.

'It wasn't all because of you, Steve.' I stop and swallow. 'I'd been bullied for years and my dad was horrid to me too. And I think the thing with you was the last straw. If it hadn't been you, I'm pretty sure it would have been something else.'

'But you were going to go to college. You never went to college.'

'Steve, it's in the past. Please, leave it there.'

'You never went to college,' he wails. 'You never went to college.'

'Steve,' I say, softly. 'You need to go home.'

'I've left her.'

'Steve, well maybe you should go back to her.'

'Can I stay with you?' he asks in a baby voice.

'Steve, I've got a boyfriend. I'm happy now. Go back to Michelle.'

'But you're beautiful.'

'You made your choice,' I say softly.

He sobs into his hands again. There's nothing else I can say to him. There's nothing else I want to say to him. And even if there was he'd be too drunk to comprehend it. What can I do? Except turn around and head for the car. Life is all about choices, isn't it? Mum made the wrong choice with Dad. I made the wrong choice being with Matt. But I could whoop for joy that I've got it right this time with Joe King.

Al drops me off again at Rose Cottage. I pick up my big bunch of jasmine.

'Take two,' I mutter as I knock on the door. There's a bit of a wait before Joe appears, in jeans, a hoodie and a cardigan, looking tousled and a little bit better than perfect.

'Lady for hire,' I say with a big grin.

He furrows his brow.

'I thought this was our day away from each other,' he says, pushing his hair out of his eyes, but he's smiling.

'Ah ha, yes, but it's night now,' I say. I'm so cunning.

He closes his eyes and scrunches his face up. 'But, babe, I'm in the middle of writing.'

His shoulders slump forward.

'Well, I could just snuggle in your bed until such a time when you're finished and then I could soothe your aching guitar-playing shoulders with a massage, and then I could . . . I could . . . well, I could suck your willy.'

His shoulders slump forward even more.

'Are my blow jobs that bad?' I exclaim.

'No,' he chuckles sadly. 'Your blow jobs are out of this world . . . it's just . . . ' He sighs.

I stop smiling.

'Joe, what's up?'

Something's definitely up. He was funny with Mum, we never moved the rug to under the trees after she left and it was he who suggested we have today apart. It most certainly wasn't me.

He sighs again and it's the sort of sigh that sends a cold shiver down my body.

'Come on, if we're honest with each other, we'll be fine, you said,' I remind him gently.

'Come in,' he says, but unwillingly.

I don't move. Why do I sense doom?

'Tell me what's the matter.'

He tenses his jaw. 'I just . . . oh God.'

He puts his hands to his face and shakes his head. 'I don't . . . I just . . . ' he says, his face still behind his hands. He releases them and looks at me. A sad, resigned face. 'I'm just having doubts, that's all.'

'Doubts?'

'Yes, a bit of a wobble.'

'Wobble?'

'Hmmm. It's all so sudden and I came here to write. I really want to do an album . . . I shouldn't be falling in love.'

It's my turn to slump. I think I might faint, or fall, or die. Jesus.

'Jenny, I'm so sorry.'

Sorry. SORRY!

I'm breathing deeply. I'm spinning.

'Jenny, come in and sit down.'

I shake my head. I'm really dizzy now. I think somewhere along the line the deep breathing stopped and all breathing ceased.

'Jenny, come in, let me explain.'

But, I'm backing away down the drive. I turn from him. I get to the gate. I know he's still there, I haven't heard the front door close, and the light from the doorway is still being hurled down the path at me. It's better at the gate. I have something to lean on and cling to.

'Do you really mean this?' I say, suddenly spinning back to face him.

He looks in pain. He does. As though he doesn't want to do this. Then why is he doing it?

He nods.

'Why did you do this?' I cry, but not cry with tears. There

are no tears. Just my strangled voice. As though someone is killing me. 'Why?'

He shakes his head. He's got tears, they sparkle on his cheeks. All he can do is shake his head. I turn away. I open the gate and walk through it.

It was all so inevitable, wasn't it?

'How could you have been so stupid?' I hiss to myself. The venom shocks even me. 'You are so stupid, Jenny!' I scream. 'So stupid.'

I've fallen to my knees on the pavement. I didn't even notice. My bag splits open. A lipgloss tumbles down the road. A compact falls and the powder cracks.

Chapter 57

I've taken to my bed. Like a woman in a costume drama, only nowhere near as pretty. This is day two with a duvet over my head. Mother must have slept on the sofa last night. Perhaps I should feel bad about that, but I don't. Perhaps I should feel bad that I haven't done the Smiling Manifesto for two days. But I don't care. Let Matilda die, let people carry their own shopping. I like it here with my duvet curled around me like I'm something fragile. I'm not though, I'm not fragile, just stupid. So, so, so stupid. I knew Joe was going to do this. This was the reason I kept away from him at first.

He dumped me. Dumped. Lovely word that. Dumped like an old telly that will end up in a landfill in China under millions of other old tellies. Like the girl you said you wanted to spend the rest of your life with and then realised wasn't good enough. *Sorry.*

I didn't think anything could be worse than Steve Wilmot. But Joe King . . . oh, God, every time I think about him, it's like someone has put their hand in my tummy and is scooping out my insides. I don't even think he's a bastard. I mean, what he did really hurt me because I am an absolute tool with men. I was too scared to let anyone near me after Steve Wilmot and I didn't sleep with anyone else for eight years. Eight years! I mean, that's not normal. I kissed a few people in the early hours to loud music, but I'd never go home with them. Until Al. And then Matt. It's a catastrophic portfolio. But, no, I don't think he's a bastard. I can understand Joe King. He wants to write an album. Fair dos. And I'm not the woman he thought I was. I told him about my breakdown and it must have altered his opinion of me. I think the technical term for what he must think I am is a fuck up. Joe King shouldn't have wooed me. I agree. You shouldn't woo anyone so confidently. It's asking for trouble. But I shouldn't have let myself be wooed. I knew that fairy tales are for children, that romcoms are fairy tales for adults. And that the higher you fly, the further there is to fall. The bigger the smile, the louder the sob. If you are just a girl standing in front of a boy . . . don't, whatever you do, tell him that you love him!

There's a knock on the door now. I ignore it and roll further into my duvet. It must be Al. Mum's in the room with me. She's been here all the time. I haven't been speaking to her though. She should go out and enjoy herself, see the plasterer, anything but sit here with my misery.

'Fan.' It is Al. 'Fan, I've got some soup here.'

'Thanks,' I mumble into the duvet.

'I'll leave it on the side for you.'

'Thanks.'

'It'll all be fine, Fan-Tastic.'

How can it be fine, Al? I left a stable man who would have married me for one who turned out to be a rat. Everything I touch, I ruin. Everything my dad and Michelle said about me was bang on the money, I'll come to nothing, I'm stupid. So, so, so stupid.

'Well, I'm here, Fan. I'm here.'

They should leave me alone. I'll only bring them down. I wish they'd go and have some fun. He should be out snogging Gemma, not making me soup. He closes the door as he leaves.

'Jenny,' Mum whispers, and she crawls onto the bed next to me. She sits up with her back against the headboard and strokes my hair. 'Jenny, my little girl. Let me in.'

I burrow further into my duvet.

'Jenny, let me in.'

I don't respond.

'What happened?'

I don't respond.

It feels later now. I think I must have fallen asleep. Mum's still in bed with me.

'It's OK, I'm here when you're ready to talk,' she says. 'Or not. I'm here.'

I must have slept again because it's dark outside now. There's no light peeping beneath the curtains. Mum is still stroking my head. I sigh and then I swallow.

'He dumped me,' I say simply. It must have been fairly obvious that that's what happened. But it's the first time I've stated it aloud.

'Oh, Jenny. I'm sorry.'

And we don't say anything else. We don't really need to. We just carry on as we were.

There's whispering outside the door, and another knock. The door opens.

'Hey, it's me,' says Philippa.

I poke my face out, and my lips curl down and my eyes fill with tears to see her.

'Oh, bubba, come here,' she says and she sits on my bed, and she opens her arms and draws me to her. I sob into her shoulder.

She lets me cry, and she strokes my hair. I can see Mum out of the corner of my eye, smiling sadly at the two of us. And all of a sudden I feel so incredibly lucky. Lucky that there are two people here, my mum and my best friend. But that makes me cry more, because I wish I was better, for their sakes. I wish I was better full stop.

'Oh, baby girl,' Philippa says, and she rocks me. 'Oh, baby girl.' She sighs. 'Oh, bubba.' And she kisses my greasy hair, which must be above the call of duty. 'Oh, Fan,' she whispers, and she rocks me some more. 'I'll be back in a sec,' she says when I've nearly cried myself out.

Two minutes later she's back with a bottle of wine and three glasses and Al, who's carrying our telly in from the lounge.

'Could you put it there and bring us the DVD player, Al? Do you mind?'

Al shakes his head and looks at me.

'Thank you,' I snivel at him.

'Thought we'd watch Larry Lemon, the comedian's comedian,' Philippa says. 'Unless you fancy anything else?'

I shake my head.

'Mrs T? Any preference?'

'No, I don't know this Larry Lemon comedian. He's the one you were talking about the other night.'

'Ah, you'll have to acquaint yourself with lovely Larry,' Philippa says to Mum before turning eagerly to me. 'Now, Fan, I'm only allowing wallowing for one more day, and then we're going to the Reading Festival,' Philippa says.

'I'm not—' I start.

'Yadda, yadda, yadda,' she says, holding her hand up to ward off any more of my protestations. 'You have no choice in the matter, Al's going to physically carry you into the car. Have you told her your rather exciting news, Mrs T?'

Mum shakes her head. 'What? About Debbie Diamond. No.' Mum turns to me. 'You know my old friend, well, I found her on Friends Reunited.'

'She looks fab, Fan,' Philippa continues. 'Proper bonkers, sorry Mrs T, I mean that in the best possible way. So we've given Joe's ticket to her. Was that OK?'

I nod.

'Good, eh?' Philippa trills.

It's not good at all. Well, I suppose it is for Mum. But the last thing they need is me moping around with them. I won't go. I'll lock myself in the bathroom.

'I'll leave you girls to it,' my mum says, getting up.

'You can stay,' I say.

'Yeah, Mrs T, stay and watch Larry Lemon.'

'I will another time. You girls have some time for just the two of you now. But if you need me I'm here,' she says, and leaves the room.

When Al has set up the telly for us and Philippa is getting Larry Lemon ready with the remote control, she turns to me. 'The stupid thing is, Fan, I bet in a few years, or months, or weeks we'll have a drunk Joe King on your doorstep à la Steve Wilmot, crying about how losing you was the biggest mistake of his life.'

I can't imagine that scenario, largely because I never want to see Joe King again.

The two of us prop ourselves up in bed, glasses of wine in hand. This is one of the DVDs that I watched repeatedly when I was depressed before. I probably know very word. Larry Lemon walks onto the stage. He feels like an old friend.

Chapter 58

Philippa was right. Debbie Diamond is bonkers. She's right out of *Ab Fab.* She doesn't stop talking or drinking or asking Marge to stop the car so she can get out and have ciggie. Mum's delighted by her and that's nice to see. I'm in the back with my head against the window, staring out, miles away. But a stranger's chatter is oddly comforting.

'Hey' – Philippa slides her hand in mine – 'I went to Rose Cottage this morning.'

It's a jolt to hear that, but I don't show it. I don't move.

'I wanted to check the draft of my interview with Philip before I handed it in. Didn't want to annoy the man who was reading my novel by misquoting him. He said the article was fine, and then he said that he had read my book and he really liked it.'

I whizz my head round to look at her.

'That's amazing. I'm so pleased for you,' I say, and tears come into my eyes.

'He's suggested a few changes I need to make, but he really thought it was good.'

'Wow.'

'I didn't see Joe,' she says. I wasn't going to ask. 'But I heard him. Playing guitar upstairs. Sounded quite nice. Thought you should know that. At least he's doing what he said and getting on with his music. At least he's not . . . ' she trails off.

I nod. At least he's not met someone else. At least not that we know of.

'It will get better.'

I nod.

'Your mother and I went to Glastonbury moons ago,' Debbie Diamond says, she's off again.

'It was Reading!' Mum corrects her, laughing.

'I'm surprised you knew where you were, dear!'

'Why?' Philippa asks. 'Was Mrs T off her tits?'

'No, someone was on her tits though!' She whoops.

'Debbie!' Mum gasps.

'Ooh, she met a lovely man, didn't you, Pam?'

'Mum, you're blushing. Is this that Lawrence chap?' It's the first thing I've properly said to everyone. My voice has shocked everyone else into silence.

'Yes,' Mum acknowledges.

'Oh, he was a good 'un. Was that his name? Lawrence?'

'Yes, yes, I think it was. Yes.'

'Lost him, she did. Had a weekend of wicked sex and then couldn't find his tent. My fault, though, really because I made you join me on the Sunday to see that terrible folk duo. Sorry.'

'Oh, you know, that's life.'

'Hmm. Then she gets home and marries your father.'

'We all make mistakes,' I say and it occurs to me that I

probably shouldn't refer to my mother's twenty-seven-year marriage as a mistake. But my comment makes my mum and Debbie laugh, no howl. But then they both stop suddenly and sigh in absolute unison and that makes them laugh again.

Philippa nudges me. 'Is this what we'll be like?' She smiles.

'I hope so.' I smile back. Although without the twenty-seven-year lapse in friendship, I think. God, I shiver, life without Philippa, it actually doesn't bear thinking about. I squeeze her hand.

My phone buzzes. Joe? That's what I always think when my phone buzzes. When will that stop? I wonder. It's from Matt.

> Please, please, don't throw this away. We can make it work. I need you, Fan. Please let's talk.

He's been texting a lot. I haven't texted back. Yet.

'You should try and find him again now you're single!' Debbie shouts. 'Oh, Marge, services in three miles, can we stop so I can have a fag? Yes! Pam, let's search for Lawrence the Lovely.'

'Debbie, you genius!' Philippa is bouncing up and down on the seat. 'Pam, write down exactly what you remember about him and we can circulate it in an email, to be forwarded on and on to everyone's friends. *Looking for Lawrence*, we'll call it! I'll bet we could get an article about it in the press somewhere, someone's bound to know him.'

'Philippa! That's it!' Debbie claps her hands together. 'Oh, do you see the exit for the services there, Marge?'

Marge nods and flicks down the indicator.

We park in the service station car park, and just as Debbie puts her hand on the door handle to get out for a ciggie, my mum begins speaking. Her voice is quiet but her tone is strong.

'Girls, I don't want to find Lawrence. It's passed and done now. We were obviously meant to lose each other that day, for whatever reason. Searching for him feels wrong. Some things are meant to be lost.'

Perhaps there is something in the certainty of her delivery, but no one tries to persuade her otherwise.

Chapter 59

'Ladies! Ladies! Ladies!' I shout, uncrossing my legs and standing up. I wipe some grass off the back of my legs and sway a bit against someone's guy rope. 'I would like to make a speech.'

Everyone looks a little startled because I've only really spoken to Philippa today. But I've been listening to them all.

'I just want to say, firstly, ladies . . . ' I sweep my gaze around the circle, looking at Debbie Diamond in the truly hideous Rasta hat she purchased earlier, as a substitute because she hasn't been able to source any weed, at my mum glowing from booze and sunburn and dancing and catching up with an old friend, at Marge who's already snogged the fella in the next tent, and at Philippa, my beautiful, beautiful friend, who's held my hand all day while we've walked from stage to stage and from tent to tent and who is going to become a famous author. Woah, moving my head like that has made me a little wobbly.

'First of all, let's just toast this lovely pear cider!'

'Lovely pear cider!' they whoop.

'So, I would just like to make a little speech, because I

haven't said much up till this point and this isn't normally how I am. But, ladies, I would just like to say, thank you. Thank you for forcing me to come away, and thank you, Al, who isn't here, for lifting me into the car earlier, and thank you all for putting up with me and making me feel soooooo much better. Marge, thank you for insisting we sit and talk about all the awful things men have done to us and thank you Debbie, for holding the floor on this particular subject for so long. Much obliged. Feeling so much better.' Debbie has never been afraid to love and, blimey, she's loved some toads, one bloke got her pregnant, pressured her to have an abortion because he said he didn't want kids, then left Debbie and had a baby with someone else. Debbie's never had children. She held my face, with tears in her eyes, and said, 'I never had a beautiful daughter like you, Jenny,' and then she kissed my forehead. Debbie is the awesomest, I am so glad she's Mum's friend. I could hang out with her all the time. 'And Philippa, the amazingest, wonderfullest person on the planet, I love you sooooooo much, and Mum, my lovely mum, I never, ever in ten billion years— whoops, sorry,' I shout to the people whose tent I've just lurched into. 'Mum, never, ever did I think we'd be here at a festival having this much fun. And I love this little army we have created. So, ladies. Lady army, I thank you, I love you and now I'd better sit down or I am liable to have these poor people's tent over.'

I've had a bit of an epiphany today. When I took to my bed before, when Steve Wilmot had humiliated me and Dad made me feel worse, when I took to my bed in Philippa's house for ages, it was only really Philippa that kept me going. But now, I have Mum and Philippa and Marge and Al, and Debbie, I hope, she's invited me to come and stay at her house in Edinburgh any time and I'm going to take her up on that, and go to the Edinburgh Festival one day. But I realised today that I've got a pack of lovely people around me now. And that's what life's all about, and even though I won't be falling for any gorgeous musicians again, the likes of Joe King and Steve Wilmot can't hurt me, not when I've got Mum and Philippa and so many great people about me. God, I love pear cider.

Everyone is oo-ing and ah-ing after my speech.

'Right drink up, and then we go and see the Arctic Monkeys!' I command. Then Philippa and I scream. We *love* the Arctic Monkeys.

'Oh, no, I'm too old,' Mum protests.

Debbie shakes her head admonishingly.

'Mrs T, did you or did you not used to like the Stones.'

'Still like the Stones, Philippa.' Mum corrects her.

'Well, the Arctic Monkeys are the Stones of our generation and you will love them.'

'We saw the Stones at Reading.' Debbie sighs. 'With that chap. What was his name again?'

'Lawrence,' Mum says quietly.

'Lawrence! That's it, thank you. We danced to the Stones with Lawrence and he had you on his shoulders. Oh, he was a funny dancer, did a brilliant Mick Jagger impression. Marge!' Debbie Diamond is serious suddenly, and wagging her finger at Marge. 'That chap, the one whose mouth you had your tongue in, get his number, do it. Now! Go on, off you go, don't lose him, don't do a Pam and Lawrence on us. *Now!*'

Marge does as she's told and gets right up and pops into next door's tent. She hauls her fella out, types his number into her phone and then drags him along with us as we all make our way to the main stage.

I almost can't remember the old Mum. The one who Dad would shhhhhh and shout at. Someone has swapped her for this laughing, dancing woman.

'Philippa, can I use your camera?'

Philippa smiles and nods and turns her back to me so that I can extract it from her rucksack. She points towards Marge, as I zip it back up.

'I know! Unbelievable,' I holler over the music. 'You'd think they'd need to come up for air at some point.'

Marge has been snogging the chap from the next tent whose name I'm still not sure of for the whole of the Arctic Monkeys' back catalogue. We're onto the encore songs now. That's how long they've been at it. While they've been snogging, Mum and Debbie Diamond have been dancing, well, jiggling.

Before the Arctic Monkeys came on stage Debbie Diamond took a sip from her hip flask.

'Girls,' she declared. 'We won't embarrass you. Of that I promise you.'

'No, there's nothing worse than an over-fifty making a fool of herself on the dance floor.'

'Well, there is, Pam, it's two over-fifties making fools of themselves.'

'Oh, please!' Philippa snorted.

'If you want to dance, dance!' I shouted, holding my arms wide and stomping along to the warm-up music, and because I'd had a lot of pear cider it struck me as a good metaphor for life.

Anyway, after approximately half a song they adhered to my advice and have been engaged in some pretty awesome rock jiggling ever since. They stand with their feet rooted to the plastic-cup-littered ground, their arms out at forty-five-degree angles from their bodies, frantically nodding their smiling heads to the beat. It's quite something to behold. They look as though they're being driven down a bumpy street at great speed.

I turn on Philippa's camera and take a few shots of the band on the stage. Philippa starts pouting in the direction of the camera so I get a good one of her too. I catch a sneaky one of Marge and blokey and then turn to Mum and Debbie Diamond. Debbie sees the camera and immediately puts her arm around Mum's shoulders. Mum opens her mouth and smiles. Her eyes are shining and her cheeks are rosy from fun and sun. She looks beautiful. Debbie accidentally jiggles onto Mum's foot, Mum pretends dramatically that she's in agony. The Arctic Monkeys launch into a Rolling Stones cover and they both leap into the air. I keep snapping away taking pictures of the two of them, my mum looks so full of joy and life, I don't want to stop.

Chapter 60

'What are you having?' Matt asks.

It's just a drink! I said yes to a drink, that's all. It doesn't really mean anything except that I felt bad that he was texting all the time. Although, I won't have a drink drink, because I'm still hungover from Reading, even though I've been back three days. He looks tired. It quite suits Matt to look tired, somehow. There's something a bit terrifyingly driven about him when he looks in the peak of health and fitness. Something indomitable. The vulnerability he has when he's tired and a little low is endearing.

We're in a pub I've never been to before, the other side of Nunstone. A country pub, with real ale and pork scratchings on the table. I tried one. It nearly broke my jaw.

'Oh, um, just a Coke.'

He nods and heads to the bar, leaving me fiddling with a beer mat, hoping my jaw will recover.

He comes back with a Coke and half a bitter and sits on a stool opposite me. It seems such a small seat for a big man.

'Thanks,' he says, 'for meeting me.'

'Thanks for the drink.'

'Pleasure. How are you?'

'Um, all right. How are you?'

'All right.' He nods and then sips his drink. 'I miss you.'

I nod. 'Hmmm.' I smile sadly.

I don't suppose these sorts of drinks are ever a laugh a minute.

'So, are you and Al . . . ?'

'No.' I shake my head.

'Right.'

He takes another sip. He should have got a pint really.

'How's work?' I ask after an uncomfortable pause.

'Busy, you know. Got the big yearly bash soon. You could still come with me . . . ' He tails off and looks out of the window. 'How's your work?'

'I'm off work at the moment. There's an enquiry into whether I accidentally killed an old lady.'

He looks so shocked I laugh. But then I think of Doris and I stop.

'Hopefully, it'll all be OK.'

'Yes.'

I look at him. My Matt. Funny old handsome Matt, with his unbelievable drive and work ethic. His unshakeable notions of how things should be done and ordered. And I smile at him.

'What?' he asks.

'Nothing.'

I feel incredibly calm. Oddly so. Perhaps it's the quiet old pub. Or perhaps it's because the storm has passed. Perhaps it's because although we're totally different, I feel safe with Matt. Who knows? I'm sure Philippa would have a theory.

'I'll get to the point, Fan. I haven't cancelled anything. Partly because I just couldn't bring myself to. Partly because this all seemed so not you that I hoped, I hope' – he looks straight at me with his tired eyes – 'We might be able to salvage us.'

I nod.

OK, here goes.

'The thing is.' I stop and look down. 'It wasn't just Al. There was someone else too.'

'Bloody hell, Fan, is there anyone you haven't shagged!'

I don't know why I'm laughing.

'I don't think it's very funny. Who was this one?'

'The— oh, God, just someone I met.'

'And is it serious with him?'

'It isn't anything any more.'

He nods. He's finished his drink already. He puts his glass down and shuts his eyes.

'Oh, Fan,' he says. 'Why do I want you so much?'

I shrug. 'I really can't imagine.'

'I must be mad.'

'Bonkers.'

'Anyone else I should know about?'

I shake my head.

'You get me, Fan. No one's ever really got me before. What did I do?'

'Nothing, Matt. It so wasn't you. It was all me. Well, maybe you booking the golf club when you knew I didn't want you to.'

'Fan, your idea was sweet and I thought about it, but who'd clear up? Who'd set up? It would take a week to sort it all out and then we'd start our married life having to take down a marquee and give people back their potato salad bowls. And I rather fancied being on a beach with a cocktail looking at my wife in her bikini.'

I smile. He's got a point.

'So what do you reckon?'

'How do you mean?'

'Shall we have another go?'

'But . . .'

'Or do you think there's still more for you to get out of your system?'

'No.' I laugh sadly.

'Shall we just have a go? I don't want to marry anyone else.'

'But can you forgive me?'

He looks at me and nods. 'You hadn't really slept with anyone before me, had you? I'm thinking it was a reaction to the proposal. Like you said, it was a shock, we hadn't even lived together.'

'Hmmm.'

'But I think if we do this, you should move in with me. I don't think I'm cool with you living with Al.'

'What about my mum?'

'She can stay with Al.'

He reaches towards me and takes my hand. 'I want to make you happy. Let me make you happy . . .'

I look into his eyes and I think about the days I spent in bed after Joe King dumped me. I never want to feel like that again.

I nod.

Chapter 61

'Look! Look, it's in,' Philippa says, thrusting a copy of the *Tiddlesbury Times* at me as soon as she's opened the door. 'It went in the paper today.'

Is There An Angel In Our Midst?

Television cameraman receives
anonymous note offering him kind advice

David Derman, 35, was recently down in the dumps, he had been working abroad and was finding it hard to readjust to life in England. One day he looked in his camera bag and found a small envelope with a note inside. The 'angel' wrote that he or she had been in the doldrums before, too, and offered a list of ten things to do that might cheer him up. The angel called the list the Smiling Manifesto.

Dave says, 'I've been following the advice and it's got me smiling again. Now I'd like to discover who sent it as I want to thank them.'

> The *Tiddlesbury Times* is keen to uncover the angel in our midst, too, and would like to hear from you if you have received any notes from an anonymous well-wisher, or you think you may know who is writing them.

'Who do you think it is?' she asks with a wink when I hand it back to her.

'No idea.' I smile.

'It'll be interesting, won't it, if people do come forward.'

'I'm a bit worried we'll hear more tales of our terrible matchmaking.'

'Oh, bummer, yeah.' She laughs. 'So come up.'

I follow Philippa up the stairs.

'I have to tell you something,' I say once we are in her room.

'Why do I have a feeling it's going to be one of the worst things you've ever told me?' she says seriously, plonking herself on the bed and fixing her eyes upon me.

'I'm going to marry Matt,' I say.

'Please don't do it,' she says, not missing a beat, as though she was expecting it.

'I'm doing it.'

'What does your mum say?'

'I asked her to be happy for me. I don't want to fall out with her and I don't want to fall out with you. I was fine with Matt before all this Joe stuff. I just want to get back to that.'

'But the Joe stuff, surely it's made you realise that there is someone out there who'll love you for you, who'll make you feel alive and glow.'

'Yes, and then he'll crap on me from a great height.'

'No, no. Please don't.'

'Philippa, I love you more than anyone in the world. But you need to realise that I know what's best for me. You don't. You do about a lot of things. But not this.'

'Oh, Fan. What can I say to you?'

'Nothing. You don't understand.'

'Urrgghhh,' she groans in frustration. 'But, Fan! I do! I think I understand you better than anyone. I understand that for years and years you tried to make your horrible father love you, but it didn't work, and then you fell for Steve Wilmot and he broke your heart, and you didn't want to have your heart broken again. And then you met Matt, and something about him bossing you around feels familiar and safe for you. But it only feels safe because that's what your dad did to you. And you'll end up like your mum and we won't be friends for twenty-seven years and you'll find out that Matt has another girlfriend and somewhere along the line you'll lose you. And I don't want you to lose you, Fan, you're awesome! I give you a list of ten things and you do them for six years! Six years of meeting mavericks and helping kids with their homework and giving people flowers that you barely know. And the Tidds Tour – how you came up with that, I'll never know, but I bloody love it. And the dress code, I say something for a laugh and you run with it till it's a bloody adventure, and the musketeers, man, the Musketeer Missions, they're mental, but they're one of the highlights of my life. No, you are, Fan, you're the highlight of my life and I know how hard stuff is with your depression, Fan' – oh, God, she's trying not to cry – 'I really do know, Fan, how hard it is. And when you came off the antidepressants, Fan, it was the proudest I've ever been of anyone. I wish I could give you confidence. All the confidence in the world. Because I know people meet you and you've got pink hair and you're funny and they must think you're the most sorted person on the planet. But I know that somewhere in you is this belief that you're worthless. And you're not, Fan! But Matt, he doesn't know any of this. And I don't think you'll survive with him. I think you're very good for Matt, but he's not very good for you.'

'I've said I'll marry him.'

She kicks her bed frame. 'Ouch, that really hurt.'

'Please, just be happy for me.'

'I can't be happy for you. I can't be there, Fan. Put yourself in my position!'

'Please, Philippa. Please.'

'Fan, no. I'm not coming to your wedding. What do you want me to do? Smile. Tell you the golf club is lovely?'

'Yes.' That's exactly what I want her to do.

'I can't.'

I wait for her to change her mind. But she doesn't.

'I'd best be off.'

'Yep,' she says, but she doesn't look at me.

Chapter 62

Well, I'm back where I belong. I let my guard down. No, I let myself down, by getting close to Joe King. Still, it could have been worse and at least I'm here again with Matt. At least he was sensible enough to know I was behaving out of character, and he waited for me. And Philippa will come round. I have to believe that Philippa will come round.

Being with Matt is already starting to feel familiar again. I hope I'll stop comparing him with Joe King soon. I suppose it's only natural that I should compare them. But I feel so guilty doing it. I feel so guilty all the time actually. Hopefully that will pass soon as well.

Matt likes to put the telly on after sex and catch up on a bit of news or football. It's good, it means I can zone out. I don't think I can be perky at the moment. Post-coital Matt is not at all like Joe, Joe would ask me questions and questions about myself as we lay entwined in bed after sex. What was the first single you ever bought? If you won the lottery tomorrow, what would you do with the money? How did you get the scar on your chin? When we have our first child what shall we call the little fella? He'd really said that, when we have our first child . . . crazy. Or he'd play me a song on the stereo, and we'd lie there naked, our legs twisting around each other's, our toes touching, listening to some beautiful folk song. Or he'd reach out of the bed and fetch his guitar, and then sit up in the bed and play me a song himself.

Sex with Matt is different to sex with Joe King too. Well, of course it would be. With Matt it feels like something he has to do. Not a duty, as such, but a biological need that should be met. It's not bad though. Not at all. But Joe King, well, Joe King was a sorcerer.

You can't fall in love at first sight. Well, maybe you can. But you shouldn't.

'Do you want me to buy you a new dress for my work do?' Matt asks, during the adverts.

'Oh, no, I'm sure I've got something.'

'Really? I don't mind.'

'No, I've got loads of dresses.' I smile. 'But thank you.'

'Nothing too mad, Fanny,' he says, and he must mean it because he turns his head from the telly towards me.

'What are you trying to say?' I joke.

'You know, just that it's my work do. I want us to make a good impression.'

'Course,' I mumble.

'Maybe run a few suggestions by me in the next few days, so we've got time to go out and get something if we need to.'

'OK.'

'And maybe . . . ' he stops himself.

'What?' I ask.

'Well, don't hate me for this, Fan, but I was thinking about your hair.'

'What about it?'

'I was thinking it might be good if it could be a more natural colour. Don't get me wrong, I like the pink, it's kooky.' He fingers a few strands idly, and smiles to himself. 'I fell for you with crazy hair. But, you know, you've got to grow up sooner or later.'

'Oh,' I say.

'If I'm going to be a partner, I don't think we should entertain clients with you with pink hair. I don't know what the Japanese would make of it. Or the Germans. They might think you're on drugs.' He laughs. 'I think we should play it on the safe side.'

'Hmm. What do you think? Blonde?'

'I thought brown, Fanny. I think people would take you more seriously.'

'Oh, oh, um, OK.'

'And I was thinking about that too, your name' – he props himself up further in bed. He's on a roll now – 'I think I should try to call you Jenny. Fanny is a bit too ... a bit too ... a bit too ... something, well, you know what I mean.'

'Hmmm. Anything else?'

'No! Sorry. Does that all sound awful? It's just when I'm a partner ...'

'Yeah, it's fair enough,' I say, turning away from him. I close my eyes. I want to go to sleep now.

'Jenny, are you all right?' Matt asks, turning the volume down slightly.

'Hmmm, course,' I say, but I can feel that the area under my eyes is a little wet.

Chapter 63

'Al?' I knock lightly on his door.

'Fan-Tastic! Where you been?' he shouts cheerfully. I hear a few clomps, then the door opens and his smiling face appears. The smile quickly drops to a frown.

'What's up, beautiful?'

'Nothing. Can I have a word?'

'Course, come in. I was just trying to give it a tidy. Gemma might be . . . well, you know, don't want to expect it, but she might want to come back tonight and if she does . . . '

'You want it to be nice for her.'

'Yes. What's up, Fan? Still Joe King?'

'No. No, I'm fine.'

'I ran into him yesterday, Fan. I hadn't called him, you know, I liked the guy but what he did to you was unforgivable, if you ask me. Anyway, we were in the supermarket yesterday evening, looking at microwavable curries at the same time. Sad bastards. He looked dreadful, Fan. I don't get the bloke. He said he'd been doing his music. Crazy musicians, eh?'

'Hmmm. I'm, um, I'm OK. I'm back with Matt.'

'Oh.'

'Yeah.'

'Is he going to twat me again?'

'No, sorry about that.'

'Fan, I'll take a punch for you till the day I die.'

'Thanks. But I hope you don't have to again.'

'So . . . Wow' – he sits on the bed – 'Matt.'

'Hmmm. The wedding's back on.'

'Oh, well, congratulations.'

'Thank you.' I smile sadly and fiddle with my ring.

'I don't know whether Matt will want me at the wedding.'

'Oh.' That hadn't occurred to me. But I couldn't do it without Al. I might not even have Philippa there! 'Al, you have to come, please!' I'm aware of the panic in my voice.

'Yeah, course. Can't not see you walk down the aisle,' his comforting voice calms me.

'Thank you.'

'You look sad, Fan.'

'Yeah, but I'll perk up soon. Just some big adjustments. But it's right to get back with Matt, of that I'm sure. The only thing is, well, I'll be moving out.'

'Oh?'

'Hmmmm.'

'I suppose you would be, yeah.'

'Hmmm.'

'End of an era, eh?'

'Yeah.'

'Bloody good era, Fan, I've loved living with you.'

'Me too.'

'God, we've had some laughs, haven't we?'

I nod. 'Can Mum stay here? For the time being anyway, till we work out what we'll all do.'

'Yeah, course.'

'Do you think I could have a hug?'

'Any time.'

I walk into his open arms, he closes them tightly. It's the longest hug we've ever had.

I leave Al and head towards my room. Mum's room. I knock on the door.

'Mum?' I call. There's no answer. 'Mum?'

I gently open the door. She's not here. I walk in, kick my shoes off and lie down on my bed. I look about my room. I was so proud when I moved in here. It felt like such an achievement to be able to afford to move out and share a flat, even if it was above a kebab shop in Tiddlesbury. Rather than recovering from a breakdown at my friend's dad's house, moving into a flat share felt like something that I should be doing. Yes, I was proud and excited, but nervous too, hence the Smiling Manifesto pinned to the back of the bedroom door, it's currently covered by a year planner because I didn't want Mum to see it and I worried I'd rip it if I took it down. The nerves vanished quite quickly when I got here, though, because everything was so much fun: Fashion Fridays, nights at Bomber, the Tiddlesbury Tours, Musketeer Missions, clothes, comedy, dancing, everything, it was all so much fun. The end of an era. You've got to grow up sooner or later.

I look about me. Matt doesn't have room for all my clothes, I know that without asking. Perhaps I could put some in storage, but will I even need them all now? Will Philippa and I carry on with Fashion Fridays? Oh, I hope so. It feels as though everything is ending just because I'm moving out and marrying Matt, but it doesn't need to. In a day or two I'll get some bin bags and start seeing if there are some clothes I could do without, try to get used to the idea of parting with them.

I climb off the bed and look at my rail of black clothes. I'm sure Matt will want me in a black dress for his work party. I pull out the more conservative of them and lay them on the bed. As I pull one from the rail the black T-shirt dress with the heart on it falls to the floor. I pick it up, hold it to my nose and sniff. I want it to smell of Joe King, but it just smells of log fire. I toss the dress into the rubbish bin across the room. Then I try on a fitted black cocktail dress. I've always liked the simplicity of this dress. Normally I'd team it with a black-and-white animal-print belt and my pink hair. But I think Matt will prefer it without the belt. I look in the mirror and try to imagine me with brown hair again. I haven't had brown hair for years. But I probably should go back to my natural colour at some point, dying it brown will be the first step. I'm surprised I've got any hair left, I've dyed it so many times.

I kneel on the floor and feel under the bed for a shoebox. I pull it out. Then I sit on the floor and take the lid off. It's my box of memories, old letters and photos, bits I didn't want to throw away. I flick through the pictures, loads of Philippa and me in our Fashion Friday outfits. One taken on the night we met Matt, when we were dressed as air hostesses. Our big smiles look like we're about to have a very good night. I take that one out to keep. I flick through more. So many big smiles. We start to look younger and younger, until I see one of us in the burgundy Tiddlesbury Remand uniform. Here we are. There's me with brown hair. Philippa's dad took this photo, I remember it clearly. We were revising for exams in the garden. We're lying on our tummies on the grass, surrounded by books and empty crisp packets, smiling and squinting slightly in the sun. It was pre me sleeping with Steve Wilmot, and I look almost carefree. I'd been offered a place at a performing arts college. Philippa had already been offered a trainee position on the *Tiddlesbury Times*. I wonder what that young girl, Jenny Taylor, would say to see me now. I wonder if she'd be disappointed if she met me. I look at her. She had thought the worst was over. Poor thing. I rummage further in the box, I come across the two well-worn photos of Steve Wilmot that I'd cut from the school magazine, and just one photo of Mum, Dad and me. I sit back and look at this one.

'Wow,' I whisper. You absolutely wouldn't recognise the woman in the photos as my mum now. She's holding my dad's hand, her head is bent down and her eyes are turned up to the camera. It makes her look meek. She's smiling, but her eyes look glazed, like she's somewhere else entirely. Oh, Mum, were you really so unhappy? So unhappy for years and years? I think of who she is now, with her Victoria Beckham bob and her penchant for a bit of rough. Was this woman suppressed under this lady in the photo all the time? I was so unhappy at home, it never occurred to me that anyone else might be. I sigh.

I hear a door slamming in the hall. I put the photos back in the box.

'Oh, there you are!' It's Philippa. 'Look! Look!' she throws some printed sheets of A4 paper at me. 'That's not all! Fan, it's amazing.'

I pick up one of the pages and start to read.

Three years ago I was in Nunstone for the pub quiz at The Nags Head with some friends. I went up to the bar and bought us a bottle of wine then I came back to the table and we drank the wine and struggled to complete the IMPOSSIBLE general knowledge round. When I returned home that night I found a note in my bag. It was written on a pretty card. I have NO IDEA how it came to be in my bag (my friend is convinced it had something to do with a girl who asked us where the loos were – but she was nowhere near my bag!).

Anyway the note said *after you bought a bottle of wine tonight the barman who served you turned to his colleague and said, 'She is the most beautiful girl who comes in here.' Thought you should know.*

Cutting a long story short, we're getting married in November and would very much like to thank the angel who left that note.

'Philippa! They're getting married! Do you remember them? She was proper gorgeous too. Tiny thing! Oh, my God!'

'I know!'

'Oh, my God!'

'I know!'

I look at her and we both giggle.

'Amazing.' I shake my head. I pick up another.

I used to park in the same place for work every morning. One day I returned to my car and found something underneath my windscreen wiper. It was an envelope with the words OPEN ME! I'M NICE on the front. So I opened it and inside was a little card which said *Hello, I am a little note to say that you look like a lovely person – every day you make all the people you say good morning to smile.*

I've still got the note. It's stuck on my bathroom mirror. It reminds me to smile and be friendly when I wake up feeling grumpy and wanting to go back to bed.

'Ah, she used to park round the corner from the surgery. I was one of the people she would say good morning to. She doesn't park there any more. I miss her on my walk to work.'

I pick up another.

When I was going through my divorce last year, I felt too down to join my workmates for lunch so I would sit by myself on a bench in town eating my sandwiches. One day I found a note on the bench when I arrived, labelled *For the lady who sits and eats her lunch here*, it said *Sorry to see you crying – I would have come over and offered you a hug but I didn't want to scare you – so this is a less scary version of a big hug – may the bad days quickly pass.*

I can't tell you how much that meant to me. And the bad days did pass.

'Oh, bless her, she was getting a divorce. I wondered why she looked so sad,' I say.

'There's more, Fan! The paper wants to publish them. Disgruntled Dave is beside himself. Although, he's saying he may want us to do something about it on camera. I don't know what we should do about that. You know, what with us being the ones sending the notes.'

'Yeah, bit of a mess that. I still can't believe that couple are getting married because we sent her a note,' I exclaim.

Philippa's face drops as soon as I mention the word 'married'. It doesn't just drop, it visibly twists itself into an expression of fury.

'Oh, here you are, girls!' It's Mum, she's smiling and she's carrying a few unopened letters and an Oxfam bag. 'Oh, you girls, I've had the most wonderful day, I spoke to an agent about you two, I sent him the Tiddlesbury Tour. Oh, he was such a nice man, I felt as if I'd known him for years. He likes the DVD! He's going to invite you in for a meeting, he might take you on and get you presenting work,' she chatters on. But she stops suddenly as soon as she glimpses Philippa properly.

'Philippa, what on earth's the matter?'

'I was just thinking about Fan marrying Matt.' Philippa's jaw is rigid. Even my mum's amazing news about us possibly meeting an agent hasn't distracted her from her fury.

'Ah.' Mum nods.

'What do you think, Mrs T?'

'Well . . . ' she says very gently. 'Well, ultimately it's Jenny's decision . . . '

Philippa's nodding, her jaw still clenched tight. I've rarely seen her like this in all the years I've known her. I think I've only seen it once, when she didn't want her mum to move to America. My beautiful friend Philippa, turned ugly by rage.

'Philippa, stop it,' I say, standing up and trying to reach out to her. 'Mum's just told us some really good news.'

'I DON'T KNOW WHAT TO DO!' she shouts.

'Just be my friend, please,' I plead.

'HOW CAN I?' she screams, and quickly spins round and storms out of the flat.

I look at Mum. She opens her mouth as if to say something.

'Please, Mum, I don't want to fall out with you about this again. I'm marrying Matt, don't say anything against it. Please, I couldn't bear it,' I say quickly.

Thankfully my mum nods and doesn't say whatever it was she was planning to.

Chapter 64

'You'll get used to it,' Matt says, kissing my shoulder as I stand wrapped in a towel looking at myself in the mirror. I've just dried my brown hair for the first time, ready for Matt's work do tonight.

'So weird,' I say, staring at my reflection. 'It hasn't been like this for years.'

'It suits you,' he says. 'You're naturally beautiful as you are.'

I smile at him in the mirror, but he's already heading into the bathroom.

Maybe it does suit me, but I feel like someone I don't know. I don't even recognise myself. It's the strangest sensation. I can't help but feel that this is the face that looked back at me in the mirror when I was depressed. I so don't want to be that girl again. Mind you, it always takes a while to adjust to a new colour.

'I really want to put on a hat.'

'Don't you dare!' Matt calls from the bathroom.

'No, it wouldn't go with the orange backless number I'm wearing.'

'Very funny. Fan, Jen, you need to be ready to go in half an hour.'

'Yep.'

'I mean it, Jen. Can't be late for the reception drinks.'

'I know.'

'I'm just getting in the shower.'

I blow breath through my lips and wander to the window of Matt's bedroom. My bedroom, I suppose, although it doesn't feel like it yet. I look out at the car park and the high gates at the entrance to the development, and the field beyond it. Then I blow my breath through my lips again and step into my very plain, conservative dress and I don't add the animal-print belt. Then I walk back to the mirror to apply make-up.

'Who are you?' I find myself whispering to the girl in the glass.

Chapter 65

'See, it'll make a great venue for the wedding,' Matt says.

'Hmmm.' I try to smile, I really do. But I'm just not feeling it. We're walking along a corridor lined with framed pictures of men in horrible jumpers. The last thing this place says is party. The only fun party you could have here would involve desecrating it – with the right combination of people and booze, these gentlemen's faces would end up covered in marker-penned willies and people would play naked midnight golf before bonking in the bunkers. That would have been just the sort of wedding that Philippa and I would have enjoyed, before all this. But I guess my and Matt's wedding will be a bit more traditional.

Oh well, it's just a day. At least they'll do the clearing up.

Matt's holding my arm as he steers me into the unimaginatively titled Function Room. It's as horrible as I knew it would be: white tablecloths that stretch to the floor and those horrible narrow chairs with carpet on the back crammed around circular tables. Lining every wall are plaques full of club members' names and lists of etiquette. It screams rules and regulations. Oh well, at least there's a disco set up and a dance floor cleared, I'll have a little dance later. That'll perk me up. I wonder what Philippa's up to this evening.

'Smile, Jenny, you're on show,' Matt says, just before we stop in front of a young chap holding a tray of drinks. I wonder whether this was the bloke who asked to touch Philippa's boob at the Doris ambush. I smile to think about it.

'That's better,' says Matt. 'We shouldn't have too much booze. Grave error getting wasted at the work do. So we can have a drink now or save it until later.'

'I don't suppose you do Jägerbombs?' I ask the young man.

'I wish.' He laughs. Yes, I bet he was the boob feeler.

'J-e-n,' says Matt, and looks about him to check no one heard.

I take a glass of champagne. I feel like getting wasted. I feel like drinking so much I can't think, but I'll make do with this one glass of champagne.

'Jen, don't flirt with the waiting staff,' he whispers, leading me away. 'Right, we'll greet from the top, Jenny. Are you ready?'

'I am very ready and at your service,' I say, and then take quite a gulp.

'Right, Mr Neville first, ah, damn, he's just started chatting to someone.'

We stand still for a moment. I can sense Matt wondering where to go next. Out of the corner of my eye I spot a very attractive older lady walking quickly towards us. I turn towards her. Wow. She takes good care of herself. She has a figure that she's obviously sweated to get, and a strong face with prominent cheekbones and a sleek jawline, covered perfectly with what I bet is hideously expensive make-up. She's tanned and turned out and oozing an aura of money. She's probably in her late forties, I must look like a clumsy girl next to her.

'Matt, darling.' She smiles.

'Moira!' Matt says, and he kisses her on both cheeks. 'This is Jenny.'

'Ah, Jenny.' She says my name as though she's heard a lot about me. She's giving me the once over. I stand still and smile.

'Lovely to meet you, Moira.'

'Tell me, Jenny, do you ever get to see this handsome man of yours, because he works all the time.'

'I know!' I exclaim. 'I keep trying to persuade him to take a sicky and stay in bed and watch telly for the day, but he's so committed he won't.'

Matt looks frozen. Moira gives me an odd look and then throws her head back and laughs. I decide I quite like Moira.

'Is he wonderful in bed, darling?' she asks me.

'No, but he's learning,' I say.

Again she howls.

Matt smiles uncomfortably like a man who's just been embarrassed in the presence of his boss.

'I don't mean it, darling,' Moira says, winking at him.

'Do you have a nice man?' I ask.

'That's debatable,' she says in a deep voice. 'If you'll excuse me . . . ' And she sashays away.

'Wow, she's awesome,' I say, as I watch her go.

'Hmmmm. Now, Jenny, let's go and introduce you to Mr Neville and please no funny stuff.'

No one's dancing yet. We've finished the dinner, and the music's been on for an entire hour, but there's still not a soul on the dance floor. I was quite happy to start the dancing off, it only takes one, but Matt said no. I feel sorry for the DJ. He's obviously panicking. He played 'All Night Long' at half past nine. Still nothing.

You know a party is rubbish when you look forward to going to the loo to have a break from it. They're actually very nice toilets. So that's one positive to getting married at the golf club. Oh, what was your wedding venue like, Fan? Oh, the toilets were nice, very spacious. I lock myself in a cubicle. I put the toilet lid down and sit upon it. I don't even need to go. Probably because I've only had one drink. One drink on a Saturday night. I shake my head at the thought, I hear two drunk girls burst in to the Ladies giggling, it makes me think of Philippa and me.

'Ah, ow.' One of the girls is panting. 'These shoes are killing.'

'Take them off!'

'If I take 'em off I'll only have to put 'em back on again. Then it'll be worse.'

'They look nice though.'

I smile. So like Philippa and me.

'Bit shit, isn't it? What time do you think we can get away to Tiddlies?'

'Oh, not yet. Did you see Matt brought his woman with him?'

'Hmmmm. She looks even more miserable than the last one. Do you remember her? Really pretty, amazing skin, but face like a someone had force-fed her lemons.'

That's me and Trudi they're talking about. Oh, dear, I thought I was doing a good job of pretending to be enjoying myself.

Right, I must really concentrate on smiling when I get back out there.

I listen to the sound of make-up bags being rummaged through.

'He's marrying this one though.'

'Poor girl. No wonder she looks down.'

'He's such a bastard.'

'Handsome though.'

'Do you think this one knows about him and Moira?'

'Everyone knows about him and Moira.'

'She probably doesn't.'

'What do you think he says he does every Friday then when he's off boffing boss lady?'

'No idea, squash or something.'

'Man, I am so glad I'm single sometimes.'

'Didn't think anyone could look more miserable than the last one.'

'I feel sorry for her. Maybe we should go and chat to her.'

'Oooh, you know what we should do?'

'What?'

'Write a note! Like that thing in the paper.'

'Oh yeah, an anonymous note.'

'It's a list of ten things, can you remember what they were?'

Their voices are high with excitement.

'No more than two hours of telly!'

'Yeah! Yeah! Do a good deed was one of them, um, um, bugger, what else?'

'Have you got a pen?'

'No.'

'Oh, me neither.'

'Sod it, shall we go and get a tequila.'

'Yeah. Let's go. Ow, my feet.'

I don't know how long I've been sitting in here. It could be fifteen minutes. It could be fifty. It's as though I've floated away from myself. I need to snap into some sort of gear. I need to do something but I don't know what. Matt will be annoyed with me for staying in here so long. I'm surprised he hasn't sent someone in to find me. Maybe he's too embarrassed. One thing's for sure, I need to get out of this toilet. If my legs will carry me. I'm suddenly not sure that they will.

I take a deep breath and lift my weight off the loo. I wobble for a second but remain upright. Phew. I open the cubicle door. A me with brown hair looks at me in the mirror opposite.

'Hello,' I say. 'Bit of a balls up,' I add. My reflection agrees and nods back. 'You're really, really bad with men,' I tell myself. Again, I agree.

The brown hair's actually not that bad, but I wish I hadn't played down my clothes and make-up so much.

I take a big, really big, deep breath that almost makes me dizzy and walk out of the toilet as confidently as I can. I try to keep my head up and my shoulders back. I make my way back to the ghastly Function Room. Matt is hovering by the bar, he literally leaps towards me.

'Jesus, Fan, where the hell have you been?'

'I thought I was Jen now.'

'Where were you?'

'In the toilet, I did tell you.'

'Not for half an hour! What the . . . ?' Matt looks at me with alarm.

I'm struggling to take my ring off. I didn't want to do it dramatically, but my finger must have swollen up this evening. I'm having to tug and tug.

'I'm just trying to take this engagement ring off, Matt,' I say quietly.

'What the . . . ?' he hisses back.

'I just found out about you and Moira and I don't feel so good about the wedding now.'

'Shhhhhh,' he sputters.

'Everyone knows about you and Moira, Matt, I don't think I really do need to shhhhh.'

'Well, er, Jenny, listen, you can't talk, you . . .'

'Yes, I did. If you're going to say, you slept with someone else. Yes, I did. But I told you, Matt. I didn't try to deceive you. Not that it matters.' I look into his despairing face. 'Come on, we've both had other partners during our engagement, it probably isn't the best indication of a blissful marriage.' The penny drops. 'Was this all because you wanted to be made a partner? You thought you'd stand a better chance if you were married?'

I have never seen a man look as uncomfortable as Matt does now.

'But we were all right together. It wasn't as if . . .' he trails off.

I've finally got the ring off. I hold it out for him. He looks at it.

'I don't know what to do, Fan,' he says and he really does look very lost.

'Well, just concentrate on your work,' I say, which sounds a little ridiculous.

He opens his mouth but nothing comes out. He's not taking the ring so I clutch it back in my hand.

'I'm going to go now,' I say, and then for some reason I add the words, 'I hope you do get made a partner.'

And then I turn and I walk away, just as the DJ starts playing 'Sex on Fire'. I stretch my arms in the air as I walk and I think of Joe King.

The cold night air slaps me as I step outside. It knocks my confidence. I freeze. How could I have got it so wrong? All of it so wrong. Repeatedly. If there was an award for 'Woman With the Worst Love Life' I would definitely be in contention. In fact I'd be raising the cup above my head right now. At least there's a taxi coming down the driveway. I hope it'll take me back to Tiddlesbury. Back to the flat. Back to Mum and Al and pyjamas and my Larry Lemon DVD. Back to where I should have stayed.

The cab pulls up in front of me. I step towards it to speak to the driver, just as the nearside back passenger door opens, and out steps ... out steps ... this is the strangest thing ... out steps my mum.

'Jenny,' she says, as though *she's* surprised to see *me.*

'Mum!' I exclaim.

'Are you leaving already?' She looks tired, incredibly tired. And she sounds tired too. She's almost slurring her words.

I nod. 'What are you doing here?'

'Oh, Jenny, I just couldn't sleep. I had to see you.'

'What? Why?'

'Well ... '

'Actually, Mum, let's get in the cab, and get him to take us home.'

'But what about Matt?'

'Matt and I are no more,' I say. 'And we never will be again. He's been bonking a lady partner at his work.'

Oh,' she says, and her shoulders seem to rclcasc. 'Oh, that is good news.'

'I've had better, to be honest, Mum.'

'You can call that nice Joe King,' she murmurs.

I sigh at the mention of his name. I think I'll always sigh when I hear the name Joe King.

'Well, I could if he hadn't brutally dumped me.'

We climb into the back of the taxi and tell the driver to drive us back to where he just came from. I take Mum's hand.

'So let me get this straight, you got a cab at ten at night, to come to Matt's work do, where all his partners were, in order to talk to me.'

'I just wanted to see you,' she says dozily.

'Why?'

'I just knew you would be here, and I wanted to see you.' She smiles.

'But why right this minute?'

She shrugs. 'Sometimes you have to do what's on your mind there and then.'

I shake my head and laugh.

'Have you been smoking the doobies again?'

'Maybe.'

I turn my face towards hers and smile. She smiles back and I squeeze her hand.

'I love you, Mum,' I say, and I stop myself from saying 'even though you are bonkers' because I love her just the way she is.

'And I love my beautiful girl,' she replies.

Chapter 66

He looked me in the eyes and proposed to me when he was having an affair with someone else. Did they lie in bed talking about me? Blimey, they must have thought I was really stupid. She must have been with him when I told him I'd slept with someone else. He wouldn't let me up to his flat and his hair wasn't even wet even though he said he'd had a shower. Bonking Moira, that's what he'd been doing. He even invited her to our wedding. Thank goodness I found out when I did.

I've just been on a very long run. I added miles onto my normal route but nothing seemed to exhaust me. It was as though my whirring mind was propelling me.

'Hey, Al,' I call, as I stand by the kitchen sink draining a pint of water. 'Why aren't you at work?'

'I'm very ill.'

'Oh, right. Sorry about that.'

'No, I overslept so thought I'd feign sickness, how you doing this morning?' he says, stopping and leaning against the door arch on his way to the bathroom.

'I seem to have a lot of . . . a lot of . . . ' How can I describe it? 'A lot of "arrrrrrgghhhh" to get rid of.'

'I can't think why,' Al says. I sat up with him last night, after Mum went to bed, and I ranted and I ranted and then I ranted some more.

'Ah, it's my fault you overslept. Sorry.'

'No, you're all right, it's my fault for setting my alarm for seven tonight. Fan, I meant what I said last night, if you want me to hit him.'

I smile. 'You're very kind but no, Al. Where's Mum? Has she gone out?'

'No, don't think so. I didn't hear her go out.'

I look at the cooker clock. It's nearly half past eleven.

'She can't still be in bed. Can she?'

'She was exhausted last night,' he says.

'Yeah.'

'I put her post under her door first thing, I'm sure she called "thank you". And I think I heard her making tea earlier.'

'Oh, maybe she did go out, then.'

I check the kitchen table and the fridge in case I missed one of her 'morning all, just popped to the shops' notes. But there isn't one. I head to her bedroom door.

'Mum! Mum!' I call. 'Mum! Mum!'

'Mum!' I call again, knocking on her door. 'Mum,' I shriek, knocking again.

There's no response.

'Mum?' I try again.

I turn the door handle, and open the door a few inches.

'Mum.' I smile, she's propped up in bed. 'Hey, I thought

we could . . . ' I start. But then I stop. '*Mum!*' I exclaim when I see that a cup of tea has fallen from her hands and spilt all over the duvet. I rush to the bed. She's not moving. At all. She doesn't even respond when I start shaking her arm.

'Fan, calm down!' Al is shaking me. 'Try to keep calm,' he is shouting at me. He's shouting at me because I'm screaming. I'm screaming and I hadn't even realised.

Chapter 67

Al called an ambulance. They came in minutes that felt like hours.

'Is she allergic to anything?' an ambulance man asked.

'I . . . I . . . I don't know,' I responded.

'Is she on any medication?'

'Oh, um,' I remembered the paper pharmacy bag that I'd seen that day in her case. I dashed towards the case and opened it, wide this time. 'Oh my . . . ' I said. There wasn't just one paper pharmacy bag, there were plenty. I clutched at two and upturned them on the carpet, packets of pills spilling to the floor. I turned towards the ambulance man. 'Um,' I said again, as I hurriedly reached for two more bags.

'How long has she been ill? he asked me urgently.

'I didn't know she was ill!' I cried.

The ambulance man looked at me in surprise. Then he left the room to radio someone. The other ambulance men had Mum on a stretcher by then and were wheeling her out of the room. Al appeared beside me. He put his arms around me. I gasped into his chest.

There aren't many things that I don't like, however, if pushed to come up with something, I would probably say secrets and lies. But it took years to realise this. Life at home with Mum and Dad was clearly full of secrets and lies, Dad was bonking Sue and I was being bullied, but no one said a thing. I thought we were past all that, but my mother has been staying with me for six weeks and she's been keeping a monster to herself.

I sit here, now, in the hospital, holding her limp hand, looking at her drugged, sleeping body, and I wonder how and why she did it. And how I didn't realise. The doctor said, 'Did you not notice any changes in her behaviour?' Well, yes, but I thought she was having a midlife. Except I didn't say that, I just nodded. Did she have headaches? Oh, yes, terrible headaches but I thought they were stonking great hangovers, although I didn't say that either, I just nodded again. Loss of memory? Yes, a bit, but I put it down to the dope smoking. Again, just a nod. Has she been sleeping a lot? Well, yes, but my dad was having an affair with her friend, I thought she was sleeping to block it out. Again, just a nod. But, no. It wasn't a midlife or a menopause, malignant cells were growing on her brain. And she knew. She knew. Knew it was untreatable, knew at some point they'd swell to such a size that she'd lose consciousness. But she never mentioned it. The doctor said that from her records she was told four months ago that she'd have approximately six months to live. It would have been about the same time she found out about Dad's affair.

The doctor also said she might not regain consciousness. He said I should prepare for the worst.

Chapter 68

She didn't regain consciousness. I sat by her for thirty hours and just before 7 o'clock this evening she slipped away. Slipped away. I think that's the best way to put it. Like when you're at a party that you've had enough of and you say, 'I'm just going to slip away.' Unobtrusive, without wanting to cause any fuss, I'll just slip away. That's what my mum did.

In many ways, everything makes perfect sense now but then at the same time nothing does.

Little tears have been trickling from my eyes but I couldn't say how I feel. I have so many questions and I know they'll never be answered. Why didn't she tell me? Why did she come to stay with me? Didn't she want to go to Rome or see the Northern Lights? Was she afraid? Was she in pain? But most of all I just want to hug her. She lay on the hospital bed and I put my arms around her and I pretended that she was hugging me back. I want to tell her that I love her. I told her as she lay lifeless, but I wanted her to hear it. I thought our new relationship was just the beginning. It was actually an ending. But most of all I want to say thank you to her for giving me this time. And to say I hope she enjoyed it as much as me. And to say, Mum, I'm so proud of you. And I want you to be proud of me too.

I didn't get back to the flat until gone 11 p.m. Al was already in bed. It must now be the early hours of the morning. I'm in the bathroom. Sitting on the floor in my bathrobe. I got out of the bath ages ago but I don't want to leave the bathroom because Mum's bits are everywhere. It's as though she's still here. And maybe she is.

'Mum, ' I whisper. 'If you're here, I love you.'

I curl myself up in my bathrobe and lie upon the bathroom floor until morning.

Chapter 69

The funeral will be just a small affair at the local crematorium, with a picnic afterwards on the common across the road. I was getting into a tizz about where to hold the wake, but then I remembered Mum saying how we often over-complicate things, and really it's sometimes enough to feel the wind on our skin or the ground underfoot. It felt right to do something outside, and every weather forecast (I checked sixteen) assures me it will be fine on the day. At some point afterwards, I'll take her ashes and scatter them. At sea, I thought. I keep remembering the delight on Mum's face as she paddled in the sea at Skegness. Most people have to organise a funeral for a parent at some point in their lives, I'm trying not to feel sorry for myself, and at least having something to do takes my mind off this overwhelming ache I have inside. It doesn't feel like an ache that will ever go away either, just something that I'll have to get used to.

Philippa and Al have stayed with me. They've been wonderful. They even went through Mum's address book and papers and sent funeral invitations to all the people they could find, so that I didn't have to. They've both gone back to work today. This is my first day alone and that in itself feels like a hurdle to overcome. They've both been calling and texting me repeatedly though. Al, largely to discuss his menu plans for dinner, Philippa to read me the responses the *Tiddlesbury Times* has received from people who were given anonymous notes, twenty-six so far. So, in spite of everything, I've been hearing a lot of good news.

So when I'm not on the phone to them, I'm bearing up, as they say, getting by, moment to moment. Philippa wrote a lovely obituary about Mum in the *Tiddlesbury Times*. It went in today, along with the photo of Mum dancing to the Arctic Monkeys, she's smiling and squinting in the sun. We put that one on the order of service too. I hope that's the way Mum would like to be remembered.

The funeral is only two days away, but I haven't been able to get hold of my father. There was no answer at home and then when I called his work I was told he was on a three-week holiday. No one seemed to know where he'd gone. One chap thought Florida, another said he'd mentioned a cruise. They both said he would be on email for anything urgent. But I emailed and I haven't heard from him. In the first email I just said, please contact Jenny. But then when he hadn't responded after twenty-four hours I had to tell him about Mum. There was no answer at Sue's house either. So I can only assume that she's with him. I think that Mum went to Sue's house on the day she was diagnosed. I just have a feeling. She hinted that she'd known about the affair for years. So that must have been the catalyst to confront it. I don't think she even told my father that she was ill.

'Hey, Mum,' I whisper.

I've been talking to her a fair bit. I'm hoping Mum's found Doris and they're having a glass of cheap fizz.

The hall buzzer goes. I look at it but don't move. I may be feeling strong but I'm not sure I want to see anyone. The buzzer goes again.

'Mum, should I get the door?'

I really will stop doing this at some point, I promise. For some reason, though, I'm already up and I'm lifting up the receiver of the intercom.

'Hello?' I say. My voice surprises me for some reason.

There's no answer. But I feel as though someone's there. It seems surreal. But then nothing feels as it should at the moment.

'Jenny Taylor.'

I close my eyes. I have to swallow. Isn't it strange how some voices can make you instantly feel like crying?

'Hello,' I say, my voice quivering. 'I don't think I want to see you.'

Perhaps I'm not as strong as I thought. It's Joe King.

'Oh, Jen. I know. But I'm afraid you need to see me.'

I shake my head and have to swallow again.

'No.'

'Please.'

I lean against the wall.

'Joe, what do you want? I'm ... I'm not great at the moment ...'

'I know ... I know about your mum,' he says gently.

Now I'm crying. It's his voice. His bloody kind voice, the voice that whispered to me, 'Can I help? Can I do anything?'

when he held me on the pavement the day that Doris went to hospital. The voice that said, 'I'll be by your side,' when I spoke about seeing my old school bullies. It was the voice that I thought would stay by me.

'Oh, Jenny.' He's crying too. I don't like hearing him cry.

'People will think you're mad crying into an intercom system.'

'Let them.'

I buzz him in.

I open the door. I can hear him walking up the stairs, not quickly, not slowly, but steadily. It suits me. I try to regulate my breathing before I see his face. He's on the landing now, walking towards the flat. Now he's here. He's in front of me. Joe King, in his biker boots, and his black jeans and his grey hoodie. It's the Joe King as I remember except there are tears down his cheeks and his mouth is twisting as he tries not to weep. I want to comfort him. But I don't move. My chest heaves and my eyes fill again with tears but I don't step towards him.

We stand still, our irregular breathing oddly similar. I don't know why we're doing this. It doesn't look like it's good for either of us. I don't know what to say.

'Do you want a cup of tea?'

I'm so British.

He nods and half smiles and shrugs and then follows me through to the kitchen. Mum's obituary is lying open on the kitchen table.

'Such a great picture of her,' he says and it strikes me as being a bit of an overfamiliar thing to say about someone you only met once and didn't seem to particularly get on with.

I keep my back to him while the kettle boils and I get the tea ready. When I eventually turn around with the cups, I'm newly shocked by how upset he looks.

'Listen, you,' I say, trying to jest. 'My Mum died, I'm supposed to be the more miserable of the two of us.'

He looks down at his lap and nods. I place the teas on the table and sit down on the furthest chair from him. I can't be too close. I still want to reach out and touch him. He's sucking his bottom lip. He seems far, far away. Eventually he looks up at me, sighs a tiny sigh and looks back down at his lap.

'I knew your mum was ill, Jenny.'

'Say that again ...'

He nods. 'I knew ... I knew she was ill. Really ill. She came to the pharmacy right after I started there. She had loads of stuff on prescription. I said, "We'll be able to hear you rattle with all this." Maybe I shouldn't have said anything, I'd never worked in a chemist. Anyway, she laughed, and when she came back to pick them up she'd had her hair done. So we had a bit of banter. Then she came in again not long after and she was glowing, and I said, "You look great, you don't look at all poorly." And she seemed thrilled, but she said, "I am though, it's my brain, I always suspected I was ill in the brain. But it's my secret." That was it. And I'm just working in a shop, Jenny, I didn't know what to do or say! Then when she came in again, I said, "how are you doing?" and she said, "OK. I think I've got a little while left and I'm living it." And I said, "Do you want to talk about it?" and she smiled and said, "Thank you, but I haven't told my own daughter so I shouldn't really talk to you." I said, "fair enough." And she said, "Do you think that's wrong of me. To not tell my daughter that I'm dying?" And I thought about it. I didn't say anything. She said, "I just don't want everything to be about my dying, I want it to be about my living.' And I thought about it. And I nodded, and I said, "I'd probably do the same." I was already in love with you. And then we had your mum over for tea.'

He stops speaking suddenly and starts to cry, as though it's a relief for him to have finally poured it all out.

I get up and give him some kitchen roll. I leave it in front of him on the table.

'I didn't know what to do. I didn't want to hurt you, Jenny. I'd never hurt you. Oh, God, I feel sick.' He half laughs and wipes his face with the kitchen roll. ' I still don't know what I'd do differently. How I'd do it better. She asked me not to tell you. How could I be with you keeping that a secret? But then I didn't want to not be with you. I hate secrets, Jen. But this wasn't mine to tell. Oh, God.' He puts his head in his hands. He exhales. 'You said that since you'd met me you'd neglected your mum, and I thought, I've got to step aside, let you guys have time together. So that's what I did. But I didn't want to hurt you. Oh, I hated to hurt you. And I know you probably can't forgive me. But' – he swallows, and runs his fingers through his hair – 'that's what happened. Anyway, after the tea, your mum came and visited me. She gave me a letter, she said, "This is for Jenny, after I'm gone, hopefully I'll get to tell her before I go, and then I'll come and tell you and we can throw this letter away. But if I don't get a chance, for some reason, if the old brain wants to speed things up, then can I ask you to give this to her?"'

He pulls a square envelope out of the front pocket of his hoodie and pushes it along the table towards me. *Jenny, my beautiful girl* it says on the front.

'I best get out of your hair,' he says, standing.

I look up at him, at this beautiful man.

'Will you be coming to the funeral? It's the day after tomorrow.' I whisper.

'It's up to you,' he answers quietly. 'If you want me to.'

I nod. 'The dress code is The Rolling Stones.'

We lock eyes and let our breathing synch for a moment. I never notice my breathing with anyone else, yet with Joe King, it's as if our respiratory systems are desperate to dance together. He steps away from his chair and walks towards the door. I follow him. He turns when he's on the threshold so we're facing each other.

'Jenny, I'm so sorry,' he whispers.

'It's OK.' I mouth the words.

I look into his kind, wretched face. And he looks down at me. And, as if at the same time, our arms open. Mine find his back, they pull him towards me, and his hands land on my shoulders and draw me into him. His head rests on top of mine. I can hear his heart beating. I don't want to leave this embrace and I don't for a long while. When I do I say, 'Will you go home . . . ' Joe King looks at me and nods sadly. But I hadn't finished because what I was going to say, and what I do say, is, 'Will you go home and get your guitar and come back?'

Joe doesn't answer.

'If you want?' I add.

'I want,' he says.

Chapter 70

My beautiful, beautiful girl,

Oh, Jenny, I'm sitting up in your bed writing this to you. I look about me and I see all your hundreds of fabulous outfits and I hear you chattering and laughing with Al in the kitchen. Yet there's a tear in my eye already, because if you're reading this then . . . well, then . . . I'm no longer with you. And I am so sorry I didn't have time to tell you. I wanted to tell you myself. But I also wanted us to have this time together, without such a black cloud hanging over us. If you think this was wrong of me, Jenny, I am so truly sorry.

Jenny, my darling, I'm going to say something, which will be a shock. So I hope you are sitting down and I hope you will forgive me. It's something I promised Jack I wouldn't tell you. But as I'm no longer about, as such, I feel I can. I wish I hadn't promised. I'm starting to feel you've been unduly punished by secrets, Jenny. And again, I am so, so sorry.

In 1984 I went to Reading Festival with Debbie and met a man called Lawrence. Jenny, I am almost positive that this man is your father. Not Jack. I'm so sorry, Jenny. I had been seeing Jack, and before Debbie and I went to the festival, he proposed, I hadn't answered him, I was to make my mind up there. And I did, I decided not to marry him. I fell in love almost instantly with this man called Lawrence. Oh, he was lovely, Jenny, funny and caring and he had a way of looking at the world that made you excited to be alive. But I lost him. Still, I came home and told Jack I didn't want to marry him. But Jack persisted. He was very persistent when he wanted something. Then I found out I was pregnant. In all honesty, I wasn't sure whose it was. I told Jack this. But he said he'd marry me anyway. And that seemed like a good thing, Jenny. I hope you can understand this. I wanted you to have a father. So we married and you were born, but then Jack and I couldn't have any more children, we tried but I never got pregnant and I think that's when he started to resent you and me. He never trusted me, as you might remember. So no, I shouldn't have married him, but I did and I thought I'd made the most of it. But me marrying him made no one happy, and unhappiness grows, it seeps into everything, until you forget that happiness is even an option. All I ask of you, Jenny, is that when you find happiness, cling to it, defend it. But somehow I know you will.

I don't think I'm the only woman who looks back on their life and thinks, well if it wasn't for my diabolical decisions in love, I would have aced this life malarkey. But Jenny, I had a good ride. And although I could have used another forty-odd years, as we both know, when it's your time it's your time. And you have to be grateful for the time you had. And mine was good. I had good love and bad love and good friends and bad friends, I saw sunsets and cities, I laughed and I cried, I made mistakes, but don't we all? And I did some good, I helped some people, but best, best, best of all I had a beautiful daughter. When I look at you or think of you, Jenny, I feel so proud of you. You once said, 'We can't all be superstars,' but you are, Jenny, I think you're a superstar. You certainly shine like a star.

I will always be at your side, my darling daughter, always.
I'm so glad we had these days.
Lots of big, big hugs.
Your proud mum.

x

'Do you need a hug?' Joe King says, when I've finished reading.

I nod. He lays his guitar down on the floor then moves over to me on the sofa and he scoops me into his arms. I appreciate that he doesn't ask me what it says. I don't want to start talking about how my dad isn't really my dad at all, but some bloke called Lawrence is instead. There'll be plenty of time in the future for me to discuss all this with him. Right, now, I just want to be held.

Chapter 71

Jack Taylor always seemed an unlikely partner for my mum. He looked too tanned, too smooth, too a lot of things for her somehow. A little bit smug with it as well, a little bit 'didn't you do well, darling'. But not today. My dad – even though our blood is different I can't stop calling him my father overnight – my dad, Jack, is broken. We stood next to each other in the crematorium and I don't think he could see, his eyes were so wet and swollen. All I could hear throughout the service was him trying to breath through his blocked nose. We left the crematorium together, walking side by side into the bright sunshine to the sound of the Rolling Stones' 'Ruby Tuesday'. There in the entrance he suddenly grabbed me and clutched me to him. The other guests had to walk around us. It wasn't quite the hug I had imagined, what with it being at my mother's funeral and all. But . . . well, I don't know actually. I don't know what to feel. He couldn't speak when he released me.

'Let's meet up next week,' I found myself saying to him. 'To . . . ' I stopped there. To what? To have dinner? A drink? A coffee? To reminisce about Mum? But I found myself saying, 'Let's meet up next week and talk.'

I don't know how you go about rebuilding tattered relationships like ours but talking seemed to be the only place to start.

He nodded.

And so, here we all are. A group of people sitting on the grass in the sun. Me wondering if I could manage some hummus. The ache is still there, obviously. But there's also another feeling, one I can't quite put my finger on yet. My Mum left me her love. She spent her last months with me and now I have her love. Something I didn't really feel I had before. And that love is such a gift – I can't help but feel that it's changed everything, most of all the way I feel about myself. I'm all right, you know. Jenny Taylor's all right. I no longer feel terrified that everyone's going to leave me or start hating me. Maybe having my mum's love is making me love myself. Oh, I don't know. Perhaps I can't be relied on to make sense today. And I probably shouldn't try. But I've decided I'm going to go to college. I hope I can go part time at the surgery and study performing arts somewhere. I want to grow and learn now. I'm ready and I think she'd be pleased and that makes me smile.

'Hey, beautiful,' Joe King says, squeezing my hand.

I'm wearing my wedding dress. I did ask him if he thought it was weird, but he said that I looked beautiful and that I had to wear it. He hasn't left my side since he reappeared. We haven't said much to each other, to be honest, and we haven't done any sexy stuff. His hand simply seems to appear in mine, or I feel his arm around me when I need it. I feel lucky, and like Mum said, I'm going to cling to this and defend it. I'm not going to be afraid this time. Nope, no more fear.

I squint my eyes at the sun blazing down upon us. I'm not complaining, I'm glad the sun is smiling today for Mum.

'Do you want my shades?' Joe asks.

I shake my head and pull out the Dame Edna ones that Mum wore the day she had the hangover to eclipse all others. At least that's what I thought. I always assumed the headaches were hangovers; it never occurred to me they'd be anything else.

'Ah, I remember those!' Al exclaims, when he sees me putting them on.

'Yeah, do you remember that day? She got all overcome that you'd made a frittata. "He's a man and he made frittata, why does that make me so happy?"' I say. I love sharing stories about her.

'There are so many people here,' Philippa whispers. 'I think there's well over a hundred.'

I nod. 'I think most of them must be from the hospice where she used to work. I should go and introduce myself.'

'Do you want me to come?' Joe squeezes my hand.

'No, I'll be fine. But thank you.' I smile. That nice Joe King, my mum said. 'You should play a song on your guitar.'

'Do you want me to?'

'Why not? She loved a festival, my mum,' I say.

It makes me think of my dad, my real dad who doesn't know I exist. I wonder if I will ever meet him. I wonder whether I should search for him or whether perhaps Mum was right and some things really are meant to stay lost.

I stand up, wipe the grass from the backs of my legs and

start visiting the clusters of picnicking people. Debbie Diamond jumps up and hugs me. She's hugged me a few times already today, she's insisting that Joe and I go and stay with her for a few days. We said we'd like that very much. I leave her and walk towards Dr Flemming, in his very fitted purple suit from the seventies, so tight in the trousers I don't know where to look. He's talking with Marge, who's wearing a kaftan. She's draped over her beau from Reading. I say hello and hug them. I think Mum would have liked to have gone out with Dr Flemming really. But I think she was frightened that being a GP, he'd suspect she was ill. That's my theory anyway. When I move on, Simon the Plasterer stands up, he holds out his hand for me to shake, but I smile and hug him instead.

A kindly faced lady reaches out and taps me on the leg when we are finished. I bend down.

'Your mother was a wonderful woman,' she says emphatically. 'When we lost half our funding at the hospice, it was your mother that came up with the plan that got us through. She saved the day for us.'

She briefly introduces me to the group she's sitting with, nurses who knew Mum, other fundraisers and even some families who had loved ones at the hospice and met my mum. I feel so very proud as I leave them to carry on with my other greetings.

'Oh, Mum, I wish you were here,' I whisper. But then I close my eyes and feel the warmth of the sun tempered by the breeze on my face, and I realise that it's a foolish thing to say, because again, I feel that she is here.

When I open my eyes again, I notice a man on his own, he

is standing up and staring at me. He looks very familiar. I push my sunglasses onto the top of my head and look at him. He's stepping towards me. It looks like Larry Lemon, the comedian. The comedian's comedian no less. I look about me, he is definitely walking towards me.

'Jenny Taylor?' he says. It is him. I recognise his voice.

I nod and smile. 'You're . . . you're Larry Lemon. You are, aren't you?'

'Yes. Guilty to that, I'm afraid.'

'Oh, my goodness. Your *I Probably Shouldn't* DVD is one of my favourite things ever. My best friend bought it for me years ago. I still watch it regularly.'

'Oh, ho, thank you.'

He looks genuinely chuffed. Larry Lemon is here. I look about for Philippa, because I'm sure she'd like to meet him too, but I can't get her attention because she's talking to Dave.

'Did you know my mum then? From the hospice?'

'Oh, no, no, I didn't.'

'Oh.'

'I, er, your mum sent me, well my company, a DVD of you doing something called the The Tiddlesbury Tour.' He chuckles.

'My mum sent you—'

'I manage acts now. I haven't done the stand-up for years. Now I look after a little select group of comedians and presenters.'

'And my mum sent you . . .' I can't seem to close my mouth.

'Yes, she was quite the agent.'

'My mum sent you . . .'

'She was very proud of you.'

'Wow.'

'She called me first and told me all about you.' The way he laughs indicates that my mum went on and on and *on* about me to Larry Lemon. 'She said she thought you were very talented and she asked me what I recommended. Then she sent the DVD and I thought that you were great so I called her back.'

'Wow.'

'I really did think it was a great tape. I'd like you to take my card and call me, we can have a meeting with your friend Philippa. The camera loves the pair of you. I'm sure I could find you work.'

I really should shut my mouth.

'Jenny, I am so sorry. Forgive me. I got carried away, now is certainly not the time to be talking business. I came along because your mum and I got on so well on the phone that I was going to ask if she wanted to meet face to face.'

'Like a date?'

'Well, I suppose so, yes. But then I received the note about the funeral and well, I'm so sorry. But I just ... I just felt I should come today.'

'Oh,' I say, feeling sad for him and sad for Mum and a bit sad for me too, my mum dating Larry Lemon would have been pretty incredible. 'That's rubbish.'

'Hmmm. Hmmm,' he agrees. 'So, anyway, I'll leave my card with you; when you're ready and if you'd like to, call me.'

'Oh, yes, yes,' I say, taking it. 'I will, thank you.' I look down at the card – LL Artist Management. Who'd have thought? I will definitely call him. No more fear. I look up and it's funny because my gaze instantly finds Joe King and he's looking at me too. I smile. Not a big beam, because that isn't in me at the moment, but a little smile that says I'm so glad you are here.

'Just one thing,' Larry Lemon says, rousing me from my Joe King thoughts. 'I just wondered whether ... oh, it's stupid, really ... ' He halts, shakes his head, and places his hand in front of his chest as if to stop himself doing something instinctive.

'What?'

'Ridiculous question, but your mum, Pam, didn't ... no, no, I'm sure she didn't ... but ... your mum, she didn't ever mention seeing the Rolling Stones at the Reading Festival, did she? By any chance? Years and years ago. So silly looking back on it, but I met a girl there called Pam ... and I lost her ... silly fool ... and I've always regretted it because, well, I thought she was wonderful. It only took me a minute to fall in love with her.'

Acknowledgements

Some humungous THANK YOUs are in order! As ever, a big one goes to my amazing dad, for all the time and advice he gives me, from the first ideas to the last edit. Another to Rowan Lawton, my brilliant and lovely agent. And a big fat thank you also goes to Rebecca Saunders, a very special editor and person. The journey of this book has been unconventional, shall we say, which meant that I was a bit (really quite a big bit) of a nightmare for her. I am very, very grateful for all the kindness she showed me.

I had a glorious stint in Bamburgh writing about Jenny Taylor; the warmest of thanks go to Barbara and Charles Baker-Cresswell for putting me up and putting up with me.

Sincere thanks go to a host of amazing people at Sphere/ Little, Brown: Adele Brimacombe, Sophie Burdess, Louise Davies, Charlie King, Carleen Peters, Thalia Proctor, Jo Wickham and Emma Williams.

And last but by no means least, so much gratitude and love to my amazing friend, Dannielle, who helps me through my own dark days with her brilliant advice, irreverant wit and frigging incredible cake.

Is Gracie in love for the very first time?

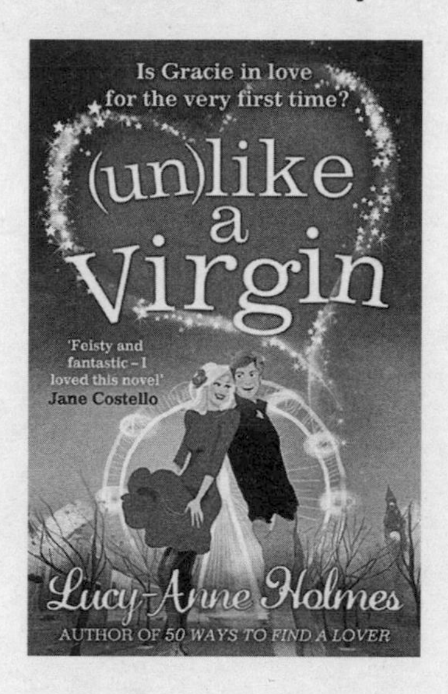

You know that bit in The X Factor, when the singer tells everyone about the rocky road they travelled to pursue their dream? Well, that's Gracie Flowers' story.

Gracie is very focused for a woman of almost twenty-six. Her favourite book is *The 5-Year Plan: Making the Most of Your Life*. And her five-year plan is going very well. That is, until she is usurped from her big promotion by a handsome, posh idiot; she is dumped by her boyfriend; and she discovers her loopy mother is facing bankruptcy.

Hormones awry and ice cream over-ordered, a dream Gracie thought she'd buried ten years ago starts to resurface. A dream that reminds her of the girl she used to be and everything she wanted to become.

*

'Hilarious, sweet and all too relatable. Had me laughing out loud from the first page. Which was embarrassing' Lindsey Kelk

sphere